Song of the Jayhawk

or, *The Squatter Sovereign*

Jack Marshall Maness

Wooden Stake Press
Denver, CO

www.woodenstakepress.com
www.songofthejayhawk.com

ISBN-10: 1940936020
ISBN-13: 978-1-940936-02-4

Cover Design: Laurie Kubitz-Maness

*Image courtesy History Colorado,
Aultman Collection (CHS.A99).*

For Sister Andrea.

"[M]en go to preach with jests and jeers,
and just as long as they can raise a laugh,
the cowl puffs up, and nothing more is asked.

But such a bird nests in that cowl, that if
the people saw it, they would recognize
as lies the pardons in which they confide."

-***Paradiso***, Canto XXIX

Introduction

It has been widely noted that one cannot fully comprehend American society without a fundamental understanding of the Civil War. Historian and novelist Shelby Foote may have explained it most succinctly, stating that before the war the country was considered a plurality, a loose affiliation of states that "are." After the war, he noted, the nation was a singular, an "is."[1] The Civil War unified the nation.

I could not agree more. The abolishment of slavery and the fundamental hypocrisy it wrote into the American story; as well as the abrogation of the mere possibility of secession from the Union, changed that narrative forever. The greatest covenants Americans share with one another owe their consecration to the men and women who gave their lives in the Civil War. But the war did not begin, as Americans are taught in elementary school, at Ft. Sumter, South Carolina in April of 1861.

The Civil War began in the newly established territory of Kansas seven years earlier, in 1854. It started with the murders of men most Americans would never remember—men like Charles W. Dow, Thomas Barber, William Doyle, and two of his sons, William Jr. and Drury. It started with the drowning of an anonymous slave in Atchison, the rigging of elections in Doniphan, the destruction of a printing press in Lawrence, and fistfights in places like Oskaloosa, Osawkie, and Kickapoo. It started because in Kansas Americans just couldn't live together. It started, literally, between neighbors.

The conditions that made this tumult possible were created by what is often considered one of the greatest failures of leadership in American history.

Unable and unwilling to settle the issue itself, Congress decreed that year that the first settlers of Kansas would decide the Western-slavery issue for themselves at the polls, calling it the principal of "squatter sovereignty." The history books tell us about those men and women who came to Kansas for this purpose, to make her either a Slave State or a Free State. The iconic John Brown is the most famous among them, and he was certainly not alone. But many of those who pioneered in Kansas came not for the fight or the cause, but for land, for the opportunity to own the fruits of their labor and build an inheritance for their children and grandchildren.

In emigrating, they soon found themselves irrevocably swept up in a maelstrom that would change the course of history. Congress's inaction made these people immensely powerful the moment they laid the first stone or log of their cabin. Humble families from all over the world suddenly held the reins to the enslavement of over four million people, the future of an entire nation and, ultimately, world history. Whether they liked it or not, accepted it or not, or were prepared for it or not, the simple farmers of Kansas in the 1850s were the most powerful people on earth. These largely poor people were not only sovereign, they were sovereigns. This novel is their story.

While I have taken artistic liberties in parts, I have made every reasonable attempt to portray historical figures and the events in which they forged their fame as accurately as I am able, and have provided a glossary to assist the reader. In these pages one can learn a great deal about territorial Kansas, its issues, and how they sparked the war and helped define contemporary American culture. But this is a work of fiction, and should be read as such. This novel and its sequels are less concerned with detailing the facts and more with capturing what I consider a transcendent reality.

This book is about the spirit of the times, the part of history that we least understand yet which most affects us. It is the reality we behold only in agonizingly brief moments, but in utter, unforgettable clarity.

Nobody is certain who coined the term "jayhawk." Though it had been used before in different contexts, most historians attribute its first use in Kansas to an Irish immigrant by the name of Patrick Devlin, others to the Free State leader James Henry Lane.

Wherever it originated, it was used increasingly in the 1850s in Kansas to denote Free State guerilla fighters who harassed Missourians and Southerners, robbed them of their possessions, and sometimes assassinated them. The notion is that both jays and hawks tease their prey before killing it.

In the Civil War, the nickname "jayhawker" was adopted by a regiment of Kansas volunteer cavalry, where it soon came to denote all Kansan soldiers; then, gradually after the war, all Kansans. It has come to embody the identity of a people and their shared heritage.

The territory's namesake tribe, the Kanza (or Kaw) Indians, did not tell many stories to whites, but they delighted in telling them to one another. One of their favorites was about a monster, the Mialueka—creatures with large beaks who tricked people into following them to the darkest recesses of the woods, or the rivers, from which they may never return.[2] I have long delighted in wondering if this story was the inspiration for the infamous Kansas "jayhawk." The librarian and historian in me believe not, but the writer knows it is so. It simply must be.

It is the truth behind the history that will forever haunt the present, a mysterious beast that emerges from the shadowy recesses of the past, for an indelible moment, and soon disappears.

Our choice is whether or not we follow.

Jack Marshall Maness
Denver, CO. December, 2013

1. Shelby Foote (1990). *Ken Burns' The Civil War: Episode Nine—The Better Angels of our Nature.* Foote's comments begin at 2:24.

2. Joseph E. Unrau (1975). *The Kaw People.* Indian Tribal Series: Phoenix, AZ., p. 18.

Song of the Jayhawk

I

Patrick thought it was wrong to hang a man for such a thing, but didn't know if he should say so. The hotter it got that summer, the more dangerous it had become to speak. August is intolerable in Atchison, and in 1855 it was unusually so—not only humid, but busy and testy. Standing in the sweltering heat beside the river that day, something drove him toward an opinion on this long-bearded man from Ohio, this reverend whose steel-gray eyes waited patiently (not unkindly, but fiercely) while the mob decided what to do with him. They should not be doing this. Pardee Butler of Stranger Creek had not committed a crime. He had done nothing with his arms or his fists. He had no rifle, no revolver, not even a Bowie knife on his person. He had only opened his big obnoxious mouth and refused to shut it, and now they were going to hang him for it. It wasn't right. It just wasn't right. But Patrick couldn't decide if he should say so.

"Drown the nigger-stealing bastard!" one man cried from the other side of the crowd.

"Let's hang him!" another shouted. "He may be a man of the cloth, and we'll make darned sure his collar's a-made a hemp!"

The men laughed, and it seemed for a brief moment that levity would diffuse the situation, but it didn't. Tones of anger and impatience soon rose from the crowd again like gnats regrouping after a good swat, and the men moved like a colony of ants toward the great elm that stood just up the bluff from the sandy ferry landing.

Patrick's heart rose to his throat, but he held both tightly. It was when he realized they were moving this old man toward the tree to hang him from it that Patrick felt both his heart and throat come unclenched. It was almost as if generations of Dugans were speaking for him, despite all his effort to silence them.

"Stop!" he cried in a faltering voice.

The mob turned like a single creature and looked at him. It was quiet enough that Patrick could hear the mosquitoes in his ears, and a jay's shrill call from a distant tree.

***

Earlier that morning, Maria realized she had lived in Kansas Territory for a year, and moving there had proven to be a mistake.

She told this to Patrick. "This is not a place to rear a child, Patrick," she said.

"I know it," he sighed.

And then there was silence. There was actually silence. For once the wind stopped, the warped sides of the structure that served as their shelter all the previous winter ceased their creaking and whistling, and there was actually silence.

"We've got to think about going back," she said too loudly. She knew what the look in his eyes meant. "We found a way here, Patrick. With God's help we'll find a way back. Back home."

"Home?"

He stood, hunched over at the waist so his head would not rub against the cottonwood planks. He'd gotten several splinters in his scalp already that spring when it became warm enough to remove his hat inside the shack.

"Boston is home to you?"

"Of course 'tis. I've lived there since I was a little girl."

"It's not home to me." He picked up a tin cup and knocked it on the solitary single-planked shelf. "It's a cold, crowded place."

Maria laughed. She leaned back while sitting on her mattress of dry leaves and grasses, returned to sitting upright, and gathered her thoughts to reply. But then she looked at her husband. A tall, thin man with bulbous knees and elbows, he looked like he was stuffed into the place, arms spilling out windows, legs out doors, like a crab crawling out of its shell. He was so close to her she had to look almost skyward to see his face, silhouetted against the shafts of light in the ceiling where the earth above the planks had begun to fall through.

"And just what are you laughing at?"

She laughed again. And she laughed again after that. Soon Maria was laughing so hard Patrick left, slamming the pathetic door to the shanty so hard it fell off and the dirt came cascading down on Maria and her bed. And that made Maria laugh more. She heard the tin cup hit a tree outside, and laughed again. Maria laughed and laughed, brushing soil violently off the bed sheets, and Patrick started walking toward town.

It wasn't like her, he thought.

It wasn't like him, she thought.

August in Atchison is so hot, they both thought.

***

A few days before, a slave named Molly had turned up drowned in the muddy-orange Missouri River. A ten-year-old boy found her while fishing. He was very still as he watched her body turn over once, on its way into shore, and slide up on the bank, facedown, hair matted with clay where the head had made contact with the sand, the eye on that side pulled open. The boy felt almost as if the river had given him this corpse, pushed it right on his lap. He tugged on its shoulder once, turning it back over to face the sky. She was the third slave he had ever seen. He looked at her face long and hard, and ran home crying.

The boy's father was a lawyer from Cincinnati named J.W.B. Kelley, a man known for his distinctive, long, curly moustache. He'd come to Kansas on May 31st of the previous year, the very next day after the territory was opened to settlement by Congress and it was declared that it would be admitted as either a slave or a free state, depending on the will of its people. An ardent Free Stater, he was horrified that his boy should be subjected to this. He went with his son back to the river and saw at once who she was. She was owned by a Kentuckian who was building a sawmill, an ape of a man named Grafton Thomassen. Kelley went straight to the mill and confronted him.

"Molly—your property—turned up at the feet of my son while fishing," Kelley told him, his moustache quivering. "He was quite disturbed."

"Goddamnit," said the large man behind the desk. "I'd a-wondered where she done got to. Is she dead?"

"Yes," said the pale Ohioan. "And I'd ask you to have her body removed. My son fishes there. He was very upset."

"Well, ain't nothin' a man can do 'bout mortality, now, is there?"

"You can bury her," came a flat reply.

"Bury her?" Thomassen's expression betrayed a huge forehead. "You want me to get a damned preacher?"

"I'd like to see the woman decently interred, sir," said Kelley. Thomassen's face betrayed the size of his skull once more, and he laughed. "Are you laughing at me, sir?"

Soon Mr. Grafton Thomassen was laughing so hard that the skinny lawyer left, slamming the door to the cottonwood shack that served as Thomassen's office.

And in walked Patrick.

"Ah!" the Kentuckian growled. "Enough laughs for one morning! The Irishman returns!"

"I'd like to work," Patrick said as he removed his hat.

Grafton Thomassen said nothing.

"I need a horse, Mr. Thomassen. I want my wife to have a wood stove before the fall."

But the man with the big, thick, knotty ears behind the desk just laughed.

"Maria is with child, Grafton. As a fellow Christian—"

"I've got all the white niggers I need, Mr. Dugan. Goddamn Irish and Mormons," said Grafton, motioning Patrick away. "But I tell you what—I just learned I now have a need for a cook and a maid. If you want to sell me that little Irish whore you got stashed out there in the woods, I'll consider it." His expression had changed from one of humoring Patrick to a statue-like obduracy. He didn't move at all.

Even his teeth seemed thick. It was like there was another head inside his head, and everything was double the width. Patrick wondered if there was room enough for a brain inside Grafton Thomassen's skull. Hitting him would be solid, satisfying, but ineffective. And it was apparent, looking at this man's knuckles, that the counterpunch could be fatal.

"There's work down at the levee," Grafton said. "Go find the Mormons. If you wanna find work in this town, find the niggers 'n Mormons."

***

When Patrick arrived at the levee after his argument with Maria, he was not in the best of spirits. He and his wife disagreed very infrequently, and he was aware that this was because, more often than not, he simply capitulated to her before expressing his disagreement; and he was equally aware that this was because, more often than not, she was right, and more often than not, he knew that she was. But he didn't admit this to her. And he didn't need to. She knew it too, and knew that he knew that she knew. It was thereby a largely happy marriage.

But the shack had still been crowded that winter. Even if it had only been the two of them and not three, counting Patrick's little brother Roger, it would have been crowded. When they'd arrived in 1854 there was very little building material to be found anywhere, and the brothers did everything they could to fortify a canvass tent with sod and cottonwood planks, hand-hewn from the banks of a small tributary to the Independence River, which ran along the southern third of the section they'd claimed. But it was astonishing how quickly the cottonwood warped. It curled like birch bark peeled from its trunk, twisted like wet hemp rope left in the sun, and left the place drafty and dirty. In the morning, the light came in uninvited, and in the evening, rattlesnakes.

It seemed there was one snake a week through much of the fall and later in the winter, on toward springtime, and Maria was usually their executioner. Patrick and Roger would dance around them with a stick, a stone, or a hoe, jabbing feebly like they were boxing a larger man, and even, on more than one occasion, letting out little girlish cries when the serpent struck in their direction. But little Maria, with her thick-set legs, iron-hard calves and thighs, and leather-tough feet and toes; little Maria, with her fiery red hair and quick, pointed gestures and movements; little Maria had had a close encounter with one in bed one night, and knew how to end it quickly, without mess, without fuss. She kept a shovel in the corner of the shack for the purpose, and taught the men to check their shoes and beds before putting any part of their bodies in them.

"Just let me know if you see a serpent, boys," she would say. "I don't need you breaking what little I possess in your ridiculous attempts to kill the poor creatures."

And sometimes (she thought in secret but Patrick knew), she would cry. Maria would kill a snake, find a quiet spot in the trees beyond the garden, and cry, not to make a fuss, but because she wondered how in the world she could ever raise a family in such a godforsaken wilderness like Kansas.

Snakes were not the end of it, either. Two mornings in January they woke to several inches of snow on their blankets, and by February Maria decided something must change. And then, just in time, it did. The earth thawed and Patrick and Roger spent the warmer days of February and March felling hardwood trees and trading for whatever lumber they could find. They began the foundation for a new cabin a couple hundred feet from the shack-tent, and by June had constructed something much better than the tent with the green warped walls and the sod roof. No longer would she hear the sand falling through the cracks at night and think it was snow in her nightmares. No longer would she dream of snakes slithering under the filthy canvas flaps.

By August, the three-room cabin was nearly complete, and they were going to move in any day now. Patrick wanted oak planks for the floor and cupboards, and wanted to insulate the bedroom. The garden and bean crop was a complete success, and by trading with the Mormons and working at the levee, Patrick would secure the extra cash, labor, and materials to make it a home. It was going to come out all right. It really was. Why, then, Maria would want to go home now was a mystery to Patrick.

"You wear the young husband's expression of preoccupation this morning, Patrick," said Harry Clegg with a little smile when Patrick arrived at the levee. "Something on your mind?"

"Maria wants to return to Boston."

"Does she now? She's got more sense than the rest of us, then, wouldn't you say?"

Clegg was an Englishman by birth, a Mormon by choice, and twenty years Patrick's senior. He'd arrived in Atchison with his wife and three children just after the river had cleared of ice. Most of his people had left for Salt Lake by now, outfitting for the long trek over the plains during the thaw and leaving in the mud. But Clegg still lived in what was called "Mormon Grove," a tent city several miles to the west along the old military road that just eight weeks earlier boasted a population of over two thousand, some twenty times that of Atchison itself during that spring and summer. The citizens of Mormon Grove, in fact, had built much of Atchison, exchanging their labor for cash and supplies, and then left, leaving a few families behind that were too ill, poor, or both for the journey, including Clegg's.

"She's got an interesting sense of time," said Patrick. "Now that things are turning."

Clegg appeared to consider this a moment. "Some women always have something on their mind, something worth listening to," he said. "A few log walls and a little sunshine won't change that, my friend." His round cheeks were red with heat and labor.

"She's with child, Clegg." Patrick let his shovel fall and poked it nervously in the sand.

"Ah! And you're wondering why she wants to go home? You've a lot to learn about wives, my friend." Clegg laughed, not unkindly but also unrestrained.

"'S'pose you're right."

Clegg turned toward the river. The swirls in the orange-brown water looked easy and peaceful, but beneath there were heaving tides of danger. "What a godforsaken wilderness is Kansas. Job had it easy."

He turned back toward Patrick and smiled. The town of Atchison had been laid out, yet very scantily settled, in sections on a clearing that sloped gently toward the west, and this verdure provided an excellent backdrop to the tall, handsome Irishman. The sun had risen over the trees across the river and light splashed on the pasture.

"But I can see an Eden awaiting you, Patrick," he said. "In time, you and Maria will find your paradise."

"God willing," said Patrick.

"Precisely, my young friend. God willing."

"And you shall find yours, Clegg."

"I do hope so, my friend, I do hope so." He paused and sat, wiping his brow with a neckerchief. Patrick joined him. "Patrick, I hope you do not consider me a heathen," he said quizzically and glanced over at his friend.

Patrick, distracted by the troubles with his wife, hesitated. He realized that moment was painful, and turned on Clegg with polite vehemence. "No! My, no! Why on earth do you ask? Is something wrong, like?"

Clegg looked down into the mud, his jowls falling forward like udders, hiding his eyes. "When I crossed the Atlantic I had not heard that the Church had allowed a man to take more than one wife. I want you to know that." The udders sank back into his face as he turned again toward Patrick.

The river seemed to swell for a moment, almost as if the moon had tugged it suddenly. "Of course." Patrick stood and patted Clegg on the back. "Of course, my friend. I will say I cannot imagine why a man would want more than one." In Clegg's smile he saw an invitation to continue. They may not share a religion or a homeland, but they could share what men the world over can share— chauvinism. "Two cows, two sheep, a flock of chickens, yes. But two women for one man? Why, I imagine one alone is sufficient toll for St. Peter."

Clegg laughed, stood, and the two began to work. Soon a large wooden dock would welcome the ferry from Missouri, and the steamboats from downstream, as far as St. Louis. The Town Company had chosen for their site a sweeping bend in the river, this reaching-out to the West, in the hopes Atchison would become the primary outfitting stop for the journey across the plains, and one day the central hub of the nation's railway system. At this moment, with the sounds of saws and hammers filling the thick August air, wielded by blacks, Mormons, Irishmen, Northerners and Southerners alike, it seemed not only possible, but destined.

Just before lunchtime Clegg holstered his hammer, wiped his brow, and looked at Patrick. He was an averaged-sized man, shorter and plumper than Patrick, and always wore a straw hat that shaded his pale, freckled face and neck.

"Did you hear of Mr. Kelley?"

"Mr. Kelley? No, I've not heard of him. Why?"

The Englishman took a step closer. Patrick could almost feel the heat of this man's body beside him. A slight breeze, the first all morning, cooled both momentarily. He spoke quietly and Patrick could barely hear him over the sounds of the hammers and saws around them.

"A young lawyer from Ohio by the name of Kelley apparently found the body of a slave in the river and went around town claiming she'd been so badly mistreated by the sawmill man—"

"Grafton Thomassen."

"—yes, Thomassen—that she drowned herself in the river."

"I wouldn't doubt it," Patrick said, looking about furtively. "Thomassen's a bear of a man."

"Kelley also complained that Thomassen wouldn't decently bury the woman. He likened the man to a savage."

"Too true and too dangerous an insult."

"That's how I see it."

"And what has Thomassen done about it?"

"Well, he stopped short of murder, I'll say that much. But just short. He beat him so badly even his compatriots pulled him off. I tell you, Patrick, not in all my days in Manchester or New York did I see a man so badly beaten. I thought his brains would spill out his skull. His face was so swollen it was unrecognizable as the head of a human being. And instead of burying the slave—Molly's her name—he hanged her corpse from a tree on that bluff over there." He pointed to the largest bluff downriver, just south of the town site. The town and all the steamers on the Missouri would have seen her, and the rope still swung.

Patrick looked away in disgust. "Jesus help them both. What did they do with Kelley?"

"A mob of townsmen banished him from Atchison. Mr. Kelley and his moustache must to be halfway to Ohio already, the poor man."

It was almost as if the great river were breathing hot air on them like a giant dragon, a serpent stretching itself from mountain to sea.

"What a place to have settled, Clegg." Patrick shook his head and sighed, stubbing the point of his shovel into the earth. "I thought—" he turned back toward the west, toward the gently sloping hill that would soon be covered by buildings, a gateway to the endless American Desert, where there was more sky than there was land to walk under it. "I thought we'd have space here. Maria and I came because we thought we'd escape that . . . jostling. The crowdedness of the world. But it followed us here. The world is too much with us."

"Oh, and it's just starting to arrive!" Clegg's eyes became larger. "I think the Americans aim to settle their differences in Kansas."

"Maria's right. It's no place to raise a child."

"No, it's not." Clegg joined Patrick's gaze, down at the mud. He was thinking of his six-year-old son back in a shanty in Mormon Grove. "But the Lord afflicts us to save us, my brother. We'll weather the storm. Just be careful the next few days. In fact, be careful whenever you're in town."

"Oh, I keep my mouth shut," said Patrick. "I always keep my mouth shut. My pappa always told me to keep my mouth shut and my bowels open, because he could do neither."

"No better advice was ever given a man," Clegg laughed. "Well, the *Sovereign* is claiming that Kelley incited Molly to kill herself. Freedom or death, you know. It says the townsmen should be on the lookout for abolitionists inciting the mass suicide or insurrection of their property. They're having everyone sign an oath condemning Kelley and praising Thomassen, Patrick, and I suggest you sign it if you're asked."

Just then, a frantic group of men pushing a disheveled man in front of them clambered down the banks toward the water, many of them screaming "drown the damned abolitionist!"

The leader of the mob, a younger man with inlaid eyes pronounced knuckles on his fingers, grabbed his victim by the collar, spun him around so his back was to the river, and produced a bucket of black paint. Without a word he painted the man's face with it, drops of it running down his gray beard.

Another man produced a smaller bucket of red paint, and to the laughter of the crowd, painted a big red "R" on his forehead.

"Goddamn right!" someone shouted. "This preacher's a rogue!"

"Goddamn Republican!" shouted another.

II

"And just who the hell are you?" one man finally said to Patrick. All the eyes in the mob were on him. The man speaking seemed to be the leader of the mob. He cracked his large knuckles, his deep-set eyes fell back in shadow, and Patrick suddenly realized who he was. He was another "Kelley," a different man than the pitiable, bludgeoned lawyer from Cincinnati. He was a Virginian by the name of Robert S. Kelley, and was the postmaster and junior editor of the town's weekly newspaper, the *Squatter Sovereign*. He had written the column accusing abolitionists of inciting Molly's suicide, and insurrection in all of Atchison's slaves (and much, much more over the last several months). In fact, Patrick had probably read everything this man had ever written, and most of it amounted to a heaping threat to Free State settlers to stay out of Atchison County.

"I am a resident of this county," Patrick said. "My farm is three miles north, on the Independence."

"A son of Lewis 'n Clark, eh boy?" said a Missourian in the crowd. "Niggers ain't no explorers."

"I am not a nigger," Patrick said in a tone lower than he'd used in a long time.

"Yer Irish, ain't ya? Irish is white niggers in my book."

"Irishmen are welcome here," interjected Bob Kelley. "All white men, all men for that matter, are welcome here so long as they understand that Kansas is to be a slave state. We've no use for nigger-stealing abolitionists in Atchison."

There was a moment's pause, and Patrick knew what made it such a pregnant one: he was to declare, then and there, beside the great bend of the Missouri, his intent to vote for Kansas as a slave state, or a free one. This was not a moment for moderation. It was a moment for speaking out, for taking sides.

But Patrick thought of Maria, and kept his mouth shut through several agonizing seconds, until a dentist opened his.

"My friends, we must not hang this man," he said, motioning to the preacher. "He is not an Abolitionist, he is what they call a Free-soiler. The Abolitionists steal our niggers, but the Free-soilers do not do this. They intend to make Kansas a free state by legal methods . . . I propose that we make a raft and send him down the river as an example."

Another pause followed, and Bob Kelley had what he was looking for. "A vote, gentlemen!" his voice squealed as it was raised, and he grabbed the old preacher by the elbow and spun him around so he faced the majority of the crowd. "The Reverend Butler intends to vote for Kansas as a free state, and we shall honor his belief in democracy by voting on his life! Hang or sail down the river!"

A cheer rose from the mob, which had doubled in size since its arrival at the bank. Almost all the men of Atchison were now present, and this mob was becoming a democratic convention. Paper and writing utensils were produced for Bob Kelley, who now sat at an overturned wooden crate. The convention coalesced around Mr. Kelley, and after voting to send the Reverend down the river, Patrick found himself right behind the skinny, pale editor as he tallied the votes. He could look over the shoulder of Kelley and watch him count each, one by one, and was quite crowded-in and stuck that position, in fact. Clegg was nowhere to be seen. Patrick wanted desperately to leave—he had no desire to see this old man hanged, which appeared more likely with every mark on the editor's paper— but it seemed he was destined to see the thing to its end. He was not in Atchison on his way west to another Zion as was Clegg. This was it. Perhaps if it was to one day be heaven on earth, it would have to be hell first.

Patrick studied the Reverend Butler. There were only a few men left to vote. Some of the black paint had run down his beard and stained his shirt, the white undershirt that had been exposed by the tearing of his overcoat at the collar as Kelley and others tugged him about the town that morning. There was something sad about him, and it was neither his age nor his current predicament. The corners of his eyes reached toward his ears, and turned down a little, almost as if they were frowning. The skin was a little elastic, too, making the eyes somewhat droopy and frumpy. And these frumpy eyelids contrasted the fierce color of their irises so much that the man was a contradiction in the center of his face. Nevertheless, Butler stood tall and erect, proud and undeterred. It was almost as if he actually wanted to hang so that he could prove not only his own personal virtues, but those of his beliefs.

And he would probably get his wish. Patrick looked down at what passed for Mr. Robert S. Kelley's shoulders, the odd creases behind his ears, the stray, wiry hairs on the back of his neck, and his knotty fingers scratching out their marks like a rodent clawing at a morsel of food lodged beneath a stone. Considering all the things this little man had written about abolitionists, Free Staters, and Yankees, Patrick knew that no matter the results of the poll, this mean, vindictive little man would see to it that Pardee Butler would hang this August day.

With five voters left in the queue the tally was, to Patrick's surprise, even. The steely-eyed reverend stood apart. His feet had begun to sink in the mud, and he pulled them out one by one, each boot making a sucking sound as he did so. The whole crowd, in fact, had begun to sink and, man by man, it pulled itself out. The color of the men's boots was now the color of the river, and Patrick noticed a worm struggling beneath the heel of a man smoking a pipe next to a tree.

For the first time, Patrick considered this, his new community. It was a tough, hardscrabble lot of men who had lived their lives on the frontier, some of them having gone to war in Mexico a decade or so earlier. They didn't own slaves, these men; they only aspired to one day, and they saw Kansas as an endless stretch of fertile possibility, a land where they could build the sort of plantations they had seen as children in Kentucky, Tennessee, and South Carolina. Their dreams, in fact, were similar to Patrick's and Clegg's. They wanted to grow. They wanted to own themselves and their destiny. They wanted to be left alone.

Nevertheless, Patrick was not going to let them hang this man. He made up his mind that when Robert S. Kelley tallied that final vote, he would speak up. He would appeal to this sentiment on Pardee Butler's behalf. He would tell them they had no more right to control the thoughts and words of this preacher from some small cabin on Stranger Creek than Washington had to control theirs. He would show them the hypocrisy of their doings, and save this man's life. His promise to himself to hold his tongue, to not get involved, to flee the end of the world and begin another world in Kansas, had to wait for sundown.

Patrick watched intently over the shoulder of Kelley as the last man came to vote. It was tied, and this man would decide the fate of Butler. He was a quiet, old man who had wintered beneath a lean-to eating snared wild rabbit and pheasant. And as the man approached the crate where Bob Kelley sat, Patrick thought there was nothing in the world that could possibly draw his attention away from the little piece of paper where the vote was kept. But just as the man indicated his preference to Kelley, and Patrick opened his mouth to begin his stirring oratory, he heard a truly shocking screech to his right, toward the river where Butler stood in all his face-painted humiliation.

A hawk descended suddenly from the sky and plucked at the gray hair of the hat-less old man, bending him forward a little, putting a slight grimace on his face. The bird, just as surprised as the man, stalled for a moment, then fluttered off into the sky again with another shrill cry.

And the men laughed as a drop of blood ran onto the black paint on Pardee's forehead.

"That bird's a-fixin' to nest on your head, Preacher!" said one.

"I'd say that bird is sent from the Almighty to condone the judgment of Atchison!" said another.

"I think he wants first dibs on your scalp!"

"I've already a-spoken for it!"

Others cracked jokes to those next to them out of the sides of their mouths, and there was general hilarity, but Bob Kelley and Patrick Dugan were not interested. They, and they alone, were aware that the final vote had been cast and the fate of the man attacked by the hawk had been sealed. They both looked at the paper at the same time.

The old man had broken the tie—Butler was to hang.

But just before Patrick could speak, Kelley stood on the crate. Patrick thought he might push him down and beat him silly, just as Thomassen had done to J.W.B. Kelley a few days earlier. He thought he might begin his speech now, pushing himself out from behind the little man on the crate. He thought he might just call "Wait!" or "Stop!" like he had before. He looked down at his boots. A corner of the crate was sinking in the mud. He saw the hawk circling above. He looked around. These men were ready to hang another man. All of the empathy Patrick felt a few moments before was gone. These men were not the same. They were monsters. They would hang him too if he spoke. Patrick hesitated, and thought he would not say anything at all. He was going to let them hang Pardee Butler. It was none of his business. He wasn't a townsman. He was a simple farmer who lived three miles away.

"You have spoken!" spoke Robert S. Kelley. "We are to make an example of this man, and send him down the river!"

The hawk, circling above, gave another shrill call, and through his own tears and the stunned silence of the mob, Patrick could see and hear something move in the brushes across the river.

Something about Atchison just wasn't right.

It did things to a man.

III

On March 21st, 1854, when Patrick wandered into the newly opened reading room of the newly built Boston Public Library and picked up a book that was lying inconspicuously on a wooden table, he found his destiny. At first he didn't know if he was allowed to read it, but after glancing at the man at the desk and having held it, the man smiled, and Patrick knew somehow from this smile that this book was as available to him as it was to anyone. All around him were more books on shelves, but this one would do just fine. It was enough to just read again. It reminded him of his mother, who had taught him as a child, and the smell of the paper and ink reminded him of hunger, of sitting beside the fire in their Cork County cottage, his fingers running over the pages, his mouth salivating as the limp soup cooked in the giant pot beside him. When there was food at all.

It had been a couple years since he read anything but signs, circulars, and the occasional newspaper, but after twenty minutes, it all came back to him, the rhythm of reading. He sat hunched over the wooden table for several hours, and completely forgot where he was.

Within ten pages of the *Journals of Lewis & Clark*, he knew he must leave Boston, go west and make a life for himself and Maria, that he hadn't left Ireland just to flee starvation and oppression; he'd come to America so he could find its interior, its frontier. He'd come to America to meet Maria and read this book. Finally, it all made sense again, just as it had when he was a boy, before the famine, before the revolution.

"How does one go west?" he asked the librarian.

"West?"

"West." He held up the book so the man could read the title along the spine. "To follow such men as these."

"You want to be an explorer?" the librarian asked quizzically.

"No. I'm tired of exploring. I want to farm."

The librarian smiled. "There are rumors that Congress shall open the lands west of Missouri for settlement soon. If I were you, I would wait patiently, save my money, and read the newspapers."

That was all Patrick needed to know. Saving, waiting, and reading were three of the seven things he could do very well, the others being praying, working, eating, and drinking (the first three of which he did quite religiously, the fourth of which he did not ever do, and with even more religiosity).

He ran to Maria's house and burst into the front room.

***

Maria couldn't remember her father's name. She'd come to think of him as a smell and a moustache on one hand, and a myth, a legend, on the other. The only complete memory she had was him leaving for work in the dark one winter, bent over at the wood stove, preparing the coals and kindling so her mother could light it easily and warm the house for the children. Maria lay very still and watched him, his hairy hands quietly doing their work, and just as he rose and turned for the door, he looked back at her, winked, and disappeared into the foggy marshes of childhood memory.

Though she couldn't remember it, his name was in fact Patrick, and Patrick's memory—his myth and his legend—came to shape Maria's childhood household and the lives within it long after his death. Pappa, as he came to be known posthumously, was referred to like scripture. "And just what do you think Pappa would say about your behavior, Maria?" her mother Maria would say. "Ah? And would Pappa agree, young lady?" Or, "Maria, lass, Pappa is turning in his grave." Maria came to think of him as a terribly expensive garment hanging in a well-lit window on Merchant's Row, something that was unattainable, unspeakably beautiful, and so totally directive of her actions that she fancied herself an instrument upon which he played. He pulled, pushed, and dragged her through her own life.

And so when she met Patrick, a newly arrived immigrant from Cork County, she knew she would follow him instead. It was 1853, she was in her early twenties, and knew she was ready for wherever he might lead her, simply because she had to escape the city that killed Pappa, that stole his hands and his moustache and made of him a hairless legend.

"I want to go to West," Patrick blurted out one March afternoon, rushing in the front door as Maria sipped tea. "I want to leave this awful wetness and stake my life on the frontier, Maria."

Her eyes brightened, and she waited for him to see it before she said, "Oh, let's!"

"So you'll come with me?"

"Oh, yes, Patrick, yes! Let's go tomorrow!"

***

And so it was. They were married that summer and Maria would be pregnant by the time the first leaves returned to the trees the following spring. Patrick saved all the money he could, helped Maria's mother maintain their small house, and made preparations for their journey westward. All they needed was fifty dollars and their health, both of which they had by the summer of 1854, and both of which were gone by Christmas.

But Patrick had a secret. He told her about his dreams of expansion and peace, his dreams of sculpting the future like it were clay that lay for his hands only, but what he didn't tell her was that he believed the world may just be coming to an end. It was crumbling and falling behind him like a bridge across a crevasse, and all his life he felt he was running west just as fast as he could to keep in front of it. And he'd come to believe the world would end in Kansas, begin anew in Kansas; that in the vast stretches of the American Desert a new existence would rise, and anyone caught east of the Missouri River would perish. They would slaughter the Irish, slaughter the Negroes, slaughter the Mormons and the Jews, and then each other. Patrick felt it in his bones like cold or hunger; had all his life. Man was all hind legs.

But he held his tongue. He said none of this to her. He never spoke of what he thought was behind them, only of what he thought lay ahead. In fact, with few exceptions, one being that of the afternoon of March 21st, he always held his tongue, and he knew that that was why Maria loved him so.

***

On his walk back home from the levee that August day in 1855, Patrick began to cry. This was the eighth thing he did very well. Patrick cried so easily his mother had once thought something must be wrong with him. But today, the heat, the arguing, the near hanging of a man, and the memories of how they had come to Kansas and how disappointing it had been, made it all too much. Patrick cried all the way home.

And the ninth thing he did very well was walk. He could walk while doing any of the other eight things he did very well—he could walk while eating, carrying an astonishing amount of food, usually atop some slice of bread; he could walk while praying, and in fact did most of his praying that way; and he could walk while drinking, for a time, anyway, until it became rather impossible—and today he walked while he cried. He wandered to the east of the path he had already worn to his farm and came upon a rectangle of logs placed on the ground amidst a small clearing in the cottonwood trees. He was surprised he had not seen it before while collecting firewood or lumber with Roger, as it was only two-thirds of a mile from the house. The underbrush had grown around the logs, which appeared to be a half-hearted attempt at the foundation of a cabin, indicating they had been there before springtime. And then he saw it.

It was a yellowish piece of paper nailed to a nearby tree, and Patrick knew immediately what it must be. During the previous fall and spring, the territory had held two elections; the eve of the second being a night when men on horseback came from Missouri and threatened settlers they should either vote pro-slave or go home. These men voted fraudulently, throwing logs down in the woods and pretending they were residences. And, being under a mile from his cabin, it meant one thing—Kansas was crowded. He'd come to expand, to have space and room, and now he was claustrophobic. He read the note:

> *"Move my cabin and I'll cut yer liver out.*
> *—Joseph James Hawkins of Missouri"*

The world was coming to an end, and he hadn't escaped it—he'd taken his little family straight to the epicenter of the apocalypse. Maybe Maria was right. Maybe they should just go home, wherever she thought that was.

And so he walked some more. He would keep walking until he was at the edge of the world, the very border of the universe. He would walk until all the strife, all the petty disagreement, all the jostles of will and exertions of power faded behind him like the sound of a steamboat up the river. Wandering into the forest to the north of his claim, he knew he had to walk until something made it clear to him that it was permissible to stop. Whether arriving or becoming lost, he would know when it was time to go home and make up with his wife. He would know it from that place of knowing inside him, just as he had before.

It came at a spring. It was the clearest water he'd seen since leaving Ireland as a child, and was incredibly contrasted to the great big dark Missouri. It almost appeared to be some sort of hallucination, impossibility in the desert, but there it was, bubbling up from the ground atop a small hill. The water ran down the southeastern slope and disappeared into the topsoil. The area around the hill was soft and supple, smelling of wet wood and leaves. He stopped, realized he'd found his thus-far undirected destination, and took another step forward. And he heard a crack underfoot.

It was a small clay token he'd broken, and looking around, he found that there were tons of them all about, scattered around the hill with the spring atop it. They were offerings, it appeared. Bones of birds and animals, man-made pottery, even some coins and the rotten remains of small carcasses that were once furry. Patrick thought of all the stories he'd been told as a boy in Ireland—of little men and sacred trees—and realized he knew what exactly what to do.

He circled the mound, leaving what he could (a coin here, a bit of handkerchief there), closing his circles ever so slightly, walking ever so lightly, until he crested the pinnacle of the hill, and he bent down and suckled the earth. It was the coldest, clearest, cleanest, most refreshing water he ever drank. He suckled again. And soon he was laughing. He suckled and laughed, sucked and chuckled, until he was truly in an uproar. And when he was done, tears in his eyes, he felt very tired, rolled over and fell asleep.

He woke just ten minutes later, felt cold and uncomfortable, yet somehow revitalized, and stood. The sun had begun to set to the west, and the sky stretched itself across the length of the earth, the shadows across the land. It was going to be one of the sunsets he had come to associate only with Kansas, the sort of setting sun that made Maria almost love the place, the light that made Patrick think, at times, that perhaps he had indeed found what he sought.

Off in the distance he saw something he did not expect. To the northwest he saw a man approaching.

He waited, knowing that the man was heading straight toward him and would speak with him. He sat down atop the hill, his backside sinking into the mud.

When the man reached the small clearing around the hill, he stopped, smiled, and said, "You better come down from there, young man. It's not wise to stay there so long."

Patrick stood and descended the hill, noticing that the man—a short man wearing worn wool, canvass, and skins—had stopped at a line of stones in the earth that, once Patrick surveyed the ground about him and noticed it, encircled the hill. The man had a misshapen moustache and an odd accent, a bit of French, a bit something else entirely.

"I'm sorry," Patrick said. "Is this your spring?"

The man laughed. His eyes were bright, his skin weathered. "Doesn't belong to me or any man," he said. "You've as much a right to drink that there water as the President. Or a slave, for that matter—even a dirty savage. But you've a-been there too long. You're not welcome anymore."

"I'm sorry. I didn't mean to offend anyone. 'Tis a sacred place, I see."

"Ha!" The man spit to one side. "It isn't any man whose welcome you've outstayed. But that plant is none too happy to see you." He pointed to a small tangle of ivy that laid about the hill, a great nest of it at the top. "Did you stick your face in it to drink?"

"Yes, sir."

"Well, let's wash you or you'll have trouble a-breathin' tonight. The name's Paschal," he said, pouring a handful of water from a canteen and scrubbing Patrick's face with a familiarity and a lack of ceremony that was not as surprising as it may have been. "Paschal Pensoneau. And you've gone and stuck your face in a bed of poison ivy. Your head'll be the size of a pumpkin tomorrow. Keep mud on it."

"I didn't know." Patrick began helping with his own washing.

"You sure as hell didn't! Don't you know you've got to leave some for seed? There's always a new season to think of, young man. There, that should do it." He had covered Patrick's face with mud and moss by now. "Let's sit."

They sat on an outcropping of limestone a couple hundred yards from the hill, and Paschal removed a small satchel of dried herbs from a deerskin bag that was slung around his shoulder. He leaned his muzzle-loader against a tree, loaded a pipe adorned with the tail of a deer, lit it and began smoking. He handed the pipe to Patrick, who initially tried to refuse it, but then acquiesced.

Patrick coughed, and asked, "What is this place?"

"Let's start with yer name, unless you want me to call you Mud Face. Yer Irish?"

"Yes, sir. And it's Patrick. Patrick Dugan."

"And you live in Atchison?"

"I've staked a claim a few miles south of here, between Atchison and this place."

"Well, you've found yourself a special place to settle, Mr. Dugan. This is the land of the Wind People. Used to be, anyway. And this place? Well, you seem to have figured it out by the look of ya. It's the breast of the Earth, Mr. Dugan. That river's her blood—this, her milk. Only you done got greedy. A rash is usually what we get when we get greedy, too, idn't it, Mr. Irishman?"

Paschal laughed, and his head leaned back so that the orange glow of the setting sun illuminated the interior of his nose and mouth. He was hairy in those nostrils, but not terribly so, and the shadows of the bones in his face were unfamiliar, long, dark, and protruded. The sun made it seem that his skull glowed from the inside out. He seemed to be of another world altogether.

"Where are you from?" Patrick finally asked.

"Ah." Paschal grinned. "The sun's a bit low for that sort of story. I'm a Frenchman by birth, obviously, but I've changed through the years, Patrick. This land has changed me."

"Where do you live, then?"

"Out on the Grasshopper." Paschal pointed west. "Mine's the first cabin round here. I'm the first white man to settle without building a fort first. I was, anyway."

"Was?"

"You see it, Patrick," the Frenchman stared deeply. "I see that you see it. I done got married to an Indian and I've changed. Man and wife tend to grow close through the years if they do it right. And in Kansas you must do right. This is a land that don't forgive."

"How long have you been here?"

"Oh, a dozen years or so."

"But I thought..."

"Ha! They didn't open it for settlement 'til last year? I just found that out myself!" Paschal laughed and packed more herbs into the pipe he'd been smoking. He struck a match on the limestone and puffed.

"Used to live right down there in Atchison. I offered my cabin there for the election last year, and after two hundred Missourians a-showed up, I realized how it was going to be. So I went west, followed my wife's people to where the folk down in Leavenworth made 'em go." Puffing his pipe, his expression become friendlier. "Patrick, white men been comin' round here for a long, long time. They just always got scared away until me, that's all."

"What scared them away?"

Paschal looked at him, turning his head slowly, opening his eyes just as wide as he could. The sun seemed to brighten for a moment, concentrating on the Frenchman's face like a candle held close to the face of a storyteller. He puffed his pipe calmly, grinned a little, and said, "You mean, you didn't see it?"

"What? See what?"

"It was watching you, Patrick. It's been watching you for a while now."

"What? What's been watching me?"

"The sun is so low, Irishman." He looked away, as if to end the conversation.

"I have to know!"

Paschal tapped out his pipe on the rock between his legs. "Oh, you'll know soon enough. It don't watch for long, Patrick. You will see it. Just look around you, for Christ's sake."

Just then Patrick heard a rustling in the brush to his left, around the other side of the hill with the spring. He looked, but saw only the branches moving, as if something had run into them. He rose and made a quick move toward it.

"Oh, don't follow it. Whatever you do, don't follow it," said the Frenchman, standing and shouldering his gun. He smiled. "You won't catch it anyway. You wouldn't want to, neither."

"But…"

"Patrick Mud Face, Mr. Irishman, come back here the next full moon at sunset, one month from now. If you don't know by then, I will tell you."

"But…"

"Just don't follow it, son. Look for it, but whatever you do, don't follow. Your body will do it, and you'll have to stop yourself."

And Paschal disappeared just as quickly as he had arrived. Soon he too was a rustling in the bushes, and all that was left behind was the sound of birds in the trees and the rising song of the frogs in the grasses.

Patrick walked home.

***

The sun had just completed setting as he crested the small hill directly north of his farm, and he could see Roger and Maria, his little Maria, finishing their preparations of supper by the glow of the campfire. He also saw that a lantern was on inside the new cabin; that his wife and brother had spent the day moving their meager belongings there, and that the little shack to the east was now fodder for firewood. The first hard year in Kansas was finally over. He knew it now. And he realized that Maria knew it too.

He hopped down the small hill, prepared to apologize to her for leaving so abruptly this morning; for not returning promptly after work; for not listening with kindness and attention, just as he had always promised her. He was prepared to explain the day to her, right then and there, the mosquitoes in his ears, the poison ivy beginning to swell his lips, mud falling from his face like a molting snake. She turned toward him as he approached, a smile on her face. He stopped right in front of her. Roger stopped chopping wood and looked at them. Patrick looked into Maria's eyes, waiting for her to speak. And then he embraced his little wife, who said nothing. Not a thing. And he knew now that while she loved him for holding his tongue, he loved her because she didn't have to.

IV

The next morning Patrick woke to the smell of eggs. It was the first time since they left Boston that he had woken to a smell, much less to the smell of something pleasant, comforting, and welcomed. Through all the previous fall and winter he'd woken either to a sight—light streaming in between the cracks in the wall of the shack—or a feeling—usually cold. Damp, wet, cold to which the wool blankets eventually, and always, had to allow entry. After smelling the eggs he opened his eyes, remembered the ivy, and was pleasantly surprised to see the mud and moss had worked beautifully—his reaction was very minor. He saw that the day had broken, that for the first time in months he had slept past the sunrise. It was a good morning.

It was already quite hot out, and he found Roger with his shirt off outside, splitting more wood.

"I thought I would wait for you to tear down the shack, brother," he said. "I thought you might like it." Roger was a quiet boy normally, given to great fits of temper or excitement only on rare occasion, and the smile he offered at this moment was about as expressive as he ever was during normal hours. Patrick walked over.

"Thank you, Roger," he said, offering his hand. "You've been a man this summer. None of this could have happened without you." He made a surveying motion with his arm around the homestead. It was now a cabin with a large chicken coop, a modest pig sty, a truly impressive vegetable garden, and a partially cleared pasture prepared for a cash crop and a dairy or beef cow, perhaps even both one day. The brothers understood the gesture was in apology for Patrick's absence the previous evening.

"I'm very glad to be here, Paddy," said Roger, resting his axe. "Kansas is the threshold of the future."

Patrick chuckled. "I'm not sure where you get such ideas, boy, but let's hope it's less eventful around here this autumn than last."

"Oh, I don't think it will be. That was nothing. Just the beginning."

Maria came over to them with two cups of coffee. The large cup was for her and Patrick to share. They all sat down on wide logs used for chopping.

"And why do you say that, boy?" asked Patrick, aware his tone was more patronizing than he'd intended. Maria looked at her husband briefly as she handed him the coffee.

"They're all coming here," Roger said, looking East. "Some things will be easier now. We'll have food and warmth, goods and groceries, but Kansas will soon be crowded."

"Don't say that, Roger."

"It's true and you know it!" Roger said with a wide grin.

"Maybe so, but this is nothing a boy your age should worry himself about."

"You just called me a man, Paddy."

"But this is none of your concern. Your concern is this farm. These chickens, those pigs, this wood."

"And protecting them."

"From what?"

Roger smiled. "Anything that may harm them, brother. Now, let's tear down that shack!"

Roger hopped up, nearly spilling his coffee, which he gulped before bounding off with his axe toward the "old" shack, as it had already been renamed in the twelve hours that had elapsed since the onset of its disuse. He stopped just before reaching it, laughed with a little hop in his step, and struck it broadside with the blunt end of the axe head. It lurched, and he struck it again. And again.

Patrick wanted to join in but it all happened so fast. In a matter of seconds Roger destroyed what had been their home for the past year. What had been a conversation over coffee became an acute moment of violence with a suddenness that reminded Patrick of Roger as a child—there was a time, for instance, when Roger was only about two and Patrick was only a little younger than Roger was now, that the boys went out together into the yard to feed the chickens, and Roger tried to kill a rooster. The bird had charged their father, flapping its wings as loudly as it could, and Roger immediately fought it back. His arms flailing while he jumped about, he also unleashed a nonsensical toddler tongue-thrashing on the rooster, who eventually cowered in the corner behind a small post. But Roger wasn't pleased with simple submission—oh no, he wasn't finished with that rooster, and had to be pulled from the pen by his older brother.

Patrick had always believed, without ever admitting it to Roger, that had he not stepped in and restrained the enraged little boy, that rooster would have found itself without feathers in two minutes. And somehow Patrick remembered this when Roger began tearing down the shack, not because it was rare for Roger to do such a thing (though it was), but because somehow it always seemed that he may do such a thing, someday, if so inclined. For two moments, two unique moments separated by more than a decade, to define someone, seemed illogical. But this was Roger. The two-year-old who would stand up to a mad rooster when others would cry, and the fifteen-year-old who demolished a shack in the woods in Kansas, were somehow bookends that mirrored the shelf.

Patrick and Maria stood. He gave the cup of coffee back to Maria. "Well, we better clean it up as soon as we finish the eggs. It ain't gonna turn itself into firewood," he said, and thought to himself that he was finally beginning to sound like an American.

***

What Patrick, Maria, and Roger needed most now was a stove for the cabin. They almost had enough money and Patrick was due to receive one on the next shipment from St. Louis, whenever that might be (hopefully before the first frost). Maria described what she needed in this stove to Patrick while she cleaned the pan that had cooked the eggs and Roger began dismantling the walls of the shack for firewood.

"Just somewhere to rest the bread," she said, "like mamma used to have."

Maria had become a master of cooking with wood fires. She could make or bake just about anything in an open fire, knowing how to rotate the wood for heat and light, how to rotate pots and pans so their content would cook evenly, how to roast and broil, fry and boil. "Stick me a piece of cottonwood there," she would say to Roger. "No, not that one lad, a flat one. Yes, that's it, I need the light." But Maria was slowly turning a soot color, her face and hands were desiccating, and she was beginning to experience breathing problems at night. It wasn't the stove she needed as much as the flue. She was excited about the stove.

"And make it a good one, Paddy. This is not something to buy cheaply. This could cook our food for the rest of our lives."

It was true, and her excitement told Patrick things had indeed finally turned for Maria, as if the tumult of yesterday were the last throws of darkness, or winter, and suddenly spring, the day, had dawned. Still, he didn't want to make any promises about such an expensive purchase, so he waited for Maria to stop talking about the stove for a moment and changed the subject.

"About last evening, Maria," he began, but she smiled knowingly and put her finger to her lips to silence him. She was kicking dirt onto the fire, wiping her ashen hands on her soot-covered apron. "Nothing to be said," she patted him on the stomach, peeled off a square of mud with a laugh and kissed him on the cheek. "All's well that ends well."

"What do you mean?"

"I mean to say that they didn't hang him," she said knowingly. "Whatever you blame yourself for, Patrick, is nonsense. I know you and I know you take responsibility for all injustice on God's green earth. It'll kill you, Paddy." She smiled and patted her hands on her thighs.

"But how did you know?"

"Know what?"

"How did you know about what happened yesterday? In town, down by the river?"

Her brow furled. "Well, from Roger, of course."

"From Roger?"

"Yes, silly. Roger was there."

"He was?"

"Of course! But didn't you know?"

"No, I sure didn't. I thought he was here with you all day, minding the farm."

"A boy can't stay hidden in the woods all the time," she said in a hushed tone. "Besides, he told me you asked him to come."

"I did not. And I find it hard to believe that he could have been there all along without me noticing . . . unless . . ."

"Unless he was hiding from you."

"Exactly." A coal popped in the fire. "It was dangerous, Maria."

She smiled. "Exactly." Another clump of mud fell from his face, and she laughed. "Nevermind where Roger was yesterday. You need more mud on your face."

***

After Patrick and Roger finished demolishing what had once been their home, they went hunting. Both had memories of their father hunting, and of his dog Chance, without whom they thought hunting was near impossible. And to some extent it was. If Kansas had not provided the abundance of fowl, rabbit, and deer that it did, the brothers wandering around in the woods would probably be more likely to shoot each other than any sort of edible game. But as it was, they ate. And they ate well when they learned how and had time to hunt.

Not having found many dogs in Kansas, they'd developed a system where Roger was ostensibly the dog—flushing turkey and pheasant out from the underbrush—and Patrick was the triggerman. They used a short, shrill whistle to warn each other of their presence, one they learned from their father in Ireland as children. Roger hated being the dog. Tromping through the knee-high, thorn-riddled bushes seemed to release as much moisture as it frightened fowl, and at times he felt claustrophobic, as if the vegetation trapped the humidity and heat like a sauna. He always ended the day covered in ticks, and would spend an hour or two before supper removing them, sometimes needing help. He felt like a child removing his shirt and having his sister-in-law twist them out of his lower back and shoulders.

"Paddy, I don't want to kick them out any more. I get all the ticks. Let me shoot."

"I don't want a face full of lead, boy."

"Hell, Patrick, I won't shoot you."

Patrick stopped walking and looked his brother in the eye. "So you're a-cussin now?"

"And you're a-talkin' like a Missourian now?"

They both smiled.

"Please, Paddy?"

"Oh, all right. Just make sure you see feathers before you pull the trigger. If you see skin you better relax that finger of yours."

They walked across a small clearing toward a dense grove of diseased cottonwood trees that thrived in the muddy bottom despite their gnarled, knotty, dusty condition. The trees were releasing their cotton now in late August, some months later than their healthy peers, and the cotton spread across the field like little white fingers throwing fabric or sand across a table. It rained down on them and, looking up into the sky, it seemed like a blue tunnel with white polka dots and a green center. They walked through the tunnel silently, stepping lightly and carefully. Neither wanted the walk to end. It was a gorgeous tunnel.

"I'm not going to fill your face with lead, Paddy. Besides, it looks like someone else already has. What happened to your face anyway?"

"I poked it somewhere it didn't belong. Seems to be a family trait." They glanced at each other. "What were you doing in town yesterday, Roger?"

"Sticking my nose where it doesn't belong, I suppose."

"It's not that it doesn't belong, Roger. Just not yet. You're too young yet. It's not safe."

"I've got a feeling boys become men a bit younger in Kansas than in other parts of the world, Paddy."

"Aye, but they mightn't ever even become men if they aren't careful."

They reached the grove of trees and became quiet, listening for game lurking in the underbrush. The cotton had slowed its fall to the earth as the wind had receded, and the leaves and grasses fell silent. The smell of the river, a bit like a partially decomposed, floppy catfish, thickened the air as flour being added to water. After motioning with his hands to Roger, indicating what he was about to do, Patrick silently crept counter-clockwise on the periphery of the grove, and slipped between two trees. And he heard a rustling in the grass. He thought it was a rabbit or a pheasant, and he took large, loud steps toward it, kicking the grass as if it were a river through which he waded. The grass moved again, this time some twenty feet in front of Patrick, and Roger, glimpsing the feathers of a grouse, raised his gun and fired into it.

At first Patrick thought he had shot the strangest pheasant on earth, some wild Kansan fowl never before seen by a white man. But it was a boy, not a bird that emerged from the grass, his straw hat rimmed with feathers first, his muddy face next. "Goddamn Yankees!" he screamed in a voice that failed him. He ran, tripping a little, and before Patrick or Roger could react, he was sprinting toward the river on the other side of the grove of trees.

"Goddamnit, Roger!" Patrick strode toward him and removed his gun with a yank. "What did I tell you about feathers?"

"I saw feathers, Paddy!"

"What are you saying? Boys don't have feathers."

"Didn't you see his hat? It's covered in feathers!"

"No, I didn't," Patrick's shoulders relaxed and he looked to where the boy had been. He chuckled, "I suppose it was, wasn't it?" He laughed. "You scared the hell out of that poor boy."

Roger laughed too. "Almost ruffled the feathers of a ruffian, didn't we?" And they both laughed.

"Lord forgive me," Patrick said, still laughing, asking forgiveness for both his using the Lord's name in vain twice just now and of his laughing at the misfortune of a fellow human being. The boy looked to be Roger's age, too. No longer a child, but not quite a man; he didn't seem to be armed. So while he laughed, Patrick also wondered what the boy could have been doing there, if he weren't hunting. There was no cabin within several miles, and a boy of such an age would not be likely scouting for a potential homestead across the river, but he might be with his father.

And then Patrick stopped laughing.

He saw, on the distant tree in the grove, the yellow note he'd stumbled upon the day before, and he looked down. He was standing right in the middle of the square of logs that passed for the foundation of a cabin. He walked over to the note while Roger still laughed, took it down, and handed it to Roger, who read it, and then they both looked down at the square of logs.

"Oh, no," said Roger.

"Oh, no is right," said Patrick.

V

Breathless, Oliver John Hawkins finally found his brother Joseph James, who was ten years his senior, picking mushrooms along Deer Creek just to the south and east of the Dugan claim. His horse, Ninny, was grazing in an adjacent pasture.

"Jimmy! Jimmy! Some goddamned Yankees done just took a shot at me!"

"Now slow yerself, boy." Joseph James was pale only in the depth of the winter, his skin darkening, it seemed, within moments of finding the sun. Wizened eyes, a stubble beard, and pronounced, horned nose marked his face, and together with a large frame and thick buckskin clothing, he was the quintessential Missourian. "What d'ya mean by a-sayin' they 'took a shot'?"

"With an ol' muzzle loader, Jimmy! I'd just gone and found the note and the square you left last spring, just like you told me, and when I heared 'em comin' I hid in the grass, quiet like. They came right up on top a me, Jimmy, so close I coulda heared 'em a-breathin'. But I just laid there all still like, letting them skeeters eat my face clean off and the ticks a-suckin' my blood, just a-waitin' for 'em to leave. But one of 'em come up right behind me kickin' the grass like he was a-rabbit huntin', and he done kicked me clean in the ass!"

"Watch yer mouth, boy."

"Well, that's exactly what he did, Jimmy! Kicked me right in the rump, so I ran! And what'd the other one do? Why, he raised the rifle right in my face and took a shot right at me! Search me how I got away, but I a-heared 'em laughing behind me and I come runnin' right to ya!"

Joseph James Hawkins didn't hesitate. He placed the last mushroom in his satchel and whistled for Ninny, who obediently trotted to him. He hopped up on the horse into a stirrup-less saddle, gave his arm to his brother, who mounted Ninny behind him, and the three galloped off into the woods, heading west.

***

"We'd better get back to the cabin, Roger. I think we might've just started a civil war."

"Damnit. I'm sorry, Paddy."

"Don't you start cussin', little brother. We wouldn't be the first Dugans to start a war. Remember that."

"We'd be the first to start one by accident though."

"And the first to do so without cause."

"Paddy, we have cause! Those Missourians are a-stealin' our land!"

"I'd think they already have, the way you're a-talkin'."

"Paddy, they're coming and you know it."

"I don't care who comes to Kansas and who doesn't. We came to farm and make a new life. A quiet and peaceful life, and I intend to keep that alive no matter who crosses that damned river."

"That's not a life, Paddy. That's running from a life."

"Damnit, Roger!"

Patrick had a lot to say just then, stamping in the grass like a child, but he never got the opportunity, because Joseph James and Oliver John Hawkins arrived. Ninny galloped alongside them quite suddenly, Joseph wielding his Colt revolver and shouting from atop his beige mare.

"Stop right there, you goddamned Yankees, or I'll blow yer heads clean off your shoulders."

Roger began to raise his rifle at the man on the horse, but Patrick knocked it down.

"Smart man," said the unflinching horseman. "Now both a-ya drop them things behind ya. Now, boys!"

The two Irishmen carefully dropped their rifles behind them, and Oliver John, who had already dismounted Ninny, scrambled over and picked them up. He gave Roger a little kick in the back of the leg while he did so, and Roger shot a look of indignant disgust back at him. Joseph James rested his pistol on his leg.

"Now, which one of ya bastards took a shot at my brother?"

"I did," Patrick replied.

The two men held each other's gaze for several seconds. Both had the grizzled, stubble-faced look of frontiersmen, but within the world of the frontier they could not be more different. Joseph James was born in Indiana to a westward-wandering Tennessean, but had never walked upon anything other than Missouri soil until he left at a young age to fight in the Mexican-American War. He was a western Missourian through and through, wore canvass leggings with his buckskin coat, an antler-handled Bowie knife on his hip, even while he slept. He had the look of someone who had been seeded, germinated, and grown out of the rich but clay-ridden soil of the river basin.

Patrick, on the other hand, despite having learned a year ago the fabrics and clothing that held their own on the frontier, still looked like someone who had been overgrown by the land instead of having grown out of it. Still a little swollen from the poison ivy, his face was slightly asymmetrical and he appeared even more out of place because of it. Joseph James was a vine that crept along the limestone bluffs of the Missouri, and Patrick was a Rip Van Winkle who slept so long the vine grew over him, waking to find himself, unexpectedly, a part of the land. Patrick had been subsumed by it from the outside in, while Joseph had manifested it from the inside out.

"Hogwash," said Joseph James. "The boy did it."

"It was an accident. The boy thought he was a pheasant. "

"Don't you Yankees teach yer youngins to look first before you shoot?"

"It was his hat, sir. The boy saw the feathers moving in the grass. What was he doing hiding in the weeds?"

"Ain't none a yer business, sir," he replied with sarcasm. "This here's our land, and we can do what we want with it."

"I'm not sure a yellowed note and four logs make a claim, Mr...?"

"Hawkins. And they make a claim if I say they do." He raised his handgun at Patrick. "Git down on yer knees."

"Don't do it, Paddy!" Roger said immediately and with force.

"Shut up, boy!" Joseph James was even more immediate and more forceful. "Get down on yer knees, you damned bogtrotters. Both of ya!"

Patrick and Roger slowly knelt in the grass. Roger could feel ticks crawling up his pant leg, and wondered if he'd ever have a chance to twist them out of his skin. He thought about calling for Maria.

Joseph James dismounted Ninny and walked toward Patrick, the Colt leveled at his head.

"Where's yer claim?"

Patrick tried to keep his lips from quivering. "A mile north." He almost vomited as he spoke.

"Don't lie! T'ain't no mile."

"I sure hope it is," said Patrick, and from somewhere that seemed outside of him, he managed a little smile, which seemed to result in the loosening of Joseph James's arm muscles, ever so slightly.

"Get this straight, Irishman—this here ain't no false claim. I came and voted to keep free niggers outa here, but I didn't do it 'cause I'm politically inclined. I did it 'cause I aim to move my family on this side of the river and I don't want no damn nigger lovers or free niggers takin' my land or my daughters, bunch a heathens. All you is, is a white nigger. I seen Irishmen in Mexico in '48, and yer all a bunch a traitors, every last one of ya. You San Patricios traitors just as soon fight with the Mexicans, damn Catholics, than anyone else. Yer white niggers. You got that?" He leaned forward and plunked the barrel of his Colt on Patrick's head, knocking his hat cockeyed. "You got that?"

"Yes." Patrick did throw up this time, a little, and Joseph James let him finish before continuing.

"Now I don't feel like touchin' off no war today. I been to war and I don't want one today. Maybe tomorrow, but not today. I ain't gonna kill ya. Not today. Maybe tomorrow, but not today."

He lowered his pistol, walked around the kneeling Dugans and picked up the rifles, handing them to Oliver John, and mounted Ninny. Oliver John followed and fired one of the rifles a few feet from Patrick and Roger, who both flinched, sending the Missourians into a fit of laughter as they galloped off, and to the Dugan brothers' surprise, dropped the rifles at the edge of the trees.

"Come," said Patrick, standing and retrieving his gun. "Let's go home."

***

Later that evening Maria, Patrick, and Roger sat around their camp-fire. They did this partially out of habit—it had been their living room for over a year, and though they now had a much more comfortable place to sit inside their new cabin, the rock-ringed fire with limestone cooking surfaces, centered in a grove of trees, was still home to them. They also sat here because they still had to cook here, would have to continue doing so until they could purchase the new stove, and because the furniture they had purchased was still on a steamboat somewhere down river, and, unknown to them, the boat was beached on one of the many treacherous sandbars that were the bane of the Missouri River steamboat captain's existence. Once the furniture arrived, Clegg was going to lend his horse so they could cart it to the cabin, but tonight it was still a living room with campfire-flickering trees for walls, stars for ceiling, and rocks and logs for furniture.

"We can't move the cabin now," Patrick said. "Not after what we've been through, and now that…" He glanced at Maria, who knew it was now time to tell Roger about the baby.

She looked at Roger as he sipped his coffee.

"What?" he said, looking up, the light flickering on his face. He looked tired. "Now that what?"

"I'm with child, Roger," she said. "By the Feast of St. Valentine we shall be four."

Roger's reaction, both Maria and Patrick thought, was that of a man. He smiled, rubbed his eyes, shook his head, and then laughed. "The two of you just don't want this to be easy, do you?"

They all laughed, and Patrick rose to his feet, his form appearing more ungainly than usual in the orange glow of the embers. His shadow, cast against three cottonwood trunks growing together that the family dubbed the "three sisters," was even more awkward, knotty and elongated so as to be nearly monstrous. "I need a drink."

"Paddy!" Maria snapped.

"It's okay, love. Just a nip for me and the boy."

"And…?" she stood.

"Sure, if you want one."

"I'm not asking permission, boy."

"No, of course you aren't."

Once they toasted and downed the whiskey they kept on hand as medicine, Patrick repeated himself. "Well, we can't move the cabin. It's been too much work. I think Hawkins's claim beat ours, but I don't think it was very sincere. I'm sure we can prove that when the time comes."

"To who?" Roger was bordering on incredulousness. "There ain't no court in Atchison, Paddy. At least, not a real one. What you and I did this morning for that man was court round here."

"I know, Roger, I know. If only I could convince him to just move a couple hundred meters."

"Convince him?" Roger was now incredulous. "Did we meet the same bastard?"

"Watch your tongue, young man!" Maria already sounded like a mother.

"Maria, this man was a devil! Paddy wants to reason with the devil himself."

"He is not a devil, Roger. No man is. He just wants what we want and has a different way of getting it."

"No different than me." There was a terribly awkward silence that can only exist in families in which the individuals harbor deep affection for one another. Had they not loved him, Roger's defacto guardians would have understood the comment simply as a comment. But they loved him, and understood it for what it was. But Roger decided to give voice to what the comment really meant anyway. "No different than how Pappa would have handled it."

Maria buried her face in her hands.

Patrick rose, containing himself as best he could. "And look where it got him, Roger. Look where it got him!"

Roger stood and faced him. "And look where your way got us, Paddy! Stuck in the middle of nowhere on our knees at the mercy of a monster!"

"Listen to me, young man! You're the one who went off half-cocked! Had you been just a mite cautious…"

"Cautious! You aim to be cautious around here, Paddy? Then we're all damned! Damned, I tell you!"

Patrick gritted his teeth. "There are better ways, Roger. Ways Pappa never tried."

"I'm going to bed."

"Good."

As he left, Maria stood, reached up, and wrapped her arms around her husband's neck. "Be patient with him, Paddy. He's got the fire of youth in him."

"He's got the fire of his father in him too."

"I know." She smiled. "And so do you, God help us all." She plunked him in the chest with a knuckle and turned toward the cabin. "I'm off to bed, Mr. Dugan. Off to my bed in my new home!"

"Enjoy it, love. You'll have a new bed soon to match."

"I know it. You've a lot of work to do tomorrow, love. Come to sleep soon, will you?"

"Of course. I'll be right there."

Patrick watched as his little wife shut the door—tight and latched!—behind her, and the lantern was extinguished in their room. He heard Maria and Roger speaking in soft voices in the dark, and knew things would be settled by morning. He knew that he and his little brother would often be at odds in Kansas, that one day Roger would need to strike out on his own, and as long as Patrick could keep him safe until he was fully grown, it would be okay. Things were going to be okay.

Then the specter of Joseph James Hawkins, atop his horse, behind the revolver, was raised in his mind. He and that little rat of a boy that scurried around beside the scruffy man on his scruffy horse, were not going anywhere anytime soon. Maybe Roger was right. Maybe the Missourians were coming in force, along with half the men of the South. He'd heard in town, from Clegg probably, that there were yet more boatloads of Free Staters coming from the North, too, financed by the New England Emigrant Aid Society. He'd met some of the first boatload of them during his trek west with Roger and Maria. Some seemed rather normal, but others were fanatical, even violently so. Yes, they fought a good cause, perhaps, one he could agree with—no son of his father could ever do anything but hate any form of bondage—but some of them seemed bent on conflict, also like his father. No, he didn't trust them either. Kansas was becoming a battleground. Roger and Clegg were right.

But so was Maria. He looked at his cabin, his garden, his pig sties and chicken coop. Behind the cabin there was a lot of clearing to be done if they were to expand their cash crops, but it would be done. Now that the furniture was on its way and the stove within reach, he would hopefully sell enough crops to buy a horse and plow by the fall. And next year would be even easier. If he could only protect this—his little quarter-mile section—then the rest of Kansas could go to hell. Let the Americans sort out their politics in Kansas if they like, he thought. Let them have their civil war wherever they might want to. He would keep it at bay. He stood tall and lit his pipe. He would hold back the hordes of humanity if he had to. He would stand between the world and his cabin, his little wife and his little brother, an immovable force of nature.

He smiled, puffed his pipe, and remembered the whiskey. For two or three years now he hadn't had a sip, but now he felt the aroma in his throat. Just another nip, he thought. I was almost shot to death today, nearly so yesterday, and I held it all back twice. I faced the devil himself on horseback. I deserve just one more sip. So he turned, found the flask beside a stump, and walked back to his previous spot by the fire. Slowly, relishing every twist of the cap, licking his fingers, he prepared himself. He took one more drag from the pipe, lifted the cap, now full of whiskey, to his lips, and let it slide down his throat. Ah, it was nice.

And when he opened his eyes he saw something move in the trees just a few meters away. He remembered the conversation with Paschal and held still. He wouldn't follow, he told himself, tightening the cap on the flask. No, not even once. He wouldn't follow it, whatever it was, and it wasn't going to show itself, anyway. No, it was gone. So he strode, dropping the flask, toward the trees that had moved. He would just look. Just a little peek.

But after just two steps it emerged from between two trees. At first he thought it had to be the whiskey, but after blinking and rubbing his eyes, he knew it wasn't.

Standing before him was a giant bird, with a broad, thick, curved beak, long feather-less legs, and eyes the size of his hands. It blinked, and was clearly watching Patrick. It gave out a little squeak, and then a shrill, ear-splitting squawk that startled him and made him turn toward the cabin to see if Maria or Roger had been woken by it. And when he turned back, it was gone. The trees were moving a little, and he began to run toward them before he heard the Frenchman's voice, "Whatever you do, don't follow it."

VI

The pulpit was made of pine. The second he saw it, Patrick wished he hadn't come. He had never wanted to come, but decided, in consultation with Maria, that it was best he did, for Roger's sake. Roger had been honest, after all. He could have crept away to Big Springs and been secretive about his doings, as he had twice in the last two weeks, sneaking out under the light of the moon without a word, just a satchel over his back. But this time he invited his older brother, handing him a circular announcing the convention over the new supper table, which had arrived that morning along with several other pieces of furniture, and which he and Clegg had carted up to the farm.

"Free State Convention!" the circular read. "All persons who are favorable to a union of effort, and a permanent organization of all Free State elements of Kansas Territory, and who wish to secure upon the broadest platform the co-operation of all who agree upon this point..." Patrick knew the language. It was almost as if it was his mother tongue that he'd left behind in the mother country. The convention was to be held at Big Springs, some fifty-five or sixty miles to the south, "for the purpose of adopting a Platform upon which all may act harmoniously who prefer Freedom to Slavery. Let no sectional or party issues distract or prevent the perfect co-operation of Free State men. Union and harmony are absolutely necessary to success. The pro-slavery party are fully and effectually organized. No jars nor minor issues divide them. 'United we stand; divided we fall.'"

Their father would be proud. Roger was taking up the banner of freedom.

During his moonlit escapades over the last fortnight, Roger had actually gotten a personal invitation this convention. That a party could include a mere boy in its platform deliberations was shocking to Patrick, and it told him, he felt, a lot about this movement. It was, at least in Atchison County, rather desperate.

"They think I'm seventeen," Roger confided on the way to Big Springs.

"I see," replied Patrick, holding his gaze straight ahead. Maybe they aren't desperate, he thought, maybe they're just stupid.

Clegg had loaned them his team of two horses and wagon for the trip, which went very smoothly in the steamy mornings of early September, and despite the wretched conditions of the roads, only one minor repair being necessary to the brake lever. They arrived by suppertime on the 4th, set up camp, and ate bread, ham, and carrots, sitting on the back of the wagon. It was a dark night, a bit cool compared to what had become a hot day, and full of stars. They considered lighting a fire, but were too tired. All about them were others who had come for the same purpose, and the flickering of campfires and sounds of distant conversations made the evening reverberate with the unordinary. Tomorrow was going to be the most eventful day in the history of Big Springs, before or since.

Roger became quiet. At length, having finished his meal, he repositioned himself in his seat, and said, with a little crack in his voice that he had tried so hard to preemptively stop, "Paddy, do you ever think about Pappa?"

Patrick choked a little on the bread that had somehow become dry, despite the humidity of the day. It was the bread, though, not the topic. "Of course I do, lad. What kind of a son would I be if I didn't?"

"I've been thinking about him lately. I wish I knew him better."

"Aye. And I'm sure, wherever he is, lad, he wished he knew you better too. Your Pappa sacrificed a lot."

"For a good cause."

"Yes, for a cause. But loss is loss, Roger." Patrick hesitated, then decided he'd found a good way to express what he meant. "You were a good cause too. We all were."

"But this is bigger than all of us." Roger hopped off the wagon, took a few steps away from it, and turned toward him.

Behind him Patrick could see the glowing camps scattered about the prairie, and he thought of all the women and children left behind so these men could convene here.

"He always told us that," Roger said. "He told us to lay ourselves down, to give ourselves to the betterment of mankind. A free Ireland is the best thing he could have given us."

And now Patrick knew why he had come. He had come for this moment. Opportunities to speak to children, and young men, at a time when they may listen are few and far between in life, and one must seize them like ripe, wild fruit, recognizing the bright color in the repetitive thicket of green, pith caught in the mundane. Reach out and harvest. "Yes, a free Ireland would have been a great gift, Roger. But the gift of a father is a hard exchange to make for it. And we never had a choice."

Roger turned away, hands in his pockets, and looked out over the gathering of wagons. "I would have chosen as he did."

Patrick waited a moment. He'd seized the fruit, he thought to himself. It wasn't there anymore for the taking, and wasn't as sweet as he'd have liked. "So be it," he said, climbing into the wagon, pulling a wool blanket about himself, and lying down.

Roger followed and lay next to him. "I love you Paddy. I'm glad you came to Big Springs."

"I love you too, lad. I'm glad you invited me."

***

The first speaker at the pine pulpit was a gentle Bostonian now living downriver in Lawrence, the Chairman of the convention. Charles L. Robinson was a doctor and politician who had written the text of the circular that Roger had given Patrick. He was a balding, round-headed man approaching forty with bright, engaging, soft blue eyes that could find consensus between devils and angels if they ever wanted to. And his audience that September day liked him very well. They agreed he was their leader. They listened attentively and nodded their heads, but they shuffled in their seats— cottonwood stumps, mostly—and they yawned.

Then, just before noon, James Henry Lane stepped to the podium. Jim Lane had more magnetism in how he rose to speak than Robinson had in the most important lines of his entire speech. He glided and floated toward the front of the gathering, which had decided to reconvene outside the small community building, under a grove of walnut trees, due to the nice weather and large crowd. Robinson had come to this moment after many months of careful planning, meetings, and with the help of an extensive network of financing reaching back east, but Jim Lane had arrived in Kansas with a rifle, a knife, a beaver-skin hat, a bearskin coat, and an incredible gift for oration. He was ugly, to be sure, and this fact was underscored as he removed his hat and revealed the wildest head of hair in Kansas, but there was an undeniable beauty in his presentation. Each piece of the man was horrid, but as a whole he was as compelling a man as any west of the Mississippi.

Robinson was a man people followed in the best of times, Lane in the worst and, between them, they could lead a bonafide revolutionary political movement.

As Lane rose that day, hunger beginning to distract and unsettle his Free State brethren, he knew that it all began here. His unremarkable stints as Lieutenant Governor of Indiana and as a member of that state's delegation to Congress didn't matter anymore. The people of Kansas were as fertile as her soil, ready to be tilled and seeded in neat rows like the ranks of soldiers he colonelled in the war with Mexico, and harvested when the time was right. Nothing held Jim Lane to Indiana anymore, not even the wife he'd twice sought to divorce, and twice been denied. The second he rose to speak that September day in Big Springs, Jim Lane was as Kansan as anyone.

As Lane turned and faced his audience, Patrick looked askance at his brother. Roger had the appearance of someone who believes they are in the presence of greatness, and Patrick knew now that the issue was not that he should not have come, it was that he should not have let Roger come, with or without him. The night before in the wagon, under the stars, he knew why he had. That morning when he saw the podium he wished he hadn't, but when he saw the face now at the pulpit, he knew that being in Big Springs meant that he'd brought his little brother right into the center of the end of the world. He'd come so far to escape it, the apocalypse, only to see it follow, but at least he had his claim to cordon off and make of it a sanctuary on the plains. And he should have locked Roger on that land. This boy's midnight escapades and this trip to Big Springs were like shaking hands with the devil.

"Nooowww..." Lane bellowed from the podium, throwing the syllable across the room like it was water and he wanted to soak everyone in it, his palms planted firmly upon the top of the podium, bending forward as if following through on this throw, his elbows stuck up in the air, making him look like some sort of insect. "Why have you come to Big Springs, today? Why have you come to Kansas?"

If truth be told, that was all it took for Lane to make Roger a believer. And Patrick knew it. He nudged his brother.

"I'm hungry, lad. Let's go see what we can find to eat."

"Shhh."

He tugged harder on his brother's arm and smirked. Though it was serious, it reminded him of poking his little brother at the supper table as children.

"Paddy! Not now!"

"I'll tell you why you came to this Territory! I know why. I know why you have come because I, too, have come for that reason."

Every syllable was given its proper time, enunciation, and emphasis. Each was accompanied with its very own gesture and facial expression, as well, a sort of physical consort that mimed the language and accompanied it to the listener's head, where one went to the eye and the other the ear. Lane's listeners were also watchers. He orchestrated as he spoke.

"When I ask myself why I have come here, and I look deep into my heart and soul, I find an answer, and I find that this answer is not mine alone. I hear your voice speaking it," he pointed at one man, "and yours," and at another, "and yours, young man!" he concluded, pointing at Roger. "We are all here for the same reason this young man is, and I want you all to look at him."

The audience turned and looked directly at Roger.

All the blood sank from Patrick's face.

"This is the future of Kansas! This is the future of these States! He is here because he is obliged by something deep inside of him, a place of knowing, to be here, something of great meaning and importance. This young man is here because there is a great darkness wanting to spread itself across this land, a darkness that threatens to enslave free white men, and this young man—each and every one of us in this humble gathering place—is willing to put themselves in front of that great darkness and stop it in its tracks!"

The crowd burst into applause. Teeth were gnashed, fists clenched. Had Jim Lane asked them then and there to charge some great army of demons, they would have done so without hesitation.

"But moderation, moderation, moderation, gentlemen!" For now, it could wait. Lane took a breath, the men were seated, and Roger wiped the tears from his eyes, pretending to yawn.

VII

By the end of the day, the body signed its endorsement of a set of resolutions establishing the Free State Party of Kansas, and Roger was officially addicted to politics. It wasn't just Lane's oration that did it, though that was in large part responsible. Robinson's exact skill of organization—the way he split the delegates into small groups to examine drafts of resolutions, written primarily by Lane the night before, and the way the entire proceeding unfolded yet converged toward consensus—was exhilarating. It was what his father told him as a very young boy: resolute and righteous groups of citizens were always the mechanisms of progress in the world.

The resolutions stopped somewhat short of establishing a true platform, instead setting forth a repudiation of the state government established by the elections earlier that spring and the winter before—they were simply going to ignore the Pro Slavery government and establish their own. And this was the second thing Roger liked about politics—one could diminish the power of people who were not resolute or righteous. The selfish people who had elected the current state government, Missourians who voted illegally, were the very folk who had made him and Patrick kneel, fearing for their lives. Joseph James and that little squirrel of a kid of his had them so afraid they were vomiting in the grass. Their grass. The land they claimed legally and with righteousness in their hearts.

These people were not only perpetuating the evil of slavery, they were undermining the right of true land-owning and land-improving settlers in Kansas to govern themselves. Just like Pappa always said, bad people try to gobble up all the land and make tenants or slaves of the good. The ownership of land was, and had always been, the only way for people to control their own destinies. This Free State movement was not only a fight for right, as he saw it, but first and foremost it was a fight against wrong. And with this set of resolutions the movement knew now, at least, what it was not. They made the first step toward defining themselves that day in Big Springs, through compromise, procedure, and wordsmithing. To Roger, nothing could be more human than politics.

But to his brother nothing could be more human than farming. As the convention drew to a close—scheduling meetings for future dates where they would proceed to elect their own delegate to Congress, forcing Washington to decide whom to seat, thereby making it very difficult to ignore the issue of the legitimacy of the elections held thus far, and hopefully providing a catalyst for a Congressional investigation into the matter, thusly and henceforth and forthwith, etc., etc., & etc.—Patrick squirmed in his seat and made a list of what needed to be done at home. He'd left a corner of the corn field un-harvested the month before, as it had been shaded by trees most of the growing season and the stalks were less mature. That needed to be harvested. He still needed a horse and a dog if he could find one; he needed a barn, a better pig-sty and better plow, and if he was ever going to get more milk cows he better put up some hay, and soon. The sun was setting, and he wanted desperately to get out of that meeting and get on the road back toward Atchison.

He looked up from his little list and saw that Jim Lane was at the podium again. It was almost as if his wild hair was set purposely to do what it did. The sides and top were both combed forward, the top crowning into a swirling flame. His head looked like it was on fire, and it seemed everything about the man was intended to look that way. He was a charlatan, and all these people were buying his junk. Especially Roger. The poor boy even rose to his feet and let out a burst of vocal approval when Lane claimed that the Missourians were "not only stealing our government, but our land! The next time they cross that river to vote as Kansans, I suggest we remind them of that border by drowning a few of them in it!" Patrick saw Charles Robinson, sitting to Lane's left, wince, but the crowd applauded wildly, Roger a bit more enthusiastically than most. Finally, on a note of drowning, it was over. Patrick had the horses hitched to Clegg's wagon before another man left the little building, who happened to be Roger.

With Patrick holding the team steady and his back on the gathering crowd, Roger was accosted suddenly from behind, just a few yards from his wagon. It was Lane. He had passed all the men in the gathering as they clutched at his bearskin coat, just to have a word with the youngest member of the delegation. Roger turned and saw this man's face up close, its deeply inlaid lines, pointed nose, and sloping brow, hair that stood up like masts, and thought it had the shape of a barque to it. His head didn't only look like it was on fire, it looked like it was catapulting through this life at breakneck speed. This man from Indiana was like a meteor traversing the surface of the earth, and in him Roger saw everything he ever wanted to be. Even the smell of his coat was something he wished to emulate.

"I do hope you'll continue your involvement in the Free State Party, Mr…?"

"Roger—I mean, Dugan. Mr. Roger Dugan."

They shook hands.

A muscle just below Roger's left eye twitched. He rubbed it calmly.

"Well, Mr. Roger Dugan, it's a pleasure to see such young men in the Territory interested in its future. Tell me, how did you come to be involved? Where are you from?"

"Atchison."

Lane drew back and blinked. "Atchison! Why, you must be the sole Free Stater in the county!"

"It's Pro-Slavery territory to be sure."

"Indeed! Never have I seen such hatred spew from a man as that . . . who is he now? . . . the editor of the *Squatter Sovereign*..."

"Stringfellow. And Kelley. Robert Kelley is his junior editor. He's smaller than me."

"Is he now? Yes! The both of them, my word. And the town's namesake, Senator Atchison of Missouri. Do you know I met him once or twice during my time in Washington? I was a Representative from Indiana. David Atchison is a devil and a drunk, I tell you. He's well known in the capitol for his love of whiskey. 'Old Bourbon,' they call him. The vices of slavery men are endless."

"I didn't realize what the town was named for."

"Oh, yes, it's a stronghold. But we can count on your help to turn it around, I'm sure, Mr. Dugan of Atchison."

"Of course."

"Of course! The Irish never shy from a righteous fight."

They shook hands again.

"Thank you." Roger's eye twitched. "Thank you, Senator."

"Ha! I'm not a senator, son. Not yet, at least." He winked. "Call me Jim."

"Thank you, Jim."

"Anytime, Mr. Dugan. You and I are alike, you know. When we know what's right, we don't like waitin' around for it."

Roger turned and walked to the wagon, where he found a hunched-over brother with a set jaw gripping the reins with white knuckles, staring into the dying light of the east.

***

On the way back to Atchison, both Patrick and Roger thought about their father and what he would have made of the convention in

Big Springs. James Patrick—J.P. as he was known—was active in the Irish resistance to English rule while the boys were young. Most of the Irish were tenants to a handful of landlords who lived in England, unfamiliar with the plight of farmers who were essentially their share-croppers. Many could barely feed themselves, and once the potatoes went bad and people actually started starving, J.P. refused to pay his rent, stating boldly and calmly in a letter to Southampton that he needed the money to feed his family.

The moment he signed that letter he became a dissident, his sons the sons of a rebel. He joined various bands of rural agitators, then the more established and genteel Young Irish resistance, believing all along that a massive, armed rebellion was the only way forward for his people. He was shot in the leg during a standoff with the police around a farmhouse in July of 1848, captured soon thereafter, and by 1849 was either sent to Van Diemen's Land in the islands off the coast of Australia as a prisoner, or was hanged, his wife and sons never told which, as if it mattered. To them, Australia was as good as dead.

J.P. told his sons that if anything ever happened to him they should take their mother somewhere where they could own land. "With fertile soil a man can have all the good things the Lord can offer," he told them. "Go to America, and move as far west as they will let you. Own your land and you will own its bounty."

Little Roger would cry, "Not without you, Pappa!" and he would scream an inhuman scream when J.P. left the house after supper, and once attacked his father with flailing arms, the way he'd attacked the chicken as a toddler and the Kansan shack as a teenager.

It was a night after they had lost their land and moved to the city of Cork with thousands of other angry, sick, starving farmers, and J.P. had come home very late. The smell and eerie glow of flames filled the windows of their damp, dark house, and the family knew there had been an uprising. Roger attacked his father when he walked in the door. J.P. held the boy back until his arms tired, and then embraced him tightly. They cried together in the rainy doorway of their home. It would forever be the strongest memory of J.P. that Roger had, and every time it rained, he could feel the warmth of his father around him.

About half way to Atchison, it began to sprinkle. Pockets of steam rose from the soil, and the smells of frogs, slugs, worms, decaying grasses and mold wafted above the horses toward the brothers. As it began to rain harder, and the wagon slipped its way along the ruts to the river, they both knew that J.P. was there with them. The night before had been the first time since reaching America—since losing their mother—that they had spoken of him so openly; and now they thought of him just as openly. Both knew what the other was thinking, and they knew their father was sitting right between them, smiling. The yoke strained under the weight of a third man and one of the horses looked back before Patrick snapped the reins. "Ya! Mind your work! Ya!"

And J.P. must have smiled, because he knew that there was nothing he could say, dead or alive, that could ever prevent the following from happening.

"You don't have to prove him right, you know," said Patrick.

"Who?"

"Don't be daft, Roger. I don't like the looks of that Lane feen."

"Pappa would have loved him, so."

"No. No. That is where you are wrong. It was different in Ireland, like."

"'Twas nary a difference, Paddy." With J.P. there, both brothers' original accents percolated back up their throats and bubbled in their mouths. "You heard what they said, like. The Southerners want our land."

"They want our vote, Roger. They want their way of life, their slaves and plantations."

"It's wrong!"

"Let them take all of Kansas and make it the devil's land then, Roger, except our piece of it. We'll protect our quarter-mile, you and I. We shall make our own kingdom. The Land of the Dugans."

"Pappa would be ashamed."

"Watch your tongue!"

"He would be, Paddy, and you know it. We can't retreat into our little farm and ignore the storm."

"We can't stop it from raining, either! Pappa had less of a choice than we do. Calm heads must prevail in Kansas, and this Lane wants to ensure they do not. He's a provocateur."

"How could you use that word? A son of James Patrick Dugan accusing a man who stands for freedom of disobedience? What's happened to you?"

"I won't have it in my home, Roger. I won't. It's torn my family apart once already."

"You won't have justice in your home. How honorable."

The boys settled into the rhythm of the horses. Clegg's wagon was well cared-for, yet it swayed and creaked along the uncared-for trail. The rain was light and steady, and began dripping from their hats and the canvas covering the wagon. As the miles stretched themselves toward the river, the sky darkened under the growing night and clouds. A late season thunderstorm was approaching, and neither wished to end the day soaked, cold, and hungry. It had been a long few days, there was a lot of work to do tomorrow, and Patrick slapped the horses a mile outside town. He was in a hurry now.

Almost an hour had passed since the last word was spoken.

"Pat will let it in his," Roger mumbled.

"What? Who the hell is Pat?"

"Pat Laughlin. His place isn't far from here. Justice is welcome in his home."

The sky opened under a great clap of thunder, the wagon's back-right wheel slammed down into a hole filled with water, and the wind began to howl. The horses neighed and the brothers could barely hear each other.

"Is this Pat one of the provocateurs? He's your midnight tryst?"

"Go to hell, Paddy!"

The two jumped down off the wagon and went into an automated process of hoisting the wagon out of the hole, using a long plank of wood and a rope.

They yelled at each other through the noise of the storm and their work.

"I won't go to hell, boy! I've been there before and you're trying to go back!"

"What do you call Kansas? Paddy, look at this!" Roger stood and turned his palms up, indicating the mud and filth around them. "Kansas is hell!"

Patrick rushed over to him, stumbling a little as his boot stuck in the mud. "It's not yet!" He jabbed his finger at Roger's chest. "Not until young, fiery men like you make it hell for the rest of us!"

"If I've got to go through hell to do what's right, Paddy, I'll do it!"

"Not on my farm you won't!"

"So be it!" He dropped the plank of wood, just as the wagon crested the lip of the hole and the horses pulled it clear. "I'll go to Pat's!"

"Don't do it, Roger." Patrick's voiced settled a little. "Stay with me." He offered his hand. Roger didn't accept it, so he placed it on his brother's shoulder. "Stay with your sister and me. Maria loves you. I love you." He placed his free hand on his brother's other shoulder, and looked at him deeply. "I need you, Roger. Your cause may need you, but so does your family. I need you to help me make a new life here in Kansas, and put all this behind us."

"It's caught up to us, Paddy. We're running out of West."

"I know. But we'll protect our farm. The rest of the world can crumble around us."

"No, I won't let it."

"Damnit, you stubborn mule! Your father died and orphaned his children for this cause! It may have been right but what did it do to us, Roger? It was selfish! He should have put his family first! You're doing as he did and mistaking integrity for selfishness, you pig-headed ass!"

"No! He would be proud of me! I'm speaking out for what is right and you're hiding in the woods, you coward!" Roger turned toward the east and took a big breath. Just below a small ridge, which was the crest of a bluff crowded with trees that fell steeply to the river bottom, he saw something move. He turned back toward Patrick. "I need this, Paddy. Goodbye brother. Our father would be ashamed of you."

Looking again toward the river, he thought he saw a large, beautiful bird blink at him, and tears came to his eyes as his chest filled with a comfortable warmth. He began walking toward the river.

The rain, which had been coming intermittently in light sheets, steadied and increased as Patrick called, "Don't do it, Roger!" The wind had stopped, and though the rain was louder now, his voice carried over the wet plains, and Patrick knew his brother could hear him. "Don't do it, brother! Come back to us! I need you."

But Roger kept walking.

They'd been through famine, uprising, transatlantic crossing, the loss of their father and death of their mother, and the building of a home out of wilderness, but it was to end here on this windswept prairie in Kansas. Patrick watched as his brother disappeared into the trees just below the ridge. Darkness set in over the land and he could no longer see the trees. All was shadow. The rain began to fall torrentially, and he climbed back into the wagon to begin the final mile home.

The world was indeed coming to an end, right here in Kansas.

VIII

When Patrick returned to his new home without his brother, Maria was livid. She came after him with a shovel like she did snakes (even though snakes in the house were much less frequent now that it had actual walls and doors, she still kept a shovel in the kitchen behind the new stove), cornering him in the bedroom, and before he could stop her, she gave him one good swift whack in the leg. As he watched her fiery eyes glare at him beneath her red hair, Patrick felt sorry for all the snakes she'd killed that way. She was scary. Damned scary. Those snakes died in terror, to be sure.

"Damnit, beor! That hurt!"

"What were you thinking, Paddy?! And don't call me that—we aren't in Ireland."

"What was I thinking, woman? I didn't run away; he did!"

"You're bigger than he is, you stupid goat! Stop him! He's your responsibility! (And don't call me that in English, either.)"

"He's not a child anymore, Maria."

"Of course he is! Have you lost your head? 'Not a child…' He is a child! He's just a boy!"

"Maria, he's not. I can see the resolve of manhood in his eyes. Besides, if you wrestle a boy that age, he'll never forgive you for it—the humiliation."

They sat down after Maria lowered her weapon and replaced it behind the stove, her beloved stove, which she patted lovingly, as she always did when her hand passed within arm's reach of it.

"What are we to do?" she said.

"I don't know."

"Where did he go?"

"I don't know."

"Where did he leave you then?"

"I'm not sure. About a mile up the road, I think."

"Patrick Dugan, you are worthless!"

"Aye, that may be." He put his head in his hands, thinking that he was glad his elbows had a table to rest on. Roger had helped him build the table, of course. "He told me Pappa would be ashamed of me."

Maria stood, circled the table, wiped her hand on her apron, then on his back. "Well, he's wrong in that, boy. You know that, Patrick."

"Yes, I s'pose I do, girl. I wish the boy could have one more day with Pappa. Then he'd know him for Pappa too, not just the infamous J.P."

"I know," she said, sitting down. "My father was always a myth, too. Our whole block would speak of him as if they owned his memory more than I do. Can you imagine that? A grocer knowing a man better than his own daughter."

Patrick looked up, rubbed his eyes with the back of his hand, and then placed it on hers, which were folded neatly on the table. "I reckon we're the rocks in a bed of diamonds, Maria."

She laughed. "Well, we've done right in coming to Kansas, then."

He laughed. "Yes." He looked out the window.

An owl was just outside, its hoots carrying into the kitchen.

Patrick sighed heavily.

She squeezed his hand. "He'll come back, love. Just you wait and see."

"Oh, Maria, I don't know. To ask that boy to farm in the midst of all this is a task for the likes of Job himself. You should have seen him in Big Springs. He's naive but well suited for it. As long as he can keep a level head, he'll be fine, but you know Roger—when his axis tilts, summer is winter before you've had time to bat an eye."

She let his hand go, sighed, and sat down. "Any idea where he could have gone?"

"Just before he left he mentioned a man who lived nearby. Laughlin, I think. Do you think I should fetch him?"

"I don't know, Paddy. Maybe let's wait a few days and see if he comes home on his own. You may as well ask about in town and see what you can find out."

"But there's so much work…"

"I'll do what I can tomorrow," she smiled, and Patrick could see the soot in her wrinkles.

"But Maria…" She stood, moved next to him again, her hand on the back of his neck, and he lay his palm flat on her stomach.

"You may as well get all the work out of me that you can now, lad, while you still can." She placed her hand over his, bent toward him, and they kissed. "Now, for a spot of tea and some dry clothes. Would you like some toast, too?"

Patrick smiled and stood, looking out the window at the trees shaking the water from their leaves. Somewhere out there, his little brother was finding a place to rest.

***

When Roger arrived unexpected at his new home after the convention in Big Springs, soaked to the bone and without a horse, Pat Laughlin's wife was livid. How could a boy his age be left to his own devices on a night such as this? She hurried about the one room cabin, fetching dry clothes, a clean towel, even fresh linens, and warmed a bowl of parsnip soup. She even offered to butcher a chicken before her husband put a stop to it.

"Leave the man be, lass," he said. "You've done enough and he's grateful, but we've got politics to discuss now."

"Man? He's no more'n a boy, Pat. What are you, Roger, fourteen?"

"Seventeen, mum."

"Ha! Seventeen! You lads and your political parties. When there's so much work to be done the women's fingers are rubbed raw, you're off to your parties as soon as the moon gives you enough light to walk without falling flat on your face. Well, I hope you enjoy your parties."

"Conventions, like," her husband corrected her.

"If it were left to the men, this land wouldn't have a single crop in the ground or wooden frame clear o' the grass. We're here to settle and all you want to do is go to parties."

"Political parties, lass," he corrected again. "They have conventions. It's not the same . . . Oh, never mind. Leave me and the man be, would you?"

Pat Laughlin's wife shuffled over to the corner of the cabin with a candle, cup of tea, and her knitting. She glanced up at them every now and then as she knitted, almost as if he were a boy in trouble and was supposed to sit in his chair without moving until she said so.

"Tell me about Big Springs, Roger," Laughlin sat back in his chair with his fingers interlaced behind his head. He was ugly, Roger noticed for the first time. Big, misshapen ears, a crooked nose, and dark eyes that were hard to track.

Roger relayed all the necessary information, wondering why Laughlin hadn't come. The Free State Party was going to completely ignore the already established government set up by the bogus territorial elections held by the Pro Slavery Party last fall and this spring. They were going to elect their own delegates, write their own constitution, starting in Topeka.

"Who are the party leaders?"

"It is a righteous cause, Mr. Laughlin. We are blessed to be involved."

"The leaders, lad, who are they?"

"Oh." He pulled the circular out of his jacket pocket. It was smeared with rain, and he attempted to read it. "Rob...Robin..."

"Damnit boy! Who are they?"

"Robinson, that's it. C. Robinson. Charles, I think."

"From Lawrence, no doubt?"

"Yes, sir. Oh, and Jim Lane. An Indianan, James H. Lane. A fantastic orator."

Laughlin smiled, more inwardly than out. "Lane and Robinson, eh?"

"Yes, sir."

"I'm sure they can be found in Lawrence."

"Yes, I'm sure they can be."

"Well, we shall find them, lad, and do what we can to contribute to our noble cause." Roger smiled through a mouthful of bread, and Laughlin glanced over at his wife, who looked ever so briefly up from her knitting. "And so what do we owe the pleasure of your visit to?"

Roger choked a little on the bread before swallowing it. "I've run away."

"What?" Laughlin said in a low tone because he could sense his wife's ears perking up across the cabin. "Run away from whom, laddie?"

"My brother. My sister." He ripped another bite of bread away from his fingers as if he were shearing the bones of a small animal. "They don't understand the Free State cause."

"What?" cried Mrs. Laughlin as she leaped from her rocking chair so forcefully that it recoiled back from her and slammed into the wall. "An orphan in our midst! Sweet Mother in Heaven!" Her back arched and she placed her hand on her chest as if she were having trouble breathing.

"Sit down, beor! A man can't be an orphan."

"There you go with your 'man' again," she said, beginning to repeat all the motions of a half-hour ago—fixing bread and butter, warming soup and coffee, finding dry clothes—before realizing she'd already fed and clothed the orphan and there was nothing more she could do. "Can't you see he's not a man? You call him 'lad' yourself."

"Well, he ain't no orphan."

"Don't you start talking like these territorial heathens, either," she said. "You sound like a Methodist."

"Well, leave the boy be, lass. He's not an orphan—he's just struck out on his own, that's all, and should be commended for it. There comes a time in every man's life—"

"—when he has to do what he knows is right—" interjected Mrs. Laughlin with rolling eyes. "—yes, yes, I know. You sure know how to choose the night to become a man, Roger." She slapped the back of his neck lightly with three fingers. "It rains harder in Kansas than in all of Ireland at once and I think half the Lord's bathtub spilled over tonight. Why did you leave home, again? Did I hear you starting to spout some political nonsense? You're as bad as my husband."

Laughlin smiled at Roger. "She doesn't understand, my boy."

Roger smiled patronizingly at the woman standing above him, her hands on her hips, "My brother Patrick is a coward."

"Now, that's no way to speak of family!"

"It's true, Mrs. Laughlin. Our father was a hero and a martyr. He was either hanged or banished for his involvement in Young Ireland. We never knew which."

This gave both of the Laughlins a start. Mrs. Laughlin began to busy herself about the stove, and once again realized she had nothing to do. She sat at the table and twisted the ties of her apron around her fingers.

"But Patrick, my brother, doesn't want to have anything to do with the Free State cause here. He's a shame to his father's memory."

"Oh, the Virgin bite her tongue!" Mrs. Laughlin stood, turned, and sat back down.

Her husband leaned back in his chair and put his hands in his lap, squeezing them tight together. "And he won't allow you to do what you see is right."

"Not so much."

"But he makes it difficult, so?"

"Well, not so much, actually. He took me to Big Springs."

"Then what are you doing, lad?" broke in Mrs. Laughlin. "You'd rather sleep in a cot in the corner of this little shack with us two than be with your family? Let me tell you something, lad..." She stood and clasped the boy's face in her calloused, muscular hands. Her husband reached out to stop her but she pushed him off with an effortless shrug. "In the end, when the Lord judges you, you won't have a party, a cause, a resistance, rebellion, or movement standing by your side. You'll have your brother. He'll be by your side till the end of days. Those men you met in Big Springs will be long gone by then. Causes—what you say is 'right'—come and go, but love lasts forever. Love isn't always right, but it's eternal."

She sat down and Laughlin waited until she was well clear of him before he retorted, "Nonsense, woman! Right and wrong are what the Bible teach, not foe and friend. Righteousness trumps loyalty every time. God is more than love, He is righteousness. He is Justice. Isn't that right, Roger?"

Roger, who hadn't stopped eating, looked at the two on either side of him, the table between them, with a peel of bread sticking out his mouth. He realized, as he chewed and swallowed, that this was exactly the question that he had answered today, and he had answered it for himself.

"That's right," he said. "Courage means sacrificing what's good for your family in exchange for what's good for God's family. My brother is a coward and a traitor," he said unconvincingly and paused. "The men at the convention are heroes. Men like you." He looked at Pat Laughlin with the most serious expression he had. "I want to do what is right, not necessarily what is loyal."

With a cheer from the man and a sigh from the woman, the Laughlins busied themselves with making a bed for their new boarder.

And as Roger drifted to sleep he saw Laughlin smiling at his wife, telling her all the plans he had for himself and their new boarder. It was going to be an interesting autumn in his new home. There was no telling what might emerge from the darkness of the Kansan landscape.

IX

The full moons of Kansas are a little fuller than most. And it was during such moonlit nights that Patrick missed books the most. Since leaving Boston he had really only read the *Sovereign*, and while it was informative—from it he learned that Kansas was to be the epicenter of the apocalypse, for nobody could be so stupid as its writers unless the world were coming to an end—it wasn't very good reading. The small, misaligned, smeared columns didn't help the ridiculously inflammatory rhetoric that somehow managed to squeeze itself between and among so many punctuation marks that it looked like a chicken with ink on his feet had walked all over the paper. One could only amuse oneself with bad writing and editing for so long. After a while, the reader wanted a professionally edited and restrained narrative. Bob Kelley and his boss, John Stringfellow, were idiots. Patrick chuckled to himself. And Stringfellow was a medical doctor. Imagine someone who could barely put together a two-dimensional piece of paper putting a body back together. God help us all.

Just as his eyes closed, still smiling, Patrick woke with a start. The moon was full! It was September 25th! He was supposed to have met Paschal, the Frenchman, at the spring at sunset to learn more about the odd bird that led his brother away from him.

He stood, dressed, told Maria he was going for a walk, unhitched a new gelding he'd purchased from a Mormon man on his way to Iowa City to join next season's mustering, and who he'd named Zion. He raced north through the shadows of trees, wondering why on earth the Frenchman would have waited several hours for him. Still, he thought, it was worth checking.

As the woods opened to the clearing in which the spring rose from its mammatus mound, he stopped Zion and listened to both of them breathe.

The moon was high in the sky, and the spring reflected its light in all directions like a lighthouse beacon back in County Cork. Everything was silver; the trees looked almost as if they were glowing, and the great river could be heard somewhere in the breeze. It was on nights such as these, and places such as this, that magic lived, thought Patrick, and things are born.

And then he saw Paschal.

He emerged from the trees as if he hadn't left them since their last meeting over a month ago, as if he'd stood right there at the edge of the copse all along. He stepped into full view in the clearing, the gray light of the moon falling on him like water, and the silver of it as it careened off the spring gave him an almost inhuman quality, like a spirit or a ghost. His beaver-skin hat and raccoon shoulder-wrap seemed like the robes and mitre of a pontiff, and he carried his musket like a staff, his deerskin satchel like an incense casing swinging on a chain. He had a beatific, yet somehow also ornery (almost sinister) smile on him as he approached.

Without thinking, Patrick knelt before the approaching figure, expecting to kiss its ring.

"Tell me, Patrick Mud Face," said Paschal, showing his teeth, "do Irishmen always greet people this way?"

Patrick laughed and stood. The silver dulled a little. "No. No, I s'pose they don't."

"Ah, that's a shame. I could get used to it!" He clapped Patrick on the shoulder, and looked into his eyes. "I missed you at sunset, my boy."

"Yes. I forgot, Father."

"Father!" said the Frenchman with a chuckle. "My, you are so reverent it's irreverent! So respectful I'm offended! Don't you know I'm more man than any other man? Please, do me the honor of being indifferent to me!"

"I don't understand," said Patrick with a smile and a shake of his head.

"Good! Come now, let's sit."

They walked over to the limestone outcropping they sat on in August and took the same seats. Paschal removed the pipe and herbs from his pouch, and in silence they shared the first tokes. The moon centered herself directly above and behind the spring, and Patrick didn't know if his eyes were watering from the smoke or the bright light of the moon as it dove toward the western horizon.

At length, Paschal began. "You have seen it. I see it in your eyes." An expression of sadness and compassion spread across his face. "And it has taken someone from you. I'm very sorry for that, son."

"My brother."

"Ah, your brother. What a hard thing to lose to the bird."

"So it is a bird?"

"Yes, a bird, if you like." Paschal smiled, smoke wafting out his mouth. "Or a tree, a rock, a buck, a beaver or a raccoon. Whatever you like, Patrick. But yes," he sighed, "feathers and beaks make birds in my book." He gave a long slow grin and, smoking as he lounged across the limestone, he reminded Patrick of the caterpillar in Lewis Carroll's *Beyond the Looking Glass*, which he'd read as a child. "And that beak, eh? That beak!"

Yes, the bird's beak was striking, now that Paschal mentioned it. It was more or less proportionate to the body of the giant bird, but it still had a quality to it that was almost surreal. In thickness, length, color, and apparent power, it was almost mesmerizing. It was as if this beak of this bird could crush the earth itself, and Patrick said so now.

"Of course, Irishman! This beak can indeed crush anything. And those feathers, eh? Those feathers, Irishman!"

Yes, the feathers were also striking, now that Patrick thought about it. On first glance it was a camouflaged bird, the earthy sepia tones of Kansas running along each feather and section of its body, like most semi-flightless birds. But when one looked closer, this was no ruddy-colored pheasant or common sandpiper. No, if you looked long enough, this bird became blue and red and yellow all over like it had dropped from some South American rainforest right into the heart of the Missouri River Valley. Exotic, extravagant, opulent— even words like these didn't describe the color of these feathers, nor their texture. They seemed to be the softest down in the world, as if they could incubate the egg of life itself, and Patrick said so.

"Of course, Irishman! Those feathers could indeed give birth." Paschal took another long, slow drag from his pipe, handed it to Patrick, and stretched out even more upon the rock, extending himself to such an extent that he looked unnaturally elongated, like a dead chicken. The moon had sunk a little lower and the spring had ceased to reflect its light in all directions. It hung directly in front of them, so big it seemed it could be touched. And he began his story.

***

"Now, Irishman, let me tell you about this place.

"First, this place is not what you think. What you call 'Atchison' was once an island, and its first documented resident was a cow. She fell asleep beside the river one night, and seeing the water run past cool and brown in front of her when she woke, thought she'd turned over in her sleep. But when she turned around and walked away from the river, she found there was water there, too, so she walked up to it, bent over and drank, and turned back around, doing the same on the other side of the island. She did this half the day, muddy-faced

Irishman, circling along the shore for an exit like an ant, and finally, realizing she was entirely surrounded by water, that an island had formed itself around her overnight, she spun around four times, looking at the trees and grass and finally the sky, and with a groan sat down, flicking her tail.

"One July day in 1724 Captain Etienne Vengard de Bourgmont, commander of French forces in the colony of Louisiana, happened to discover what came to be known as Cow Island a few years later. She could have been rescued. But the gentleman and his officers, on a diplomatic mission to the native tribes upriver—which also served as a less-than-diplomatic statement to the Spanish, who had wandered almost this far north—proceeded to eat her.

"Bourgmont just happened to be at the front of the procession when they arrived at the bank of the great Missouri River and attained a view of the cow and her new island home, stranded amidst the rushing silt of the river. She was of much the same hue as the muddy water; and the trees, having been flooded upon the creation of the island, had also taken on the brown of decay. Bourgmont noticed the cow, despite her camouflage, and wondered how on earth she found herself stranded in the middle of a river, how long she'd been there and how she survived. But something else caught the attention of the woman next to him, Wah-Shinka Wako, an Osage squaw who was instrumental in Bourgmont's ability to communicate with the Indian chiefs. It was something blue and red, something moving quickly and disappearing into the brush on the island, something the size of a man, but something that appeared to have feathers and a very large, long, shiny beak. Indeed, Wah-Shinka Wako thought it might be a giant bird.

"'The Kanza tell of this bird,' she said, turning to Bourgmont with a wry smile and addressing him by the name she'd given him, I'n-Ta-Tse Shinkah (which meant 'Heavy Eyebrows,' and which was the only Indian phrase she would not translate for him). 'It tricks men into following it into the forest, toward the river, and they are never seen again.'

"'Nonsense,' he said without turning his attention. 'That, mademoiselle, is a cow.'

"Three days later, the Captain fell ill, was carted back to the river and returned to Ft. Orleans in a canoe, never to return. And the French, of course, never settled this place. Neither did the Spanish."

Paschal took another long pull on his pipe and continued. His French accent had remained, but all the Missourian and Kickapoo dialects were gone. It was as if some historian were speaking for him.

"Exactly eighty years later, in July of 1804, Lewis and Clark stopped at Cow Island. They found no cow, but a horse there instead. Perhaps the Indians stole and placed him there, thought Mr. Lewis. Or, a failed attempt to swim the river somewhere far upstream brought him there, thought Mr. Clark. But Sacajawea knew better. 'Fools,' she thought (as she had often thought and would think even more often in the months to come) as the horse slipped away into the dense brush near the western shore of the island, 'they know nothing of islands.'

"'Don't follow it,' she told Mr. Clark as he began to give orders for it to be captured.

"'Nonsense,' he replied. 'Such an animal is a tiding of fortune, my lady.' And with that, he sent a man by the name of Joe Fields after the horse.

"Three days later, discovering that three Indian paths intersected at the summit of a hill across the river, Mr. Fields was bitten by a snake, carried back to the river, and returned to St. Louis."

Paschal removed yet more herb from his satchel and refilled his pipe.

The moon sunk a little lower.

"I followed Lewis and Clark here, Paschal."

"What is that you say, Mud Face?"

"I followed them here. I read their diaries in Boston and decided to come West."

Paschal started with a little chuckle but was soon laughing heartily. Patrick looked at his boots. He felt ashamed.

"No man follows another man, Patrick," said the Frenchman. "Men follow only themselves."

Patrick thought he understood the joke now and said with a smile, "Or giant birds!"

But Paschal became rather serious, sat up, and within inches of Patrick's face, looked deep into his eyes. The stubble on the Frenchman's face seemed like steel wire, and he smelled as much like oil as he did the smoke that crept out the corners of his mouth. "And you still think there is a difference?"

He lay back on his elbow, puffed his pipe, the curls of smoke rising into the light of the moon, making a convergence of silver light and silver fire in a plume above his head, and continued.

"Exactly fifteen years later, in July of 1819, U.S. Army Major Steven Long joined a detachment of his on Cow Island, the detachment having spent the previous winter there establishing a small fort they named 'Cantonment Martin.' Traders and trappers who had traveled the Missouri in the years that followed the Lewis and Clark expedition had met with aggression from the Kanza braves who stood watch and hunted along her banks, and though the Major's objective was the exploration of Yellowstone, he sought to secure westward routes along the way. His parade up the Missouri River Valley was a show of force and power.

"A month later, Major Long held a council with Kanza chiefs, warned their aggression would be reciprocated if continued, and had even had a steamer built to impress upon them the severity of his threat. The Western Engineer, as it was called, chugged upriver to the great horror of the Kanza. Its bow was a giant blue serpent, its mouth and tongue painted red, and through it the exhaust screamed and steamed. The Western Engineer raised its flags and fired artillery from its starboard cannon into the high bluffs on the western bank overlooking the river. The shells broke the limestone in the bluffs and the skeletons of the Kanza ancestors tumbled out of the stone, some of them rolling down into the water.

"A non-aggression treaty was agreed within the hour, and within a decade the Kanza—the People of the Wind who buried their dead in the bluffs that are the horns of giant monsters with thrones in the depths of hell, and who knew of the bird for centuries, had lost many braves to it—were moved. I followed them here, Patrick, with my wife and her people, the Kickapoo, but then we were moved to the banks of the Grasshopper. We are a sick and sad people in our new land, but the Kanza, the people shaped by these bluffs, these trees, this river, and which were in turn shaped by them, fare even worse. They may not see the next century, but they will live in this land forever. In its name and its soil."

A silence followed, the moon almost set, and finally Patrick asked his question. "But Paschal, who is this bird? What is this place?"

Paschal sat up again and a look of sadness crossed his face.

"This is a land of ghosts, Patrick. It is a haunted place. This mound and this spring, they are not just the breast of the earth, they are the gates of hell, Irishman!" Paschal's look of sadness left suddenly and he laughed again, an eerie, foreign laugh to any speaker of any language, and sighed. "I see the poison ivy has left your face, but the stain has not, my young friend. The stain will be with you forever." He sighed again, stood, and faced east, toward the river.

"The Wind People believed the world began here, Patrick. They believed the world was once a giant river with a single island floating in it, and some say that island was the shell of a simple turtle. The Great Spirit put men and women on that island, but they became too many, Irishman, and the world became a very crowded place, so crowded that children could no longer fit on the island and were drowned in the muddy water. So the women pleaded that the island be made bigger, and the turtles and beavers changed the course of the river so the island could grow. Some say that island was Cow Island.

"But as they diverted the water it created more than just that island. It dug down into the bowels of the earth, and on this side of the river it exposed these lofty cliffs, these rocky bluffs, which are really the horns of great monsters that once lived well beneath the water of the world. But now they are here, with us. The Kanza buried their dead in these banks, Patrick, on this side of the river, in a sitting position so they could welcome the rising sun, right in the laps of monsters."

"So it's this side of the border, Paschal? Where the Kanza buried their dead? You're telling me Atchison is being built on an Indian graveyard? Is that what's wrong with this godforsaken place? As the white men move to this side of the border, they find only strife and warfare?"

"Border, Irishman?" laughed the Frenchman. "What border? That is what I'm trying to tell you. Rivers change their course, they grow and shrink, they dig and build, they shape our lives. These islands we live on come and go, but those monsters remain, these ghosts stay with us a long time, and the river is forever." He stood, and though Patrick felt Paschal had set up a camp on the limestone, within seconds he had all his belongings back in his satchel and his walking stick was in his hand. He was a self-contained town, this Frenchman from along the Grasshopper.

"When men forget that islands come and go and that rivers slither across the land like snakes, Patrick, they sin. They commit atrocities and sacrileges. Their breasts swell and become bigger than their heads. They harden, Mud-Faced Irishman, and what hardens may one day break."

Paschal turned toward the moon, and without any kind of departing ritual, began walking away.

"But, Paschal, will I see you again?" called Patrick.

The Frenchman turned all the way around and faced his questioner. The moon was directly behind him now, and the longer Patrick looked, the more the light bled into the man, almost subsuming him entirely. A breeze moved across the clearing from the east, and Patrick could smell the river, mud and fish and wet vegetation. He felt like he could smell the giant horned monsters' breath, or the skin of the bird. Decay was all around him, and so was growth.

"I do wish you would listen, Patrick. You must learn to listen. If you cannot, how do you expect to teach others?"

And the Frenchman walked off into the moonlight and the rolling hills to the west.

X

Roger had lived with the Laughlins for nearly two months now, but had yet to purge the sense of disquiet that perched on his shoulder the rainy day in September when he moved in, curling into sleep amidst the hushed tones of his hosts. He thought it was due to the fact that the entire territory was restless—that Kansas was a wilderness and a battleground—and didn't attribute his unease to the household he now called home. But throughout the last two months he had done little but attend meetings of agitated people (righteous and dedicated to their cause, yes, but agitated nonetheless), and he understood that this must have an effect on him. I'm tired, he thought. Yes, that's it. Tired and anxious. Anxious for what's to come, whatever that may be.

Arming oneself, in fact, is an act inherently dedicated to anxiousness, and that is what Roger Dugan and Pat Laughlin had being doing ever since the rain became cold and the trees began settling in for their winter slumber. Pat had become instrumental in forming battalions and platoons of the Kansas Legion, a quasi-military arm of the Free State Party. He'd left the politics to the likes of Jim Lane and Charles Robinson, preferring to correspond with investors in Boston who would send money and guns, and with homesteads who would accept both in exchange for their loyalty to the cause. They would muster at a moment's notice, these Legions of Free State Kansans, and he, Pat Laughlin, would help lead them. Plus, he usually found that a few extra dollars wound up in his pocket, and if they didn't, some of the guns that could be sold. It was remittance for his services, after all—one couldn't expect all guerillas to work for free, as Mrs. Laughlin said.

"Of course they expect it," she would say in her loud voice, glance at Roger lying in his bed in the corner, take her husband by the arm and continue in a whisper. "Read the letters, Pat. They are paying you to do their dirty work."

She said much of these sorts of things after Roger went to bed but before he went to sleep, and he would hear bits of it as he drifted off, then dream strange dreams where he was lost, confused, and hurried. And this contributed to his sense of disquiet. Mrs. Laughlin's whisperings carried the agitations of the day into the night, and Roger had little respite from it, without realizing it. He didn't know the meetings of the Kansas Legions continued in his sleep, that they followed him into his dreams through the whisperings of the woman who fed and sheltered him.

"They know nothing of freedom," she said one night in late October, her eyes holding her husband like a strong hand. "Do you think these people really care about slaves? They just want Kansas to be a place where they can succeed, just like we do, Pat. They think if they keep the slaves out of Kansas they'll keep the plantations out, and if they keep the plantations out they'll keep the plantation owners out, and if they keep them out, they'll keep the rich farmers out altogether, and they will become the rich farmers."

Pat sat and listened to his wife intently, glancing every now and then at Roger, then a slip of paper on the table, then at Roger. He rubbed his eyebrows with his forefingers and pinched the base of his nose as his wife continued. "And the Missourians are just afraid the slaves will be freed and become land-owners themselves. That makes sense to me! I used to think the Free Staters made more sense. But now look at them. Just look at them—they're doing the dirty work of the rich abolitionists in New York and Boston. No, Pat, I say we do it. I say we tell the Sons of the South everything. It's a good price and things have changed. There is more freedom for us in slavery. Hell, if they free the niggers, they're liable to enslave the Irish!"

After a moment, Pat Laughlin let out a long, loud sigh, and with one more glance at a sleeping Roger he snatched up the paper, stood, and put on his coat, shoving the paper into his pocket.

"My Pat!" said his wife. "My brave Pat!" she said and kissed him on the cheek, a girlish smile crossing her face. "The things you do for me!"

"It's not just for you," he said. "It's for the good of Kansas. It's what's right."

"Of course it is!" she replied, patting his shoulder and turning toward the stove. "I'll have some warm bread for you when you get back."

Laughlin left the cabin, looking back inside over his shoulder as he closed the door slowly and quietly on the sleeping boy.

***

Patrick stepped into the cool night feeling like he had all the energy in the world. It'd been so long since he'd been this drunk, it was nice to have an opportunity to actually enjoy it. Drinking with Clegg had been nice, and the two complemented each other, but he always thought that if he ever got back to doing this thing that he did so very, very well—drinking—it would be a little more fun. Instead, it had been a night of almost ten whiskeys (every sip of every one sweet as honey) and wallowing in lost loved ones.

Patrick had come to town looking for a way to sell his newly harvested gourds, and found Clegg standing aimlessly on Commercial Street with his son and a few possessions, almost as if he were waiting for Patrick. Not having seen his friend at work for many weeks, and without very much thought, Patrick followed him into the Pioneer Saloon, and they spent the next four hours around a wooden table, feeling heavier and heavier, as Clegg's son ran in and out of the place, playing under tables, flirting with women and doing tricks for drunken men.

"It's a sin, you know," Clegg had said as they arrived.

"Yes, of course, like. I'm Catholic, Clegg. And Irish. If anyone understands sin as well as Mormons, it's the Catholics. And the Irish."

"I try to stay sober, Patrick. But I'm lonely."

"I know."

"I miss them."

"I know. I miss them too."

Patrick was grieving for his absent brother, Clegg for just about everyone and everything. His wife and two daughters had died of cholera the previous summer, just as they were ready to leave for Salt Lake. Forced to bury them in an unmarked grave in a small wood outside Mormon Grove, he had lost the motivation to leave with the rest of the train. He ran out of supplies and money in the next couple months, spent much of the winter in bed while Little Joe Clegg wandered the camp with an equally unlucky young girl, then began work at the levee, where he met Patrick. And then he'd disappeared.

"They just showed up one night and made us leave," he said, downing a whiskey.

"Who?"

"The Missourians, Paddy. They took the Grove away from us."

Patrick felt the whiskey inside of him expand, warmly. "What do Southerners have against Mormons?"

Clegg guffawed. "The 'Mormon War of 1838,' they called it. Chased us out of Missouri. Their governor even ordered our prophet executed."

A loud group of men entered and sat next to them. Patrick and Clegg moved to a table near the back instinctively. "But what changed?" continued Patrick when they were finally seated and Joe had been corralled near them. "They left you alone out there for over a year."

"The *Sovereign* wrote about how we kept to ourselves out in the Grove, how we are hardworking, law-abiding," was Clegg's answer. "They needed our labor, Paddy. But there's enough of that now without needing polygamists. Funny how business makes friends of enemies, isn't it?"

"And the reverse."

"Yes, and now we've been camping out ever since, wherever we can."

The two sat in silence for a moment, and though Patrick knew what he was going to say next, he wanted the silence to mark the moment first. He wanted his friend to know he was serious.

"Clegg, why don't you and your son winter with us?" Patrick looked over at Little Joe, who was tugging on the pant leg of a very mean looking man, who shooed him away.

"Oh, that's kind of you, but…"

"But what? You can help me with the farm and we'll work at the levee. You'll be in Salt Lake before June. Do you have a better choice?"

"Not that I'm aware of," he said with a chuckle.

"Perfect! We'll even keep each other sober. You can teach me how to be a patient husband and father, and we need the company. We need each other, Clegg."

"I don't know, Patrick. Maria is pregnant, and…"

"Exactly! She's alone all day while I'm in the field or in town. Having a child there with her would be wonderful."

Clegg motioned to the whiskey glass in front of Patrick. "Maybe you should think about it, and ask Maria first."

"Nonsense. It's settled already," he said, standing. "Come now, Clegg. We'll go fetch your son and your things right now. I've got the wagon and it will be easy. Come, now," he said, helping his friend stand. "Let's step into the cool evening." He smiled a big smile, and Clegg half-heartedly returned it. "I need to get out of here. You need to get your son out of here."

A man was yelling at the boy, whose lower lip started to quiver. Patrick grabbed the boy's hand and with his other held the boy's father upright. He felt light, impenetrable, and irrepressible. Yes, the world may just collapse around him, but anyone on his little section of Kansas would be safe. Patrick Dugan would save the chosen ones.

***

A week later, at a meeting of a nearby chapter of the Legion, a man stood suddenly as Laughlin was speaking. "Traitor!" he cried. "You are a hypocrite Irishman! You told the Law and Order Party everything!" He turned and addressed the crowd, which numbered about a dozen. "Men, I have reason to believe that Mr. Pat Laughlin has decided to spy on us for the enemy. He's given our names and places of residence to the Southerners, and now they know each and every one of us, whether or not we're armed, and what our plans for the coming winter are! He's a traitor to our cause!"

The man's name was Sam Collins, and Roger had seen him before at Free State Party meetings, as well as one or two Kansas Legion meetings. For some reason Roger liked this man, though he'd never formally met him, but as he stood and accused Laughlin of treachery, Roger felt the blood boil in his veins. He didn't know if he should speak, but he did. "Liar!" he yelled, and a few other men rose and repeated it.

The meeting degenerated into a shouting match, with three or four supporting Laughlin, the rest taking Collins's side. Roger was dumbfounded. He had no idea where such an accusation would arise, but he had the odd feeling that he was tossing in his bed, almost as if he'd dreamed this before.

Collins and his allies left abruptly in a hail of curses, which left Pat, Roger, and three others in one of the men's houses that had served as their meeting place. The man was a bachelor and had but one chair and one table, at which Pat now sat. There was a very odd silence, and it was apparent to all of them, Roger included, that the unspoken question in the room would soon be answered by Laughlin.

"It's true, lads," he said with a sigh, removing his hat and running his fingers through his sweaty hair. There was a certain compassion for the hair, but not the man.

"Then get outa my house," said the bachelor. "And don't never come back or I'll blow yer head clean off."

Pat stood and, as if in a dream, Roger followed him. They stepped out into the cool night, and though he wanted to speak, Roger couldn't think of anything to say. Words like "betrayal" and "disappointment" escaped him. He felt ill, and not knowing where else to go, he followed his host.

They strode through the Atchison night, Roger only now beginning to realize how it had grown since he'd last been there. Double, even triple the amount of structures lined her streets, which were more rutted and muddy than ever, soaked if not in rain, then in horse and oxen droppings. The sounds of drunkenness filled the air, and it felt to Roger that his ears were opening gradually, like they did after he was ill. And his nose followed, then his skin, and finally his eyes. It was as if he were waking from a slumber, and only now, in their return, realized that his senses had been failing him for almost two months.

They made it to the edge of town in a few minutes, where Commercial Street became a dusty road leading west. The sounds of men, horses and buggies faded, and in the trees frogs and crickets came to the fore. The moon was full, and the road was light as day, but the trees were dark and crossed with long shadows. Roger felt awake now, and turned to the man on his right, who walked with a slump in his back, his hands in his pockets, and his head darting about him like a squirrel on the ground.

"You're a snake, Pat Laughlin," said Roger, and as Pat opened his mouth to reply, a man stepped out from behind a grove of trees. Roger thought he saw something steel in one of his hands glinting in the moonlight. It was Sam Collins, and Roger felt a sudden wave of compassion for him. He must have children and a lovely, loyal wife, and family somewhere east that loved him. His face shone in the moonlight like a ghost, so white and indistinct, but never did Roger feel a man was more of an animal. He could smell the two men, and tell their smells apart.

Collins opened his mouth, began to raise his hand, and Roger's hearing and sight disappeared as suddenly as they had just returned gradually. He smelled gun powder, saw red, felt as if someone had clapped his ears with hands made of cement, and just as suddenly as it had emerged from the trees, Sam Collins's face was gone. Raw, bloody flesh and bone was left in its place. It was torn wide open right down the middle, and fell to the ground.

Laughlin had a clenched look to him, from his still-extended arm and hand to his jaw. His pistol still smoking in his hand, he turned to Roger and began to speak frantically, almost as if he'd forgotten Roger was there.

But Roger couldn't hear him. He experienced, much to his great surprise, a feeling he hadn't had in years, a feeling that he hated now more than ever. It was fear and regret, a great ache welling up inside his body.

He turned and ran, as fast as he was able, crying loudly, back down Commercial Street, in to Atchison, eventually screaming something about "murder!" He ran and cried out for what seemed like minutes, but less than twenty seconds after entering the town he ran into something broad, soft, and very familiar. His hearing began to return again, and so did his skin and nose. He buried his face into this familiar softness, and breathed deeply through his nose, smelling it. He embraced it and could hear himself crying, under which was a rising voice that also reverberated through his skull, saying his name, "Roger, Roger, Roger, what's wrong?" He let his body go and slumped into the familiarity completely, sobbing uncontrollably as he realized what it was. It was his brother, a slight scent of rain to him.

***

While Roger cried, Patrick looked around and saw, several hundred yards down the street at the edge of town, a man stop running and holster a pistol beneath his coat. The man turned around and walked in the other direction. Patrick knew Roger had been running from him.

"What does he want, Roger? What happened?"

"What's happening to us, Paddy?" came a muffled rely in the voice of a very young, upset, younger brother. "What is this place doing to us?" His hat was falling between his face and his brother's shoulder.

The lightness of knowing a loved one is safe came also with the heaviness that they may not always be so. Patrick pulled his brother to his chest, not knowing if it was to anchor them to the earth so they would not float away into the blue of the sky, or if it was to keep them from sinking.

"It's a haunted place, Roger," he finally replied. "It's not your fault. Come now, quickly—into the wagon."

Clegg swayed beside them, his son clinging to his pants leg. Patrick shepherded and steered them around the corner and felt as if he alone lifted these three men and boys into the wagon by himself in one giant sweep, leaped into the seat, and soon the four were racing out of Atchison to the northwest.

Patrick felt as if he could hear and feel the earth crumbling behind him in an apocalypse, and he was just a step or two in front of it. He had to get to his land, his Zion.

XI

Joseph Clegg had spent much of his conscious life in the ditched-in farm of Mormon Grove, watching friends and family leave or die. Surrounded by the trenches that had pent up the emigrants' livestock, the world to him was an oval of shady grass, what would have been a tranquil resting place upon the threshold of the plains; but was, instead, an insular commune of suffering. Crossing the ditches meant life. Staying within them meant death.

He smiled now and looked out at the gathering thunderstorm to the west as they travelled north in the rickety wagon, leaving behind them the shouting and laughter of the Pioneer Saloon, heading for the Dugan farm. Suddenly it began to rain, and the boy let out a shriek of joy. He caught the water in his hands and rubbed it in his hair. He leaned so far over the back of the wagon that his father snatched and snapped at him several times. The light of the moon still shone from just leeward of the approaching clouds and Clegg felt very heavy, imagining his son bouncing out of the wagon and being crushed beneath its wheels. Roger felt much the same, thoughts of his father floating in the smell of the rain.

It turned into a rare storm for October, more like one of July or August than fall. The moon was clouded over and the world became very dark, loud, and wet.

Patrick could barely see the road, much less avoid the water-filled ruts and giant puddles that were already forming. Just over two years old, Zion was too young to help. Instead he lurched at every thunderclap, recovered frantically from every slip in the mud. It hadn't rained like this in months, and the entire party had quite forgotten how violent the skies of Kansas can be. An angry sky to the northwest, towering above them, presaged that it was going to get worse over the next half hour or so. And then Patrick realized they had lost their way.

He soon realized that they'd turned off the trail just a quarter-mile below his claim, and knew he could wind his way through the trees to his house. But that would take him right by the little square of logs the Hawkins brothers claimed was a foundation for a cabin, which he'd sought to avoid ever since their confrontation in August. He had no idea if they'd ever actually returned, made any improvements, or even if they were actually serious about homesteading or were just harassing anyone they thought was a Free Stater. But he had no choice. The wind had become so fierce, and a brief outburst of hail twice spooked Zion into a gallop. He had to get home. Maria would be worried and would smell the whiskey on him. There wasn't enough time in the night to explain how Roger, Clegg and his son, and the whiskey had found their way to him that October evening. And he still didn't know what sort of trouble Roger had gotten himself into, or if it posed this pathetic wagonload any further danger.

A bolt of lightning struck just ahead of them, and in it Patrick could see the Hawkins claim. It had indeed been built upon—a little anyway—and he thought he saw in the flash of light the form of a man. It appeared to be white, almost like a cloud, the steam from a ship or sawmill, or even a ghost, so bright was the lightning. But another flash revealed it was Joseph James, bent over something near the log foundation. His body was unmistakable, the way it hunched and lurched, and it was making rather frantic movements. Somehow Patrick was drawn to it, and so was Zion, the night storm, and the lay of the land. He had no choice but to drive his team straight for the man who two months ago had threatened his life.

As they approached, Roger climbed into the seat next to his brother and squinted into the rain. He too knew exactly where they were, and couldn't believe what he saw.

Joseph James was hunched over his little brother, who seemed to be underneath something. As they came within fifteen feet of the forms, Joseph James looked up and waved to the group. Oliver John was stuck under a fallen tree, wedged between it and part of the foundation of the cabin. He wasn't moving.

"Goddamnit," said the Missourian as he reached the wagon. "Just figgers I'd a-need help from the likes of you."

"Do you want our help or not?" Roger screamed through the wind.

Patrick turned harshly to correct Roger, but over his shoulder saw the giant bird move in the trees, glancing back at him. Perhaps he'd followed it to the Hawkins claim. But it was too late.

"A course I need yer help, boy! Mah little brother's a-dyin' under that tree!"

"Why should we give a damn?" Roger said, trying to grab the reigns. "Let's move on."

"We're helping," said Patrick, and hopped down.

It took several minutes and lots of yelling, but Joseph James, Patrick, Clegg, and Roger (who tried as hard as anyone after a moment's hesitation, mostly out of anger and resentment toward his brother and the belief that eventually this would prove to be a mistake) were finally able to lift the tree off Oliver John. The tree had fallen across his pelvis, which had broken in several places and caused the majority of his pain, and his left leg, which looked like something on a butcher's table.

"I thank you fer yer help," Joseph James said contritely, as if it were shameful to need help with such a thing. "But we'll be on our way now."

"Good luck," said Roger.

Clegg looked at Patrick. Little Joe was crying in the wagon and he turned toward it.

"The name is Patrick," he said, offering his hand. "Patrick Dugan."

The wind picked up.

"Joseph James," he cried into the wind. "Joseph James Hawkins!"

"Joseph, you know as well as I do your brother won't survive the ride across that river. Come with us."

"No."

"Well, he's your brother, like."

Joseph James spat. He spat when he was nervous. And he didn't speak when he was nervous. So with a sigh from Roger and not another word from anyone, they picked up Oliver John and took him to the wagon as he screamed in agony. He lay in the back moaning, his brother and Clegg trying to stop the bleeding. Joe Clegg was crying, trying to hide his face in the corner. It wasn't fun anymore. He hadn't realized bad things happened outside the Grove.

Just as he hopped up onto the seat, Roger saw Oliver John's feathered hat lying in the trees. "Goddamn heathen," he muttered as he hopped down and retrieved it, tossing it angrily into the back.

Patrick steered the Zion as gingerly as possible toward home, but the young gelding was impatient and oblivious to the plight of his human passengers. The light inside the Dugan cabin looked warm to the men and boys, and they knew a woman was inside, just from the color of yellow it emitted. Patrick thought about how he would explain his wagonload of men to Maria, but also thought perhaps he didn't have to. He would know the second he saw her. Her eyes would tell him. An odd quiet fell upon them, as the rain and wind let up and Oliver John's and Little Joe's cries turned to heavy breathing only.

Roger thought about Sam Collins. His wife must know he was dead by now. And he thought about Pat Laughlin. His wife must know by now he was a murderer, though she already knew he was a traitor. All her talk about loyalty must have meant something else. In the last handful of hours he'd seen more blood and flesh than in all his life. He'd seen dead bodies before, starving people, and he'd witnessed his mother die on the boat a few hundred miles off the coast of America, but he'd never seen the likes of Collins's face and Oliver John's leg. Roger leaned over the side of the wagon and vomited into the mud. His brother patted his back, steering with the other hand.

Clegg thought about his wife and daughters. All his life he'd been an optimist, but the world seemed very bleak to him. His son's cries were bothersome, and he felt ashamed for it. Oliver John's blood disgusted him. He didn't like what he was becoming. He felt the whiskey well up in his stomach, and he scrambled back to the end of the wagon and vomited into the mud. If only I owned that little patch, he thought, just that little circle of American mud to call my own, everything would be all right.

Joseph James thought about his mother back in Missouri. She was sick again. He thought about his father, who he hadn't seen in five years, and who'd left his mother for a younger woman, leaving his bastard sons in Missouri. In those first few years of Joseph James's life his mother didn't eat well, and was sick on and off ever since. And he thought about Del, his wife. She was pregnant and didn't get along well with his mother, whom she had to nurse during illness and suffer in health. They'd have it out tonight, for sure, wondering where the boys had done got to. He looked deep into his brother's eyes. He could see that Oliver John was in a lot of pain, but he would make it. There was not a drop of death in his eyes. Hawkinses were tough, he thought. They could take a lot of hurtin' before they died, and somehow, for some reason, they always did.

Oliver John thought about the canvas covering him and the wagon. He was thankful for it. It felt like drowning while he was pinned down under the rain outside, and Oliver John didn't like water. Every time he and his brother crossed the Missouri, he got real nervous. He didn't trust that river as far as he could throw it, and you can't throw water too far at all. He knew that one day that river would wind up in his lap, just like the tree had. Flash, bang, and next thing you know you're a-starin' at the heavens with a face full of rain and pain. The canvas looked endless, like the stars, and Oliver John closed his eyes. It felt good to get some rest

"Wake up, Oliver John!" his brother yelled.

Why wouldn't they let him go to sleep? He was so tired. Because he was a-layin' in the river, that's why. He could feel the water run underneath him. Yes, he'd have to get up and nap on the bank.

"Take it easy, brother," Joseph James said. "You ain't goin' nowheres."

So why wouldn't they let him sleep? He felt so wet. Some man's face appeared and wiped the sweat off his head. That felt good. Ready for sleep now. Tomorrow he'd feel better. Tomorrow they'd go fishin', he and his brother. Yep, they'd spend the day at the river together, just the two of 'em, and listen to the water slink past. And they'd catch some good fish. Yep, rivers is hard to cross, but they sure do give you what you need if you sit there patient like.

XII

When Maria opened the door on that stormy night in late October and saw her drunken husband, runaway brother in-law, two lonely Mormons, and two filthy Missourians, one of them horribly injured, she knew exactly what she had to do—put them all to bed with a warm cup of tea. But they all stood there soaked to the bone, saying nothing, so totally helpless that she had to laugh, thinking how pathetic and stupid men can be, and then realized it wasn't polite to laugh at guests as they stood in the rain at your front door, bleeding to death.

"Mother of God! Put him in the bed fast, lads!"

She swept them in and began to scramble about for as many lengths of fabric as she could find. They'd have to clean the hunched-over Missouri boy and wrap him up before he could sleep. She'd have to be quick about it. She could smell vomit on these men, and if there was one thing about men that she hated, it was when they smelled bad from some sort of effluvium that belonged inside their bodies. She heated water for tea, warmed biscuits and ham, washed carrots and radishes, fed the men and nursed the boy—and even managed to kill a snake in the process—all single-handedly, without fuss, complaint, or hesitation.

Soon they were all warm and sleepy, even Oliver John, who'd been given as much whiskey and iodine as he could handle, and she told them where to sleep.

"You'll sleep with us in here, Roger," she said. "Oh, and welcome home. It's good to see you, lad. Come here to me, boy." She clasped his face in her hands and looked into his face. "What's the matter?"

"Nothing, Maria."

"Nonsense. I know my little brother-in-law. Come, let's talk."

Patrick, Roger, and Maria stepped out into the wet night. It was well past midnight, and the moon could be seen almost directly overhead, the storm having passed completely as if in apology for itself. They sat down near the fire pit that had fed them before the cabin was built. It was familiar and almost sentimental for them.

"He was a traitor to the cause," Roger began in a quiet voice. "Laughlin, the man I went and lived with. He betrayed us."

"There's more to it than that, boy," his brother said without looking up, twirling a blade of grass between his fingers in the dark.

"He shot someone," Roger freely admitted. "He shot a good man." Roger's face fell into his hands and he began to cry again. Maria rose and as she placed her hand on his back to comfort him, he jumped up. "No! That's not the trouble here! We have the enemy in our house! In your house!"

"We don't have enemies in this house, boy," Patrick replied with restrained anger. "We don't need them in this godforsaken place."

"They'll take your land, Paddy! They're takin' the Mormon's land! Look at this pathetic old womanizing drunk you have—"

"Stop right there, Roger." Patrick stood stiffly, pointing at his brother. His anger was even more restrained now. "Clegg is a good man. Yes, the Missourians ran him off his claim, just as they would me if they could." He straightened himself. "We are family men. We are not pathetic."

"For not defending your families you are!" Roger's voice broke a little, and he wiped spittle from his lip with the back of his hand.

"Nonsense."

"What are you doing, Paddy? Do you really want those two barbarians in there? A slave-owner and a polygamist? What century are you living in? Barbarians living with your wife and—" He motioned to Maria's belly. It had begun to show in his absence.

"I can protect my children, thank you, Roger," she stated calmly.

"Well, you're making it more difficult for yourselves. We need to rid Kansas of these people."

"'These people'?"

"Slavery and polygamy, Patrick! They have no place in a free society!"

"Listen to yourself, brother. What do you suggest we should've done? Left them there to die in that storm?"

"Yes! When God does the work for us, we should accept it."

Patrick straightened again and took a deep breath through nostrils as distended as an overworked mule's.

Maria stood up between them. "Boys, boys, let's go to bed. Roger, we need to know if you're in danger."

"In danger? We're all in danger, Maria!"

"From the man who shot the other man. Paddy said you may have been followed here."

Roger turned, shaking his head and scratching the front of his skull vigorously. "I don't know. Laughlin chased me but I don't see how he could have tracked us here. He knows I live—you live—in these parts, but not exactly where." He looked up again and replaced his hat. "But why worry about the wolf at the door when you have a lion in your bed?"

"Well, as you so adamantly state, Roger, this is my house and I will decide who is the animal in it."

"So be it."

Despite their agitation, the boys slept. Only Maria lay awake in the cabin, listening to the men breathe and snore, smelling them, feeling their warmth radiate. They all slept through the night, except Roger, who Maria caught standing over Oliver John before sunrise, bending down so his nose almost touched the injured boy's, as if he were trying to smell the boy's breath or examine his teeth (which stuck out crooked as he slept). She watched him very carefully and quietly. It was a very odd expression that fell along his face, one that was so ambivalent it was almost indiscernible. It was either Christ-like compassion, like a moment with a mirror during grief; or it was downright scorn, like a vengeful assassin's final glimpse of his prey. Maria held her breath as Roger held his pose over the injured boy, thinking that at any second he would either go back to bed or he would clasp the boy's throat and choke him to death. It seemed like an eternity. She closed her eyes, and when she opened them, Roger had gone back to bed.

Maria lay awake in an almost panic until the rooster crowed. She hated herself for doubting Roger's intent. She hated herself for holding her breath because she felt he might start strangling Oliver John at any second. She hated herself for thinking her brother-in-law—to whom she felt like a mother—would ever do such a thing. She took a deep breath and rubbed her belly, and then, for the first time, she felt a kick. She held her breath again, and felt another kick, and then another. She smiled and then began to cry. Soon she couldn't control her tears anymore, and she cried like she did when she killed snakes.

She had to get out of the house, so she rose, surveyed the house strewn with the bodies of men—tall men and short ones, religious men and profane ones, men as healthy as ox and those who almost died last night, all of them relatively young and quite dirty—and slipped out the door into the morning light. She would cook them eggs, find one of them to fetch a doctor in town, set the rest to work, and nurse the injured one. All the while the next Dugan boy would squirm and thrash inside of her.

***

On his way to town, Patrick wondered why he had to be the one to fetch the doctor. Joseph should have done it. It was his brother that needed help, after all. But Oliver John had woken in terrible pain, and wouldn't keep any whiskey down. The only thing that comforted him was his older brother's presence. Maria didn't seem to trust Roger, for some reason, to fetch the doctor, and Clegg busied himself with his son. That left Patrick, and Maria was clearly in charge of the arrangements anyway, which was a good thing.

But after the incident with the Reverend Pardee Butler at the river in August, Patrick had hoped he'd never have to directly interact with an editor of the *Sovereign* again. Despite Bob Kelley's having saved Butler's life for some unknown reason, he still was without question the provocateur of the whole affair. Why a man would do so much to incite so much violence, only to squash it in the end, was beyond reason. Kelley was such a mouse of a man, it seemed his boss, the senior editor and doctor J. H. Stringfellow, could only be a rat. There had to be another doctor in the area by now, but Patrick didn't know where he might find one. It worried him, because he knew Maria should see one soon, but he wasn't sure what he could do. The very idea that the senior editor of the *Sovereign* would deliver his son was unacceptably ironic.

"Of course," Stringfellow said. "Let's go straight away."

Just like that, Patrick and Stringfellow were riding out of town together. Patrick had expected more out of the interaction. He expected the man of the editorials to be the man he met, and that he would have to prove somehow he'd voted for the Pro Slavery ticket if he were to receive medical attention. But no, Stringfellow had simply asked a few questions as he gathered his things, and that was that. The man wasn't in fact an idiot; like a lot of intelligent men, he just wrote like one.

"This town has grown," he said as they left it. "So much of what we envisioned has come to pass."

"Excuse me, doctor—who is 'we', so?"

"A Cork County native, so?" he replied, a cigar clenched between his teeth. "I haven't heard that accent in some time. Quite some time. 'We,' Irishman, is the Atchison Town Company. I'm a founder, along with my junior editor, Robert S. Kelley, and the esteemed Senator David R. Atchison, along with a host of western Missouri's best and brightest." He spat, then plucked a stray leaf of tobacco from his lip, wiping on his mare's neck.

"Ah," was all Patrick could say.

"Ha! Your tone betrays you, Irishman. A Free Stater, I assume?" His tone was less threatening that Patrick may have imagined it.

"No, in fact, I'm not. I'm just a farmer. You'll be happy to know the injured boy is a Missourian, Doctor. We came upon him and his brother in the rain last night and took him to our cabin."

"You, a Free Stater, came upon the enemy and are nursing him?"

"I'm really not a Free Stater, Doctor. I'm just an immigrant looking for a peaceful place to farm."

"Ha!" Stringfellow nearly choked on his cigar, coughed it out, and began laughing. He laughed so hard that his considerable girth shook his horse; so much so that the shake could be distinguished from her gait. "Peaceful? Kansas? Oh, Mr. Dugan, you're sorely mistaken. This is the soil that will give rise to the next revolution! You'll find no peace here, my friend."

"Yes. I discovered that the day I picked up your paper."

"You read the *Sovereign*, do you?"

"'Tis all I have to read, Dr. Stringfellow." Patrick had tried to control his tone, but disgust shone through.

"Well, if it's that distasteful to you, perhaps you'll prefer this garbage." He withdrew a book from one of his bags and handed it to Patrick, who felt his heart jump upon seeing it. It was a book! An actual book, thick with pages full of print; an actual book with hard covers, title pages, imprint information, and even a labeled spine; it was an actual book with paragraphs, standardized spelling, complete sentences, and a professionally-sewn binding; an actual book that he could read over and over in the moonlight, no matter what it was about! He nearly came to tears thinking about it, and how it had been so long—almost eighteen months—since he held one in his hands. "*Uncle Tom's Cabin; or, Life Among the Lowly*," he read on the spine.

"Yes, and never was a more blasphemous block set and imprinted upon a page," said Dr. Stringfellow. "It's become the Abolitionists' Bible, Mr. Dugan. It's in all the hotels and drawing rooms of Boston. Imagine," he continued, having finally succeeded in relighting his cigar in the wind, "an entire nation worshiping some woman from Connecticut. It truly shows the perverted nature of the cause of the Yankee. You have it backwards."

"I'm just a farmer, Dr. Stringfellow," he replied with disinterest, thumbing through the pages as best he could while still holding the reigns to Zion.

"Ha! A man from Cork County Ireland is not just a farmer these days. You've seen enough disease, starvation, and revolution to last a lifetime. It's a shame you're a-fixin' to see so much more." He puffed his cigar, and said through the exhale, "and where did you live before Kansas?"

"Boston."

"Of course you did. Of course you did. Well, I expect you will like this book, Mr. Just-a-Farmer from Boston. I expect it will change your life, in fact. Soon, I am quite, quite sure, you will be raising arms as well as corn, and we will meet again in far different circumstances. But for now, we must focus on the task at hand. For now, the Hippocratic Oath takes precedence to the Constitution."

He drew long on his cigar and let the smoke trail out his nostrils. It dragged behind him in curls as his mare made her way along the path, making him look like a Chinese dragon. "Now, tell me more about the injuries of this poor Missouri boy, this son of the earth."

***

Oliver John knew it was getting hot outside, hotter than it had been in the last few days, anyway. He could still feel that change in temperature, despite the tightly-clad walls of this house, the likes of which he'd never slept in before. And he could feel it despite the fact that his hands and feet, knees and ankles, his ears and brow and nose, had all begun to tingle strangely. All the nauseating and sharp and dull and global pain that emanated from his pelvis and shot like lightning down his left leg had fallen into the background, like a wind making its way down a valley, and in its place came this strange tingling lightheadedness.

He breathed deeply, could smell the man and woman who lived here, as well as all the smells of autumn—sticky leaves and sap, rutting deer, wet soil—and he smiled. He was so tired. Never had he breathed so deeply.

Oliver John opened his eyes when a bolt of pain shot down his leg, and for the first time he began to remember what had happened. They'd just decided to leave and begin the trek back home across the river when the wind picked up something awful. It seemed like August had visited October all of a sudden the way the storm blew in. Then he couldn't hear anything, or see anything, neither. All he could do was smell something, like a burning carcass, and feel rain on his face. It was hard to breathe at first, all that water and wind rushing in at him like a stuck pig. Then he realized he was on the ground, could feel the water soak in on his back, so he started to stand. But he was stuck. Only then did he feel the pain.

The first thing he thought of was Delilah. She'd be sittin' in her chair in the corner of the shack knitting away, when the storm blew in from the river, and she'd be scared for him. She'd know, all right, she'd know. Del knew things before they were known. She'd know he was stuck here just the way she knew Pappa was leaving again for that whore up in Indiana. The second time, anyway. First he'd come and had Joseph James, stayed a bit, then left, and then he'd come back to Missouri and had him, Oliver John, before leaving again. Why Pappa didn't just stay in Missouri and raise his family was one of them questions in life you just never did figure out the answer to, just like why he ever bothered comin' back in the first place, if all he ever did that for was to just turn around on his haunches and up and leave again. Men do strange things, Del said, and don't you be one of them. You stick with your brother and you listen to him because he's a good man, takes care of his mamma and his wife and his little brother and never so much as says a word in complaint. Nope, Joseph James was a better pappa than Pappa ever could be, the way he chases them Indian whores around like he does. He can have his squaw up in Indiana for all she cared. He was too old anyways.

"Jimmy!" he thought he screamed into the wind. "Jimmy, I'm stuck!" But it may not have ever come out. He could open his mouth and breathe, now and then, but lying in this bed in this nice big tight-walled cabin, he wasn't sure if he ever did yell what he intended to yell.

There were a lot of colors, things like needles sticking in him, and still the rain just beating down on his face, so much that he thought he'd drown. And his brother. He thought of Del first, of Pappa a little, but all the time he was under that tree Oliver John knew his brother was there. He could hear and smell and feel him all around, trying to get the tree off, trying to pull him back up from the hell he'd been pinned down into. And really, Oliver John was never really all that scared. He knew that his brother was there for him, and he knew that Joseph James Hawkins could not only pick up this little ol' tree, he could move mountains and hell itself if he had to, for the sake of his family. Jimmy had said on more than one occasion that if he had to fight a war all himself—if he had to hold back the Yankee hoards with one hand tied behind his back—he'd do it, just so his right to Kansas land could be upheld. He was done with this farmhand hogwash—sorry Del—he was gonna get some land and anchor the Hawkinses to it for the next ten—no, the next hundred—generations.

Oliver John had begun to fall asleep with this thought in mind when he heard his brother yelling in the adjacent room. "You just back off there, young fella!"

And then there was a loud crash, the sounds of a struggle, and to Oliver John's utter horror, the sound of his brother's breath in a struggle. He'd only heard that sort of breathing from Jimmy when he was straining himself something awful when he worked. And then he heard him grunt, just grunt out loud. He was in a fight! Oliver John's body, like a reflex, recoiled and tried to jump out of bed. He fell out of it, heard himself scream, and began yelling. "Jimmy! Jimmy! I'm a-comin' brother, I'm a-comin'! You just hold 'em off a little while longer! I'm a-comin' brother! I'm a comin' to get ya and them fellers better watch out 'cause I ain't takin' no prisoners!"

XIII

What this little Yankee had been saying was just not fit for polite company. And though Joseph James couldn't decide if he was in polite company or not, he figured he may as well act like he was. They'd saved Oliver John's life, after all. He had to remember that. He was in their debt. But this little sonofabitch sure had a mouth on him. This was the little bastard who'd taken a shot at Oliver John in the grass a couple months ago, and though he'd helped lift the tree, Joseph James didn't think Roger could be trusted. He could see it in his eyes, just the way he saw it in them damn Mexicans during the war. He was hell bent on revenge, this little Irishman.

"The 'Law and Order Party'? —is that what you call yourselves?" Roger raised his voice, standing now. "A party of rigged elections and bogus legislatures, a party that enslaves his fellow man? That's what you call yourselves?"

"Watch yer tongue, boy." Joseph James almost spat at Roger's feet. "This here's your house and you done me a great favor, but I can only take so much of them lies a-fore I'm honor-bound to do something 'bout it."

"Lies! What lies? Your party fights for oppression. These people you name our counties after, Atchison and Doniphan, they trick you stupid ignorant barbarians into fighting their wars for them, and they not only enslave the blacks, they oppress you, too."

"Don't you dare speak ill of Alexander Doniphan! He led us from Leavenworth to Santa Fe right on into Mexico! He did more to expand this country and its freedoms than any man. He's a man the likes of which you ain't never seed! All you is, is a starvin' Irishman, anyways. Bet your daddy's still a-gettin' drunk back in Ireland."

"My father is J.P. Dugan! He did more to fight off the Crown than your little colonial revolution could possibly fathom. You Southern Americans are worse than the English! Perfidios Albinon!"

A second later, the two were grappling like bears over a salmon carcass, dancing around the table like young people at a line dance, and they jarred the table enough to break a glass or two. Then they heard a thump in the next room, a scream from Oliver John, and the front door opened. In walked Patrick, Stringfellow and Maria as Joseph James rushed to his brother's side and Roger rushed past his brother's side, on out the front door.

"Roger, where are you going, brother?"

"It's them or me, Paddy! I won't sleep another night with a pair of barbarians!" He turned and stormed off toward the creek.

"What the hell kind of a household are you running, Mr. Dugan?" asked the doctor as he removed a stethoscope from his black bag and walked across the room toward the cries of the injured.

Patrick and Maria looked at each other with sadness in their eyes.

After a moment, Joseph James reappeared. "Doc wants to be alone with the boy," he said. "I'm sorry 'bout your brother, Patrick. I'm in your debt, and I'll get Oliver John outa here just as soon's I can, but that boy's got some kinda mouth on 'im."

"What happened?"

"He shamed Alexander Doniphan!"

"And…?"

"I shamed his—your—father. Don't know nuthin' 'bout him, but we tussled a bit and he stormed outa the house."

"Damnit."

"I didn't mean to run your brother outa here, Dugan."

"I'm sure you didn't. Look, where's Clegg?"

"I thought they was with you."

"No, they stayed here."

And in walked Clegg and his son. "What's upset Roger?" Clegg asked, removing his hat. "I saw him running through the woods, almost as if he were chasing something in the hunt."

"Which way did he go?"

"Southeast. Toward Atchison."

"Thank you."

As Patrick rushed out the door, Joseph James called after him, "Don't take that young buck of yours! Take Ninny! She's run down many a Yank in her time!" Though she hadn't come with them the night before, and Patrick knew she'd never been hitched at the cabin, there she was, standing ready right where she should be.

And ten seconds in, Patrick knew she was the best horse he'd ever ridden, and also knew that no one but Joseph James had ever ridden her alone.

***

Patrick returned not having found Roger, but having sighted the great bird once again. He knew he'd lost his brother as he saw it, and decided that Paschal's insistence that it not be followed didn't necessarily mean one couldn't curse or throw stuff at the thing. So he did. Patrick hurled every dirty word he knew and every stick or rock at hand at the bird, but it just blinked. It stood there next to a thicket of trees, the coward, and looked around with the blank eyes of a beast, just blinking.

"You stupid pigeon!" he yelled. "Come and get me! C'mon! I'm not afraid of a goddamn overgrown turkey!"

But it just blinked.

"You dumb feather-head! What kind of a ghost are you, stealing little boys, anyway? If you have something against me, come and have it out, you coward!"

It turned its head a little, bent over, stood up again, and blinked. A little peep found its way out of the giant beak.

"You're just a big nasty chicken! Those colors don't fool me, you egg-laying bastard! You're nothing but a big duck! Quack, quack, you dummy!"

The bird looked around, and seemed to blink right at Patrick. Another little squawk came out, almost inquisitive in its tone.

"That's right, you big dumb chicken! I'm not afraid of you! My wife and I will feast on your breast! Mmmm . . . just look at those legs! I bet a little buttermilk would dress that drum nicely!"

Another squawk, a little louder this time, was definitely directed at Patrick.

"Ah! Don't like that, eh? Well I'm going to be scrambling your children tomorrow if you don't give my brother back!"

But the last part of the sentence couldn't be heard, not by the bird or anyone else within a mile, because it was overwhelmed by an incredible screech from the bird, almost ear-shattering in both its volume and pitch. The thing had looked directly at Patrick and emitted the sound in his direction. This thing was definitely offended, and was arguing back.

"Shut-up! Just shut-up!"

But it did it again, and without another thought Patrick had found himself chasing it into the woods. He went twenty yards before he realized it, turned back, mounted Ninny, and went home, his ears ringing.

"Patrick! Paddy! Are you deaf?" Maria had to step in front of him to get his attention when he came inside the door.

"Oh, I'm sorry, love—I've a bit of a ringing in my ears."

"Where's Roger?"

"I couldn't find him. He just disappeared into the forest."

"Nonsense. Boys don't disappear in the trees."

"Ain't nowhere else for 'em to disappear," Joseph James said. "Pardon me, ma'am, but anyone grows up in these parts knows them woods so well it's like a home to 'em. Oliver John's like that. You might mistake him for a pheasant if you ain't careful." He shot a quasi-humorous glance at Patrick. "You know that boy ain't had a skeeter, chigger, or tick since he was two? No jokin'. The boy's a part of the land."

"I suggest you listen to the gentleman," said Stringfellow, who emerged from Oliver John's room, drying his hands on a small towel. "That young man inside that room there is about the toughest I've ever seen, and I've treated more people between here, Platte City and St. Jo than anyone else. That boy's an ox. But he's in a helluva lot of pain." He wiped his hands on a towel.

"What's broke, Doc?"

"His pelvis, his leg, hopefully just that. Are you his father?"

"Older brother."

"Well, I'm afraid you're going to have to impose yourself upon these folks for a few weeks."

"What? I need to get him home to his—"

"Well, his ma's going to have to come here to see him. That boy needs to be bedridden until the first of December. That is," he added, turning to Maria, "if you'll have him."

"Of course. This is a Christian house," she said. "Our love is unconditional."

Dr. Stringfellow chuckled. "Yes. Well, you'll need to know how to bathe and turn him on his sides so he doesn't develop sores on his skin. You'll also need to keep his pelvis and thigh stable while you do it. I'll leave you some more morphine, but I suggest you brace yourselves—he's going to be in a lot of pain for a long time. If he were a horse, we'd shoot him." He dropped his towel unceremoniously on the table.

"Can he work the winter wheat, Doc?"

"I don't expect so, Mr. Hawkins. I'm sorry. You'll have to find another farmhand this winter."

"We are the farmhands, Doc. For one more winter, anyway. We're squatting on this side of the river until sometime after Christmas."

"God bless you, young man! I assume you know about the troubles and you will vote with your conscience if you are so asked again? The Free State Party is drafting their own constitution in

Topeka in clear violation of the Territorial Government rightly elected by the people and recognized by the United States Congress."

"Oh, yes, sir! I voted twice already and I aim to improve my claim. I am a registered member of the Law and Order Party."

"Ah, were you a Blue Lodger too?"

"Of course! Done heard Senator Atchison himself speak twice!" Joseph James hopped up on his chair and proceeded to imitate the Senator's booming, grating style of public speaking. He anchored his thumbs under his arms as if they were suspenders, protruded his belly as far as he could (which was rather unconvincing given his gaunt, wiry frame, but the suggestion was effective) and sharpened his drawl a little to sound like a West-Missourian who spent half the year in Washington. "Sons of Missourah!" he boomed. "If I may impress upon you the urgency of our situation, I would hope your feet would already be moving to Kansas while your ears remain in Platte County to hear my humble thoughts. Kansas must be a slave state or the Union is lost!"

Dr. Stringfellow was laughing, Maria had busied herself somewhere else, and Patrick was pecking at the floorboards with his toe.

"The Blue Lodges, Mr. Dugan," Stringfellow turned politely to the other man in the circle, "were gatherings across the border that Senator Atchison, myself, and others began as a way to galvanize our people against yours. Kansas belongs to Missouri, Irishman. Remember that and you will be allowed to keep your claim. Neglect it, and..."

Patrick decided to hold his tongue. He could solve nothing here and now, with these two men. Perhaps if they were to attempt to force him off his land, he would fight. Responding to idle threats was the domain of the fearful.

"Now, he ain't a-gonna ferget it anytime soon, is you Mr. Dugan?" Joseph James was smiling and took a step toward the others. "Naw, this here's a good Irishman if I ever seen one. He coulda left Oliver John to die in them woods, Dr. Stringfellow. And I've seen enough a-that before, in the Mexican War, folks a-treatin' one another like animals." He paused and looked at Patrick. The next sentence was directed more at him than Stringfellow. "And if I'm to be honest, which I always aim to be, I couldn'ta blamed him if he had left him to die after what I done to him." He turned back to Stringfellow. "This man ain't political, Doc. He's just a farmer, the most respectable kinda man in the world, if you ask me. His brother might be another story, now."

"Yes, well, farmers can vote in this country, Mr. Hawkins," Stringfellow mused.

"Yer damn right!" Joseph James stomped his boot so hard Maria was startled. She spun around from her stove, and Patrick decided he could not hold his tongue at this—he had just finished the floor!

"Mind the floorboards please, Joseph," he said.

Joseph James grinned and apologized.

"Yes. Well, I need a ride back to town, Mr. Hawkins," Stringfellow looked at his watch, "and I wouldn't mind a ride from a farmer of similar political—as you call it—conviction."

The two soon rode off. Maria hurried to the other room to check on Oliver John, and Patrick stepped outside. Sitting on top of his cabin, like a weathervane, was the giant bird. It blinked, shuffling its feathers a bit.

"Goddamn you," Patrick said under his breath. "Why are you nesting here? I can't avoid following something that comes home to roost, now, can I?" He picked up a rock and hurled it at the beast. It plunked him right in the eye, and bounced off down the roof, but the bird merely blinked. And blinked again. "All right, you dumb bird. You're welcome here as much as any man, I suppose, so make yourself at home. Can I get you some tea?"

And the bird, with a surreal movement that seemed to spring him toward the sky, opened his giant wings, and rose into the tops of the trees. The wind from his flight was heavy and cold, like the October storm of the night before, and it turned toward the west and disappeared behind the top of the forest canopy.

Patrick stood still, absolutely dumbfounded. He didn't know if it was beautiful or terrifying. The bird was both at once, really, and suddenly he wanted to know more about it. He wanted a name for it, and he wanted to speak with Paschal. He began to blink and breathe again, and moved toward the cabin, but the bird came screaming back over the trees from the west, heading east again, and the leaves stirred below it as it flew overhead.

Just like that, peace could be interrupted, thought Patrick. Strife and bloodshed could sweep across a land just as easily as this bird could soar above it. It was going to be a long, long winter in Kansas Territory, one way or the other.

XIV

The November air of 1855 was filled with the sounds of work. In the twenty months since the territory was opened for settlement, the population of Kansas had more than tripled, and most of it was busily hammering and sawing in preparation for the winter, a winter that would be colder than any of them could imagine. The new population, as a rule, was entirely segregated. Free State towns like Lawrence and Topeka were replicated in smaller, somewhat calmer settlements like Osawatomie and Oskaloosa, and Pro Slavery hubs like Atchison, Lecompton, and Leavenworth had smaller counterparts in Franklin and Baldwin. For every Free State settlement there was a Pro Slave enclave nearby.

The land was settled for conflict.

The Mormons, for the most part, were gone, and there were many primarily apolitical families outside the small but growing towns there simply to squat a claim and make a new life for themselves in a new land, and they also kept mostly to themselves. They came not for peace or war, but merely for the right to toil and reap the rewards of that toil. They congregated in like-minded settlements merely for protection, should it come to it, but preferred to mow grass with scythes and clear tree stumps and rocks with beasts and ropes. They thought about their sons and granddaughters as they did this, knowing that one day Kansas would be a great state in a strong union, and these beneficiaries of such sweaty toil would lead the happy lives of the free. Only in one little place was all this stark segregation not the case—Patrick's farm.

Here, throughout the month, lived two deserted Mormons, two Pro Slavery bastards whose father had left his mistress in Missouri for his wife in Indiana, and a young Irish couple that had fled the potato famine, seeking only a peaceful farm to call their own. These two were Free Staters, but they preferred not to prefer.

It was the oddest corner of Kansas—nobody outside the farm knew about it, and nobody inside the farm wanted them to know about it. They had enough trouble as it was, getting along together in the little house. Joseph James tried sleeping outside as much as he could, or spent time with his mother and wife across the river, but he always came back to the little cabin, because that's where his little brother lay. They kept to themselves in this manner on the farm, much to Maria's dismay. She knew that if they roosted together they'd find love. But as the weeks dragged on, she knew they wouldn't do that, even though they slept under the same roof, and she knew that that could only mean one thing—war.

"Patrick" she began one night in bed.

"Don't say it, girl. I know it."

"There's got to be a way. I don't want to start all over again, but maybe if we moved farther west..."

"Well, that's our only other option. I don't want to do that again, at least not in the wintertime. We'll just have to be patient, so. I'm sure by the spring we'll know who is to govern Kansas once and for all. That should be the end of it." He paused, and turned to her. "Don't you think, girl?"

"I don't know," she sighed. "We have this God-given chance to see the troubles of Kansas right here under our own roof. If we can't get Joseph James to talk to us—you saved his brother's life, you're helping rebuild his cabin, and you've opened yours to him and his family—then I don't see how people like Stringfellow and . . . could ever stop short of war. Ever," she said, rolling over to go to sleep, knowing that Patrick knew she meant to say "Stringfellow and Roger." And she was right. Patrick knew it, and knew that she knew that he knew it.

Patrick had indeed begun helping Joseph James rebuild his cabin, with Clegg's help—over a ridge southeast of where it began. The two men agreed upon this without words, and it was a sort of compromise. In exchange for Oliver John's life, Joseph James had given Patrick rights to the claim they had only begun to dispute. They just picked up the cabin and moved it closer to town. By the third week of November it was framed, and soon it would be time to move Oliver John and the Hawkins women into it, because with simple walls and a roof it was already better than the farmhand shack they lived in across the river. Patrick would have what he needed— land to farm, the right to keep its bounty—and so would Joseph James, which just happened to be the same thing, only a quarter-mile away. A long quarter-mile away.

But for other boundary disputes it wasn't that simple, and on November 21st, a Free State settler by the name of Charles Dow was shot by a Pro Slave settler by the name of Franklin Coleman just outside Lawrence. Word spread quickly up and down the Missouri River, along the Kansas, and immediately curled its way along the meandering path of the Wakarusa, on whose banks the shooting took place and where the disputed land lay. It was a boundary dispute, one the two men had hotly contested every time they saw each other during the past two months, but it didn't matter. One was a Free Stater, the other Pro Slavery, and everyone knew it. That was enough to be a declaration of war, for the Law and Order Party to become the Kansas Militia and the Free State Party the Kansas Legion.

It was enough for the Sheriff of Douglas County, a man who still lived in Missouri but who'd been appointed by the Territorial Legislature (that had been elected the previous fall by invading Missourians), to attempt to arrest a friend of Dow's for "inciting violence." And it was enough for a small group of men involved in the Kansas Legion to attempt to "rescue" this man from Sheriff Sam Jones's custody. And that was enough for the Sherriff to appeal to Governor Wilson Shannon for three thousand troops, and enough for the Governor to call the Kansas Militia to action. It was enough for Doctor and Editor-in-Chief J.H. Stringfellow, who was also the Speaker of the House for the Territorial Legislature, to become General Stringfellow; it was enough for his junior editor of the *Sovereign* to become Colonel Robert S. Kelley, and enough for Senator Atchison himself to become General Atchison once again (he'd been an officer in the Missouri Militia during the Mormon War of '38), and for them all to muster their forces and march toward Lawrence.

A sitting senator of the United States Congress was now leading irregular forces to battle in a territory of the United States.

And this shooting was enough for Charles Robinson, the balding man with piercing blue eyes who chaired the Big Springs Convention and who helped found Lawrence, to become General Robinson, Chair of the Lawrence Security Committee; it was enough for Jim Lane, the mesmerizing orator of that Convention who had since chaired a constitutional convention at Topeka, to become Colonel Lane and Secretary of the Security Committee.

Robinson had another title, that of Governor, as he had been elected the previous month by the Free State Party as their governor, and Lane had been elected to the United States House of Representatives, though he went unrecognized by that body. Their constitution, which abolished slavery but also Negroes as citizens of Kansas under the premise that "the best interest of Kansas is that it be populated entirely by free white men," was also not recognized by Congress. Nonetheless, to Kansans there were two Kansases, two territorial governments established under two diametrically opposed constitutions, each with its own executive, legislature, and delegation to Washington. And these two governments were now armed and ready to fight each other, because for many of the men and women of Kansas, Coleman killing Dow was enough, quite enough.

The Wakarusa War had begun.

***

On the balmy night of December 1st, 1855, one of the Kansas Militia men camped outside Lawrence was Joseph James Hawkins, standing tall and proud atop Ninny, wielding a saber that the Militia had stolen from the armory in Liberty, along with their cannon from Mexico, "Old Sacramento"; and inside the town, helping defend it under command of the Security Committee, was Roger Dugan, clutching his Sharps Rifle that had been sent from Boston by Henry Ward Beecher of the New England Aid Society in a box marked "Bibles," ready to do whatever his new boarder, Col. Lane, asked of him. Since leaving home a second time in October, Roger had found his way to Topeka, where he heard the final negotiations for the Topeka Constitution, as it had come to be known, and where he'd silently disagreed with the "Negro Exclusionary Clause." What's wrong is wrong, thought Roger. Why exchange bondage for banishment? That's all his family had done, in fact, by leaving Ireland to escape English rule. Had his father had his way, they would have fought until they won, and Ireland would be free. He wasn't going to make the same mistake Patrick had. He wasn't going to run away. He was going to defend Lawrence, Kansas, or die trying. By Christmas he would either be a hero or a martyr.

"You want me to shoot that damn smile off yer face boy?" Sherriff Jones rested the butt of his shotgun on his right thigh.

"No," Roger replied with a smirk.

"That goddamn white nigger's smirk's gonna be the straw that breaks this camel's back, boy. Who the hell are you?"

"A legitimate citizen of Kansas, sir. And now, by necessity but not by conscription, a soldier in the Lawrence Defense Forces."

Roger had heard the term "border ruffians" before, but he'd only met two—Joseph James and Oliver John. The term aptly fit them. They were hairy, dirty, smelly, hunched over, and ragged. But Roger more or less assumed that they looked and acted this way because they were the poorest of the poor, and while he was right about that in the case of the Hawkinses (they were as poor as anyone they knew), their appearance and behavior was not unique in western Missouri. Roger learned this fact the morning of December 2nd, when Sherriff Jones rode into town in front of a band of twenty dragoons, every one of them as rag-tag as the other—dirty faces and shirts, coats of every color, cut, and pattern, hats with flimsy and torn brims, boots with holes. Roger had laughed as they rode up in front of the Free State Hotel, the largest man-made structure in Kansas at the time, and halted their horses.

Jones and the men adjacent to him laughed at Roger's impertinence. Their horses impatiently shifted their weight. "You're a soldier, lad? You look like a little Irish brat, if you ask me."

Roger's blood boiled. He imagined himself shooting Samuel Jones in the belly and watching him bleed to death in the street, blood running out his mouth and nose and ears. But he remembered the training he'd received the afternoon before, and held his rifle steady, standing still and straight. He glanced around the twenty men that were staring him down. An odd sense of calmness came over him, and he saw someone he recognized. Roger wanted this moment to last as long as it could.

"Well, at least my division hasn't anyone living with the enemy in it."

"What's that, boy?"

"That man there," he pointed his finger, careful not to move his rifle an inch. "His name is Joseph James Hawkins. He's living with a Free Stater up in Atchison County. I know 'cause I helped save his little brother's life two months after I tried to kill him. Shoulda done it right to start."

"Go to hell, you scumbag bogtrotter!" screamed Joseph James from the back of the party. "I'll kick your little ribs in, you bastard!" It was the first time Joseph James had ever called someone else a bastard. He swallowed hard, dismounted Ninny, and made a run at Roger.

Other men grabbed his collar. "Not without orders," they said.

"I'll kill you, you little sonofabitch. I'll kill you yet."

"Then where you gonna live?" Roger retorted. "With Governor Robinson?"

"Ain't no governor a-livin' in Yankee Town, boy," interjected the sheriff. "The governor of this territory is Wilson Shannon, in Lecompton, and I am here as his emissary, as an officer of the law. Now, I know you Free Staters don't give a damn 'bout the law, but I'm here to enforce it." His patience grew short. "Goddamnit, you little bastard, I'm a-tired a talkin' to a child. Go get your commanding officer."

"Gladly." Roger turned and went inside the hotel, where the Security Committee was awaiting Jones's arrival. "Excuse me, General. Sam Jones is here to see you."

"Show him in, lad, show him in and offer him a glass of water."

Roger turned, walked through the little lobby to the front door, and for the first time he felt the warm well of nervousness rise in his chest into his throat, but he didn't know why. "The Governor will see you now, Mr. Jones." His voice cracked.

"You mean, 'Mr. Robinson will see you now, Sheriff.'"

They stared at each other.

"Git the hell outa my way," said Jones, pushing Roger aside.

Roger pushed him back.

Joseph James balanced his saber in his hand and took a step closer. Nobody blinked or breathed. They all knew that if one shooting over a boundary dispute could lead to a siege, then a single blow to the head could lead to hundreds dead, wounded, and captured. It was a hard decision to make, and before anyone made it, Charles Robinson appeared in the doorway.

"Gentlemen, my, my gentlemen! Whatever is taking so long?"

***

The sheriff and his posse left town as quickly as they had come. His prisoner, and the men who had "rescued" him over ten days earlier, were no longer in Lawrence, according to Robinson and the Security (now Defense) Committee. The town had washed its collective hands of these men. They opposed slavery, would fight to the bitter end against it, but did not see how going to war over this matter could help in that end. Yes, they saw the sheriff's office as illegitimate, and that illegitimacy had everything to do with the slavery question, but theirs was a grand cause, not a petty one. Dying in Lawrence over the authority of Sam Jones was not what they had in mind when they moved to Kansas Territory, and they wanted a peaceful end to this Wakarusa War. Even Jim Lane wanted to negotiate, because the best fighters know not only when to throw a punch, but when to pull one. Let the sheriff have his damned badge for now, he thought. We won't end slavery by defeating this little man from Platte County.

So within another day or two, Governor Robinson sent a delegation to Governor Shannon, requesting an interview. Robinson and Lane knew that Shannon would allow Jones's posse to lay siege to Lawrence if he felt his authority was undermined, but also knew that if Shannon were told that the prisoner and his rescuers were no longer in Lawrence, there could be no pretense for a siege any longer. If Law and Order were the objective of the Kansas Militia, then they had completed their mission. If the destruction of Lawrence was their mission, then they could no longer be considered on the side of the law. They had to appeal to the Governor's sense of justice, and though Lane had his doubts, Robinson was confident.

"Shannon is Pro Slave," Lane said one night. "He is their man. I don't see any difference between sending for him than sending for Atchison, Stringfellow, or Jones himself. Shannon wants to see Lawrence in ashes as much as any of them."

"I don't believe so," retorted Robinson. "He may be Pro Slave, but he is a Pro Slave politician, and a Democrat from a Northern State at that. And like any politician he simply wants control. I'm betting that Shannon has been misled, and believes that we're in usurpation of his power. No, something else is at play, and if we're to speak with him directly, I believe we shall discover and address it. He will call off these hordes when he realizes that it is we who are abiding by the law, and that we will not let Lawrence burn without a very bloody fight."

"The laws of the unlawful!" boomed Lane, pounding his fist on a desk. "And if Shannon does call them off, who's to say they'll listen?"

Roger overheard these men's voices from outside the door, and eavesdropped on this part of the conversation. When he heard Lane's fist pound on the desk—something he'd heard many times by now—he burst inside, unable to control himself any longer. The two men looked at him, one, small, squat, calm, and a face of the affable; the other, tall, gaunt, his face twitching and lined with a lifetime of expressiveness. Robinson was seated behind a large desk, his fingers intertwined and resting on his belly, round as a clock, and Lane was standing next to him, his body angled like the hands of a clock at one in the afternoon. Robinson was dressed like a seasoned traveler, in a suit that would do on the floor of a western legislature as well as in a saloon, while Lane was dressed more like one of the men outside erecting the barricades across Lawrence's main thoroughfares in case the Missouri cavalry came galloping down one.

"Yes?" asked Robinson. "Private, do you have something to say?"

"No, sir," Roger said sheepishly. "No, no . . . I . . . I'm sorry. Forgive the interruption, General."

The two men smiled. Robinson produced three cigars from a box on the shelf. "Don't leave, Private. Enjoy a cigar with us and join the conversation. My friend and I are at an impasse. Not an uncommon occurrence let me assure you."

Lane laughed. "This is my boarder, Charles. Roger Dugan. He has all the fire of the Party in his Irish blood, he does. He'll tell you how to handle these mongrels."

"Please, sit, Roger," Robinson said, gesturing to a chair. "May I call you Roger?"

Roger nodded and sat.

Robinson rose, handed Roger the cigar, and helped him light it. He returned to his chair, lit his own, as did Lane, who also sat. "Roger, I think you may have heard our dilemma. Do we send for the Governor, or no?"

"You—" Roger coughed on his cigar smoke, suppressing it awkwardly. "You are the Governor, General."

Robinson puffed his cigar. His chair creaked as he leaned back. "Imagine that. Both titles at once. Well, Wilson Shannon is the Governor who is recognized by the United States government. We must remember that. Until the Congress realizes the territorial elections were falsified, the voters intimidated, we will do nothing for our cause if we openly rebel against the sitting legislature."

Lane sat next to the desk now, his legs so long that they angled up before down, as his knees were taller than the seat of his chair. Even at rest he seemed cocked with a spring. He looked like a spider in the corner of the room, all legs, and even at rest it seemed he may scurry off with awesome speed in a fraction of a second. "But we do nothing for our cause if we appease an illegal, immoral government," he said.

"Exactly!" Roger's tone, volume, and gestures betrayed his enthusiasm once again, and he sat back, puffed his cigar, and tried to remain calm.

"You agree with Colonel Lane, then, do you, Roger?"

"Yes, sir. Of course, with all due respect, sir, what's wrong is wrong is wrong. Our cause is one of morality, not politics. We cannot compromise with evil."

Lane, who had been smiling wryly throughout Roger's response, exclaimed, "Here! Here! You should run for governor yourself, Mr. Dugan!" and clapped his knee.

Roger fidgeted with his cigar but didn't attempt to smoke it again.

"Yes," said Robinson. "Well, gentlemen, perhaps you are right. If the government does support Shannon in this endeavor, and Jones in his attempt to assert his authority, we must wonder why mere farmers bark at our gate, and not Federal troops. I'm sure that the President has no interest in a civil war erupting in Kansas."

"Exactly!" Lane exclaimed.

"Yes." Robinson paused and stared at Lane. "And neither do we. Surely, Shannon has sent for troops from Leavenworth, but they have not arrived. We must know Shannon's position in this. Let us continue to fortify the city with embankments, men, and weapons—if the Missourians come, we will repel them—while also seeking to safeguard our Lawrence by more peaceful means. We shall write Shannon a letter to ascertain his plans to secure peace in his territory. Colonel Lane, I will draft the letter; will you please call a meeting of the Security Committee? We will sign it together and dispatch our bravest to Shawnee."

"Yes, sir." Like a spider, Lane was up and out the door.

Roger began to follow him, his cigar no longer alight.

"Young man," Robinson said, "a word, please."

Roger halted at the door.

Robinson took his time in standing, stretching, and strolling across the room, and placed his arm on Roger's shoulder. "You must remember that to fight for what is right, you must love what is right, not hate who is wrong. You must remember that, or your hatred will consume you, as it has our friend Jim. Remember that." He took Roger's cigar from his hand. "Now, go and do your duty to God and country."

Roger turned and left the room, and within seconds bumped into Lane, who was returning with two members of the Committee. Lane clasped both of Roger's shoulders, held him at arm's length, and smiled, looking him straight in both eyes. He patted his shoulders, and smiled even broader. "You have changed the course of history, young man! You keep that burning inside of you. Never let it quell."

XV

To His Excellency, Wilson Shannon, Governor of Kansas Territory:

SIR—

As citizens of Kansas Territory, we desire to call your attention to the fact that a large force of armed men from a foreign State have assembled in the vicinity of Lawrence, are now committing depredations upon our citizens, stopping wagons, opening and appropriating their loading, arresting, detaining and threatening travelers upon the pubic road, and that they claim to do this by your authority. We desire to know if they do appear by your authority, and if you will secure the peace and quiet of the community by ordering their instant removal, or compelling us to resort to some other means and to higher authority.

Signed by Committee

Thus wrote Charles Robinson in the five minutes James Lane had been gathering the Committee, and thus signed the Security Committee within five minutes of having read it. And thus was in the breast pocket of C.W. Babcock later that night, as he and a small contingency of the defenders of Lawrence rode through the dark toward the Governor's residence in Shawnee Mission. And thus was in said pocket when a band of Ruffians on patrol stopped Babcock and his friends.

"Whoa there, men. Just where on God's earth are you all off to this time a night?" Joseph James cocked his head and looked down his pronounced cheek-bones at Babcock. It was a clear night, the moon a quarter full and in wane, and it was crisp and cold. Most of the men wore gloves, but Joseph James did not. His hands were red with purple tinges, the knuckles white on the reins.

"To see my sister," replied Babcock. "She and her child are ill and need assistance. Word reached me this evening at supper, though it was sent three days ago."

"Where? Oh, lemme guess: Yankee Town?"

"Yes, sir. I freely admit that I was in Lawrence. My sister's letter was detained by, well, by your men."

"And you're a-doing what in Yankee Town?"

"I'm sure you quite know. Defending it from marauders."

"Marauders? Ha! That don't sound like a respectful word, now does it, boys?" The other men chuckled. "If your town was under attack from marauders, why'd you leave it for your sister? Ain't she got a man ta take care a her?" For the second time in his life, and as many in a week, the word 'bastard' came into his mouth. He swallowed, turned his head, and spat.

"Yes, but she's my blood, sir. Lawrence has ten-dozen men to defend her. My sister has but one, and is in grave danger. My nephew is an infant, and I fear will not have survived to see my arrival. I am ashamed."

Joseph James paused, thinking of Oliver John up in Atchison, still lying in the bed of two New Englanders. Oliver John had just begun to walk around again, and the memory of that sight of him walking so tenderly, but with such a great smile on his face, brought tears to Joseph James's eyes for the first time in many years. He'd forgotten what it was like to cry, and almost missed it.

"Very well, then. I wish you and your sister the best, sir."

***

Joseph's men protested quietly, but were immediately silent when their patrol leader told them to "mind yer damn manners." They knew he was a veteran of the Mexican War, had fought in it quite young, and though the Kansas Militia had a somewhat disorganized system of hierarchy, he was clearly their superior. His service to C Company, the 1st Missouri Cavalry under Col. Doniphan, whose regimental coat he wore this night, was all the knowledge they needed to obey. All the men of western Missouri knew and loved Alexander W. Doniphan, and they respected the volunteers who'd rode all the way to Mexico and back in the '40s.

"Well, Cap'n," said one of these men, who rode an old ailing horse, as the messengers of the Security Committee rode away, "what now? S'pose them men is a spy. We gonna wait here all night ta see if they come back with a cavalry?"

"No," Joseph replied, moving Ninny alongside the tired old mare his compatriot rode. "We're not. We're gonna keep a-movin' clock-wise 'round Yankee Town till we gits up to the river, just like Atchison a-told us to. One thing ya gotta know 'bout being in the military, boys—don't think and don't ask questions. Just do as you're told and you'll be safe." He paused. "Or not. But it's yer only chance."

"Well, it's a-gittin' cold, and I'm famished," said the same man. His old horse had shifted her weight a little and turned so that the little moonlight there was now shone in her rider's eyes.

Joseph James had never quite looked hard at this man's face until now. It was incredibly dirty, his eyes were droopy and bloodshot, and it was absolutely impossible to guess his age. He could be twenty-five as well as fifty. And in his eyes there was not a hint of battle. Whatever happened this night, this man would do no good to anyone.

"I think I'll have to keep a little warm somehow." The man produced a flask from his inside breast pocket, unscrewed it, and raised it to his lips. Joseph James slapped it away. The whiskey spilled on the rump of another man's horse. "Hey! Whatdya gone and a-do that fer?"

"You are on duty, sir. You are on patrol. There is no boozing on duty in my command."

"Well, I dunno who you think you are or what you think this here operation is, but this ain't the Mexican War, Cap'n, and hell, you ain't even a real Cap'n. We ain't even a real army. I'm just here to fight. I just wanna wipe out that sonofabitch town and I'm a-waitin' three days with no action! I'm here ta wipe out Lawrence! That whiskey is part of my rations!"

The other men cheered tentatively, and they were right. Ten gallons of rectified whiskey had been ordered and would be later approved by the governor. Another gallon of brandy for the officers. All in all, they would spend almost $12 on booze and only a little more than that on ammunition.

"Yer here to die if you drink that on patrol."

"Well." The man slipped his right leg over the old mare, who was starting to steam from her skin just a little. "I guess I'll just defect from this here command." He picked up the flask and downed what was left in it. Struggling to mount his mare again, the horse reeled from the man's imbalance; the man said something none of the others understood, but they laughed.

"You think this is funny?" shouted Captain Joseph James Hawkins. "It's a disgrace to the State of Missourah, to Senator Atchison, and to the South. To you men, this is also a great disrespect. If we were ambushed here, this man would endanger all our lives. Get outta here, you fool!" Joseph slapped the old mare on its hindquarter with his cold bare hand and it rode off toward the north, then the west, then the north, then the east, and finally, toward the north and the camp of Col. Atchison's Kickapoo Rangers. "Now, men, keep yer damn mouths shut and your eyes open. And spread the hell out!"

***

As he rode through the December night, Joseph James began to remember the long ride to Mexico he'd taken as a young man—still a boy, really—in Doniphan's command. His father, George Sherman Hawkins, was still living with them, on and off, and Oliver John was very young. His mother was still a happy, pretty woman in 1846, with long blonde hair and slender fingers. She still smelled good, too. In the decade that had passed since he left, he'd thought quite a bit about what had happened at home while he was away, because it was so different when he got back. But he hadn't thought much about the war itself.

In those ten years, as Sarah Sally aged so dramatically, her skin sagged and began to stink, her hair grayed and her fingers shortened and widened, he'd wondered a lot if it were somehow her fault that Pappa had left, returning to his Cherokee mistress (or wife, maybe?) up in Indiana. George Sherman was a jovial man who was full of energy and facial hair. His skin was wrinkled and tough, and his hands were thick and strong. He'd lived in four states since leaving Tennessee as a young man with his bronze-skinned mistress and slender blonde wife, and Sarah Sally always suspected he had yet another family in each of them, including Rebecca, the wife of the Indiana clan. That "Indian whore" was his only consummate companion through all his wives, and Sarah Sally wondered how in the hell she put up with George's dalliances. She would wait outside the homes of other women, sitting quietly on her horse, wrapped in a blanket, knowing that he would return to her. He always did.

"If I was her," Sarah Sally used to say, "I'd a-feed his scalp to the coyotes. But what do them Injins know 'bout any a-that? They's just squaws, after all. But not me, no siree. If that sonofabitch shows his face round here one more time, I swear to heaven I'll wipe it clean off his skull. White women know how to get respect outa their men."

But she never did wipe the face off George's skull, and one particularly warm fall day in 1846, while one of his bastard sons was marching to war for his country several hundred miles away, and the other was playing in the mud out back, George Sherman Hawkins and his face once again left Missouri with the Cherokee woman he'd loved since he was twelve, and for good this time. George went out to Oliver John and bade him goodbye. He found the boy crouched, covered in earth to his knees and elbows, and had a feeling he was too old to play in the mud. He stood above his son, who looked up at him, squinting into the sun. George took a step to his left so his head would shadow the little creature kneeling beneath him.

Oliver John looked up, seeing the silhouette of what he knew to be a man by the shape of its shoulders, and what he knew to be his father by the way his legs bowed out below the knees. He couldn't see his face at first, and his eyes hurt so he covered them with his forearm. Then he could see him, and his face was dark. It was different, too, more different than it had ever been before. Somehow this man was still his father, but not. This man didn't love him. This man's face was like the face of a stranger at the general goods store, who looked at him too long in one of the aisles when they were alone there together. This man, standing above him on this warm day when the birds were chirping and there was even a bee or two, even though the leaves weren't on the trees now and the flowers had gone to bed, was so strange he wasn't even a man anymore. He had face with lines too deep, curved, long, and spread out to be human. He was a puppet that had dropped out of the sky and landed here in cool November mud.

"Pappa?" he asked.

And the face changed back. It was his father again. It bent down and handed him a hat with a feather in it. And it smiled and picked him up with arms that didn't dangle like a puppet's, and it said a lot of things and smelled good, was scratchy and familiar, but Oliver John never remembered the things this face said. He only remembered the shadowy puppet standing above him, and the feeling of the new hat in his hands.

And he rode off.

That night Oliver John dreamed that he was in the cornfields with his pappa and big brother Jimmy. Suddenly Pappa reached down, grabbing him under the arms, and flung him into the sky. He tumbled through it, seeing the yellow corn, blue sky, yellow sun, and brown earth rotate around him like a lollipop until the colors bled together. Then abruptly he felt himself return to the ground, stuck under a small grate, shaped and sized something like a cattle guard.

"Pappa!" he yelled. "Pappa! Pappa! I'm stuck! Come 'n get me, Pappa! Come 'n get me! I'll drown here, Pappa!"

But he heard his father's heavy footsteps move in the other direction, swishing the stalks aside until the world went quiet.

***

But Joseph James didn't think much of his father leaving on the night of December 4th, 1855. He'd thought so much about it over the last decade that it had become something that drove his life and most of his decisions. Oliver John was his boy now, and he had two wives—Sarah Sally and Delilah J. When he rode back into Missouri after the Mexican War and found them, half-starved and sick, he knew his dad had left and he was the man of the house. He knew that being a farmhand the rest of his life was not an option. He knew that it was his responsibility to give Delilah J. and Oliver John a better life, and if Mamma wanted to do it with them, then so be it. And he knew that Del would understand that. Hell, if she hadn't killed Mamma while he was away, she could stand another ten or twenty years listening to her whining, surely.

Tonight, back in his regimental uniform, atop a proud and brave horse, and carrying his rifle, Joseph James began to think about Mexico. He'd volunteered with the same sort of hopping enthusiasm that Oliver John always showed, and before he knew it he was marching out of Leavenworth far out in the grasslands of Indian territory, wondering how in the hell those people could ever live out there with no water or shade. Folks did what they had to, he supposed, and these Indians were either forcibly removed there, in which case they could only make do with what they had or die, or they were born of that land, and the harsh, dry, windy, barren land was none of that to them at all, but the very origins of life.

He soon found himself in the desert, where they had built actual homes out of clay, even carved them right out of the rocks. It almost seemed that for every part of the country they rode through there was another kind of Indian, another kind of person that rose right out of that earth, and they were a part of it. And here he was, he and his Missourian brethren, riding roughshod over it, ready to take the land from a government hundreds of miles to the south. Growing up a farmhand and a bastard, Joseph James knew that in his world the most important thing was the owning of land, and the right to inherit it. But here in New Mexico the whole concept seemed laughable. Whoever claimed to own it, the land would be the land, totally indifferent to deeds and borders and claims. The land had its own ghosts.

He had made friends with some of the men, and they ruffled his hair and wondered at the sharpshooting of such a young man. But one fellow soldier in particular didn't ruffle his hair, because he was the same age as Joseph, from the same county, and they had grown up together since they were both little boys. In the march toward Mexico, and in the long days in the saddle of October and November, Joseph had come to consider Daniel Baumgartner his brother. Just like some of these Indians belonged where they were, he and Little Dan belonged in western Missouri. You could tell, just by looking at them, that they were brothers by virtue of geography. Soon Joseph James realized that he wasn't fighting for Texas anymore, that what once seemed so important was no longer. He realized that he was fighting for Little Dan Baumgartner, for Oliver John, and for his mom. He wasn't fighting for this land. He was fighting for Missouri.

And on Christmas Day, 1846, he found himself doing just that.

***

"Tell us 'bout the War, Cap'n," one of the men asked. The horsemen had clustered back together after having "fanned out" as Joseph James had instructed. They were nearing the bridge over the Kansas where they would reconvene with Atchison's Kickapoo Rangers, under whose command they had been sent on patrol, and were forced together by the lay of the land.

"Well, I'll tell you that if you'd a been there, you wouldn't a done what you just did."

"What's that, Cap'n?"

"Huddled up like a bunch of ducks on a frozen pond. Don't you know not to do that when you're a-bein' hunted?"

"Ain't nobody round here, Capt'n. No more 'n two men could a hide in them trees."

"That's all it takes, with them Sharps rifles," replied Joseph James. "One man with one good eye coulda killed us all right there." He stopped Ninny and looked around.

They had come to a ridge that overlooked part of a road below, and could see the Kansas River in the distance. Lawrence was not far off, a faint glow just shy of the horizon. From here they could safely light a fire and still hold a commanding view of their environs.

"Ya'll hungry?" he asked.

"Yessir!" they replied in unison.

"All right then, dismount and light a fire. I'll tell you 'bout the War over a nice supper." He reached in his saddlebag and produced a pheasant and two rather large squirrels, all of them rather stiff with frost.

The men cheered. They hadn't had any meat—and not much to eat at all at that—since leaving their homes in Missouri some three days earlier. They thought they'd cross the river, camp out a night, burn Yankee Town to the ground, camp out another night and celebrate, and be home for Sunday supper. A nice weekend in Kansas Territory, they thought—a little hunting, a little hooch, and a great big bonfire. But here it was already Wednesday night, and nothing had happened. They were getting hungry and bored.

"How'd you know ta bring them critters?" one man asked between deep breaths that he exhaled into the smoking kindling. It had been a dry fall, and fires were easy to start.

"What the hell do you mean by that?" Joseph James replied as he held a squirrel by the tail and gutted it into a small hole he'd dug at his feet. "Do you plan for the sun to rise every day?"

"No, sir, I just thought this'd be over by now. I didn't think to bring much food. I came here for a war, not a siege."

"Well, hunger you can plan for." He squeezed the squirrel with both hands until its excrement spilled out, "but war you cannot. When men gets to fightin', you got to expect the unexpected, my pappa always said. 'Cept he meant it when women get to lovin'."

The men laughed, and one of them field dressed the other squirrel while Joseph James started plucking feathers from the pheasant. "Here, you finish this," he handed it to the man who'd started the fire. "Lemme have a snort of that."

"Yessir!"

"Ah, now that's nice on a December night," he said as he finished his gulp of whiskey. "Now, 'bout the War, gentlemen."

XVI

Between whiskey and roasted meat, the men watched the moon fall toward the plains and the stars stretch across a depthless sky. And they listened to Joseph James tell the story of the Battle of El Brazito.

"Col. Doniphan gave us the day off," he began, "bein' as it was Christmas."

"Christmas?" interrupted one man. "I thought it was in February."

"That was the Battle of Sacramento. Everyone's done hearda that. I'm tellin' you about my first battle, about Doniphan's first battle (of the war, anyway, 'cause he'd done the Mormon War of '38 too). Well, he gave us the day off 'cause we needed the rest. More 'n every other man had saddle sores worse 'n you ever seen before, and half the goddamn dust in Mexico was in our noses, ears, and hair. That's one helluva dirty country, Mexico is, and I tell you it ain't no stroll in the woods to ride through it with a thousand horses." He took a sip of whiskey, poked the fire, and continued.

"Most of the men spent the morning sleeping, drinking what coffee they could rustle up, and smoking whatever would burn right. Lots of cards, too. Col. Doniphan included—he was a-playin' cards when the word came."

"What word was that, Cap'n?"

"Word that the damn Mexicans aimed to celebrate the birth of the Lord by killin' a few Missourians, that's what. Our scouts spotted a few clouds of dust on the southwest horizon, and we knew just what they were up to. We were all more annoyed at the interruption of our cards than excited 'bout a good clean fight."

The men chuckled. One rose and urinated a few steps away from the fire.

"Just as calm as can be, we all mustered under our flags and lined up as the Colonel ordered. It wasn't until we saw them uniforms that we got a little skittish."

"What uniforms?"

"Boys, them Mexicans can sure look perty when they aim to! They wore sharpest red coats any soldier wore since the English was here. Big tall hats with brass on 'em, and feathers or hair a-stickin' out of 'em like pheasant." He pointed to the head of the bird that they were currently eating. It lay on the ground next to the fire.

"And most of 'em wound up just like that one!

"More 'n one, I can tell you that! But a-fore then, our infantry was ordered to lay flat in the grass. I dunno what a-took them Mexicans so long gettin' there—maybe they took a siesta 'long the way—but I know a few men fell asleep right there a-waitin' for 'em to charge us. But once they did come, and started a-firin' right at us, all them hoofs a-shakin' the ground and that big ol' howitzer goin' off—hell, I dare you to find another group of country boys that'll sit there in the grass just a-waitin'."

"Why'n't you all git up and let 'em have it?!"

"Under orders, men, under orders. Doniphan ordered us to wait, so we waited. That's what this whole damn operation to help Sheriff Jones is a-lackin', and sorely at that—discipline. Why, Atchison's barely able to keep the likes of you all on one side of the river without drownin'! Can't imagine these here Kickapoo Rangers layin' down calm-like under fire."

"But we ain't facin' the army of a nation, Capt'n. We're a-facin' a bunch of yellow-bellied Yankees!"

"Them Yankees are defendin' their homes, men. Whether we think their homes should be there or not isn't the point no more. They's defending their own, and a man defendin' his home is as nasty as a coon caught in a hole."

"We's defendin' our own too!"

"The hell you is! A man defendin' his home ain't gonna drink what you's drinkin'. The will to fight and the discipline to do it smart, that's what we need. If them Yanks were up in Missourah, you'd be wearin' and a-feelin' your sharpest."

"Wasn't them red coats a nice target, though, Capt'n?"

"Damn right they were!" The men laughed. "I can't tell you what goes through your head as they come at you. You're a-hearin' them hoofs and bullets, hearin' your heart beatin' in yer ribs, and you glance up now and then and see a long wavy red line comin' right at you. Then you hear the order, and it's the nicest thing you ever heard. You get up and fire, and scream like you ain't screamed before never in your life. In our case, Doniphan did it so well, that was it. We fired, and they ran.

"'Every man for his turkey!' I heard Doniphan yell, and it was exactly like a turkey hunt—Mexicans runnin' this way and that, those big feathers a-floppin' in th' air. I just took off after one." The men laughed again, and a pause followed.

Joseph James took another drink of whiskey, then another. He stood, stretched, and looked at the long arc of stars overhead, laying itself out across the sky just like the Mexican army advancing down a ridge south of El Paso nine years earlier.

"And then you collect yourself. You cheer and hug your men, and realize the last twenty minutes of your life you'll never forget. You look around, 'cause you don't see him. 'Dan!' you yell, 'Dan! Danny Baumgartner!' And when you find him, all covered in blood, you realize you lost the battle. That the Mexicans went runnin' for the hills, but the only thing you cared about in that godforsaken place is a-lyin' there in the dirt covered in his own blood."

After a longer pause, in which Joseph James sat back down and swigged the whiskey one last time, one of the men said, "But there weren't no dead at El Brazito, Capt'n. It was a whuppin'."

"I know it, son. I know it. But one of them seven casualties you heard about was Dan Baumgartner, my best friend. He lost an eye at El Brazito." He paused. "Dan spent the mornin' drinkin' his Christmas cheer, gentlemen." He paused. "That boy hadn't drunk more 'n a glass in his whole life, and that morning he had three." He paused again, and sighed. Suddenly he jumped up. "Don't matter. We marched all the way to Mexico City and won. That's all that matters. We done drug that Old Sacramento cannon all the way across the Mexican desert as a trophy. That cannon means more than the brass and steel and lead in it, boys." He sighed, looked down at the tin cup he'd used to shoot the whiskey, and tossed it the ground by the man who owned it. "That cannon means Dan's eye was worth it." He stomped on the fire with a heavy boot. "Let's go."

Within an hour they had crossed the Kansas and rejoined the main camp of Atchison's Kickapoo Rangers, where they found several dozen men drinking loudly around several fires. Joseph aimed to find Atchison's tent to report on his patrol, and when he found it, discovered the United States Senator dancing and jumping up and down on the stump of a felled cottonwood. He stumbled off of it, toward the fire, where several men saved him from falling in, and escorted him to his tent.

"Gooddamn drunks," Joseph James said to himself. "If them Yanks only knew, we'd be as easy as ducks on the water."

***

Near the end of the week Roger was marching along the barricades erected across Massachusetts Street when he saw a remarkable wagon roll into Lawrence. Much of his company noticed it, but only Roger became fixated as it rolled past them as they absentmindedly kneeled, stood, marched—kneeled, stood, marched. They had been drilling this way all week, and any disruption to the routine was noticed and welcomed.

"Private!" his Captain yelled. "Young man, there ain't no beauty in all of Kansas Territory that can excuse a distraction such as this!"

Roger heard this, and heard his compatriots laugh, but did not respond. He simply couldn't pull himself away. Nothing in his drilling and discipline could ever pull him away from something as inspiring as this.

The wagon was full of five men, all of whom looked alike, and the driver looked to be their template. From a hundred yards away the color of his eyes could be determined—gray. Steel gray, much like certain horses or cats, or the moon in a fog. His hair was close-cropped and turning a similar color, and he rode straight in the seat. The barrels of guns stuck out every which way from the wagon, and the hair of the men and canvass of the wagon fluttered in the wind as the wagon roared down the road in a muted cloud of dust. And a long sword, fitted alongside the driver, glinted in the sun. Several swords came to light this way. This wagon was prepared for battle, and these men were prepared for war. It looked like a chariot of the apocalypse pulled by either a vengeful god or a demon.

Roger let out a burst of excitement. Surely, today, something would finally happen.

And it did. The night before, the body of a Free Stater from Indiana by the name of Tom Barber was brought to town and laid in state in the Free State Hotel. He'd been shot in the back by Indian agent and Pro Slave settler George W. Clarke, right in front of his brother, and was unarmed at the time. Clarke apparently bragged that he'd sent another "damned abolitionist to his winter quarters," and the defenders of Lawrence were about to find out about it. Barber's widow arrived in town just minutes after this battle wagon had, and all of Lawrence was gathering at the hotel.

"Let's let the boy lead, then," Roger's captain announced. "Mr. Dugan, march us back to headquarters!"

As his company arrived, Roger saw the tattered wagon and the men it conveyed parked outside the hotel. There was a general commotion about the place, and as the captain dismissed his company from drills, Roger found his way inside, where he aimed to find Jim Lane, who would explain everything to him.

But he found a crush of men, including the gray-eyed man with the sword, next to whom he found a spot and stood, waiting to see what might unfold. What followed was something he never forgot.

It was the shriek of a woman, a shriek that was grief itself given voice. Mrs. Barber had just been brought to see the body of her slain husband, and with her cry the men of Lawrence reached their breaking point. Cries went up through the lobby of the unfinished hotel, and the boots of the men muddied the floor where their heads had lain the night before. They were tired of waiting. They wanted action.

And as usual, Robinson and Lane found themselves at the center of the room. And as usual, Lane counseled action, Robinson deliberation.

"The Governor is coming this very evening," Robinson shouted. "He will see that we are in the right and our beloved Lawrence will be protected."

Lane stood on the same bench Robinson had just bounced down from, and with his exceeding height he commanded the room. "Nonsense!" he cried. "What about Thomas Barber? What about Charles Dow? The governor elected by this bogus legislature is too late for them! The laws of Lecompton are not applied to them! The poor widow you hear grieving upstairs is not assuaged by a visit from Wilson Shannon, Dr. Robinson!"

Just then the man beside Roger, who rode in town upon his wagon of Armageddon, unsheathed his sword and raised it into the air. "The blood of vengeance will assuage her!" he shouted, and an uproarious cheer rose from the crowd. For a moment it seemed even James Lane had lost control of the crowd. The man returned his sword to its sheath, a wry smile of contentment on his face, and he noticed Roger staring at him by his elbow.

He smiled. "It's nice to see a young man your age fighting for freedom," he said. "You know, many of the heroes of the Good Book weren't much older than you. My sons, for instance, make me prouder than any of the other men here."

Roger glanced around the man who was speaking to him. The speaker was surrounded by the younger men from the wagon, who looked just like him. They were his sons.

The old man offered his hand to Roger, and all the tumult of the room slipped away like floe along the river. He could hear this man sharply, see him, feel his hand as he grasped it, better than anything he had seen, heard, or felt, in years. It was like a rebirth of childhood being around this steely eyed demon.

"John Brown," the old man said. "Pleased to meet you."

***

Forty-eight hours later, with all the angry men of Kansas ready and willing and able to finally fight it out, they all went home, and the Wakarusa War ended as quickly as it had begun. All hell finally broke loose, but not the hell they had imagined, planned for, and desired. This hell did not come of war. It did not come from James Lane's tongue, David Atchison's weight, the anger of Sam Jones or John Brown's sword. Nor was it quelled by Charles Robinson's solidity or Wilson Shannon's polish. It was a hell born of cold. It was a hell born of ice and wind. It was the hell of Kansas in December.

Saturday morning broke mild enough. The sun was out and shining on Joseph James's camp on the north bank of the Kansas. A breeze from the south and west rose up in the mid-morning that was cool enough for the men of the Kickapoo Rangers to keep their blankets handy, but warm enough to keep some of them standing in a sunny sand bar next to the river. Joseph was among them, and he lingered in the warmth beside the river, drinking coffee with a hint or two here and there of corn mash. He laughed in the sunlight.

The sun shone, too, in long-shadowed streams into the lobby of the Free State Hotel, where Roger slept. It made some of the men in the hotel stir, look out the window, and notice clouds forming in the northern sky.

Snow was on its way. But as the day wore on, and the marching continued, it seemed to be a giant northerly thunderhead. Looks like a thunderstorm, they said. But from the north. In December.

And sure enough, by sunset, everyone was huddling. They were finding the weather over the last year or two was actually mild, and that Kansas had yet to unleash her full fury on any mass of settlers and their sovereignty. They were finding that there was another kind of storm, one that didn't necessarily involve rain, snow, or hail; one that was also somehow all three things put together, along with a tornado or two thrown in for good pace. It was the Kansas ice storm, and on the night of December 9th, 1855, it effectively ended the Wakarusa War.

"Hell, I'm a-goin' home," the Missourians said the next morning. "Ain't no use a-helpin' Jones if alls you doin' is a-sittin' in the ice a-starin' at a campfire." They'd endured a night of sub-zero temperatures, double-digit mile-an-hour winds, and piercing precipitation, with little food in their bellies or shelter around them, and after a week of camping out, eating little, and drinking much, they were tired. They wanted to get back across the river, have a nice meal, and get some sleep.

So the hell of the weather interrupted the hell of war, and men like Robinson and Shannon, who had worked very hard at negotiating a treaty, rejoiced. A reception was held at the Free State Hotel, which even Sheriff Jones attended, and Wilson Shannon drank perhaps the most heartily of all. The weather had helped what was already a lively and effective negotiation, as he saw it, and Robinson agreed. They'd averted a crisis, perhaps even prevented a civil war, and Shannon, for one, was going to celebrate accordingly.

He drank enough not to notice how Jim Lane and Sam Jones stared at each other across the table, and later, across the room. Jones nodded and smiled at Lane as he left, then pulled his buckskin coat up over his ears as he walked out into the cold night. Lane smiled and sipped his wine. Shannon may not have noticed, but Robinson did. Roger noticed, too. And Lane knew they noticed. This wasn't a treaty. It was just cold outside.

And Senator Atchison promised this was so. He told his Kickapoo Rangers from his cottonwood stump, "By God, we will fight yet, boys!" Dr. Stringfellow agreed. He spoke to his company, telling them that Shannon was a damned liar and a turncoat. And all through the ride back to Missouri, the men resented their being inconvenienced so; they felt that leaving Lawrence intact was an utter failure, that squandering this opportunity to have it out was inexcusable.

Even Lane knew that even the Free State celebrators were somehow disappointed in the week's events, as they knew, too, that the thing must be done. Lane was certain that Roger, at least, was disappointed. "You are a young man yet, Roger," Lane told him, taking his drink away and clasping him on the shoulder. "And now you have seen how this works," he motioned to the gathering with a sweeping movement. "Now you must go somewhere more at the heart of this," he said. "Go among the people. You will see what I mean. You will see what I did, what I learned about how to get where I am now. Go among the people and you will see where true power comes from." He thumped Roger on the chest. "True power," he said, and walked away.

Two days later, as the Defenders of Lawrence disbanded in the streets, leaving the materials of their dismantled earthworks on the sides of Massachusetts Street, Roger began to see what Lane meant. Groups of settlers were congregating around the hotel, their wagons encircled, their voices and steam from their breath rising in the cold December air. Some spoke louder than others, and those others appeared to be listening. From the top step of the hotel Roger could see that this was the true leader of the movement, this organism that breathed and moved around the square like a colony of ants, seething and writhing as one. All the conventions, committees, elections, and titles were only the rudders. Lane and Robinson could only steer this ship. It propelled itself.

In all the voices he heard from the top step of the Free State Hotel that day, one came to the forefront of Roger's attention after a few moments of listening. It was forceful in its conviction, unyielding in the tone it chose for itself. And after a moment, it was quashed. Then Roger could see where it was coming from—a small scuffle ensued, and he could see the man who'd introduced himself during the burial of Barber, the man with the steel eyes and sword. John Brown. He was attempting to stand on something to speak but was being prevented.

Roger made his way to the center of the commotion and finally found Brown, still struggling to speak, as several men held him back and others held those men. "Don't incite panic!" one yelled at Brown. "Who gave you the right to declare war?"

"God almighty has declared war against slavery!" Brown yelled in rebuttal, "This unholy institution must be eliminated! I am but His faithful servant!"

He raised his sword into the air and was then finally overcome by those who sought to restrain him, pulled down from whatever he was standing on. He sheathed his sword and climbed onto his wagon. He stood high atop the seat of his wagon as his sons mounted it from all sides. His face shone in the sun, which had just shown itself, his eyes hauntingly fixed on some distant point. "If you fight not for the Free State Party, but for Freedom itself, follow me!" he shouted. The crowd was not ready for John Brown, but Roger was.

A great shadow cast itself over the crowd, and though everyone looked skyward to see what it was, only some saw the silhouette of a great bird, and only those who saw it heard it give a great cry over the din of the gathering.

The clouds closed upon the sun once again, and as John Brown rode out of Lawrence, the winter returned with fury.

XVII

Ninny kept slipping on her way back to Patrick's farm. She kept slipping the rest of December, in fact, as she helped move Oliver John, Sarah Sally, and Delilah J. to their new home in Kansas. She slipped hauling their bed, stove, stolen lumber, butter churn, and cold press, and spilled the contents of their home all over the broken muddy roads of northeast Kansas. She slipped crossing rivers, climbing hills, getting up, or sitting down. It wasn't her fault— everything was either mud or ice, all month, and it only got worse as the winter of 1855-56 progressed. The only thing Ninny didn't drop that December was Oliver John. She carried him as gently as a mother would a newborn, and Joseph James had never been prouder of an animal in all his life.

This all began the day after Joseph returned from the Wakarusa. He wasn't feeling too good that night, having been drinking in the bare sun in the morning only to sober during a long, cold ride north. By the time he arrived at the farm he was in a horrible mood. He spat outside the door and then kicked it in.

"Mr. Dugan. A word, please," he said, keeping the door open.

Patrick had been outside working on a new barn and was warming himself by the fire. Clegg was sitting next to Maria at the table, and his son was playing on the floor with some rocks.

"You could close the door while you wait for him," Maria said.

"Sorry, ma'am. I'll wait outside."

As he shut the door and turned to feed Ninny, Joseph James realized he hadn't gone in to see Oliver John, and that he hadn't seen him in over a week. Oliver John would have heard his voice, too, so Joseph went back inside and headed to the bedroom.

"Knocking is considered polite in this household."

"I'm sorry, Maria. Can I see about Oliver John?"

"Of course. You'll be glad to know he walked all the way to the barn and back today."

"He did? Is he in much pain?"

"I think so, yes."

Joseph removed his hat. "Well, I'm much obliged for your helping him, ma'am."

"Of course, Joseph. That's what neighbors do where I am from."

"Of course."

Oliver John was asleep when Joseph James entered the room; he stood a few moments, watching his sibling sleep. He could still see the boy in him, and Clegg's son playing with rocks in the other room reminded him of Oliver John's penchant for collecting objects as a boy. He would gather sticks, rocks, leaves, bones, bits of metal, and anything else he could find that was somehow interesting in its color, texture, shape—anything useful in acting as something else—and bring them inside. He was always scolded for this by both Sarah Sally and Delilah J., however, and he would place them in a pile outside the front stoop. Outside one cabin they had during much of Oliver John's early boyhood there grew a large pile of these objects, and the farmer who owned the land commented that it looked like "half of Missourah was on the front stoop."

In this young man's sleeping face, Joseph James could see the boy that did this so clearly it was almost painful. He scratched his beard and then lightly touched the boy's face.

"He's going to walk, you know," Patrick said as he came in. "He's spent from yesterday, but he's on the mend for sure. He stood right there, tall and proud." Patrick pointed to a spot on the floor next to the bed. "Seems like he's grown an inch or two in that bed, like."

Joseph James nodded. "Well, I don't know what to say, Patrick. I still just don't know what to say."

"How about telling just me what you wanted to speak to me about outside."

Joseph James looked at his neighbor, a man he'd once threatened, a man whose goodness compelled him to assist even those who threatened him. He sighed, a twinge of pity uncurling in his gut. "It's about Roger. I came here a-fixin' ta fight with you," he began. He could see the concern clearly on Patrick's face. "But then I saw my brother, and how you a-took care of him." He swallowed, picked up Oliver John's feathered hat from the bed post and wrung it in his hands with a sigh. "I saw your brother in Lawrence, Paddy."

Patrick lost his color. "Well, wh-what was he doing?"

"He was a guard at the Free State Hotel."

"Wh-what were you doing there?" At times, Patrick seemed like a child to Joseph, lost in a world of adults who'd long since forgotten what it was like to be young. "Where have you been the last week?"

"Camped outside Lawrence." It felt as if he were explaining women to a boy. He wondered what motivated this lanky man from across the sea, how he couldn't understand why, when he'd struggled so long for it himself, a man would fight for his home. "You haven't read the *Sovereign*?"

"No, I've not gone to Atchison in a few days." Patrick began to pace the room. "I've been busy up here."

"A war nearly broke out, Patrick. How busy could you have been?" He shook his head with a sigh, grinning in incredulity. "We sieged Lawrence. They were in open rebellion. A last minute treaty—and this damned storm—stopped it."

"And what about the hotel? What were you and he doing there?" Was it that Patrick couldn't believe his brother would be involved, or any man?

"He was guarding it, like I said a-fore. I was part of a detachment that went into town to speak with the Yankee leaders, who were based in the hotel. Roger was part of the hotel guard, I believe. I met him on the front steps."

There was a pause, Patrick turned to leave the room, hesitated, then stopped. "W-was he in danger?"

"Hell, yes he was!" Joseph stopped. The enthusiasm in his voice seemed more hurtful than he wanted it to be, and he began again. "I'm afraid he was, Patrick." Glancing at how tall Patrick was, he felt silly speaking to him like a child. "Everyone in Lawrence was," he said harshly, increasingly irritated with his neighbor. "There were twelve hundred mad-as-hell Missourians who wanted to burn that town to the ground and slaughter everyone in it." He paused, and though most of the anger he'd directed at Patrick when he arrived had subsided, he couldn't let his pity confuse the fact that this strange man needed to be personally warned, yet again. "And I have to tell you, Patrick, that he was probably more in danger 'n some."

"What do you mean by that?"

They were still standing next to Oliver John's bed, and when its occupant moaned and shifted a little, they made their way outside, trying not to meet the eyes of Clegg or Maria, who simply let them pass.

It was cold outside, windy, and, to speak, they had to stand shoulder to shoulder with their backs to the wind.

"I ain't much for diplomatic talk, Patrick, so I'm just a-gonna put this the only way I know how—your little brother's one ornery sonofabitch. As we rode up on the hotel, he did everything he could to pick a fight with the sheriff, and then with me."

"With you?"

"Sure as hell. He told all the cavalry I was living with you."

After a pause and blowing into his cold hands, Patrick replied, "So?"

"So, most a those men don't take kindly to their folk a-livin' with Free Staters."

"We aren't Free Staters." So innocent. "We aren't anything. We're farmers."

"Oh, hell, Patrick, you've been in Kansas long enough to know that ain't possible. You have to choose a side." Removing his hat in frustration, he rubbed his eyes. Patrick couldn't possibly be this good—or stupid. "And I've known you long enough to know that's a lie." The wind subsided a little and they were able to lower their voices. "You're just a-tryin' to stay out of it, and I can respect that, but I know how you'll vote."

"I ain't votin'," Patrick said decisively.

He smiled at Patrick's choice of words. "Well, yer startin' to sound about right, that's fer sure!" But then realized it was a ploy, an attempt pretend he really was neutral. "I'm sure you can imagine, Paddy, that Roger was a-tryin' to get me in trouble."

"Did he?"

"Well, no. But he did himself. That's what I'm a-tryin' ta tell you." Joseph James stepped away, faced the wind and Patrick, and through a tight face rose his voice again. "I threatened him, Patrick. I'm tryin' ta tell you that while I respect you—that I'm grateful for all you've done for me—I ain't friends with your brother. He may've lifted that tree off Oliver John, but he'd just as soon drop it back on 'im again if he ever got the chance."

"I'm not too sure about that, Joseph. He's an idealistic, passionate young man, but he's rarely violent."

"Don't give me that! Hell, he's Irish!" His arms flailed somewhat wildly, then he shoved his hands back in his pockets and retook his position aside Patrick with his back to the wind. "Look, all's I'm a-tryin' to say is that if Roger's ever here again, you just do your best to keep us apart. It's best for all of us."

Patrick turned into the wind and looked at Joseph James full in the face. "Joseph, I do understand what you're saying, but Roger is my brother, and I love him dearly. I have to warn you not to hurt him."

Joseph James studied Patrick's face, hunched against the wind, maybe, but also in anger. He laughed. And he laughed again. "Hell, that makes me respect you even more, Patrick! You know what's important, and I respect that." He offered his hand, and it was accepted. "We're different on some issues here and there, but when it comes down to it, we're just family men, you and I, just a-tryin' to do what's best for our kin. Who knows, maybe someday when this is all over, you and Maria can come over and have supper with Del and me. You may even get to meet my mother, unless God spares you the honor. I 'spect we've got a lot in common."

Patrick smiled and released Joseph's hand. "We all do, Joseph. Every one of us. We just don't listen."

"Nope! We sure as hell don't. And that ain't gonna change," he said, feeling the pity again. "No time soon, anyhow, and you got to start a-realizin' that you can't say outa this, Patrick. You just can't. Nobody can." Patrick's expression now, for the first time, looked adult-like. Perhaps he wasn't as stupid as it seemed. Maybe he knew something that other's didn't. Maybe he'd learned something. Maybe he just really was that good. Or, maybe he was just afraid. "Welcome to Missourah, Patrick. Welcome to the West. Welcome to Kansas. Ain't nobody came to Kansas to start agreein' with folk. We all came here to get the hell away from the rest of the world, for one reason or another. Only trouble is that the world followed us to Kansas like a goddamned stray dog, and if you don't turn around soon, it'll bite ya clean in the ass."

***

For the first time all winter, on Maria's insistence, Oliver John sat up and they all ate supper together as a household. He was still largely bed-ridden, so the rest crammed their way into the room and ate around the bed with him.

Little Joe Clegg had taken a particular liking to Oliver John in the last week or so, and he did everything he could to get close to the injured boy while his dad did everything he could to keep his son away from Oliver John's pelvis and legs.

"Son, Oliver John is hurt. Gentle with him, please."

"It's all right, Mr. Clegg," Oliver John said. "The boy ain't a-tryin' ta hurt me. Leg's feelin' right well at the moment anyways, and he's 'bout as light as a pup." He tossed Joe his feathered hat. "Here, try this on, son."

"I think you're on the mend, Oliver John," said Maria as Joe put the hat on his head and bounced around the room. She smiled at Oliver John like a mother does her own child. "I do believe you shall be walking by Christmas."

"I reckon so, ma'am, thanks to you and yourn. I'm much obliged to you all. You done took good care a me."

"The boy is right," Joseph James interjected. "And you done took good care of me, too. That cabin's shapin' up nicely. I 'spect we could a-move in there any day now."

"Not in this weather!" Maria said with a mouthful of stew.

"Well, that cabin's already nicer than what we've got over in Missourah. I aim to move the womenfolk over as soon as they's ready, startin' tomorrow. I kin get back to my regular life now that the Yankee uprisin' in Lawrence is over —for now anyway."

This last sentence silenced the group with the exception of Little Joe, who bounced on the bed a little, picking at potatoes in his stew with Oliver John's hat on backward. Patrick, Maria, Clegg, and even Joseph James didn't really want to talk about it, but it seemed unavoidable.

"You think they'll rise up agin, Jimmy?" asked Oliver John. "Will we put 'em down if so?"

Joseph James snorted a bit as he chewed, swallowed, realized he couldn't spit so he swallowed again, rubbed his mouth with the back of his hand, and said, "I shouldn'ta spoken like that in this company, Oliver John. I'm sorry, everyone."

"It's all right," Clegg chimed in. "I don't quite see how an English Protestant turned Mormon, a Catholic Irishman turned pioneer, and a Missourian farmhand turned land-owner can dine together without finding some sort of delicate conversation topic." He smiled so genuinely, it set the others at ease. "I'd like to know the answer to Oliver John's question, myself."

Clegg had been sober over a week, had started working in town again, and was looking and sounding better than he had since September. His son curled up on his lap, and Clegg finished his stew around and over his body.

"Well, they all signed the treaty," Joseph said, wiping his mouth again. Soon he'd have to go outside and spit, he thought to himself. Swallowing was getting more difficult, especially the fattier chunks of venison.

"Who did?" asked Maria. "Who is starting all this mess anyway?"

"The answer to that depends on who you ask," Joseph answered.

"Well, once it was made, who took it upon themselves to clean it up?" she asked.

"The Yanks involved are them boys from Boston that you probably a-read about in the *Sovereign*. Charles Robinson, all them that founded Lawrence and wrote that piece of paper in Topeka last month."

"You mean the state constitution?" asked Patrick.

He looked at Patrick, holding back a glare. "No, I mean the piece of paper that they call the constitution." He looked back at his stew and turned it over with his spoon. "Never mind that, though. It's them boys on the Yank side, the leaders of the Free State Party. Robinson and a man by the name of Lane. And on our side—sorry, the Law and Order side—it's Sheriff Jones, Senator Atchison, and Dr. Stringfellow, the man who set you up right and good, Oliver John."

"Yessir. I remember him."

"He's a good man," Joseph nodded.

"What about Alexander Doniphan?" Clegg asked, putting down his bowl and embracing his son.

"How the hell—excuse me—how do you know about Doniphan?" asked Joseph.

"Mormons know Doniphan quite well, Joseph."

"Yes, that's right. Somethin' 'bout the Mormon War of '38. Well, I ain't seed Doniphan's involvement at all. The whole thing would probably be over by now if he was there."

"Why do you say that?" Clegg asked gently.

"I fought under Doniphan in the Mexican War, Clegg, as a part of the 1st Missouri Dragoons. Damn proud of it too." Joseph James sat now, but straight in his chair. "Not for a-takin' Mexico, necessarily, but just in my associatin' with a great man."

"And why do you think this great man would have ended this conflict in Kansas?" Clegg was still gentle, and his age began to show in his patience, something the others did not yet possess.

"Doniphan's a man of action, sir. A man of discipline, decision, loyalty. He wouldn'ta let us half-starve, freeze, drink too much, and bore ourselves out there. He woulda gone in there and a-showed them Yanks what for. Alexander W. Doniphan is a great man, a man of the law. He knows an order is an order." His enthusiasm was almost embarrassing, but kept Oliver John's rapt attention.

"I can see your affiliation with him is strong, Joseph, and that fighting for him in the war was important to you, and I do agree that Doniphan is a great man." Clegg stood his son, then himself, and turned his body a bit. "But I must beg to differ that this greatness is because he 'knows an order is an order.' In fact, my association with him leads me to believe he is great due to his refusing to follow an order."

"General Doniphan insubordinate?" Joseph's incredulity was totally embarrassing. Even Oliver John looked into his bowl and winced. Perhaps from pain.

"Well, I suppose so, yes. His orders were to have our prisoners executed. Without trial, without due process, he was to have our prophet hanged in the town square. He refused."

"No."

"Yes, indeed, Joseph, indeed. In fact," he turned more toward his interlocutors, "you might say that your colonel saved my prophet's life!"

"Right," Joseph nodded, "the one ya'll think is Jesus."

"We don't think he's Jesus, Joseph." Clegg chuckled a little. "We just consider him a prophet sent by God. And your General Doniphan saved his life."

"Well, hell, guess he's an even better man than I thought, a-savin' Moses like that!" Everyone laughed. "Funny how life is, ain't it, Mr. Clegg? You go to sleep on one side of the bed and wake up on the other." Joseph James chewed his last mouthful of stew, and set his bowl carefully on the bed next to his brother's feet. "I think this calls for a drink, don't you?" He directed the question at Maria.

"If you like."

"I do like! But none of that stuff from back East. I gots some good ol' mash, imported right outa Missourah."

Soon they were all standing around Oliver John's sick bed with a glass of whiskey, and Oliver John sat up as straight as could be, joining in the toast.

"To great men," said Joseph James.

"Amen," said Clegg. "And to common heroes. May they one day unite us all."

With that, the oddest household in Kansas toasted to common heroes.

XVIII

By Christmas, all the Hawkinses were Kansas residents and Oliver John was walking, carefully and painfully, but without help. For the first time in a generation there was more reason for the Hawkins family to hope than worry, more in the future that excited them than in the past. But still, Sarah Sally didn't see it that way, and still, she worried a lot and talked about the past. She drove her sons and daughter in-law up the walls of their new home in Kansas.

"Them damn Yankees," she said. "They'd a-made that bastard father of yours proud. Ain't nothin' harder for me to see than somethin' that a-made that man happy."

She was referring to the election of December 15th, when the Free State Party's constitution, drawn up in Topeka, went to the residents of Kansas for a vote, and passed by large margin. Also passed was a separate "Negro Exclusionary Clause," which disallowed the residency of any black man, woman, or child. Free Staters had decided they didn't want any blacks in Kansas, free or slave.

Andrew Reeder was now their delegate to Congress and would soon leave for the capital, and it was becoming clear that most of the true settlers of Kansas were Free State sympathizers from western states such as Ohio, Indiana, Iowa, and Illinois. They won this election handily, despite significant voter intimidation efforts in places like Leavenworth (though these efforts were little compared to those of 1854 and early 1855). The race to populate Kansas was being won by the North.

"That George Sherman woulda loved this," she said. "Goddamn nigger-lovin' Yankee sympathizing sonofabitch."

Her boys hated it when Sarah Sally talked that way, not only because it disparaged their father, but because it was so unbecoming of the young mother they fondly remembered. "For the life of me, I can't a-figger out why you done moved me to a nigger-lovin' state," she told her eldest son the morning of Christmas Eve. "Why Missourah ain't good enough for you is beyond me. Maybe you should move up to Indiana with your father."

"We own the land here," said Delilah J. "We reap what we sow in Kansas. Back home, Mr. Anderson reaps what we sow. And like the Good Book says…"

"Don't you go a-quotin' the Good Book on me, girl," snapped the mother in-law. "I a-swore on that thing a long time ago and ain't had nothin' but heartbreak ever since. It ain't a good book to me. No, sirree, that there is a curse of a text. A downright goddamn blasphemous pile of horse shit."

Joseph James cringed as his mother pointed across the room to the family Bible. He knew as well as she did it was more than the word of God—it was his family heritage, the only remembrance of the Tennessee Hawkinses George Sherman took with him, and now, the only tie to them her sons had.

"If you children only a-knowed what I been through," she said when she saw her son cringe through is yellow beard.

Little did she know it, but Joseph James did appreciate what she'd been through. During all those long marches in Mexico, he realized what it was like to leave your home and lose your best friend, just as she had. But he didn't understand why she held Rebecca and the Indiana clan against him. Why she took her hatred of George Sherman out on Joseph James. The son was nothing like the father. He was not only loyal to his wife, he was loyal to his brother and his mother. He sweated and bled to keep them all fed. He was proud of it.

"If your grandpa could only see what's become of me," she told her sons, "he'd be ashamed. We were a proud family, I remember that much. Not like your father, and all them goddamn Hawkinses."

Joseph James spat. Since he was a child, he'd wondered why she didn't love him the way she loved Oliver John. He remembered sitting on some hard, cold, wooden floor somewhere crying, just barely able to walk, while she muttered and cursed and pinched her lips. All he wanted, all he ever wanted, was for her to pick him up, fold him in her arms. But she didn't. She went about her business and let him sob. He remembered how it ached, like fire, in his arms and his chest, as he reached for her. He remembered the water in his mouth and the vomit, and her stiffly patting him on the back as she moved him aside and cleaned it up like it was poison, saying something about loving him in a voice that didn't matter. Just didn't matter.

"I'm a Hawkins, Ma," he said now, crossing his arms over his chest. "Like it or not, yer a-talkin' about me when you say those things."

And with this her eyes sunk into crescents like elm leaves in October. "Why, I don't mean you, son, you knows I don't." She began to cry, looking into her son's eyes and stroking his face as he wrenched it away like a child. "This ol' world ain't big enough for us all," she muttered. "There ain't no man or god that can bring us all together again. We done exploded into a million pieces a million years ago, and ain't nobody gonna put us together again."

***

On the last day of 1855, the Dugans and the Cleggs rode south to visit the Hawkinses. Joseph James had visited a couple days earlier to invite them, delivering a hand-written note his wife Del had scrawled on a scrap of parchment.

> *Dere Maria,*
>
> *I'd a be good n honurd if you n yourn visited me n mine for a nise supper n some mash (or maybe some wine if I kin find sum-I knows a proper ladie like yerself mite prefer wine) to selebrate the new yere. I'm sure you agree 1855 wus pretty hard n I'd like to see if we all cant make 1856 bettur togethur. Also, I cant say enuf bout how you done took care a my Olee when he got hurt so bad. He aint my child but I done just bout raised him myself, so hes like a sun to me. That means I owe you everything, and tho we never met you shuld consider me your most loyal frend. Id a do anythin for ya, Maria. Anything. Plus, since we both with child Im a hopin our little ones will stop all this nonsense and make Kanzas better n our dum men have a made it so far. I hope you agree.*
>
> *With respekt and gratitood,*
>
> *Delilah J. Hawkins*
>
> *p.s. pleaze rite me back and tell me what you think—Jimmy will ferget whut you say.*

After she read it, with some difficulty, and smiled, Joseph James said, "She don't write too good but she sure means what she writes."

"She writes perfectly, Joseph."

"She's a good woman, Maria, I'll tell ya that." He put his hands back in his pockets when he realized Maria aimed to keep the letter. "Well, whadya think? I'm sure she means to take them Mormons too." He winked at Clegg, who laughed. "It'd mean a lot to her, Maria. We owe you and Patrick."

"Nonsense. You don't owe us anything at all, Joseph, but we'd be delighted to accept your invitation." She turned to Patrick, who had read the note over her shoulder. "Paddy, do you think we could bring a chicken or two?"

"I don't see why not. And some whiskey."

"Now yer talkin'! This here's a celebration, just as Del says." He faltered a bit. "I gotta warn you 'bout my ma. She's kinda an old porcupine, that one."

"I'm sure she's a lovely woman, Joseph."

"Nah. No need ta reassure me, Maria. She ain't the kindest nor the most delightful woman you ever met. Just be warned. Okay then! I'll tell Del..."

"No, you will not, boy! Delilah asked me to write her back."

"Aw, hell, I kin remember what you said for a few miles! Plus, she probably'll have to have Oliver John read it to her."

"She will get her reply in writing, Jo—*Jimmy*."

"Yes, ma'am," he beamed.

They arrived before the sun set, cold and wet. Little Joe Clegg had impressed everyone on the trip, having helped Patrick several times as the wheels of the coach got wedged in muddy ruts. Everyone agreed he'd grown so much since arriving at the farm; his father positively beamed as they said this: his face glowed brightly, a little like his head felt when he drank, but now he was the picture of health. Clegg didn't look tired anymore, and he'd regained the weight he lost. His chest stuck out again, he was strong and quick for his age, and the wisdom and humor he'd had all his life was back. He was proud to bring his son out into the world again—it was the first time the boy had left the farm since they arrived in the fall.

Maria and Patrick, however, didn't feel so well. Both were worried sick about Roger, and though their guests made them feel like they were running a proper Irish household, they were tired. Nursing an injured boy and a recovering alcoholic, building a cabin, a barn, and a farm, all after a truly exhausting move west and the miserable winter of 1854-55 in their cottonwood planked shack had left them needing a break. And Maria had another reason to feel not so well—she was nearly due, but something was wrong. Despite this being her first pregnancy, she knew it. She was hoping a commiseration with a fellow expectant mother might help her decide what to do. She didn't want to see Dr. Stringfellow, and didn't want to worry her husband.

"Maria, Maria!" yelled Delilah J. as they arrived. She ran up to the wagon and helped down Maria, who she'd already decided was her long-lost sister. "I'm so glad you came!"

Maria was truly excited to be on the first visit of her life in Kansas, but being so tired and worried, Delilah J.'s enthusiasm was a bit annoying. "Hello, Delilah. Good to see you," she said, climbing carefully from the wagon seat.

"My! You're frozen to the bone! Come in and get some warmth."

Soon they were all enjoying as lavish a meal as they'd had in over a year, and even Sarah Sally, who sat as grumpily as she could in the corner of the room, had to admit to herself that there was something truly special and enjoyable about December 31st, 1855. Turkey, chicken, pheasant, eggs, radishes, potatoes, beans, carrots, and corn; whiskey, potato wine, tea, and even a little cake Maria was able to make with sweet potatoes made them all happy.

Oliver John played the fiddle, Patrick the flute, and Joseph James tried to dance on the table, but cracked one of its legs. It was an evening of plenty, of warmth, in a winter of scarcity, cold, and suffering. A small glimmer of light in the depths of darkness.

Little did they know that it would be the last such evening of the season—by February, Kansans would be nearly starving and freezing to death, and both New Englanders and Southerners alike would be contributing to charities that would deliver goods and supplies to the frontier.

Later in the evening, the two adults who did not drink much at all—Maria and Delilah J.—found a moment to themselves by the fire while the men sat around the supper table and Sarah Sally fell asleep in her rocking chair under her quilt.

"You don't look too good, Maria," said Delilah J. "I ain't a-knowed you too long, but I do consider you a sister to me, and I knows when a sister is sick. Tell me what's the matter, hon."

"You're a very perceptive woman, Del, but the truth is, I don't know myself. I'm tired, I know that much, but I do feel like something is wrong. I just don't know what."

"With the baby?"

"Yes, I suppose. I don't know. What should I do?"

"Why, see a doctor."

Maria laughed. "I was afraid you'd say that."

"I know a good doc over in Missourah. He's nice 'n gentle. Won't hurt you much at all. He's old as the devil, but a nice man at that."

Maria sat up. She had a sudden burst of energy. "You do? Could I contact him?"

"You contact him? Maria, you're about ta give birth, woman! Send Jimmy! He'll do it."

"Oh, you're so busy with the new cabin and all, and it's so cold…"

"What is wrong with you, Maria?! You saved his brother's life!"

"Oh, I don't think it was that…"

"Nonsense! Jimmy told me he was as good as dead when you got him. He was green, wasn't he?" Maria nodded. "Well, all the Hawkins men turn green b'fore they's about to die. That's what Jimmy says anyways, what his daddy used ta say when he was around. You saved Oliver John's life, and we owe you for it. And even if that weren't true, what the hell else is men good for? Mine's here to fetch the doctor for me, that's one thing. I ain't gonna venture out in this cold with a child in me, and I sure as hell aint gonna let you do it either. Jimmy'll go in the morning and let you know when the doc kin come. Dr. Williams is his name. A good man."

"What's that, Del?" Joseph James called from the table, a few feet away. "What'm I doin' in the morning?"

"Never you mind, Jimmy. You just watch that mash 'cause you gotta ride Ninny 'cross the river tomorrow."

"Aw, hell."

"Watch yer mouth! There's children here."

They all looked over at Oliver John and Little Joe, who were both poking Sarah Sally lightly in the toes with sticks and rocks, making them wiggle as the old woman snorted in her sleep. And they laughed.

"That reminds me," said Joseph James, leaning very heavily on the wobbly table he'd partially broken earlier in the evening as he stood with effort, "I better check 'n make sure that old girl's still alive. It's cold out."

"You mean your horse or your mother?" said Del.

***

Just before dawn on the first day of 1856, Patrick woke to what sounded like his wife breathing heavily. His head was pounding.

"Shush!" he snapped at her, but remembered she was pregnant. They were wrapped in quilts on the floor beside their host's fire, and as he leaned up on one elbow, he thought she might be cold and he would need to stoke the fire. He rubbed his eyes, reached out his hand to place it gently on his wife, and was startled when her hand suddenly grasped his.

"Paddy, Paddy, something's wrong!" she whispered in a panicked voice.

"What is it?" He was wide awake now, and could see pain and fear in her face. His little Maria, the slayer of snakes, mender of broken bones, rarely looked so afraid and anguished.

"The baby. Something's wrong with the baby."

Patrick lifted up the quilt and saw blood on Maria's legs. They looked at each other in the eyes with the pale cast of fear, the look that never needs to say anything. They both knew that whatever was happening was going to change their lives. He went to lift the quilt up further so he could determine how much blood there was, but she clutched it to her chest.

"No," was all she said.

Patrick was going to try and convince her gently. Now was no time to be embarrassed.

Delilah J. appeared as if out of nowhere. "What's wrong?" She looked as if she'd been awake for hours, dressed, even.

"The baby," Maria said. "Lots of blood." She grimaced in pain, and a little squeal escaped her lips.

"I'll get the doctor," said Delilah J., meaning, of course, that she'd send her husband.

Within minutes, the entire household sprang into action, moving Maria to the bed, boiling water to clean her, fetching as much clean fabric as they could, and stoking the fire. It was bitterly cold out, and every time the door was opened, she shivered, so they moved the bed to the fire and surrounded it with linens hung from branches that Little Joe and a limping Oliver John fetched from outside. They spoke little, and after a few moments, as things settled and Del was busy cleaning Maria, Joseph James returned. He wasn't supposed to—he was supposed to be on his way to Atchison now to fetch Dr. Stringfellow (Dr. Williams, it was determined, was too far away for an emergency).

Patrick looked at him as he came in the door, wondering what else could go wrong this morning. It looked as if he'd been crying.

"Ninny's dead," he said. "She musta froze overnight. We'll need to take Zion."

"Yes," Patrick said, heading for the door, but Maria reached out to him across the space of the room. "No," she said.

"I'll go," Clegg stood, and seconds later was galloping off down the muddy, icy road.

Once the bleeding began to slow and Maria was as clean and dry as could be, and warm enough for the shivers to stop, Del busied herself in the kitchen, making some of the tea Maria had brought the night before, and warming whatever else she could find. Every few minutes Maria gasped in pain, but otherwise was lethargic, slipping in and out of responsiveness.

Both Little Joe and Oliver John began to cry, the little one clutching the elder's good leg as he sat at the table staring at the leftover stew in front of him.

Nobody ate. Nobody but Sarah Sally.

One way or another, we're doomed, she thought. If it ain't whoring Indians, it's the Yanks. And if it ain't the Yanks or some other man, it's the baby inside you that's gonna suck everything you got, just like this little one was bleeding his mother to death before he was even born. There's always someone that wants your land, your children, your life, your blood, and your name for their own. Someone to sweep down upon you and take everything you have.

Just then, she was woken from her reverie and her venison by a great bang on the roof, followed by four or five whooshing sounds and a horrible scratching as something giant roosted above them.

Patrick, sitting next to Maria, stroking her wet red hair, looked up.

Sarah Sally looked up.

Maria just tried to keep breathing, keep breathing.

Sarah Sally, Oliver John, and Little Joe ran outside to see what it was. But Patrick knew what it was, and so did Delilah J., and they both knew what it meant.

This was only the beginning. 1856 was going to be filled with rivers of blood.

XIX

Maria labored and bled all day and into the night. She labored and bled long enough for Dr. Stringfellow to come and go, pronouncing her "fit to meet her Maker" when he saw how much blood she'd lost. She labored long enough for Dr. Williams to arrive, deliver her lifeless son and pronounce it dead, and return with yet another doctor who'd had a good deal more experience with stillbirths in little women. "She ain't big enough for babies," he told Patrick. "She might bleed to death. You might like a son but I don't think this one'll give it to ya, if she does make it through this. The next one'd kill 'er for sure." Maria labored, in fact, until after the baby was buried, the bleeding stopped, and she fell into coma-like sleep.

Nobody thought she'd make it. Patrick even started trying to find a Catholic priest who would administer last rites. But after sleeping for three days and dreaming dreams she'd never forget, Maria Dugan sat up and sipped broth. Later that day she had some milk, more broth, and a bit of bread the next day. And a week after the stillbirth she was walking. Slowly and painfully, but she was on her feet.

"Looks like yer a-fixin' to show me hows to do it, Mrs. Dugan," said Oliver John. "Here, take my arm just the ways I done took yours a-fore Christmas." And the two limped around the cabin together a few times, trying not to laugh as Joseph James said they looked like "two cripples a-dancin'."

A few days before the first full moon of the year Maria and Patrick moved back to their farm. And they were sad.

Clegg and Little Joe found quarters in Atchison, and Clegg had a full plan to join the exodus of Mormons from Nebraska in the spring (it had since been deemed by the Church that Atchison was too dangerous).

So what was for the last part of 1855 a crowded house full of the breath of a dozen lungs and the promise of two more was now just a married couple with no hopes of a child. Even Roger was gone. They thought about him often, but had heard nothing. Perhaps he'd move back if he knew the Hawkinses were gone. But there was little chance of finding him.

The first few months of the year were going to be so cold, too, that it was going to be hard to keep busy, other than by chopping firewood, and there was a limit to that sort of work. So they were not only going to be sad, grieving for their lost child whom they'd buried just outside; they were also going to be lonely and bored as well. Sadness, loneliness, and boredom rarely do a marriage good, and once again, Maria's thoughts returned to Boston.

"I've let you work too hard, girl," said Patrick on one of the first nights they had alone together. Maria was still weak, and cried a lot. "It's my fault. You worked too hard."

"That's not it, Paddy. You know it, boy. That work had to be done. Without it, we'd all be dead, not just the baby."

"I shouldn't have taken Oliver John in."

"Nonsense! The Lord will hear what you say and judge it, Patrick Dugan, even in your grief and self-pity. Oliver John is not responsible for this child. We are."

"But Maria…"

"Don't you see, you idiot? I told you Kansas is no place to rear a child! That's all it is. This is no place to bear and raise a child. Do you know how many children die here?"

"No."

And neither did she, but had either of them known, they may just have moved back to Boston. If it wasn't cholera in the warmer months, it was under-nourishment in the colder ones, at least during the winter of 1855-56. One of the few successful births in Atchison County had been that of Dr. Stringfellow's son. With his access to medical supplies and an easy conduit back to the relative civilization of western Missouri, as well as its sympathies, his child was born in the summer of 1855 and had clean water. But few others were so lucky, especially families like the Dugans, and the infant mortality rate was staggering among the pioneers of Kansas.

Arguments like this one, fueled by Patrick's self-pity, insecurity and guilt, and Maria's growing feeling that he was not capable of handling the rigors of pioneer life (and she was unwilling), got bigger and bigger as January turned to February. They grew into arguments over petty things, as disagreements over important things often do, and began to eat away at the mundane diurnal rhythms of life. They argued over where things belonged in the kitchen, how quickly one can open and shut a door in winter, how to properly make tea, stoke the fire, boil eggs, and feed the pigs. They snatched quilts away from each other, kicked each other's boots out of the way, and started to wish they'd left the old shack intact so Patrick could finish the winter there and they could keep separate.

The worst argument came on the night of February 20th, the full moon. Maria had attempted to persuade Patrick into at least considering a return to Boston (which is all she really wanted, because she, too, wanted to stay in Kansas if things were going to improve), but it irritated him.

A few minutes later they were arguing over the tea. She'd let it steep too long, he said, and it was bitter.

Well, Patrick had two feet and two hands and could have done what he liked with the tea, Maria replied. She wasn't his handmaid. He needed to be braver and take care of himself.

"What is that supposed to mean?"

"What do you mean 'what is that supposed to mean'? You speak English, do you not?"

"'Braver.' What is that supposed to mean?"

"Bravery, Patrick! It's a word in English! Don't be so cowardly you can't fix your own tea! That's what I mean!"

"Fix my own tea? Bravery! Tea? You know good and well that I know what you mean. Don't pretend you don't, so."

"I have no idea what you are talking about."

"You're a smart lass, Maria. You know what I mean."

"What then? What?"

They had been circling the kitchen table like prized boxers, but now Patrick sat. He said as if he were made of marble, "I thought you loved me for my moving here, for wanting a peaceful life, for not being my father, for holding my tongue. But you lied, or you changed since. You want a 'brave' man." The marble cracked with his voice. "You want a revolutionary, a rebel. Someone who will speak out. Like my father, and yours. Like Roger."

More disgust could not possibly fit in Maria's face. "Roger! Your little brother who is practically like a son to me but breaks my heart with sick worry all the time? Patrick, are you insane?" She shook her head somewhat wildly and had to move a strand of her hair from her face. "I want a man who will do what he feels is right as he understands it at the time, and when you're sober, that's exactly what you do. I don't want a revolutionary; I want a man who can fix his own goddamn tea!" She yanked a chair out from the table as if she planned to sit in it.

A moment of silence reigned. It was the first time Maria had ever said "goddamn," and they both knew it. Patrick thought they might start laughing, it was so out of character.

But Maria was in no mood to laugh. She said something she'd never said before because she'd never been this mad at someone she loved this much. She wanted to run and cry or slap him silly. She did neither. She felt frozen with anger, and then suddenly, she doubled over in pain.

"What? What is it?"

"Never you mind!"

"Maria, are you in pain?"

"No! Just leave me alone. I don't need you."

"Maria!"

"Go away, Patrick. Just get out of here." She waved her hand at him and looked up through her hair.

And he left his wife standing by the stove, clutching her abdomen and obviously in a great amount of pain. He wasn't even all that mad at her, and knew he shouldn't leave. But he didn't care.

For Maria it was the worst argument they'd ever had because of the acute anger she felt; but for Patrick it was a malaise, indifference, and lack of love. Right now, he just didn't really care about her. Never would he think it possible that he'd walk away from a woman in pain, especially his little Maria. But he did, and with every step he felt better about it.

When he looked up and saw the full moon, he thought he knew why. He was to return to the spring and meet Paschal again. Yes, yes, that was it. He wasn't leaving Maria, he was destined for another meeting with—whatever Paschal was. Whatever the bird was, and the water of the spring and the bluffs. God was leading him to a communion of some kind, a greater destiny. Poor Maria. She just didn't understand. She didn't know how important this place was, this land, this little bedrock of the earth that would stand through the entire apocalypse, every last piece of it.

Patrick sat down, pulled out a flask of mash, lit a pipe, and waited for the Frenchman to arrive.

But Paschal never arrived, and sometime after midnight Patrick left the spring, staggering his way off the rock, wondering how he had been wrong about this night. Surely all the last weeks meant something. The baby's death, Maria's wanting to go home—there had to be a way of understanding this. He'd follow anyone who could lead him to a greater understanding of his life. And, just as he thought this and just before he stepped from the clearing and into the trees, the bird stepped out from between two trees, almost as if it just emerged out of the forest itself. It looked at Patrick. And blinked.

Patrick looked and blinked too. He rubbed his eyes.

It was still there. Just standing and watching him. It opened its beak as if to speak, and only a faint squawk came out.

"Who are you?" he asked. "What are you?"

It squawked again and blinked the mechanical blink of a bird, then motioned its head into the woods toward the river. Squawked again, blinked again, motioned again, then took a couple steps and looked back. Squawked again.

"You want me to follow you?" he asked, to which the bird somehow made a gesture in the affirmative.

Patrick looked around. He wasn't sure what he was looking for—maybe Paschal or Roger, Joseph James or Maria—but he wanted to make sure he was alone. He felt warm inside, excited, like the first time he stole a little whiskey from his father, the first time he saw the shores of America, the first time he stopped off the ferry in Kansas, or the first time (and he particularly thought of this just now) he had a glass of whiskey in several years—just last fall. Looking back at the bird, it appeared to be almost smiling, as if to say, "You're alone, quite alone. Do what you feel is best. Don't listen to others. Be your own man. You know what is right and wrong. Only you."

It turned, and walked.

And Patrick followed.

***

In March several ferry boats arrived full of South Carolinians. They'd heeded the call of Senator Atchison and private fundraisers in the South, and came to Kansas in the spring, because surely the Wakarusa War was only the beginning. The future of Kansas—and of the Southern way of life—was still at stake. Despite the fact that the majority of the current residents were Free State sympathizers, the future population of Kansas was as yet undetermined. Hundreds of settlers had left the Territory during that winter of 1855-56, horrified that such a paradise could become such a hell as the seasons changed. Surely, nobody really knew Kansas, perhaps particularly Atchison. Nobody knew if a family could really thrive here. Even the Kanza had struggled for hundreds of years in this odd little stretch of the Missouri. It was going to be as much a matter of squatter perseverance as it was squatter sovereignty.

Patrick hadn't returned home for nearly two weeks when Maria realized she was really sick.

March had come like a lamb, and this gave her a great sense of relief in her husband's absence. Had March been as inclement as December, January, and February, she could have died. The pain in her abdomen and intermittent bleeding had become more frequent and acute, and the more she worked, the worse it got. If Patrick didn't come home soon, she'd have no choice but to return to Boston without him.

She swallowed her pride and went to town to find him, and that is when she encountered the South Carolinians.

"Now that there's a regular pioneer-ess!" one jested as she peered in the windows of various shops, looking for her husband.

"I'll say," said another. "That one'll squeeze ya till ya can't breathe, just like a snake! Just look at them legs, boys!"

And so on. They were everywhere, milling about in the stores and out on the wooden walkway that had just been built along certain stretches of Commercial Street. They leaned up against fence posts, squatted on their heels with their backs against the facades and sides of buildings, and rode their horses up and down the streets, firing their guns and yelling.

If there was one thing Maria hated the most in men, it was when they drank too much. Atchison on this early March day was Sodom to her. It was a disgusting, dirty, and unhealthy place. No place for a sick woman. She had to get out.

Then she saw him. Her Patrick. He appeared from around a corner and was with a group of men she didn't recognize.

She looked around for Clegg, but he was nowhere to be found. The men—six of them—were loud and making their way, slowly, into a saloon. One patted Patrick on the back heavily and put his arm around him, shaking his shoulders with great familiarity.

Clearly the last two weeks had been eventful for her husband, and clearly, he'd been drinking, probably for days on end.

But she had no choice. She had to tell him.

"Patrick," she said in a voice as soft as she thought effective from this distance. But she had to take two more steps closer and raise her voice. "Pa—!"

But just then she found herself being jostled and was surrounded by more men. She could tell they were South Carolinians by their accents and, to her great dismay, she seemed to be the center of their attention.

"Why, lookee 'ere," said one, "if this ain't the cutest little redhead Irish gal I ever did see!"

"Now why would a perty Irish gal like yerself be standing outside a saloon," said another, and the rest got more excited.

Patrick turned around and saw Maria, but she didn't see him.

Once they saw what was going on and Patrick's interest in it, his group disappeared into the saloon, pretending not to notice, leaving him, Maria, and the South Carolinians standing outside.

"'Cause they ain't no brothel as yet!" The Southerners all laughed.

"Don't matter," said the first one. "I gots me a tent. C'mon now, Fiona or whatever yer name is," he grabbed her by the arm. "Let's go. I'm-a show you some of the weapons the South done brought to Kansas."

Maria saw Patrick at that moment and stood her ground with her thick set legs. She felt a pang in her stomach and a stream of blood run down her leg and drip on her foot. She looked at Patrick and felt he wasn't there, he was so drunk. "I'm sick," she said, and looked down.

"C'mon now!" said the other man, grabbing her arm again and tugging harder. "I's gots Yanks ta kill in the mornin'."

"You don't want this one," said Patrick, not taking his eyes off her. "She's sick."

The man turned on Patrick. "And just who the hell're you? Another Irishman? Hell, is this whore your wife or sumthin'?" The men laughed. Patrick held his tongue.

"I get it! She's your whore."

"She's sick." He glanced down at her mid-section.

"Aw, hell! She's broken!" said one.

"Filthy Irish bitch!" said another.

Suddenly, the crowd dispersed, moving along as if it had never paused at all, much less in order to victimize someone. This left Patrick and Maria standing alone on the crooked wooden walkway.

"I'm going back to Boston," she said. "I'm really sick."

"Don't." His body wavered but this word was steady.

"You're drunk." Her lip quivered. "You've left me, Patrick." Now her voice quivered, too, and rose in tone as if it sang a song she could not control. "All alone in a wilderness."

"No."

"Yes."

There was a moment of silence and then Maria groaned in pain. Patrick swayed and struggled to stand upright, much less move toward and steady her, which is what he knew he should, and wanted to, do. But he was just too drunk, and nothing but time could change that.

"Goodbye," she said, turned, and disappeared around the corner as Patrick stood for a moment looking after her. He could feel and hear the floor planks beneath his feet creaking as he swayed, toward her, away from her, toward and away.

"Come now," said a man from behind him. Patrick turned and recognized the man who owned the Pioneer Saloon, and who sometimes tended bar. "I've got just the thing to fix that, Mr. Paddy. Come inside and it will be all right. Look here," he pointed down to where a threshold would be if there were one. "All you have to do is cross."

XX

Roger had wintered in Pottawatomie with an enclave of Free Staters anchored by several members of John Brown's family. It was a good seventy-five miles as the crow flies from Atchison, south of the growing Free State enclave of Topeka. The family patriarch, John Sr., had arrived in Kansas the previous October, just before Pat Laughlin shot Sam Collins, in fact. He'd followed sons and brought more with him, and his sister was also about ten miles away on the western edge of the little town of Osawatomie. Roger stayed with whatever family in this little community needed him most, chopping wood, riding to Osawatomie for supplies, stoking fires, helping to warm frost-bitten toes, and, most importantly, nursing whomever happened to be sick. Flu and measles spread through the Pottawatomie clan that winter with every wind that blew into every gap in every plank-walled shanty.

It was a miserable winter for Roger, and by March he began thinking about visiting his brother and sister in-law, perhaps even moving back in with them. He'd thought the winter of 1854-55 was the first and last time he would have to suffer so, but 1855-56 in Pottawattamie was even worse. Not only was the weather horrible, the Browns and their neighbors were ill-prepared and under-equipped. They had brought more weapons than sacks of flour, more Sharps rifles than hoes, not to mention plows or carpentry tools. Kansas was a battleground for Old John Brown, not farmland. But blades and barrels do little to the snows of the prairie.

Roger didn't interact with him very much, as the old man tended to prefer the company of his sons. He seemed at times distrustful of Roger, despite constantly praising his dedication to the cause.

Once, when Roger somehow happened upon a crate full of heavy, shiny broadswords and asked John Brown what they were for, the old man replied, "Why, for the coming war, of course."

Roger felt silly having asked. The old man disappeared as silently and as stealthily as he'd arrived in the little shed, just as he always did. John Brown seemed only half-human—he was of a color and had a gait that was ghostly, a posture that was so rigid and stoic it was like a statue, and a voice that seemed animal-like. He seemed to float in and out of cabins, discussions, and incidents like a recurring dream, like he'd always been there latent and unrealized, and only became manifest when he chose.

Back in December, as the winter set in, the Wakarusa War drew to its close, and John Brown called all true soldiers of God to follow him, he had also given a speech that stuck with Roger: he told the crowd outside the Free State Hotel that to let the Missourians simply scuttle back across the river with no reprisal was unacceptable. They'd poured over the border several times now, rigging elections in late 1854 and 1855, and now they besieged poor Lawrence, all of which met absolutely no resistance. Of course Washington didn't care about them—they didn't even defend themselves. No, the Wakarusa War was not over, Brown said. He wanted a handful of brave volunteers to spend the night in the grass of the small hills overlooking the river and, when the sun rose, shoot the Missourians in their tents as they slept.

A few shouted in enthusiastic agreement, but nobody volunteered, not even Roger. He didn't know, in December of 1855, if such a tactic was necessary. He wanted to fight, but wasn't sure if sniping the enemy while he slept was in alignment with the cause for which they would do this. But as it became clearer through the winter that Washington recognized only the Pro Slavery legislature, and as the Missourians and other Southerners streamed into Kansas by the ferry-load and camped menacingly outside Free State villages, Roger began to think that perhaps John Brown was right after all. How could they simply allow themselves to be intimidated this way? Didn't they care about their way of life, about their beliefs, about the slaves? Didn't they want to protect their land, their wives, their children, their right to self-governance? Wasn't their cause clearly on the side of goodness and justice? Well, they better start acting like it, and it wasn't going to be any small gesture. No, it had to be something big, something shocking, something memorable. Something people would see and associate with Free State Kansas forever.

But what that something was and who would do it, Roger just didn't know. He did know that he wanted to be there when it happened and, as he thought it through, that it probably wouldn't happen in little Pottawattamie. Lawrence was the place to be, and he would return to it as soon as he visited his brother and sister-in-law. Yes, it was time to see if they'd finally cleansed the house of those ruffian Hawkinses, to check on their health and baby, and see if they needed any help with spring planting. As much as Patrick's refusal to fight for a Free Kansas disappointed, frustrated, and angered him, Roger wanted nothing more than his brother's happiness. Their destinies in Kansas were becoming quite different, but they both belonged here, he knew. Coming to Kansas was the best thing to happen to Roger since Pappa was taken all those years ago, and he had Patrick to thank for it. He began making preparations to return to the farm for a while, then to move on to Lawrence where he'd await the conflict that was surely on its way in 1856.

It was mid-April by the time Roger felt he'd completed his duties to the Browns and their neighbors. They thanked him, fed him, and were ready to send him on his way, when much to his surprise the old man took him aside. Roger had felt for over a month that this man wanted him to leave, and now it was time.

"Roger, may I speak with you, lad?"

Roger froze a bit then twitched some. "Of course."

Old John Brown took him by the arm and led him on a stroll through the elms that grew in a few large clusters on the north side of the creek. It was a pleasant day, though there was still snow on the ground, near the rocks and shady sides of the hills. They didn't speak for some moments, and Roger took the opportunity to examine this man, something he'd never felt comfortable doing before. Looking at John Brown seemed risky for some unknown reason, but under the dappled light that scattered itself through the budding curves of the elm leaves, he was not only approachable, he was downright paternal. John Brown could have been J.P. Dugan on that April day. Roger wanted to feel more familiar with this man who was definitely a little insane, but clearly very powerful in many ways. He didn't look it, but he was.

Brown's hair had once been shorn very close, it seemed, probably just before coming to Kansas. But it had grown out a little since, so was straggly on top of being dirty. His eyes were piercing, much like the reverend's he'd seen sent downriver last August while Patrick stood idly and cowardly by—Pardee Butler, it was. Both had steel gray yet somehow also sky blue eyes that seemed to derive their color from something inside, almost as if they glowed or shone from some inner fire or light. Brown's jaw was set and solid, his skin leathery. He was skinny and wiry but looked quite strong, and his face was as it always was—steady. The man rarely seemed to smile, frown, or pout. He never looked tired early in the morning or late at night, didn't grimace when he was cold, hurt, or hungry. He wore a patched, faded, tattered shirt and his shoes had holes in the toes. His hands felt like a harness on Roger's back.

"Roger, I've been watching you. You're young yet, have much to learn—"

Roger almost interrupted him, but Brown raised his hand to indicate he was going to qualify what he'd said.

"—which is natural, of course. God would have it no other way than for his creatures to learn the ways of the world gradually. But you are remarkably decisive for a man your age. A man any age, in fact. Roger, you have the gift of knowing. Knowing what is right. Immediately and forever. And I believe you know its importance."

Roger had watched his mouth moving, speaking these words, in amazement. "I do," he said, almost in betrothal.

"Ah, and what is right is all important, isn't it? Righteousness is the following of truth, and truth is the Word of God." Brown seemed to half-expect a response to this, an "amen" or something, but Roger didn't have one in him. "Well, I see that special gift in you—the ability to analyze a situation and know, quickly, what is right, and what is wrong in it. And I think I see in you, as well, the knowledge that the Word of God must be heeded at all costs. What is right is right, and we must make it so on Earth, no matter what earthly means are necessary."

Brown's hand was on his back. It was cold, heavy, and hard, like a hammer resting between his shoulder-blades. He agreed completely with what the old man said, but he hesitated to say so. Something about Brown made him nervous. There had to be a point to this little stroll and conversation.

Brown stopped and slid the hand on Roger's back over to the shoulder nearest him, turning him to face him.

A bird chirped in the trees above them.

"Roger, I believe you should stay here in Pottawatomie with us. You have been an essential member of our party this winter, and I must say that we owe part of our survival to you. But the work has just begun, Roger." He gave Roger a little, slow, firm, shake of the shoulders. "This is going to be a very important spring, in the history of this young nation, in the history of man, and in the history of God's Word on earth. And I believe your place this spring is here. You know what is right and its importance."

"I understand, Mr. Brown—"

"Please, call me John."

"I understand." Roger took the smallest of steps away, but tried to have the posture of a comfortable man. "I came here for those very reasons—the fact that I saw them in you and your sons in Lawrence last December. But I must find my brother and his wife. I must see how they've gotten through the winter. And after that, I believe my place is in Lawrence. I can feel it." He looked skyward and sighed. "I am to defend Lawrence."

"But you will!" Brown now took the step back so he could gesture more widely. "You will defend Lawrence. We will ride there immediately should something happen. Roger—" Brown sighed and took another few steps as if to continue the stroll, but then stopped and turned toward him. The sun was behind him now, and in the soft April light, tints of gray swirled about his head and face. "I believe I am going to need you, Roger. Not all my sons can do what I may need them to do. Owen and Salmon, yes, but John Jr. is too much the politician and Frederick, well, Frederick is delicate. I need someone like you. Someone who knows what is right, knows its paramount importance in the eyes of God, and is decisive enough to do whatever is necessary to uphold righteousness. Someone stout of heart who respects himself, and who will do anything to advance the cause of God's will on earth. We can rid this world of the scourge of slavery in Kansas, Roger, we really can." Brown held out his hand. "It's in our hands. God has given us the opportunity. All we must do is wait for the right moment, then strike."

"But, my brother—"

"Roger, family is important, I know." But he seemed impatient. "And it's hard to leave them and do the work of the Lord. I have so much left in New York, I cannot begin to tell you. I miss them all terribly. But I must be here. My soul tells me to be here. My God bids me to Kansas."

And then Roger realized how to end this. "We will join again, I promise you. But my soul is telling me to go to my brother."

John Brown smiled a smile Roger had never seen on him before. What was usually such a serious face looked strange in this joy.

"I understand, young man. I understand. To Freedom," he said, offering Roger his hand. It was warm and soft now, like a quilt or skin.

"To Freedom," Roger replied, and he left for Atchison the next day.

***

April was almost gone by the time Roger arrived. Other than the fact that it appeared Grafton Thomassen's sawmill was ready for production, in terms of structures and streets, Atchison had changed little since he saw it last October. But he could feel in the spring air a bustle that was somewhat new to the town. Hundreds, if not thousands of settlers were on their way, and there were more people with different accents wandering her streets. The European accents of first- and second-generation American-Mormon laborers were gone, replaced with a variety of mature, distinct Southern dialects. But many of these accents were not heard among the bangs of hammers and hisses of handsaws; these were shouted, slurred, and raucous, spoken by men who seemed perfectly idle. And then Roger realized—these men were not here to work and farm or move farther West—they were here to fight, to cleanse Kansas of its abolitionist cancer, and by wanting to visit Patrick and Maria, Roger had walked right into a lion's den. These were his enemies, and he could be recognized, especially if he spoke.

It didn't matter much, because once he was let off at Commercial Street, all he had to do was walk to the farm with his head down. If anyone asked him anything, he'd reply with whatever few words he could speak in a Southern accent. And if he had to, well, he'd just run. He'd taken a small pistol and a Bowie knife, refusing a Sharps rifle from the Browns, but using them in his defense in Atchison would only lead to destruction.

"This here'll do it, young man," said the farmer who'd agreed to take him to Atchison. "You don't look quite old enough yerself, but I'm gonna stop here for a nice drink." They hitched the team around the side of the Pioneer Saloon, and Roger extended his hand to the farmer, who would not accept it. "Come, lad, join me for a drink."

"I'm sorry, I don't drink."

"Don't drink! Just where are you from, anyway?"

Roger hesitated a moment, checking his bag for his belongings. "Ireland, by way of Boston."

"Why, a man of mine own heart." The man opened his hands and clasped Roger on the shoulder. "Come inside and let's toast the mother country."

With some hesitation again, Roger decided to trust this man. Something about him was like Patrick. "I'm sorry. I don't feel welcome there."

"An Irishman not welcome in a saloon? Why, is the devil not welcome in Hell now, too, is that it?"

"No." Roger chuckled. "I don't drink and…"

"Ah, enough said, young man." The man waved him away, shifting his boots in the crackling mud. "One must be careful in Atchison. I understand."

"I hope you do."

"Let me tell you something about this town, young man." He turned back toward Roger, took a step closer, and said in a lower tone. "In Atchison, it's best to run. Just run."

They turned the corner and mounted the wooden sidewalk of Commercial Street, Roger deciding it the most inconspicuous way out of town. Suddenly he heard the heavy thumping of boots running on the planks. Before they could get out of the way, a running man knocked Roger over, falling on top of him. He heard men in chase shouting, and as the man struggled to extract himself from Roger, and Roger tried to get out from under the man, the two realized there was something very familiar about the other body in the entanglement. Roger smelled and began to slowly feel the warm wetness of the blood the man was dripping on him from his nose and mouth. It was all over their necks and chins and chests and the planks beneath them. Just as the man was pulled off Roger, their eyes met. It was Patrick. He had a look on his face Roger had never seen before, something that made him love his brother even more.

No time to think, Roger jumped up and threw punches at some giant man's back and shoulders, only to be pummeled himself. Soon, he couldn't tell what blood was his and what his brother's. Before he remembered to produce his revolver or knife, he found himself on the planks, being kicked in every direction. And then, like a hailstorm, it stopped as suddenly as it began.

Roger picked his heavy head up off the wood, and saw Patrick a few feet away doing the same. There were boots all around them, and mud, both wet and dry. One by one, and two by two, all the boots turned toward the street. And through the ringing in his ears Roger heard more shouting from the street.

He sat up, dizzy, while his brother did the same, and they saw an even larger group of men pushing a man through the streets. It was the Reverend Pardee Butler. He'd returned to Atchison that morning, just as he'd been warned not to the previous summer, and was now being paraded through the streets, naked to the waist.

Boots began disappearing, one by one and two by two, and Roger found himself being yanked roughly by the arm.

It was Patrick. "Let's go," he said. "Get up and run."

But Roger was watching the old reverend being jostled around in the crowd. He was reminded of John Brown, especially in the eyes. He had an irrepressible need to be involved, to protect the old man.

"Roger," said Patrick, "there's nothing we can do. We have to run."

"No," he said, standing with his brother. "We can't."

"We must. Roger, this is our chance." His look was no longer between anything—it was perfect panic. "They were going to kill us!"

"Let them." An anger was welling up inside.

"What?" Patrick sounded young.

"Let them kill us. I don't care."

"What's gotten into you, Roger?"

"You've been drinking." Now Roger wanted to attack his brother as much as he wanted to save Butler.

"I've been running for my life. Now let's go, goddammit!" He gave Roger's arm one last good yank and the two slipped around the back of Commercial Street and headed west on Kansas Street.

Through the buildings they could briefly see that Pardee Butler had been tarred-and-feathered, but with cotton instead of feathers. He was placed back in the wagon that conveyed him to Atchison and escorted out of town, still half naked.

The Dugan brothers left town and headed north toward the farm.

They didn't speak. Both did their best to clean the blood off their faces as they walked, occasionally stumbling, toward home.

Somewhere in the nearby trees, there was a squawk.

XXI

"What was that?" Roger said finally, as they neared the farm and were clearly out of danger.

"Never you mind," Patrick snapped, giving his brother a plunk between his shoulder-blades. "Just keep walking. We're almost there."

"I heard something, Paddy. Back there." He picked one last chunk of dried blood from his nose.

"Yes." Patrick seemed too tolerant of the blood left on his face. "I heard it too, boy."

"What was it?"

"I don't know." Patrick paused. "A bird. Maybe."

"A bird? What kind of bird makes a noise like that?"

"I don't know. A giant one."

"A giant one? How do you know that?"

"I don't. Big, small, whatever you like. Just don't follow it."

Roger stopped walking, demanding his brother's attention. "What the hell are you talking about?"

"The bird, Roger." Patrick wouldn't meet his eyes, but did appear more sober and less panicked now. "Don't follow it. That is—not again, anyway. If you heard it, I suppose."

"What? What's the matter with you? You've been drinking way too much, Paddy. It's disgusting."

"Mind your own business!" he said, looking into Roger's eyes now. "And who are you to talk about what's disgusting? I'm not the one traipsing around the territory causing trouble."

"What is that supposed to mean? I'm sacrificing myself for the good of—"

Patrick stepped closer. He was filthy. "Don't you give me that, Roger! I had enough of that from Pappa! You know in your heart that you seek as much fame and accolade as you do justice!"

Roger stepped back, afraid he may pounce without intending it. "Fame! Fame, Paddy!?" He rubbed his eyes and breathed deeply. "If I wanted to be famous, I sure as hell wouldn't still be in Kansas."

"Of course you would! All the zealots and quacks in America have come to Kansas! You're right at home!"

"Me, a zealot? A quack! Paddy, you selfish langer!"

"Don't you call me that!"

"It's true!" He stood even farther back now, gesturing wildly, not sure if he wanted to bloody his brother or not. "You hide from the world here in your pathetic little farm doing all you can for yourself and nobody else! There's a world outside you, Paddy, and people. Children and mothers and sisters and brothers who are suffering!"

"I am suffering!"

"Not like a slave!"

"Don't you see how I'm treated in Atchison! Don't you see all the suffering you and your Free State Party create for simple settlers like me? You people, coming here pretending to squat but not knowing the least about tending the land, cause all this and we're the simple farmers who are woken in the middle of the night with revolvers held to our heads and beaten because we speak like you! Well, let me tell you something, Roger: I am not a Free Stater! I'm not! I'm a farmer!"

"In the saloons, Paddy," Roger replied in an even, superior tone. "In the saloon is where you were beaten. I can't believe Maria is still with you if you're drinking like this."

Patrick grabbed his younger brother by the shoulders, yelling "take it back!" at him, but Roger ignored him and struggled. Soon the two were wrestling in the moist dirt of the path, neither gaining an upper hand, both considering—but hesitating—to strike the other. They disentangled, jumped to their feet, and Roger pulled out his revolver, leveling it at Patrick. It felt ridiculous, like he was holding a potato.

The two stood for a moment, catching their breath.

And then Patrick began to laugh. He laughed again, and laughed some more. Soon his laughter was well out of his control.

"What?" Roger said forcefully at first, and then repeated it several times in successively gentler ways until he too was chucking, and then laughing. He put his revolver away, and the two caught their breath again.

"She's not," Patrick said in a way that turned from laughing to crying so quickly it was sincerely sad.

"What?" Roger asked gently.

"She's not with me anymore, Roger." Patrick began to hold back his crying. "She lost the baby. We lost the baby on the first day of this damned year. She returned to Boston."

A wind blew through the tops of the trees. "And you let her?"

"Ha. You don't know the first thing about women, boy."

"I know I would never let her do that. I'd—I'd stop drinking."

Patrick almost cried again. "Yes, well, right, so. The Cleggs are gone too, and the Hawkinses have their own cabin now." He pointed to a column of smoke rising from the Hawkins chimney in the trees a quarter-mile or so distant. "I'm alone."

They began walking again, listening to the monotonous rhythm of their boots packing down the trail to the farm. There was dead grass from last fall, but very little new spring grass as of yet. Though it had been rather warm since March, it still frosted at night and the spring had yet to fully arrive.

Roger looked over at his brother. He was pale and skinny, almost as if he were ill. Roger realized what it meant that he was alone now on the farm, and that all his aspirations about beginning anew in Kansas must now seem unattainable.

"I'm sorry, Paddy. I'm sure you miss her, like."

"I do." He stopped, kicking the dust with the toe of his boot, and picked up a stick to do the same. "And you're right. It is because I've been drinking."

"So stop."

Patrick laughed. "Perhaps I will."

Another squawk, even louder this time, rang from the trees to their right.

"Paddy, what is that!? "

"Never you mind. I'm just sorry you can hear it too." He looked in the direction of the noise. Under the shade of a tree, there was a group of mushrooms. He walked over and picked one, took a bite.

Roger took a bite as well. It was delicious, meaty and firm. "What sort of a place is this, Roger?" Patrick let the mushroom drop. "Fruit of the gods in Hell?"

***

It wasn't until much later that night, the last day of April, when Roger realized Patrick's situation was even worse than he thought. And it wasn't just that he was drinking. Surely, for a Dugan man to be drinking was disastrous, and that disaster had already taken the form of a lost wife. And it wasn't just that he was grieving. Losing his first child, and part of his dream. It wasn't even just that he was lonely. For a Dugan man to be alone in the woods actually wasn't such a bad thing, necessarily, as long as it didn't last too long. It wasn't the drinking, grieving, or the loneliness that worried Roger most; it was the pile of unread reading materials on the table.

There was almost three months of the *Squatter Sovereign*, a novel called *Uncle Tom's Cabin*, and a collection of essays by a man named

Thoreau, none of which had been read more than just a preliminary perusal. Roger could tell this was the case because the upper-right-hand corners of the papers and books were relatively sharp, flat, and straight. Patrick had a compulsion while he read where he would pull and curl this corner, and one could tell how far he'd read and how interested he was by the extent of the curling—books read to their ends had all curled pages, while those that were in the process of being read had only some of the pages curled; and passages whose pages were more curled were either so boring he struggled long with them, or so beautiful he relished them. The latter was usually the case, as Patrick was not one to hesitate skipping what he didn't enjoy. There were too many books in the world to read boring ones.

None of these books had curling to any extent, whether chronic or acute. This meant Patrick hadn't been reading for months. Coupled with alcohol and loneliness, this apparent boredom surely meant melancholy, which in a Dugan man could mean suicide as well. Roger knew and understood this. He'd heard the stories of an uncle and a cousin of their father's, both who'd taken their own lives in Ireland, and both who seemed to be very much Patrick's sort of personality. At this rate, he'd be dead before Maria forgave him. Roger would have to stay until Patrick was sober enough to realize he needed to stay sober. He got up from the table, found the whiskey near the stove, and headed outside to dump it in the stubbles of grass.

As the liquor gurgled out of the bottle, Roger could see much of the farm in the last light of April. He may be drinking and not reading, but Patrick had been working, he could give him that. The farm looked to be in very good condition—the pig sty had been repaired from what was probably a snow-induced collapse, work had been done to prepare for planting, and the vegetable garden had already been started with heartier carrots, onions, and potatoes. He'd even purchased a couple of goats, and there was a new and beautiful young horse accompanying Zion in the beginnings of a stable attached to the barn. Patrick hadn't been completely idle. His vision of Kansas was still strong enough to keep him working, and he may just have the best farm in Kansas. That was good. It was hard to imagine Paddy doing something drastic on a nice farm like this.

There were still a few ounces of mash draining out of the bottle when a heavy hand slapped Roger's shoulder from behind. It was heavier, even, than the hand John Brown laid between his shoulder blades a couple weeks earlier. But this heavy hand had the urgency of anger in it.

"What are you doing?!"

"I'm dumping your mash, Paddy. I'm saving you."

"Give it here!" He made an attempt to grab the bottle, but was clumsy and misguided.

"You got so drunk in the middle of the day, Paddy, that you fainted, and look at you—you can barely stand. The sun hasn't set yet, boy."

"I was beaten, Roger."

"Also because you were drunk! It's ruining you, Paddy! This—" he held the bottle up against the sky "—is destroying everything you came to Kansas for. Everything!"

Patrick watched the gurgle wane to trickle, turned, and went inside.

Roger followed. "And look at this," Roger slapped the pile of books and papers on the table. "You're not even reading. Look at this!" He picked up the book on top, the collection of essays. "You've not even opened this one!" As he said this, an envelope fell out of the book.

Patrick was now slumped at a chair, and he hung his head.

Roger bent over and picked up the envelope. It was a letter. "From Maria? A letter from Maria? When did you get this?"

"Weeks ago."

"Paddy—"

"I know what it says. It's a goodbye. I haven't the heart to read it."

"Nonsense! Read it!"

"No."

"Then I will." Roger made a motion that indicated he was going to tear open the envelope, and Patrick rushed toward him to try and take it away. "Read it or I will!" yelled Roger repeatedly, keeping the letter at arm's-length.

"Give it to me!" Patrick yelled repeatedly. The two held back smiles, remembering childhood taunts. Both felt guilty.

"So be it," Patrick said finally. "Read it. But I know what it says."

Roger opened the envelope slowly, but unfolded the letter even more slowly. He glanced up at Patrick once it was fully unfurled, then read.

My Dear Paddy—

I'm writing to let you know that I am much better. The doctors here are so much more knowledgeable about women, and expect I shall recover fully. They believe I lost the baby due to, as you said, being overworked, and advise rest before we attempt another. They also feel Kansas is no place to raise a child, but I have decided they couldn't be more wrong about this.

Which leads me to the second reason I am writing. Paddy, I love you. I love you more than words can express, and I want to come back home—to Kansas—to where you are. I can still see the life we envisioned when we met, and I know that you are still the man with whom I can make it happen. We are young yet, we still have a hope of children, and we still have the first 160 acres of paradise, freedom, and peace.

But you have to stop drinking. Paddy, when you drink, you are not these things. You are not the man that can make that life happen, and you are not the man I love. And you are not the man you love, respect, or want to be.

Please reply with a simple promise that you will never drink liquor again and I will book the next ferry from St. Louis.

Your loving, lonely, and forever loyal wife,

Maria Dugan

P.S. Enclosed is a collection of essays by an American named Henry David Thoreau. I believe you will find a like mind in this man.

Crying now, Patrick sat down at the table.

Roger flipped the letter toward him. "How long have you had this letter?"

"Weeks."

"You langer! You stupid, stupid moron! Here!" Roger hurriedly found some paper and a pencil, slapped them on the table in front of his brother, and roughly grabbed him by the collar. "Write! Write your reply this instant!"

"I—I—I can't—"

"Now, Patrick!"

"I—I—" He held up his hand. It was shaking.

"I don't care if you write this letter with your teeth, Patrick Dugan!" Roger's tone was reminiscent of their mother's.

Patrick steadied his voice. "A letter to Boston, Roger, will be noticed in Atchison—"

"I will take it to Lawrence and it'll be in Maria's hands in a week. Now, write!"

Patrick sighed, picked up the paper, and scribbled a simple note. "Of course I will stop. I stopped the second I read your letter. Please come home. You are everything to me. Without you there is no sun and no happiness whatsoever. All is dark and sad here."

Roger snatched it up, placed it in an envelope, and shoved it in his breast pocket, and seemed now to fill the years he so often pretended to have.

"I'll be back in a couple days. And Patrick, if I find you've had a sip of mash—a single sip!—while I'm away, there'll be hell to pay. Do you understand me? Hell!"

"I understand."

Roger hesitated. His surprise at how he'd been talking to his brother was surpassed only by his surprise that Patrick was listening. This wasn't one of his tirades. This was a proper berating and it was actually being received.

"Well, good, then . . . you just . . . I dunno . . . farm, or . . . something."

Patrick smiled. "I'll do that."

"Good. Well—I almost forgot..." He pulled a folded newspaper out of his back pocket. "I got you a real newspaper from Lawrence." He handed over the most recent issue of the *Kansas Herald of Freedom*. "Not that slop spewing out of Stringfellow and Kelley. A year's subscription as well."

Patrick picked up the paper and looked at it. "Roger?" He looked up, held Roger's eyes a moment.

"Yes?"

"Thank you."

"You're welcome. Happy birthday, Paddy."

XXII

On three separate occasions on the first day of May Patrick started walking to Atchison to get a drink. And on three separate occasions he turned back. He turned back because each time something very vivid about Maria came to him. The first was her smell. The second was the sound of her voice. And the third was the memory of the warmth and smoothness of her skin. He wept each time, returned to his cabin, and lay in bed, crying. He could see Maria in the room with him, smell and hear and feel her. He sweated and shook a lot, finally resigned himself to lying in bed the rest of the day, and when a snake slithered across the room, he laughed. He laughed because he knew that soon Maria would return and the snake would meet its end. He spent the day and much of the night sick, smoking his pipe, sweating, shivering, and even vomited once when he thought about the taste of whiskey.

On the morning of the second day he rose, ate a little breakfast, and spent an hour or two tending to the needs of the farm animals. But he soon tired, became sad, and returned to bed, wondering what was wrong with him. He felt ill the rest of the day, and only as the sun set did he start to feel better. He rose again, ate a little more, and went back to bed. He opened *Uncle Tom's Cabin* but fell asleep immediately and didn't wake until mid-morning on the third day of May. And he'd never felt better. It was like a fog had cleared from around him, a candle had been lit, or a deep breath after a minute under water. He went outside and relieved himself, had a hard-boiled egg, and lay in bed with his book.

On the morning of the fourth day, Patrick realized he had been reading for nearly twenty-four hours without cessation. He'd nibbled here and there, drank some water, used the outhouse, but other than that, he'd been reading all day and all night. He finished the entire stack of reading on his table. *Uncle Tom's Cabin*, Thoreau's essays, three months' worth of Stringfellow and Kelley editorials, and an issue of the *Kansas Herald of Freedom*. And, having finished, he'd never before felt better about being in Kansas. His dream of it being at the end of the world, far removed from the bustling and jostling of mankind and his ailments, was gone.

All the things written about in these books, and not only them, but the *Sovereign* and the *Herald* and all papers across the country, surrounded him every day. All eyes were now on Kansas as her rivers thawed, crops sprouted, and her citizens galvanized for another season's action. The eyes of the world were on Kansas, center of the apocalypse.

But Patrick felt more than ever that he could protect his one hundred and sixty acres, that a great civil war was almost certainly going to erupt all around him and he, Maria, and their children would remain safe, farming, reading, walking, loving, crying, and killing every last snake in Kansas. But being so close to the commotion now made greater sense to him. J.P. would be proud of Roger. Roger didn't need to read *Uncle Tom's Cabin* because he had a strong sense of justice that he inherited from his father. And Patrick could only hope he fought to end slavery with the principles of civil disobedience and personal independence that Thoreau extolled. Then Patrick could be proud of him too, Roger of Patrick, and the delicate balance that is Kansas, that is America, could be upheld on this little plot of land. Nothing could change this world. Not politics, not religion, not even an act of God. Patrick's cabin, on the morning of May 4th, 1856, felt like an impenetrable fortress. Twenty-four hours of reading was all he needed to make all things right in the world.

But then a knock came from the front door. It wasn't a normal knock, either. It sounded like something harder, sharper, and more pointed than a knuckle. Patrick's heart jumped as he imagined the hairy hand of a Missourian or South Carolinian banging on his door with a knife or gun. They'd seen Roger, perhaps, intercepted him on his way to Lawrence with a letter to Boston. Surely it was a letter to the Emigrant Aid Society, and Patrick was a spy in Atchison County. Yes, it all made sense now. Today—right now—Patrick was to begin defending his farm. These men had all of Kansas, all of America, to settle their differences, and he'd be damned if he'd let them fight it out on this little acre.

He grabbed his gun and went to the door. "Who is it?"

Another knock.

"Who's there?"

Another knock.

"I demand to know who is at my door before I open it!"

He heard a distinctly low grumble, a gurgle, almost a grunt. He opened the door, raised his gun to chest level, and fired.

The next thing Patrick saw was smoke, and then colorful feathers scattered in the air. It was the bird. And it stood there in the doorway, not two feet from Patrick's face, a hole in its breast where Patrick's bullet had passed. It blinked, squawked, and winked, somehow almost smiling, turned, and with a gargantuan stride in both legs and wings, flew away. The force of the air coming from its wings made Patrick breathe deeply as an infant does when a gust of wind or breath meets their face. And he cried. Patrick stood in the door to his cabin in a pile of feathers, crying and holding his gun. From over the trees he heard a fantastic shriek, and the bird was gone.

That night, he went walking. It was the night of the new moon and the stars shone brilliantly over Kansas. He felt good; lean, sinewy, full of breath, and healthy. He hadn't felt this way since December, and what began as a stroll to the spring in an attempt to meet Paschal (perhaps the new moon and not the full moon was now his calling card?) became a jog toward Atchison. As his respiration and pulse increased, and beads of perspiration percolated to the surface of the skin on his neck and behind his ears, he increased his pace. The sound of his boots on the ground and his breathing found perfect rhythmic counterpoints to each other, and soon he could see the dull light of the town ahead of him. He felt now as if he could run forever.

He slowed and decided to drop to the riverbed and walk downriver past the ferry landing. He'd never seen what lay downstream of Atchison since taking the ferry from St. Louis, and felt this dark, star-spangled night was a good chance to do so.

The town was eerily quiet, but at the ferry landing he saw a man standing next to a docked ferry, a tall pole in his hand. As Patrick approached and the man's face came into view, he seemed familiar but only vaguely, much as a relative whom one has never met but whose features recall the memories of a hundred intimates. It was not Paschal.

"Need a crossing?" The man smiled through his decaying teeth and hand-length beard.

"Not tonight, thank you, sir."

"Ah, an Irishman. Tell me, Paddy, what are you up to this time of night?"

"How did you know my name?"

"You're all named 'Paddy', aren't you?" The man laughed and his teeth reflected the starlight in the sky.

"No, in fact we're not."

"Of course, of course. Now—do you need a crossing?"

"No, I'll remain on this side of the river, thank you."

At this the man laughed rather violently and began to cough. When he recovered his breath he said, "One side of the river! Ha!

This man thinks he can remain on one side of the river! Tell me, Irishman—Paddy—do you think you can remain on one side all your life?"

"I don't see why not."

"Well, you may not see it, but it's there. Just as sometimes you will see something that is not there. "

"What do you mean?"

"I think you know what I mean. I think the Irish have a strong sense of this fact, do they not?"

"I suppose so."

"Right, so. Now—how about a crossing? I charge more for crossing west-to-east, but for you, on a night like this, I'll do it for less."

Patrick had been walking past the man slowly, but now stopped. "Who are you?" The man smiled broadly and now Patrick recognized him. "The bartender at the Pioneer?"

"Million's the name," he replied. "George Million. And I ain't no bartender. I'm the proprietor of the Pioneer, and the ferry company. I'm a town father, I am. Been here since long before any a 'em, in fact. Used to ferry folk back and forth on their way to Oregon and California, even them Mormons—say, you used to drink with one of 'em, didn't ya?—when they was off to Utah."

Patrick hesitated, deciding to ignore the question and ask his own. "Why do you want me to cross the river? Now, tonight?"

"Ha! I'm the ferryman, Patrick! There is a very big difference between this side and that." He pointed across the river at the distant bluffs in Missouri. "But one can come and go between them. For a time, that is. Then one day the fare becomes too expensive for any mortal man to pay."

"So you want me to cross because I can?"

"In a form, yes!" He laughed again.

"No thank you, ferryman. Perhaps another time. I'll finish my stroll and go home. On this side of the river."

"If that suits you."

"Yes, it suits me."

"Oh, and one more thing, Patrick." Million said, grasping his pole. "Sometimes you don't have to cross. Sometimes you awake to find the river has changed course and is now on the other side of you." He smiled and looked at the river. "Sometimes you cross by standing still."

Patrick let this fall flatly upon the sand, turned, and walked away. He continued downriver, thinking of Paschal's story of Cow Island, and soon found the river cutting into a very tall bluff of chalky white limestone. It was impassable near the water, so he climbed to the top of the bluff. When he reached the apex of the hill he looked down at the dark river slithering its way to the sea. A breeze rose to his nostrils and he drank it deeply, smelling vegetation and the coming clouds of summer. For a moment he could almost feel the vibrations of the river rising through the sediment and rock of the hill, cutting its way into the earth. Looking out across to Missouri, he could see that the river had cut its way into the distant hills at one time, and that it had meandered its way across the flood plain, this way and that, for millennia. Paschal and the Ferryman were right: the river did change its course. And it left its mark on the earth.

Though he was at the apex of the hill, Patrick realized there was a mound—manmade, most certainly—rising still higher from it, like the nipple of a breast. He sat on its east side. The vibrancy and health he felt was overwhelming, and he felt blessed that the last few months had not ruined his life entirely. As long as Maria returned safely, all would be well. This town below him could go to Hell. This war could go to Hell. His paradise would remain intact. God had saved him from the talons of this bird, and he could feel the remains of the deceased Kanza buried in the mound resting at peace. Their peace was his. Rising, he was a new man, as he walked back toward the town.

Within ten yards, however, Patrick realized that though he was descending the hill toward a town, it wasn't Atchison. There was another town downriver, and it was a good ways farther off. He turned around and confirmed it—Atchison was to his north, and there was another to the south. It couldn't be. There was no way such a town could exist without him hearing about it. He stopped in his tracks and stared at the town.

It was bustling. Though it was now quite late at night, there were horses and wagons moving up and down the main street and the long, gradually sloping but still somewhat steep ramp to the ferry landing. There was even a steamboat chugging its way into the landing (and having some difficulty), but it emitted no sound. No sound at all, in fact, was coming from the town, though it was clear there should be. It seemed as if it was daylight the way the town teemed with denizens and their equipment. It definitely wasn't Atchison, this ghostly town.

He turned away, then back again, and the town was gone. Just dark woods filled the river banks to the south. It was an illusion, the whole town, and as he realized this Patrick heard a faint moaning coming from the trees on the other side of the mound. Almost a crying sound. He walked around the hill and saw something in a tree that overlooked the river. A middle-aged black woman hanging, dead, swaying in the breeze at the noose. This was Molly, the woman once owned by Grafton Thomassen, still hanging from the tree after her drowning last summer. Then, just like the town, she disappeared, and Patrick heard the moan again.

He ran. Patrick ran all the way to his farm and started laughing. Soon he was laughing uncontrollably, because even in his fear he knew he wasn't crazy at all. The river had simply changed its course, just as the Ferryman said it would. And as long as it didn't have feathers, it was fine by him.

***

Three more days passed and he began to really worry about Roger. Had he sent the letter to Maria? Had it been intercepted? Had he even made it to Lawrence, or had he been apprehended on the way and was being held—or worse, killed—by the bands of Border Ruffians that had swept into Kansas? Would they come for him next? These questions twirled through Patrick's mind as he completed his morning chores and returned to the cabin for a cup of tea.

Someone knocked at the door a few minutes later. It was knuckles this time, definitely, and the pattern sounded familiar. Nevertheless, he opened the door with his gun in hand.

"Easy, Paddy. It's me." It was Clegg, and he was alone with a letter. "This is for you. I saw Roger in Atchison a few days ago, and only now found time to deliver it. I apologize. I've been quite busy."

Patrick snatched the letter and read it standing in the doorway, his gun leaning up against his leg.

Brother,

Your letter will soon be delivered, I promise. But there is bad news from Lawrence. Sam Jones and his drunken posse returned to instigate more violence under the guise of executing the warrants they failed to execute in December. You will soon read in the Sovereign, I am certain, that he was assassinated while unarmed in his tent one night. I can tell you this is false, that he is here, still harassing us. But I'm afraid the false reports are enough for half of Missouri to be here, ready to lay waste to Lawrence.

They have arrested Robinson, our governor, and Lane is in Washington being denied the Congressional seat we procured for him by legitimate election. Samuel C. Pomeroy is now our leader, and though I have great confidence in him, all is against us. I fear for the worst.

I won't return until I have helped repel the Missourians and the freedom of truly law-abiding citizens has been restored. Please give Maria my love when she returns, which I have little doubt she will.

Your brother, Roger.

"My, my," said Clegg, reading his friend's face as Patrick read the letter. "That boy sure does find himself in the thick of things, does he not?"

"Yes, he does. One always finds the other if they're close enough, like drops of water."

Clegg chuckled. "I'm afraid you're more like him than you think. Anyone who calls himself a Kansan must be. May I come in?"

"Of course, of course."

They sat down and Patrick poured two cups of tea and sliced some bread, wishing it was as full-bodied as it would have been had Maria baked it. He thought about butter. He wanted butter. Perhaps later today he'd build a churn and begin making some tomorrow. Goat butter sounded delightful.

"You look well, my friend," Clegg began after his first sip of tea. "You've stopped the drink, I can tell."

"Likewise!" He toasted his friend with a piece of bread, wondering why he hadn't chosen tea.

"Indeed I have. I have," he said proudly. "My only regret is that I didn't sooner. The sky is brighter in sobriety, don't you think?" He looked up as if the sky were visible inside the cabin.

"Absolutely," Patrick said through a mouthful of bread.

Clegg sighed. "Paddy, I've come to say goodbye. Joe and I are headed for Scott's Bluff, then West by the end of the month."

"Yes, Salt Lake, like."

"Indeed. Odd how Moses led his people through a desert to the promised land while our Brigham Young has led us through an entire continent of gardens in order to settle in a desert."

Patrick laughed. Clegg's self-deprecating humor had been missed. "I've read as much."

"Lovely but harsh. We are alone there, free of all who have harassed us all these years. The Garden of Eden has as much to do with family as it does vegetation, I suppose. It may be a desert, but it's a peaceful one. So far, at least. "

"I wish that were true for all of Kansas." He said this somewhat dejectedly, but not with the embarrassing hopelessness he sometimes used with his older friend.

"As do I, as do I. Paddy, I'm forever grateful for what you have done for me."

"As am I for what you've done for me, Clegg." Brushing crumbs from his hands, he lay them flat on the table and looked softly as at his friend. "Your advice and wisdom I shall never forget."

Clegg smiled. "I saw your neighbor Joseph in town and heard about Maria, and then Roger updated me. I'm sure she'll return."

"I hope so."

Clegg stood, sipping his tea, and looked out the little window over the sloping yard to the east. He could see the beginnings of what his friend had always spoken about while they worked on the levee last summer. It could truly be a paradise someday. "Patrick, I converted to Mormonism because I loved my wife and children. Mormons believe the family continues after death, and in death a proper family become gods. Families have their roots in a world before life, that we find one another in this life, and continue as a family after death. Life is just a place where the eternal is realized. In marriage this eternal union is only recognized and celebrated, but it always was and always will be. Separations are not even possible, spiritually." He looked back over his shoulder at the seated younger man, whose head was bowed as he sat hunched over the table.

"And I am a terrible Mormon. Or, I was, until living here with you and Maria brought me back. Odd, that my job is to try and convert you." He turned back to the table and sat down again. "Really, I'm failing right now as we speak in not doing that. But I see the irony. It is you who converted me, back to a religion that you don't even follow. You, your family, reminded me that even as I lost my wife and daughters that dark spring, I will see them again one day. We are an unbreakable family. And honestly, my religion teaches me that yours is not eternal, that as a Catholic you follow a disjointed church, which mine has restored."

Taking a sip of tea, he set down his cup and twirled it in its saucer. "But Maria will return. And your baby—your baby will always be with you, and there are more to come. I know it. This—" he gestured out the window, "—is your Zion. This is your celestial family. You, a Catholic, taught me Mormonism again. I can never truly thank you for that." Smiling now, he looked up at Patrick, holding the cup of tea to his lips the way a child would for comfort. "Odd, isn't it? That we sometimes learn scripture from heretics." Puffy, pink cheeks accented his lips, which were reddened a little by the tea. "Just don't tell my Church Fathers that."

"I don't think that will be a problem." Patrick stood, and they shook hands. "Clegg, I learned the same from you. Or, I remembered it as well."

"Indeed. And Patrick, my prophet tells me otherwise, and I follow him with all my heart and soul, but I believe you and I will meet again one day. Maria and Abigail shall get on fabulously. Our families will dance upon the clouds, my friend."

"Indeed they will, Clegg."

"Good, it's settled. You and I have ended all the strife of mankind. Until we meet again, Brother Patrick."

"Until then. May peace be with you, Clegg. Always."

"Goodbye, Patrick."

"Goodbye, Clegg."

XXIII

A limping, smiling, probably-too-young-to-be-here private by the name of Oliver John Hawkins struggled gleefully under a bright red adaptation of the flag of South Carolina with "Southern Rights" inscribed upon it. He held it with pride as he marched toward Lawrence, every painful step. The mosquitoes were just hatching on this day in the third week of May, and the rolling hills to the west seemed to grow bigger in the fading orange sun. To the east, the land sloped down to the river, rows of bushes and cottonwood clicking and buzzing with the noise of frogs and insects. Behind this young private, from the town of Atchison, came the newly-arrived company of South Carolinians and a force under the command of Col. J. H. Stringfellow, Lt. Robert S. Kelley and Capt. F. G. Palmer, calling themselves the "Palmetto Guards" or sometimes the "Atchison Guards." And right behind him came Joseph James Hawkins, the only soldier among them whose hunting rifle was slung perfectly over his shoulder.

By afternoon on May 21st they spilled down the slopes of Mount Oread onto Massachusetts Street like ants when their hill is flooded, Oliver John still carrying the flag of the South Carolina company, his older brother standing tall beside him. And they listened to David Rice Atchison, one-time President Pro Tempore of the United States Senate, deliver these words:

Boys, this day I am a Kickapoo Ranger, by God! This day we have entered Lawrence with "Southern Rights" inscribed upon our banner, and not one damned Abolitionist dared to fire a gun.

He looked over at Oliver John and Joseph James, both of whom had never felt lighter on their feet.

Now, boys, this is the happiest day of my life. We have entered that damned town, and taught the damned Abolitionists a Southern lesson that they will remember until the day they die. And now, boys, we will go in again, with our highly honorable Jones, and test the strength of that damned Free-State Hotel, and teach the Emigrant Aid Company that Kansas shall be ours.

Boys, ladies should, and I hope will, be respected by every gentleman. But when a woman takes upon herself the garb of a soldier by carrying a

Sharp's rifle, then she is no longer worthy of respect. Trample her under your feet as you would a snake!

Come on, boys! Now do your duty to yourselves and your Southern friends. Your duty I know you will do. If one man or woman dares stand before you, blow them to Hell with a chunk of cold lead.

When he finished, a cry rose from the ranks, which immediately broke into a whooping and hollering swarm. Within minutes, they seized the presses of the two newspapers in Lawrence and threw them in the river. They chased one of the senior editors into the river as well, laughing as he scrambled along the banks. From atop his horse, Colonel Stringfellow watched his colleague with a smile on his face, wondering if he would survive a similar escape from Atchison down the Missouri, should it ever come to it. Thank God it could never, would never, he thought.

The men left in Lawrence under the leadership of Samuel Pomeroy, a one-time U.S. Representative from Massachusetts, were mostly moderates and offered no resistance. They had appealed to the governor and the U.S. Marshall for Kansas Territory, I. B. Donaldson, for assistance, but none had been forthcoming. They knew the Free State Hotel, which had been built as a fortress with this very event in mind, would be a primary target, so they abandoned it. Having seen at least four cannon on the slopes of Mt. Oread that morning, and knowing they had only one (which Pomeroy had offered in surrender), the fortress seemed more like a death trap.

Most left Lawrence and watched it burn from ridges and hilltops, and the rest wandered the streets, taking the occasional beating, and watched some homes burn to the earth. Before nightfall, all the small pillaging had been done and everyone gathered around the tall, thick stone walls of the massive Free State Hotel to see if the invaders could bring it to its knees.

Senator Atchison, a glass of whiskey in his hand, was given the honor of firing the first shot of Old Sacramento from across Massachusetts Street, repeating, "And now we will test the strength of that damned Free-State Hotel!" But the old cannon's shot missed the hotel entirely, skidding across the street and destroying a house nearby.

Laughter rose from the crowd, and Atchison's face turned red.

"Fire again boys! And hit your target this time!"

They did, but it had little effect on the thick walls of the biggest structure in Kansas. "Again, boys, again!" bellowed the former senator.

Other cannon were fired now and men rode around the hotel shooting their guns in the air. All in all, fifty cannon balls struck the hotel, but it continued to stand.

"We'll powder it from the inside, men!" yelled Colonel Stringfellow.

Several barrels of gunpowder were exploded in the lobby, but still the hotel stood.

Finally, as the sun set and the sky glowed red above Lawrence, they lit the inside afire and watched it burn into the night. The wind began to whip through the river bottoms and the fire gutted the hotel and lit the roof so it was like a giant candle in the Kansas night. Being of the least wooden structures west of the Missouri River, the hotel smoldered down quickly, and the flag—Oliver John's flag—was taken from Governor Robinson's residence (which was in turn set ablaze) to be placed atop the great chimney of the hotel.

"A good ole Southern boy oughta hoist it up," said one man.

"This Missourian, here," said Robert Kelley, placing his hand on Oliver John's shoulder, "is the personification of Southern resiliency, boys. The weight of the earth fell on him and yet he rose from his own ashes. This boy here's a phoenix!"

A cheer rose from the men and as two of them picked their way through the crowd into the front door to see if it was safe to enter, Joseph James turned to his little brother. He had been standing apart from the crowd as it destroyed the printing presses and hotel, a scowl on his face.

"Don't do it, Oliver John," he said.

"Why not?"

"There ain't no glory in burning down a town that don't resist."

"But Jimmy, you done tol' me 'while back that this is 'Yankee Town' and we needs ta git 'em outa Kansas."

"That's right." Joseph James put his arm around his little brother's shoulder. The boy was getting big. "But this was a drunken mob and it will do no good for our cause to act this way. We'll be downright lucky if nobody innocent don't get hurt. And let me tell you, Oliver John, if that happens, it'll be a guilt hard to live with."

Just then Oliver John was swept up onto the shoulders of three men and carried into the hotel. By the time they mounted the giant stone stairwell so they could climb to the roof, the boy had forgotten all about his older brother's plea. He felt like a king, a victor, atop their shoulders, carrying the heavy hemp flag. And when they stepped onto the roof, Oliver John realized this was the tallest building he'd ever been in or on. Though it was getting dark quickly, he felt like he could see all the way to Indiana, where Pappa was, and the mountains in the West, where he wanted to go one day. Everything smelled the way it did the day the tree fell on him.

The men set Oliver John down and tapped the great, blackened chimney, indicating it was the best place to put the flag. Realizing he couldn't reach high enough to place the flag in the chimney, they hoisted him back on their shoulders and walked him over to it. A gust of wind and a lurch of shoulders almost made Oliver John drop the flag, but he held it tightly and leaned up against the brick of the chimney, which seemed loose and crumbling. He began wedging the flagpole into the crumbling mortar between two bricks, and could see the men below looking up. They began to cheer as they saw the big red flag fluttering against the darkening sky.

Another great gust of wind came and nearly took the flag out of the chimney. Oliver John held it steady, but the heavy fabric whipped around the pole, striking the loose brick and Oliver John at the same time. He realized a brick had been knocked loose, and after turning away from the flag as it whipped him in the cheek, ear, and neck, he turned back toward the crowd below and saw a single brick plummeting down. He leaned over and before he could shout an alarm, saw it strike someone below, who then fell to the floor with a muffled cry and lay motionless on the ground.

The crowd cheered on.

***

When Oliver John finally got out of the hotel he found his brother waiting for him. Joseph James knew immediately that Oliver John had seen the brick strike the bystander, a boy not much older than himself.

"They took him to camp," Joseph said. "Let's go see him."

They rode to the top of Mt. Oread and for a brief moment turned and watched the looting and burning continue throughout the town.

It was completely dark now, and the small fires that grew and died in the wind made Lawrence look like it was shimmering. The trees behind it also shimmered with fireflies, and it looked suddenly like the sky, galaxies and stars in endless, depthless blackness. The ruin of the Free State Hotel looked ancient, as if some long-lost civilization had abandoned the site long ago, and the little shacks and shanties scattered about it were the ancestors of a once great nation. Lawrence was a universe unto itself.

"Ain't nothin' ta be proud of, Oliver John," said Joseph.

"I feel mighty terrible, Jimmy."

"Ain't nothin' you did, boy. What you did was an accident. I'm the guilty one in our family."

"You didn't do nothin', Jimmy."

"Exactly. We're in the right, Oliver John," he said and turned around. They gently led their horses down the slope toward the Wakarusa and the camp that he believed now sheltered the sole Law and Order casualty of the day.

"If we let these Yanks take over Kansas, we'll all be slaves. Southerners enslave the niggers, but Northerners, they enslave the poor. I don't wanna see you slavin' away in some factory like they do up North. No sirree, that's why I'm here. But you can't enforce law and order by getting drunk and burnin' down a town. You can't do it. I ain't much of a politician, but I don't expect the country will like this, and we still got a constitution to write if we wanna be a state. No, sir. This has done more harm than good." He paused, spat, spat again, and added, "To see Old Sacramento used in that way . . . it's a disgrace to Colonel Doniphan and all the Missouri volunteers who fought so valiantly in Mexico. To see the man that once represented me in the United States Senate, the man who helped make Kansas a place I can own land and offer a better life to you and my children; to see this man drink whiskey and fire that dear old cannon on a defenseless building. It's an outrage, Oliver John. A disgrace. An affront to God, and we shall pay for it."

They soon arrived at a small cluster of tents and Joseph James noticed the horse that had carried the injured young man away about an hour earlier. They dismounted and hitched theirs next to it and poked their heads inside the tent flap.

"Pardon me," Joseph said, "but is the man who got hurt...?"

"He's here. Who wants to know?"

"Excuse me, sir." He removed his hat, spat out the flap, and wrung the hat in his hands. "My name is Joseph James Hawkins, this here's my little brother Oliver John. I'm afraid to tell you that Oliver John was the man holding the flag up atop the hotel, and we both feel awfully sorry for it. Is he...?"

"He's alive. He's my son, Ralph. But it ain't yer fault, boys. Was an accident. It's them damn Yanks is who it is. If they never a-come from Boston this'd never a-happened."

"They didn't resist us, sir."

"Mr. Hawkins." The man stood. He was tall and had to bend slightly in the tent. He swallowed and his thin, long neck produced a large Adam's apple. "Mr. Hawkins, their very presence is an outrage, an affront to our way of life. These Free Staters in Lawrence don't come here to farm, to own land, to make a free land. They come as puppets controlled by their Northern slave-masters and this damned Emigrant Aid Company. They want slavery of all poor men. We want freedom."

"I couldn't agree more, Mr...?"

"Jones. Andrew Jones."

"I understand, Mr. Jones. That's why I'm here, but..." Joseph James was thinking of Patrick and Maria, and of the night Patrick and Roger helped lift the tree off Oliver John, and wanted to tell Mr. Jones about it. But then two men noticed Oliver John kneel next to the boy he'd injured and begin to cry. "Maybe we should step outside a moment," Joseph whispered.

"Of course. It ain't your fault, boy," Mr. Jones turned to Oliver John. "It ain't, son."

Oliver John wiped his eyes and nose with his sleeve and looked up. He started to speak but hesitated. Somehow, knowing the boy's name made it worse.

"We'll be right outside," said Joseph James. "You just get your mind straight round this. We ain't a-leavin' til you do."

While the older men stood outside the tent and talked about the potential ramifications of this "Sack of Lawrence," as it would come to be known, Oliver John watched Ralph sleep. Ralph's breathing was shallow and fast, his face placid, oily, and mostly calm. The left eye, nearest where the brick struck him, was swollen a little, but the major injury, above and a little behind the left ear, was covered in cold bandages. Ralph grimaced and shifted his body a little, then fell back asleep and into the short, quick breathing pattern.

For a moment he looked dead. Oliver John could feel his own heart beating quickly, and wondered if he would go to Hell if the boy died. It was an accident, but Jimmy had warned him. In disobeying, perhaps, he'd sinned and this was God's way of punishing him. The boy, Ralph, had to live. He just had to. It reminded Oliver John of lying in the mud with the tree on him. This boy probably felt a great weight on him, too, the weight of mortality and death and fear, like the ribcage of a great dark horse heaving and writhing and throbbing as it tried to get off its rider. It seemed to Oliver John that most people didn't feel it. Jimmy did, 'cause of the war. Pappa sure didn't. People who felt that weight didn't abandon their sons and wife for mistresses. They stayed put, their boots dug into the soil, and hugged their loved ones early and often. Maybe when he woke up, Ralph would still feel it and they could talk about it.

Ralph gasped a couple times. He seemed to be in pain now, from the expression on his face. He moved some more and the wet rags that were on his wound began to fall away from his head. Oliver John reached up to replace them, but couldn't help peeling them back a minute with shaky hands to view the wound. Part of his skull was missing, and in the blood Oliver John could see bits of brain. It looked like the deer brains he'd scooped out and fed to the dogs. Shivering with a sudden chill, he put the rags back and prayed, his face shaky now. He felt ill, almost vomiting. There was no way this boy would make it, and Oliver John would go straight to Hell. He knew it, and would accept it willingly. Every time he saw Ralph's face, he wanted to be sent to Hell. It was his duty. His just repentance.

Joseph James asked if he and Oliver John could stay in the tent that night to help, and Andrew Jones agreed.

Jones fell asleep quickly, and the two Hawkins brothers lay in bed wide awake, listening to the breathing of the injured young man. Suddenly, it stopped.

Joseph James got up on one elbow and touched Ralph's face.

Oliver John knew he was dead. He could feel the devil on the other side of the canvas, smiling contentedly.

Joseph James reached up and closed the young man's eyes. "We'll tell his pappa in the morning." He clasped Oliver John's face in his hands. "Listen, this was an accident, Oliver John. That's all."

"It's a guilt that will be hard to live with."

"I wish I wouldn't-a said that."

"But you did. And it's true."

They lay in silence for a few minutes, hoping the boy's breathing would return to the sounds of the night, joining the chorus of frogs and crickets. Somewhere in the distance a coyote howled. An owl called. All around them was life. Between them was only death.

A great screech came from above the tent. "Don't listen to it," said Joseph. "It's just that damned bird."

Another few moments of silence passed. Oliver John believed he could feel the weight lift from the boy. He imagined all the tents scattered over the land, and the fires burning in Lawrence. Just as he began to wonder where all the men were, he heard a rumbling approach from the top of the hill. The Law and Order men were returning from a night of looting and drinking. Their boisterous noise surrounded the tent and jostled it a little.

"Damned drunks," said Joseph James.

Oliver John began to cry as the raucousness increased, and finally stopped as the noise died down and the men found their tents or lay down next to campfires in the grass. His older brother listened to him, thinking of sleeping under the stars in the Mexican winter, lonely, afraid, confused. He knew that though a shot had never been fired at Oliver John that day, this was his first battle, his El Brazito. For days now, as the Missourians gathered and excited one another, climaxing in the burning of the hotel, the landscape had been noisy. But now, as the exhausted men finally all slept at the same time, a perfect silence settled over the prairie, and the Hawkins brothers lay next to their dead compatriot, knowing the other one was awake and eventually one would say something.

"I don't want to fight anymore, Jimmy."

"Neither do I, son. Neither do I."

"Can we stop?" he asked in a shaky voice.

His brother's was as steady as the river. "We're done with this war. We'll go back to our farm and stay put." Oliver John could imagine the look on his brother's face in the darkness. "Our farm. Can you imagine that? Our farm. We'll go there and never leave again. Come war or storm or flood or damnation itself, we ain't leaving that chunk a land for nothin', ever."

Oliver John smiled, and then began to cry again.

"It's okay son," Joseph scooted over and snuggled with his brother. "It's not your fault, son."

***

Roger didn't see the brick fall. As soon as he saw the inscription "Southern Rights" flying atop the Free State Hotel, and that a Hawkins was the bearer of it, he turned away in disgust. Where was the Governor? Where was Lane? Where were all the men of the Kansas Legion and the battalions that were ready to die in defense of Lawrence just last December?

For a month now, New England abolitionists had been shipping boxes of rifles marked "books" or "Bibles" to Lawrence, and for what? Just because the politicians no longer supported them, did that mean their cause was no longer worth fighting for? And why would a politician defend a cause that didn't defend itself? Someone had to do something. And Roger knew within five steps who that man would be. John Brown of Osawatomie.

He found his brother's new horse and rode south out of Lawrence at a full gallop until he saw a group of what looked like Missourians gathered at Blanton's Bridge. This crossing of the Wakarusa had been the scene of several murders and arrests over the last year. Roger knew that approaching it now, unarmed, with Lawrence burning behind him, was not the best of ideas. So he returned to town, found a stash of Sharps rifles in a Kansas Legionnaire's house where he'd once dined with Robinson and Lane, and waited.

As a quiet set on the town that was so complete the smoldering of timber could be heard as if all the houses were infested with termites, he escaped Lawrence to the west in the dead of night and headed for Osawatomie, where the Browns were surely gathering for whatever reprisal they had planned.

At Dutch Henry's Crossing (the intersection of the California and Oregon Roads on the Pottawattamie, where one Henry Sherman had operated a supply store for over a year now) a group of bedraggled Missourians milled about with rifles and shotguns on their shoulders. Roger saw them from a comfortable distance, and also the surrounding territory—there was little way to circumnavigate the crossing without being seen.

He'd have to try and pass through it.

They would harass him, certainly, and hopefully that would be the extent of it. But they may do more. Roger wasn't in the mood for taking more insults from men such as these.

With about a hundred yards between them, Roger kicked his horse into a full gallop. About twenty yards away, he began to scream and raised his rifle at the men.

They scattered, dove into a ditch beside the road, and scrambled for their weapons.

Roger screamed and fired, riding right through the crossing.

Looking back, he saw one man writhing in pain on the ground. He'd hit one! Dammit, he'd hit one! Those ruffian bastards! Now how did they like harassing Free Staters? There was more where that came from. And he realized he could turn around. He didn't have to keep going. So he did.

The men had gathered around their fallen comrade and called for help inside the store.

Henry Sherman was outside now but was in no mind to rush to the Missourians' aid. He only wanted their business, and already had it. They were arguing as to who should go where for help when Roger rode back through and shot a man in the shoulder. He wheeled again, fired, and all the men ran for ditches and trees, Sherman crawling into his store, unsure about who was attacking whom. Two men lay wounded in the dusty road, and though Roger tried to steer his horse forward and trample them, the horse instinctively avoided their bodies. He stopped and looked down at them. They were flushed and pale and moist in the face. "Greetings from County Cork, gentlemen!" He pointed his rifle down at the man.

"Excuse me, young man," came Dutch Henry Sherman's voice from behind. "I do not want that sort of behavior here at my store. This is a place of business and all are welcome."

Roger wheeled the horse and aimed his rifle at Henry now, still smiling. "You just saved this man's life, Henry," he said. "That makes you a sympathizer. And you take their business, which makes you a supplier. That makes us foes, and I should shoot you."

Sherman stiffened and took a half step back. "Please. Don't."

"Refuse their business and I shall let you live."

"I will."

Sherman relaxed a little. "And if I'm asked why I refuse, what shall I say?"

And then, without knowing what he was saying or what it meant, Roger replied. "Tell them the jayhawk made you."

XXIV

It took some time, but Roger realized a while later that he'd heard the term "jayhawk" once before, from an old Irishman in a meeting of the Kansas Legion he'd attended with Jim Lane. The old man had said they should "go jayhawking" in Missouri, and from the ensuing conversation Roger gathered that it meant stealing horses and supplies, waking up the women and children in the middle of the night, and generally just scaring the hell out of folks.

Little did he realize that with the Sack of Lawrence, the landscape of Kansas was going to change dramatically. The deputized forces of Atchison, Stringfellow, Henry S. Pate (the new captain of the Kickapoo Rangers), and Sherriff Jones enjoyed the support of the authorities in executing their arrest warrants, but the destruction of privately held property was certainly illegal. In the coming days and weeks, Roger's ambush at Dutch Henry's Crossing was going to be far from isolated. Illegality was going to be met with illegality, because non-violent resistance didn't work. Even Governor Shannon's horses would be stolen by the jayhawkers, and before dawn on the 22nd, it was clear that Kansas was going to bleed that summer.

As he continued to ride west toward Osawatomie in search of the Browns, Roger remembered his brother and sister in-law. Maria should have her letter by now and be planning her journey from Boston. Patrick should have planted most everything by now and even be beginning to enjoy young lettuce. Perhaps he'd butchered a hog, as well. With help he should be clearing more trees and prairie, but that would probably have to wait until he had help. It made him sad to think about Patrick farming up in Atchison. They should be jayhawking together, sons of J. P. Dugan, ensuring the Southern aristocracy didn't do to Kansas and the West what the English did to Ireland. They should be freeing the land for all men, not jealously guarding and sowing a hundred and sixty acres of it. He wondered if Paddy would avenge him if he were killed. He wondered if Paddy loved him as much as his Free State brethren did.

As the California Road approached its crossing with the Marais Des Cygnes River, Roger saw another group of men. This was a much larger group, about thirty, and he could determine from a distance that they were heavily armed. Rifles and sabres abounded, and as he approached cautiously, he recognized the sabers. It was the

Browns, certainly, and they had assembled a larger force. Roger kicked his horse into a trot and held his rifle above his head.

"Whoa, there!" a man pointed his small pistol at Roger.

"We know him," said John Brown Jr., who had been elected as captain of the group. "He is a friend."

"I bring news from Lawrence," said Roger, slightly out of breath.

"It's been attacked."

"Yes, and the invasion was met with no resistance. It's all over."

A silence ensued. For weeks now the territory had been expecting an entrenched Free State defense to a frustrated Southern offensive. The press thought so, the settlers thought so, the politicians thought so. Why a town would build its hotel as a fortress and then not defend it didn't make sense. All the work over the last two years seemed now fruitless. Tens of thousands of dollars had been raised, thousands of settlers had come and suffered through terrible weather and illness, all for the opportunity that yesterday afforded, and it wasn't taken. And now there was every reason to believe the Ruffians would run roughshod over all of Kansas. Everyone was in danger.

"Over?" croaked Brown.

"It's quite over, like. The town is short of food, and no more mouths are needed, so. There is very little to defend, and I expect the Missourians will be dispersing today after a peaceful night's rest."

This infuriated the men. The Missourians had once again terrorized Kansas and gone back home, having had to pay no more cost than a little inconvenience to their families. After riding a few more demoralizing miles toward Lawrence and asking questions of Roger, born of disbelief and for which he had no answers, the men decided to do what men in the throes of indecision often do: they ate.

All through breakfast John Brown spoke hurriedly but discreetly to his son, who mostly nodded in apparent agreement, but had the facial expression of concerned disagreement. The two looked very much alike, thought Roger, but seemed quite different in their mannerisms and in the way they approached the others.

Finally, Junior rose and addressed them: "Gentlemen, your attention, please. I know we are of separate groups—the Pottawatomie Rifle Company, the Pomeroy Guards, and those of you who came to us independently—but since you have elected me your captain, I feel we should make our next decision as a group. And, being a group that is fighting for freedom and democracy, I submit we vote. We can either move on toward Lawrence, or we can disperse and wait for our next opportunity. Those who lose the poll must follow those who win."

"Let's go home!" one shouted. "It's over."

"On to Lawrence!" shouted another. "It's only just begun."

"I say we disperse. I'm hungry."

"We just ate, you idiot!"

"A vote, gentlemen, a vote!"

The election was conducted much in the same way Bob Kelley had conducted it last summer when the Atchisonians decided what to do with Rev. Butler the first time around, and Roger put himself in the same place his older brother had that time—right behind the man tallying the votes. And he watched intently as John Brown Jr. tallied each man's preference. Some seemed almost dispassionately assured; others were hesitant.

Old man Brown stood on a stump. "Men, as you vote, I encourage you to consider why you are here in the first place. Both in Kansas and on this road to Lawrence. Whatever has happened in that city cannot change why you are here. It can only make you more resolute. And remember: God sees your vote."

Despite what seemed to Roger as a very logical appeal from the old man, the vote was close. And the last man tipped the scales: they were to disperse.

But John Brown Jr. looked at his father and rose. "On to Lawrence," he said.

* * *

By nightfall they had reached the claim of the Pomeroy Guards' captain, Mr. Shore, and decided to camp. The afternoon's ride had left the men tired and listless. Many did want to push on, but to what end they didn't know. The group was somewhat directionless and with every passing hour they became also more anxious. Over any hill could be hundreds of marauding Missourians. A man from Osawatomie produced a bottle of whiskey, and a few drank, but most were either too nervous or too intimidated by the scowls of the Browns, once they saw it being passed around.

The next morning the old man was the first awake, nearly ninety minutes before sunrise. Roger was the second awake. Brown already had a fire going and was grinding raw corn kernels between two rocks. Once they were pulverized enough to make a sort of flour, he added a little water, rolled the dough into balls, and let them cook on hot rocks in the fire. Roger arrived just in time for the first, soft batch.

"Try it," said the old man without looking up from his work.

They were good. Chewy, filling, a little gritty but satisfying. Roger was somewhat surprised by the amount of work necessary for so little food. So he began grinding kernels alongside the tanned, wiry man.

They worked for almost thirty minutes in perfect silence as the sun splashed over the prairie. The grass was halfway up to the knee in most places, and the yellow-orange of the sun as it rose accented the green of new growth. Roger had fallen in love with the smell of Kansas mornings, especially in the spring and early summer. It was as if the earth had a body odor unto itself, and being in the Missouri River valley was like being adjacent to one of her major arteries. She pulsed in eastern Kansas, the earth, and when she woke on May mornings, she was in heat.

"There's nothing as humble as morning," Brown said, popping a corn pellet in his mouth. "To wake before the earth and work toward a simple meal is an honor to God." His rigid, square jaw rippled with tendons as he chewed.

"I've always enjoyed morning," said Roger, beginning to wonder when the others would wake. "I've long felt that the first to rise is ahead of time. If the sun has risen before you, it seems like you're always trying to catch up."

The old man smiled and looked at him. Brown rose, picking up his grinding rocks, which made a pleasant clicking sound in his hands, and moved closer. "I'm very happy you came back to the Pottawatomie, Roger. It seems we both missed our chance to defend our rights."

"Yes. It's just begun, so."

"Indeed. It's time we stopped reacting, don't you think? These heathen Missourians have sacked our capital, and now they have bludgeoned one of the few politicians who stands for what is right, all to no reprisal."

Roger surmised Brown was referring to the beating of Senator Charles Sumner of Massachusetts, who had just been attacked while seated at his desk on the Senate floor by Representative Preston Brooks of South Carolina. Sumner had delivered a two day diatribe that would come to be known as the "Crime Against Kansas" speech, in which he viciously and personally attacked Brooks' cousin, himself a senator, for collaborating with Stephen Douglass of Illinois in the certification of false Kansan elections and total disregard of her true, generally Free State squatters.

"I think we must, at least once, become the aggressor," Brown intoned. "So far we have the money and the settlers, but not the will to defend either. So far we have been martyrs of God, but not soldiers of God. Once we show that we will defend our God-given rights with all our might, that we will take it upon ourselves to execute God's will on earth, the end will be at hand. God is on our side, Roger. Don't you think?"

"Well, yes, I think so."

"Roger." Brown stood, rolling a handful of hot corn pellets in his hand like dice. "Roger, this isn't going to work, this march on Lawrence. There is nothing to do there. The time to stand is gone, and I fear that if we do not take some strong stance now, the battle will be lost. This continent," he said, spreading his arms from the rising sun to the west, "this vast continent will be a den of subjugation and oppression, an affront to God." He paused a moment and then added, "It will be our fault, yours and mine, Roger. Because we can do something about it, right here and right now."

Roger's knees were aching, but he stayed in his squat, somewhat enjoying the pain. "What do you have in mind?"

"There are men who have harassed and troubled their God-fearing neighbors for a year now, and it is only a matter of time before they attack them. I have in mind to disallow that, and in doing so let all of the South know that while they may come to Kansas, and they may vote here as they please, they will not intimidate us. Their way of life is illegal and immoral, and I believe we have been given an opportunity to enforce God's Law on earth."

Roger stood now. "Who are these men?"

Brown smiled. "There are some near Pottawatomie whom I fear will attack my sons' families if they are not prevented. I propose a group of us return west and later tonight show these men that we have the might of God with us." He wandered over to a tree and picked up a broadsword that was leaning up against it, raising it as if to examine it. It seemed very heavy. "God will judge these men. His judgment with be swift and unequivocal, and it will strike them down." He let the sword swing to the earth.

Just then, two men emerged from their tents. "Good morning, gentlemen," said Brown. "Care for some breakfast?"

***

By mid-morning Brown had had similar conversations with many more of the men, and several of them, including two of his sons, separated themselves from the group and set to sharpening some of the broadswords. John Brown Jr. also held consultations with many of the men, and the general sentiment was that despite voting in favor of it the day before (or so they thought), it didn't make much sense to head for Lawrence. They learned, just after breakfast, that the captive Gov. Robinson was going to be moved to Ft. Leavenworth. A plan developed wherein the party would ambush Robinson's captors on the way from Lawrence to Leavenworth and set him free. Junior was going to lead a party east for the ambush; the intent of his father and his smaller group sharpening the swords, nobody knew for sure.

Roger sat quietly during all these discussions, watching the sharpening of the swords and the hurried glances from the others. He was deciding what to do. It seemed that whatever the old man had planned would be drastic, sudden, and unpredictable. His son's plan seemed ill-conceived but logical, its motive clear. Part of him thought about being on his knees at the end of Joseph James Hawkins's gun, Patrick shaking like a leaf, and of his countless conversations with Jim Lane. This part of him wanted to follow the old man with the piercing eyes and immovable mouth, to wield a heavy sword into battle and crash into his oppressors. This was the part of him that shot the men the day before, the part that understood the meaning of "jayhawk." The other part remembered the convention at Big Springs and his conversations with Charles Robinson. This part could feel Maria's hand on his shoulder, her warm smile, and reading by the fire with his brother. Clearly, he decided, the former must come to fruition. Politics had gotten righteousness nowhere. And if more men like him were in Lawrence on May 21st, it would have ended quite differently. He would go with the old man.

He rose and began to walk over to the group of men sharpening the swords.

Brown stood and met him before he reached them.

"I want to go with you," he said.

"Why?"

"I know right from wrong, dark from light, good from evil," Roger said, as the old man smiled. "But I must know what you have planned."

Brown's smile disappeared immediately. "Why?"

"I have limits."

"There are limits to the will of God? You would question the destiny He has set for you?"

"Of course not. But…"

"You would, like St. Thomas, need to see the wounds of Christ? You would need to see the covenant itself before yielding to it?"

"No, but…"

"But nothing. You had better not come."

"Mr. Brown…"

"No, Roger. No. You are young yet, and curious, and inquisitive. Until you learn to decide and follow blindly the path that God has set for you, you cannot accompany such a mission. Your path lies with my son."

"Mr. Brown, as a member of the Free State Party and a citizen of Kansas, I still must know what you're going to do."

Just then another man approached. "John, I urge you to be cautious," he said quickly in interruption, betraying his nervousness.

Every muscle in the old man's wiry frame rippled, and he took a step forward. He was almost shaking with vehemence. Had a knife or sword been nearby, Roger may have stepped between them.

"I am tired of this word, 'cautious'," Brown said. His voice didn't scream it, but everything else about him did. It was the loudest sentence Roger ever heard uttered, and as soon as it was completed, they all heard the shriek of the giant bird in the trees to the west.

***

Roger mounted his horse and rode east with John Brown Jr. and the rest of his men, arriving on the road between Leavenworth and Lawrence in the late afternoon.

It was dry and hot, and as they waited, deciding where to go next, Roger began to itch. Chiggers, which had plagued him since moving to Kansas almost two years previous, were now particularly bothersome. It was very early in the season for them to be so prevalent, but they filled his waistband, ankles, underarms, and groin area. The mosquitoes, too, had had their way with him the night before, and he felt like one giant feast for the swarms of Kansas. Ultimately, he was a chunk of meat, nothing more, just like the horse breathing heavily between his legs.

"I don't see any evidence of a large party having come through here recently," said a man who had been sent to scout down the road toward the river. "Either they haven't brought Robinson this way yet, or have brought him another way."

Everyone looked at Junior. He hesitated, looking east to the river, north toward Leavenworth, south toward Lawrence, and west, toward Topeka and his father. Everyone wondered what the old man was up to.

"Let's scout Lawrence," he said. "All we have is hearsay about its status." He looked at Roger. "We don't truly know how damaged it is or if there are Ruffians left."

This suggestion met with silence.

"I will go," Roger volunteered.

Another man volunteered to accompany him, and they were gone until almost nightfall.

"The Free State is burned," Roger said upon return to the group of languid men and restless horses, flicking their tails from the gathering insects. "But most of the rest of the town is intact. It's almost deserted." He turned to Junior. "Has Robinson been through?"

The men looked at him, but he didn't reply. "No," said one.

Junior mounted his horse. "Men!" he started. Some drank their coffee, some swatted mosquitoes, some stoked the fire. "Men!" he said in his loudest, lowest voice. "Stand up!" They slowly stood and he continued. "I have been contemplating our dilemma and have arrived at this revelation. We must remind ourselves about what we're fighting for…"

"We ain't fightin', we just sittin' here gittin' ate!" They laughed.

"Our cause, gentlemen! Our cause! What is our cause?!"

Several men called out both sarcastic and sincere causes, and everyone chuckled, including Junior. "For freedom! For land! For our rights!"

"We're fighting against an immoral institution!" shouted Junior. "An affront to God!"

The men grumbled. Some nodded, some shook their heads.

"The rest of the world has progressed past the age of slavery, and in Kansas the United States are deciding if we are to travel forward on God's path, or regress along the trail of the devil. We have the ability, those of us seated—standing—here on this road, this very road this very evening, to make that decision. This is not an issue of squatter sovereignty. This is an issue of abolition!"

"No! Yes!" There were shouts and grumbles in both agreement and disagreement.

"Yes, it is! We can abolish this shameful sin our forefathers have shackled us with! It bears down upon our backs like giant chiggers and mosquitos!" Laughter. "Yes, it does! It sucks our blood and desiccates our souls. But we can squash this bug! We can! We can flatten it upon the collective skin of this nation just as that man just did!" More laughter. "So I suggest, gentlemen, we not languish in waiting any longer. Let us not tarry here on this road. Let us not ambush Robinson's captors. I propose that we free a slave!"

Junior scanned the eyes of his men, something his father had told him to do when wondering about their thoughts. Some were wide in a sort of astonishment. Some rolled in an unconvinced manner, and some squinted not only from the setting sun but from utter suspicion.

"There is a cabin on the other side of the town of Palmyra," Junior began, encouraged by the fact nothing had been said in rejoinder. "There are two slaves in this cabin, and we will set them free!"

With that he raised his Bowie knife in the air as if it were a cavalrymen's saber and rode to the north. A few men followed, dragging along behind him on old tired horses. Roger, though he liked Junior and agreed with most of what he had said, did not. He felt paralyzed at this point, wondering what the men who departed with John Brown were doing. Somehow, he knew that sitting on this road was meaningless, no matter what they did.

And, when Junior returned with two slaves—a man in his forties and his meek yet pretty daughter—it became clear that this was indeed the case. The two knew no more about what they might do with freedom in Kansas then they would with an igloo.

Some of the men exchanged short words, and as the two slaves slapped bugs off their arms, they voted to return the slaves to their cabin. "C'mon, miss," said a man from Osawatomie to the girl, "let's get you home."

Roger sat on a log scratching his chiggers as the girl grasped the man's arm and gladly hopped into the saddle in front of him.

"I'm going home, too," said a young man seated next to Roger. "We can't make Kansas a free state by freeing all twelve of her slaves."

***

The next morning it was decided by the remaining men (mostly just Brown's Pottawatomie Rifles) that they would return home and await further developments. Roger hesitated. He considered riding north for Atchison to see if Patrick had heard from Maria. Especially once they were accosted by a small company of U.S. soldiers on the Santa Fe Trail and politely, but definitely told to disband. Clearly the army was going to try and neutralized the situation, and organized, roving bands of militia were not going to be terribly successful. Something more drastic and secretive was needed, something the old Brown was planning, and these were not the men who would do it. Roger could return to Atchison, see Patrick, then head for Lawrence, where surely men like Lane would return and the true Free State movement could strategize a response to the Sack of Lawrence.

But he rode on, still paralyzed by boredom, bugs, and inaction. He was tired and hungry and knew the Browns would feed him and give him a place to rest until he decided what was next. Plus, he could see what the old man had been up to, perhaps, and possibly participate in any further plans he may have had.

When a rider approached from the west along the trail, his horse exhausted from a prolonged gallop, Roger knew he was about to learn just what the old man and his odd band of followers were up to.

"Five men have been butchered on the Pottawatomie!" the man yelled. "Brutally mangled! They say old Brown did it!"

Everyone looked at Junior. One man slapped a mosquito from his face, blood smearing down his cheek, and a swarm settled on them. One man vomited.

"Well, we can't just stand here as food for insects," said Junior. "Let's make it as close to Osawatomie as we can and bed down for the night."

A few hours before sunrise that night, Old Brown rejoined them. Roger heard the horses ride into camp, and the voice of the old man giving directions to his followers. How he would have known the location of his son and the Rifles was not clear, unless it had all been planned.

He lay restless until the sun rose on a very different Kansas the morning of May 25th, 1856. Suddenly, the day was night, the night was day, and nothing made sense. I am a criminal, Roger thought. An accessory to murder.

XXV

As June wore on and the morning steam faded away into the heat of summer, Patrick really started to worry. When he read in the *Sovereign* about the shooting of Jones, Robinson's arrest in Missouri and "the glorious victory in Lawrence," he knew Roger must be in danger. He also read that the day after Atchison's raid on Lawrence, Senator Sumner was bludgeoned with a cane on the floor of the United States Senate, and knew what was coming. Even the Congressmen had taken out their clubs: surely, the world was indeed beginning to collapse, and if Maria or Roger didn't make it back soon, well, there wasn't much of an Eden to protect north of Atchison. Without family, a Kansas farm is really just of bunch of chiggers, ticks, and weeds.

With Clegg gone he felt increasingly isolated as well, and with the press of the *Herald of Freedom* rusting in the mud of the Kaw, all his connections to information on the Free State movement were gone. Should something happen to Maria, to Roger, or if anything happened that may impact them at all, he wasn't sure how he'd find out. Through the *Sovereign* and rumor in Atchison, perhaps, but he didn't want to brave his old haunts in town, lest he start drinking again. He may languish for years on the farm, unaware of the fate of his family, a total irony considering what the farm was supposed to be. He decided to pay a visit to the Hawkinses. He hadn't seen them all year, had never met their newest child (if it had survived). Perhaps Joseph James had taken part in the raid on Lawrence, too, and had knowledge of the fate of her defenders.

On his walk over (Zion was tired from a day of clearing stumps from along the creek), he realized that this was yet another thing he did very well: worry. He should add this to the list: walking, praying, reading, drinking, waiting, saving, eating, and worrying. Just two years ago, when he read the *Journal of Lewis & Clark* in the library in Boston, he didn't worry so much. Jumping headlong into a marriage and a move to the wild frontier gave him nothing other than the occasional headache. But now, with Roger off trying to start a war, Maria somewhere (and anywhere, really) between the middle of the continent and the Atlantic, and Clegg somewhere around the hundredth meridian, he had started to have trouble doing many of these things he did very well. Reading was a chore. Waiting was impossible. Eating (and the preparation it required) was almost hateful, it was so mundane. Worrying had become the only thing he did, other than work.

"Well now! Lookee 'ere!" said Joseph James as Patrick arrived. "My favorite Yankee!"

"Good to see you, Jimmy." He offered his hand. "I trust the summer finds you well, so?"

"You gotta stop it with them Irish sayin's, Paddy. 'So'? So what?" He dropped Patrick's hand and patted him on the shoulder. "We're good, thanks. Doing as well as a Kansan can expect, I s'pose."

"Yes. It's been an eventful fortnight."

"Well, come on in, Paddy, come on in and see my daughter!"

"Yes, of course!"

They went inside and in a bit of a reversal of his expectations, Paddy found Del asleep on a chair and Sarah Sally up and about, tidying and cleaning and arranging. The baby was twitching while it slept on Del's chest. Oliver John was not in the house.

"Don't mind her," Joseph said, nodding toward his mother. "She's decided she's a mother again." Joseph James was smiling.

"Watch yer mouth! I love my granddaughter. Not like some."

Joseph turned to Patrick, still smiling. "Ma's a different woman nowadays. Ain't nothin' like a baby to put a fire under a woman."

"A good baby," she retorted. "Not like some."

"Well…" Joseph leaned in toward Patrick, pretending to whisper, but spoke loud enough for his mother to hear, "I gotta tell ya, it's a blessing. Del ain't been all that well since the baby was born and we're quite blessed my mother is here to help." Though her back was to him, Patrick could see the old woman, by the stillness of her hands as she dried a clean cup, was touched.

"Now then, what brings you here, Irishman?" Joseph motioned to the table and they sat. "The Pottawatomie murders?"

"The what?"

"Don't tell me you haven't heard about it?"

"No, I haven't."

"Patrick, just how busy are you up there on that farm?"

"Busy enough to keep his family happy," Sarah Sally chimed in. "Not like some."

"Shows what you know," her son retorted over his shoulder. "Five men were butchered with cavalry swords down near Osawatomie," he continued. "Dragged outa their beds in the middle of the night and chopped up to pieces like sides of beef, right in front a their women and children. A Free State revenge for Lawrence, I guess. How's that for freedom lovers?"

"Who did it?" Patrick said through a clenched jaw.

"They say a man by the name of Brown. He and his sons."

Patrick turned pale. Roger was involved. "Mother of God."

"Sure as Hell, as much as both sides seem a-pushin' ta make this a drunken brawl, this is fixin' to be a real war. Captain Pate rode outa Platte City last week with two hundred dragoons on their way to find Old Brown, but he ambushed them down near Palmyra. The Battle of Black Jack, they're a-callin' it. The coward don't seem to know the white of surrender 'cause he shot a man under it. Musta took thirty prisoners and hid in the bushes. Word is Brown killed twenty down there, and now there's Missourians and cavalry outa Leavenworth all over the territory a-lookin' for 'im, burnin' and lootin' and shootin'. I'd be careful, Patrick. It's only a matter of time a-fore this spreads. They say Jim Lane's raisin' a whole army up north to march into Kansas." He hesitated, looked at a cup on the table. "Is uh, is Maria back yet?"

"No."

"I hear they're a-shuttin' down the river, friend. Turnin' anyone from the east back or…"

"Or what?"

"Or worse. Arresting them, maybe, I dunno."

Patrick stood, dazed. All his worries had come true. The world was coming to an end and he'd failed to keep out of it. Roger was an instrument of the apocalypse.

"And Jim Lane—well, let's just say he's a Free Stater to actually respect wieldin' a weapon. He ain't no tenderfoot Yankee out here a-learnin' how to shoot killin' jaybirds. He fought with us in Mexico, over at Buena Vista, whiles we was marchin' on the Sacramento. His Third Indiana was no joke. Yep, this here's a war, Paddy. And I don't think this one's got no articles of war. This here's a mob, on both sides. This is just terrorism."

Patrick shifted on his feet, not sure where to go or what to do, but knowing that the time had come. Kansas was personal now. "I— I've got to go."

"Go where? Ain't no safer place than right here, Paddy. Stay a while."

"No, I—I've got to find her. And Roger."

"Paddy," Joseph James stood, a look of concern on his face. "Ain't nuthin' you can do right now. Listen, bunker down for the summer. It'll all calm down in the fall, and if this winter's anything like the last..."

"Help me, then, Jimmy." He felt desperate now. If this man was going to warn him about dangers of which he already knew too well, he'd better just help. "Help me find them."

"Paddy, listen—"

"I've got to find her." Patrick turned and burst out the cabin.

"Paddy, don't. Paddy!" Joseph James called after him. "Paddy, don't go a-wanderin' out, Irishman! Kansas ain't safe no more! Paddy! Listen to me!"

Joseph James Hawkins watched as Patrick Dugan jogged down the trail back to his cabin, and smiled. His odd neighbor from across the sea had finally reached his limit. "Hey! Take my horse!" he shouted. Patrick took another few steps, slowed, and returned. "He ain't no Ninny but he'll do," he said, somewhat unconvincingly. "Ralph's his name." He watched as Patrick mounted and rode somewhat languidly, as if both horse and rider were lost deep in thought, in the direction of his farm. He stopped, pulling his rifle out of the saddle blanket, and propped it over his shoulder.

"You goin huntin', Paddy? I could use me some venison if you want someone to go with you."

Patrick didn't answer. He still seemed lost in thought, Ralph staring ahead as if it were the most familiar path he'd ever considered riding. Haze in the southern sky seemed to be rising from a Kansas that was burning. Patrick looked toward it, then toward his farm.

Joseph James knew that Patrick was finally realizing he had no choice but to choose. He couldn't just be a farmer. He knew that Patrick would turn the horse toward the south—toward Lawrence, Leavenworth, Pottawatomie, and Osawatomie; toward Black Jack Springs, where the first battle had already been waged, and toward Franklin, Fort Titus, Hickory Point, and the Marais de Cygnes, sites of battles yet to come—and he did. Spurring Ralph into a two-legged charge, he held the rifle held above his head. As Ralph's front hoofs came back to the dirt, Patrick let out a yell, a battle cry, a shriek not unlike the call of the giant bird, and galloped off into the south.

Joseph James took a bite of a tobacco plug, spat, and chewed. "Welcome to Kansas, Irishman," he said to himself. "You have finally arrived."

***

Patrick rode right into the Free State Hotel and asked the first person he saw, a boy younger than Roger, "Where is Old Brown?"

The boy smiled and chuckled. "Wouldn't you like to know?"

Patrick seized him by the throat and stuck the tip of a knife in his temple. "Why, yes, yes I would."

"I don't know where he is, mister! Out in the bush somewhere!"

"Where?"

"Anywhere! I don't know!"

Across the lobby, a man shouted, "A ruffian! We are invaded!" and general tumult writhed its way over the spacious lobby toward Patrick like ants from one food source to the next. It surrounded him before he had time to remove the knife from the boy's head.

"Let him go, you rogue."

"Tell me where Brown is." Patrick was almost surprised by how forcefully he'd said it, and by the size of the crowed to whom he'd said it.

"Half of the United State Army is looking for him," said a man that Patrick soon realized was a leader among these men. "If we did know we would not tell you. Are you friend or foe, Irishman?"

"Neither. I just want my brother back. I want my wife back."

"Put down that knife and perhaps we can help you. Keep it there and you're likely going to spend the next few days locked in a storage closet."

Patrick lowered the knife. "Who are you?"

"Samuel C. Pomeroy. And you?"

"Patrick Dugan. My brother Roger was with Brown the last few weeks. I'm afraid for his safety. And my wife was supposed to return from Boston weeks ago."

"I see your dilemma," replied Pomeroy. He had an oddly shaped head, and the way the hair curled from it, like an ocean wave, made it even odder. He looked like he may be thinner right now than he usually was. "It's one many of us share, and all blame can be placed on these Border Ruffians. They have disrupted our peaceful squatter existences."

"And now they must pay!" came a voice from the back.

"Indeed they must." Pomeroy shouted over his shoulder before turning back and lowering his voice. "Patrick, the Missourians have surrounded Lawrence with a series of forts. They're trying to starve us of supplies, stopping every wagon along the roads, looting and pillaging across the land, and also hunting for Brown's party. They seem to have more luck in the former than the latter. Your brother is every bit as safe as you are."

"I'm going to find him."

"And your wife has probably been turned back at one of the ferry landings. She is safer that way. As long as she stays on that side of the river, she's safe."

"I'm going to find her as well." Patrick sheathed his knife, turned, and began to leave.

"Mr. Dugan!" called Pomeroy, "stay here and fight with us. It is the best way to rescue your family."

"I'm no friend, nor foe," repeated Patrick, "I fight for myself and my family."

"It is a lonely battle you wage, Irishman."

Patrick hesitated. "On the contrary," he said. "Now, I'm going to tear down this fort at Franklin, as you call it, so. Anyone who would like to join me is welcome."

As it happened, the gathering at the hotel was discussing just such an operation, and all Captain Pomeroy had to do was give the volunteers—very young men and boys in two different companies, one from Lawrence and another from settlements along the Wakarusa, no more than twenty in sum—an affirmative nod for them to set out behind Patrick. They didn't follow him, per se, but kept an eye on him, something he did not do in return. Patrick rode south toward Blanton's Bridge, crossing the Wakarusa, and approached the little hamlet of Franklin from a northern ridge in the dead of night.

The Free Staters had split up by company, fanning out across the country in order to reconnoiter and avoid ambush. They were to regroup along this ridge by 2 a.m., and attack before dawn. They arrived with Patrick a little after the appointed hour. He hitched Ralph to a tree, unsheathed both knife and rifle and slowly descended the ridge.

One of the Lawrence men tried to stop him. "Irishman!" He scuttled behind the tall Patrick, hunched over in the dark. "What are you doing? We're supposed to rendezvous with the Wakarusa company!"

"Do it, so," he replied without looking back.

The man stood erect now, incredulous. "What are you doing?"

Patrick stopped and turned. "Looking for my wife and brother."

"But how are you, one man, going to do that?"

"I shall ask politely, and if they will not help, I shall shoot them." He turned and continued down the slope.

"You can't do this alone!"

Patrick paused as if considering this, but then continued, glancing at all the men. "I'm not alone."

The man sighed, looking frustrated. "Goddammit, let's go boys!"

The Lawrence party rose from their crouches and descended the ridge behind Patrick, and just as they came within the range of a Sharp's rifle, they came under scattered fire from the town.

"Get down, men!"

The Free Staters returned fire, lying in the tall grass just outside the little town. Patrick squatted behind a rock and assessed the situation. His dad had always told him not to fire blindly, but to use your eyes more than your trigger. "You can only shoot at a house for so long," he said. "The people just won't come out." It appeared both sides were doing just this: the Pro Slavery forces were firing at the darkness outside the town while the Free Staters were firing at the town. Langers, he thought, amazed at how fearless he felt inside.

Just then Patrick saw a man run from one house to another and fired at him. Missed. He saw another but wasn't loaded in time. Another, and another miss. Patrick was starting to have fun. It seemed they were firing nowhere near him, as he was off on the left flank by himself. It was like hunting rabbits. Big hairy rabbits with broad, stooped shoulders. Patrick looked around some more. The men—boys, really—on the Lawrence side were crawling this way and that through the grass. They'd be covered in chiggers and ticks in the morning and their wives—mothers, really—would not be happy. That was funny.

The Missourians ran this way and that between the buildings, totally disorganized, out of breath, and groggy. That was funny too. And Patrick started laughing. He looked around at what was becoming, at least to him, something truly absurd and comical, and started laughing again. And he laughed again after that.

Soon Patrick was laughing so hard both sides could hear him. It scared one or two of the Missourians a little, thinking perhaps a maniacal Indian ghost was out there in the grass somewhere. But others could see the lanky Irishman dressed like a farmer, his back against the rock, laughing uncontrollably while he loaded and fired his rifle now and then into the town.

Then, without warning, a cannon was fired from behind the bulwarks of the town. It had been packed with nails and, whistling eerily, these scattered about the prairie, digging into the soil and bending the grass like wind.

"Ohhh-ho-ho-ho-ho!" Patrick yelled, still laughing. "Yes! Yes! Do it again, so!"

A few moments later they fired it again, and Patrick was laughing so hard now he was crying, stomping his feet on the ground, his long bent legs tucked close to him. He looked like an ant, all joins and appendages twitching sporadically, almost frantically. "Yes! Yes!" he shouted. "Shoot the cannon, you apes! Shoot us all, you dumb langers! Ha ha ha ha ha!"

***

The Wakarusa Company had become lost along the Wakarusa on its way to Franklin and, having heard the gunfire in the distance, were now descending on the town. They heard Patrick laughing, and they thought it may be a madman. "Sounds Irish," said one, "but someone that crazy has got to be a Ruffian." They decided to circumnavigate the town and loot it rather than join a confused fight and potentially harm, or be harmed by, their comrades. Many of the Missourians withdrew at this point, shutting themselves in their homes or retreating to the south or east; it was getting light out and nobody really wanted to get hurt. The Free Staters looted all the weaponry and foodstuffs they could. They weren't able to commandeer the cannon, though. They had forgotten Old Sacramento may be stored at Franklin and didn't bring anything to carry it back to Lawrence with. They left it in the street, scratching their heads.

***

And all the while Patrick laughed. He laughed, watching his compatriots try and figure out the cannon dilemma. He laughed, watching them try to find their horses in the grass as they yawned, stretched, and swatted the waking mosquitoes in the breaking light of dawn. He laughed, as they mounted and rode northward, disappointed their little excursion wasn't more productive. Patrick laughed as he stood, wiped his face, and found Ralph. He laughed at the fact a horse was named "Ralph," and he chuckled all the way back to the Hawkins farm.

Kansas wasn't the end of the world. It was dangerous, yes, but not yet apocalyptic. It was a playground game invented by stubborn, stupid boys with too many printing presses, rifles, and knives on their hands.

***

Patrick wasn't laughing anymore as he arrived on his farm after having returned Ralph. Kansas was still dangerous and Roger and Maria were still out there somewhere, caught up in the tumult of the world. As he approached the cabin, he happened to look skyward, and against the backdrop of brilliant blue he saw the tiniest wisp of smoke rise from the chimney, almost as if it were soot whipped up by a breeze and sent twirling into the sky. But it wasn't soot, definitely. It was smoke. Someone had used the stove since he left. Someone had been here.

Just then, the jayhawk alighted on the roof of the cabin and blinked at Patrick.

As he always did, Patrick stopped everything he was doing when he saw it, almost as if it transfixed him. "Get the hell out of here," he said. "You heard me! Go on! Shoo! Shoo, you filthy pigeon! Get off of my cabin!" He waved his arms above his head, and the bird screeched, then flew away.

Patrick decided he would knock on the door like a stranger and see if anyone would answer. He heard movement inside when he did, and knocked again.

"Who is it?" He heard Roger's voice.

"Roger? It's me!" Patrick swung the door open, but Roger was nowhere to be found. "Roger? Roger! Where are you, boy?"

Then heard and saw his little brother cowering in a dark corner, a rifle in his hand.

"Roger, Roger I'm so glad you're alive! Come here."

Like a trapped animal, Roger flinched.

Patrick saw a strange, listless glistening in his eyes. He looked scrawny and sweaty. "I believe you're ill, son. Come, let's get you to bed."

"They'll be back, Paddy. They'll be back."

"Who? Who's been here?"

"The mail. They'll bring the mail back, Paddy. The *Sovereign* and the letter. They know about it. They know all about us."

"What? You mean the paperboy's come?"

"The paperboy."

Roger was still squatting in the corner, shaking a little. The poor boy was delirious with fever. It reminded him of Roger as a younger boy, sick and afraid on the boat from Ireland, and he was overcome with compassion for him. Tears welled in his eyes.

"The paperboy, the editor, the lieutenant, the post-master, the…"

"You mean Kelley? Bob Kelley's been here?"

"And a bird. A demon, Paddy, a demon."

"All newspapermen in Kansas are demons."

"But, yes—I mean, no—a bird, Paddy, a giant bird. A real bird, a giant winged demon."

"You saw it?"

"Yes."

"Don't be afraid of it, boy. Don't follow it, and don't be afraid of it. It's just like any other bird."

"They'll be back, Paddy."

"Yes, I'm sure they will. Now let's get you to bed."

Sweating, Roger gave the rifle to his brother with only a small hesitation. Patrick caressed him on the way to bed. He could feel the little boy left behind in Roger's arms, the baby in the flappy, spongy skin of his cheek. That little boy who attacked the rooster, who followed his brother fishing, who sat in the living room playing with three broken toy soldiers would always be there, no matter how many big thoughts he had, big dreams he pursued, or big people he befriended. Roger would always be Roger.

Patrick sat with him, feeding him sips of water, until a knock came at the door.

"Who is it?"

"It's Robert Kelley from Atchison, Mr. Dugan. I've come to deliver your mail."

***

It could be the bird in disguise, thought Patrick. Or it could indeed be Kelley, for any number of reasons. Maybe he knows that I know that he knows Butler should have hanged last August. Maybe he knows I took part in this skirmish south of Lawrence last night. Maybe he knows my wife is in Boston (if she is) writing letters to Kansas (if she is). Maybe he knows Roger was with Brown during the Pottawatomie murders, and that Roger is either here now or once lived here. Maybe he knows I'm Irish, or Catholic, or the son of an

Irish rebel, or that I have Free State sympathies, or all of the above. Maybe he wants to be sure I don't participate in any Free State politics, like the constitutional convention in Topeka scheduled for next month. Maybe he wants me to renew my subscription to the *Sovereign*. Or maybe he just has mail for me.

"Who is it?"

"Mr. Dugan, it's Robert S. Kelley, the Postmaster in Atchison. I have a letter for you."

"I'll retrieve it in town tomorrow."

"I'm afraid that won't do."

"Can you slip it under the door, then?"

"I'm afraid I must decline that suggestion, as well, Mr. Dugan. I really must deliver this letter with a few words from myself, if you'll be so kind as to appease me."

Patrick opened the door, the rifle still in his hand, half-expecting it to be the jayhawk again. But it was Kelley. He looked even more like a mouse than he did that portentous August day that now seemed so long ago. His nose and moustache twitched a little as his lips curled around his yellow teeth in a strange attempt at smiling.

"May I come in, Mr. Dugan?"

"You have mail for me?"

"I do." Kelley produced a handful of letters from inside his overcoat, but pulled them away as Patrick attempted to grasp them. "Ah, ah, ah. I'm afraid I must deliver them with some context. May I come in?"

"Yes, but don't consider it an invitation." Patrick opened the door wide enough for Kelley to barely slip in.

"Now, now, Mr. Dugan," Kelley began as he removed his hat and coat, "that doesn't result from some Irish superstition, does it?"

"Why, yes. It certainly does, like."

"I understand. I consider myself an uninvited and perhaps unwelcome guest, Mr. Dugan." He sat without being asked, and Patrick remained standing.

"Your editorials, Mr. Kelley, and those of Mr. Stringfellow, have a way of making an Irishman from Boston a little nervous in Atchison County. I'm not in the habit of making visitors feel unwelcomed, but I must say, it is I who feel I am an unwelcomed guest in your town."

"Ah, yes." Bob Kelley rubbed his just-shaven face with his hands. "Mr. Dugan, it seems to me you're the finest your nation has to offer, and thus the finest my nation has to welcome to its shores.

My days in Kansas have—as I'm sure you will understand—shall we say, enlightened me, if you will, to the fact that immigrants such as you—Free State though they may be, if pushed on the matter—are not a threat to me." He had stuttered and chopped his way through this, but now said clearly, "We have no bone to pick with you, Mr. Dugan, my Southern friends and I."

"But Mr. Kelley, the *Squatter Sov*—"

"Yes, the *Sovereign*. Mr. Dugan, have you ever written?" He stood and began to pace. "I mean, you read, I see." He motioned to the reading materials scattered about the cabin. "But do you write at all, perchance?"

"At times." He paused. "It's been some time."

"Well, it's a curious thing, writing," Kelley continued pacing. "Especially writing for, or editing, something that is actually read. You see, at first you—at least, I did—feel as if nobody would ever really read what I wrote, as if it were some sort of diary. Or—" He looked down at his boots and sighed, "—a letter to your wife." He sighed again. "The fact that I could use this machine, this printing press, and distribute my words, and those of my friends and colleagues, didn't ever mean I could impress upon them to read it, nonetheless be in any way persuaded by it."

Patrick was incredulous. "But that was clearly your intent."

"Of course!" Kelley agreed. "Yes, of course it was! But intent, you know, is so much more often the father of nothing than the father of something."

There was a pause Patrick did not expect. He filled it with, "Yes, I suppose so."

"Mr. Dugan—may I call you Patrick?"

"Yes, I suppose so," he replied, though he very much regretted the familiarity.

"Patrick, I will be honest with you. There is a sort of Northerner that is repulsive to me. There is an aspect of life in the North that is to me, well, inhumane. It is as if a man were nothing but the clothes on his back, the walls about his person, the ceiling that stands between him and the elements. Man is a thing to be pampered and primped, a pretty and pompous pussycat that struts about his stage like a goddamned show-horse." An agitation was showing through, and he covered it again. "It's either that or you're neglected like an ass left in the woods. Dignity in the North is far more dehumanizing than slavery, Mr. Dugan. Few people are free in a place like Boston. I'm sure, as an Irishman, you—"

Again, there was a pause that Patrick did not expect, but this time he didn't know what to say. Was he supposed to continue Robert Kelley's sentence, as if it were a bucket they passed along a line of men in order to bail out the story?

"—well, this, Patrick, is the sort of man that I do not want in Kansas. I don't want him on the face of the earth, in fact, if I am to be perfectly frank. The sort of man that makes another man—another white man at that, who is supposed to be protected by the powers of the Constitution itself!—feel as if he were an ass laboring in the yard. But I have no desire to take up arms against my fellow man. I do not have the constitution for it. I'm a writer, not a soldier. They asked me to command the Guards, you know, but I turned them down. I have a paper to write, and the pen is mightier than the sword, I told them. The *Sovereign* is a vehicle for preventing this sort of Northern man from settling Kansas and determining the future of the Union."

Another pause, one that Patrick did expect this time.

"Not a man like you." And with that, Robert Kelley handed Patrick the letters.

They were from Maria. All of them had been opened.

XXVI

Maria spent the spring and early part of the summer reading. She spent her days at the Boston Public Library, sitting in the reading room chair that Patrick had used when he found the *Journals of Lewis & Clark* over two years ago. She read a smattering of verse and prose, but mostly she read the papers. She read every article on Kansas—and there were many—that she could get her hands on. From the vehemently Free State editorials in Horace Greeley's *New York Tribune* to the Pro Slavery rants in the *Charleston Mercury*, Maria wanted desperately to know what was happening in Kansas. And she wasn't alone.

The national conversation in the summer of 1856 was dominated by the "Kansas Question," the "Kansas Crisis," and as Greeley finally dubbed it later in the summer, "Bleeding Kansas." So taken with the politics and lifestyle of the Kansas pioneers was the nation, that from time to time Maria even found the *Sovereign* on the long, shiny walnut periodical room tables of the library. She held these issues to her breast as if they were love letters from Patrick, letters affirming and promising his continued sobriety, the very letter she waited for. She knew that if he was sober, Patrick would be reading the *Sovereign*, too. In some strange way this meant they were close to each other, no matter the difference between Atchison and Boston. Sharing reading material is second only to sharing life itself.

Maria was more obsessed with Kansas that June than Patrick had ever been or ever could be. She was something of a minor celebrity in her neighborhood, and her family asked her about it constantly. She told them about Roger, of course, and when asked about Patrick she was vague, simply because she knew people wouldn't hear what they wanted to.

"I knew that husband of yours had no spine for such a thing," said her mother. "Either that or he's on the drink all the time."

That she was right in both statements was too much for Maria. She'd storm off to the library in a huff, and seeing those stout legs storm off like that made even her mother quiet.

What she read in the papers was terrifying. Ironically, the murders at Pottawatomie Creek weren't covered as much as they might have been, the editors preferring to dwell on the bloody drama between Congressman Brooks and Senator Sumner. But thereafter reports of marauders, mass murders, pillaging, and riots filled the columns of America's news. Maria knew from the sheer inconsistency of numbers that they couldn't all be true: how could John Brown lead a force of two-thousand to kill two hundred and fifty women and children in Franklin, when there weren't two thousand people in Kansas or two hundred and fifty people in Franklin? But she also knew that all Patrick's fears were becoming reality. She must go to him.

Still, she waited for his letter. She had to. He owed her that much.

When it finally arrived, a few days after the Fourth of July, she was reading papers in the library, and her little sister Kathy ran it to her, breathing heavily. "From Paddy," she said, and then stood there.

But Maria turned to the paper, trying to pretend it was of more interest, knowing she could never fool her sister. "The Army has dispersed the Free State legislature in Topeka," Maria said, almost as if she were addressing the table. "They squashed a democratic movement on Independence Day. Can you believe that?"

Still out of breath, dumbfounded, Kathy looked at her big sister with large, brown, fawn-like eyes.

"The Governor isn't even a permanent…" Maria said, because Wilson Shannon had resigned amid the growing chaos and his replacement hadn't yet arrived. The eminently Pro Slavery Lieutenant Governor David Woodson was in charge and intended to make his mark. All he had to do was deputize and ignore the rest.

"Maria!" Kathy shouted, immediately covering her mouth and looking about her. Her voice had echoed off the mahogany and marble and nearly twenty people stared disapprovingly at her.

"Shhh!" admonished the librarian from his courtroom-like desk.

"Maria!" Kathy whispered.

"I know, I know. Come, let's read it outside, so."

Standing in the glow of the sunlight that was dispersed by the humidity of the sea so that it appeared to drip from the buildings and clothing of the passersby, Maria read the letter, more of a note, really, and let it fall to her hips.

Kathy looked up at her and the expression Maria wore on her face would be forever imprinted on her memory and imagination. So this is love, she thought. "Maria?"

"I shall miss you so much." Maria began to cry.

Kathy tugged on her dress and hugged her big sister. She missed embracing the thighs she knew so well, but the hips and abdomen, to which she had grown in two years, were becoming just as familiar. "Maria."

"I can't do it. I can't go back there."

"Maria!"

"I know, I know. But I love you, Kathy. And Mamma."

"Oh, Maria."

"You'll come join me, won't you?" She peeled the girl off her leg so she could exact her promise. "You'll make sure Mamma follows through and when things calm down you'll emigrate, too? Keep that woman honest, Kathy. Keep her on her toes, won't you?"

"Maria!"

"Yes, I know you will. I know you will." She pulled Kathy tight again against her. "And I know one day we shall all be in Kansas, neighbors, all of us. All this will be behind us, Kathy. I know it will."

Kathy smiled and buried her face in her sister's dress. The light and smell of the sea came through the fabric, but somewhere the girl could smell the Missouri River and saturated topsoil, hear the frogs and bugs, and feel the Kansas sun on her skin. "Oh, Maria…"

***

On the train to St. Louis, Maria sat next to Abigail, a woman born the same day she was, and Abigail's son was born on the first day of the year, the same day Maria miscarried. This child was huge. Simply a monster. How birthing it didn't kill the slight Abigail was a mystery.

Abigail's arms told the tale of the boy's size every bit as the marks on her belly probably did; they were also huge. Her biceps resembled Maria's thighs in that they were disproportionately large on her frame, and she did a wonderful job of hiding them with bulbous sleeves on her blouses, as they were, admittedly, somewhat indecorous.

Everything else about Abigail was discreet and refined, but her arms evidenced that she could adapt to heavy situations that befell her in life.

And was she going to need it! This is what Maria thought as the train finally left what may be considered the east and began its journey through the western states on its way to Missouri and the frontier.

Abigail was on her way to Kansas, just like Maria, to meet her husband. He'd staked a claim in southern Kansas, down the Marais des Cygnes from Osawatomie. Abigail had gotten pregnant just before he left, so her husband had never met his son.

"He'll be quite delighted," she told Maria. "He has desired a son for quite some time now."

"Yes, so has Paddy."

"Is that your husband?"

Maria smiled. "Why, yes, yes, Patrick is my husband."

Abigail chuckled, shifting her son on her lap. "You seem almost surprised."

"Well, I returned to Boston to think on it some."

"Ha! There is a little Kansas in your speech, Maria. You know, you are the first Kansan I have met!"

"Why, yes, I suppose so. I am a Kansan."

"We need to get away to think at times, I suppose, Maria. There's no harm in that."

"No, I don't reckon so." They smiled at each other. "Patrick had been drinking too much, you see."

"Ah, yes, my husband tells me there is too much 'mash' in Kansas, but that it's the Southerners who over-indulge in it. But then, I do suppose—"

"Yes?"

"Never mind."

"Well, it's not something Paddy has touched often. Not until we moved to Kansas and his little brother, well, it's rather involved, you see..."

"I do. Kansas is a tumultuous place."

"Yes, so."

"That's why I am so excited! Life in Boston is a dreadful bore!"

Abigail was young. Maria could see it. She was not only young in age, but young in heart and mind and soul. Kansas was going to be difficult for her, every bit as difficult as birthing a giant baby, perhaps even more difficult. If that heart, mind, and soul could grow stronger like her biceps, she'd be fine. Otherwise, Kansas would eat her alive.

"Yes, Kansas can be exciting," Maria said. "In good ways and in bad. It can also be tedious. Farm life is quite repetitive."

"Oh, I don't mind that anymore." Abigail glanced down at her baby. "I suppose by that I mean that I'm accustomed to it."

"Mothering is difficult."

"Yes, it is." A smile played across the girl's face. "How many children do you and Patrick have?"

Maria's smile vanished. "Well, we lost ours."

"Oh! Please forgive me. I'm so sorry."

"You didn't know, Abigail. And we will have others, I'm quite sure, God willing. I raised my sister much as a mother would. That's how I understand your . . . plight."

"Yes." Abigail chuckled. "It can be rather difficult. I cannot imagine how those difficulties are compounded in a place like the frontier."

"You shall soon find out, my girl!"

"Yes, I suppose I shall!"

***

On the steamer from St. Louis, Maria sat next to a free black woman by the name of Myralee. Myralee (or Ms. M, as her friends called her) had been granted her freedom as a child in Alabama and soon found herself in Missouri. She was taking her two children back to their home in the western part of the state after a visit to Alabama to see her father, who was still alive, and still enslaved, by the same man who released her.

"'N jes where'n God's creation are you headin' off ta, miss?"

"Kansas."

"Aw, Lawd! You don't say. You mussa be perdy unhappy where you done come from!"

Maria smiled "I s'pose so, yes, Ms. M. Originally I'm from Ireland—"

"You don't say!" Myralee elbowed her and laughed.

"That's obvious, I know." She laughed. "Well, in Ireland we were starving. So we came to America. But there are millions of us. There's little opportunity in the East for us. We aren't as welcome as we'd like, so. In fact, they sometimes call us—oh, never mind what they say."

"Oh, I done knowed they a-called ya 'white niggers'."

"Yes, yes, they do."

"But trus' me, Maria, ain't no such thing. Only a nigger can be a nigger. Trus' me. Ain't nothing in alla God's s creation like a nigger, and only we's knowd that."

"I'm sure that's true."

Myralee's face turned out to the trees on the bank, slowly gliding by. "But we's also know we don't hold no monopoly on suffering, Miss Maria. Whatever you and your people done gone through, well, I'm sure it weren't no walk in the park."

"No, certainly not."

Myralee's destination soon sallied its way up alongside the vessel, and they parted with barely a farewell, given that Myralee's attention was on her children and luggage. But Maria would never forget her. What was a forgettable day of small talk with an Irish woman to Ms. M was an unforgettable experience for Maria.

Somehow, Patrick had it all wrong—the world wasn't coming to an end in Kansas, it was being reborn. It was a place of suffering, of fear and panic and derision, but this suffering was a necessary precursor to a resulting grace. As long as freedom won the day, all the suffering would be worth it. There would be no niggers or white niggers in Kansas. In Kansas, American democracy would find its redemption.

***

As soon as the steamer alighted at Weston, just thirty miles downriver from Atchison, Maria knew there was trouble. She could hear the shuffling of boots and raised voices on the deck above her, and knew a group of men had boarded that couldn't be passengers. The boot heels she heard thumping against the floor boards were not those of travelers who anticipated a journey on a steamship; these were work-boots, the boots of farmers and soldiers, the boots of those who sometimes slept in boots and needed them all day, all year round. These were the boots of frontiersmen, and the sound of them on wooden planks reminded her of Patrick.

And there was only one reason a bunch of Missouri farmers would board a ship at Weston in July of 1856—to rid it of its Northern cargo. These men, ostensibly, were looking for her. And there was no sense in fighting them. She gathered her things and headed for the deck, and was accosted by a man on the stairs.

"Where're you off ta, Missy?"

"My ticket is to Atchison, K.T. My husband and I squatted there two summers ago."

"Yer a fur piece from Atchison yit. Why're you takin' yer luggage up?"

"I'm assuming I won't be allowed to continue past Weston?"

"Now why would you think that?"

"I'm Irish. I'm coming from Boston."

"And?"

"And I don't expect you'll want me getting to Kansas so easily as that."

"And why would that be?"

"You assume, correctly, that I will vote Free State, and you'll disallow my rights by making me deboard."

"Why now, you sure know a lot about us, then don't you?"

Maria thought for a moment. She realized that while she knew what the papers told her, and that she knew Del and the Hawkinses, that didn't necessarily mean she always knew the intent of Missourians, or Southerners, or anyone, for that matter.

"Well, do I or don't I?"

"Who's yer husband and why ain't he with you?"

"That's irrelevant."

"Irele-what?"

"It doesn't matter."

"Well, now, if you wanna git to Kansas, it does."

"You may cease interrogating this lady," called a voice from further up the stairs. "I shall take her with me."

Before she knew it, Maria was off the steamer and walking along the main street in Weston with a strange, well-dressed, well-spoken man from Chicago. He explained he was an agent of the National Kansas Committee, and he'd been sent to the river to aid Northerners as they were denied passage to the Territory by roving bands of armed Missourians. That he would help them return home unharmed was his official purpose, anyway, and the people of Weston and Leavenworth stopped short of hanging him with this explanation as their reason. But really, he was here to offer options. "Adam Blankenship," he said, extending a hand to her. "Pleased to meet you, Miss...?"

"Dugan. Mrs. Patrick Dugan. I'm pleased to meet you too. It pains me to be so close to home and unable to get there."

He smiled. "Ah! You are the first person I've met who refers to the territory as 'home.' It's a very big continent, Mrs. Dugan—"

"Please, call me Maria."

"Maria, it's a very big continent. You don't expect the Missourians can guard all the West from North to South, do you?"

"No, of course not. But overland is—"

"Terribly difficult, I know." Blankenship was possibly the best-groomed, cleanest man she had ever met. His sharp nose and facial features seemed to complement it. "But worse is being prevented from executing your inalienable rights as proclaimed by God and government." He smiled confidently. "If you want to get to Atchison, Maria, I can arrange it."

"How?"

"There are massive overland emigrations through Iowa and Nebraska, by way of Illinois, Indiana, and the like. As we speak, General Lane is on his way through Iowa with thousands of settlers. You can join them."

"James Lane?"

"Of course. The one and only."

"Yes, I read about this in the papers. His 'Army of the North'."

"Ha! Yes, well, I believe that to be a bit dramatic, but obliquely accurate in a form. They are settlers. But their horses labor under more rifles and knives than hoes and shovels, shall we say."

Maria liked him. She liked his humor, and he had a genuine smile that contorted his entire face in a pleasant way. He looked older than what were likely his years, and his skin was rougher than most Chicagoans. "When do I have to decide?"

"By the morning. I will find a room for you for the night, but if you want to join the Army, as it were, we leave at dawn by stagecoach. You'll have to come with me to Platte City, where I'm staying. Tomorrow, we'll follow the river up to Nebraska with a family I took off a steamer a few days ago, and you will rendezvous with an attaché of Lane's at Nebraska City. You'll have to make your way from the border to there yourself; I can only escort you through Missouri."

Maria pursed her lips; it was a lot of traveling.

"You don't have to decide until sunrise. Perhaps if you wait, circumstances will decide for you. I've learned that is the way of the West."

She looked at him and stopped walking.

He stopped, and the two stood facing each other in the streets of Weston. A boy of about fifteen years passed by them, staring, and they waited for him to pass. They had to wait another moment before resuming their conversation, as the boy continued staring at them from an uncomfortably close distance. It seemed he wanted to eavesdrop on their conversation. Maria noted his features; his complexion was dark, with a face, especially in the corners of the eyes, that seemed to droop down somewhat, and his hair parted on one the side of his head and was combed over a rather egg-shaped skull. Another boy, several years younger, ran up to him and spoke. They were definitely brothers, though the younger one's eyes turned up, he was fairer, and his hair swept down over his rather protruded forehead, rather than up and over, like his older sibling.

Maria continued, "You look like you've spent time in the West."

"Ha! Because I'm leathery and wrinkled? Why, yes, yes I have. I marched to Mexico in '46, then went for broke (then just broke) in California in '49. I even spent a term in a municipal office in rural Illinois a few years after that, and traveled to Kansas two or three times trying to find a way to be involved without suffering a winter there. But I do think it was politics that took its toll on my face, not the travel."

Maria smiled. "I'll go."

"Excellent! Very good, very good!" Blankenship shook her hands and then offered her his elbow. "Shall we dine, then, Mrs. Dugan?"

"Why, yes, yes, we shall."

XXVII

Maria arrived early to the small lobby of the boarding house on Main Street in Platte City and waited for Blankenship. It had been so long since she'd been out to supper with a man, she had no idea if she was dressed appropriately or not. She didn't have much choice in the matter, for all she brought to Kansas were work clothes and her Sunday dress, there being little need for anything in between. Now, she chose her Sunday dress, thinking it more appropriate for the lady to be overdressed than the man. As long as he didn't show up in a tuxedo—and she doubted such a thing existed between St. Louis and San Francisco—she'd be okay.

He showed up in a tuxedo.

"I'm not quite sure why I even brought this," he said, noting her reaction to it. "But I'm very happy to have the opportunity to wear it." He offered her his arm. It was a familiar gesture already, and quite comfortably received.

"I'm afraid this is all I have," she said. "But you're the only person in hundreds of miles that could upstage me." Maria liked her Sunday dress. She grew tired of it in Boston, wearing it every week, but in the West she knew it was her sole connection to refinement. Sometimes at night, during that first winter in Kansas, she'd lie in bed shivering, thinking she'd cuddle with it.

"You look stunning, Maria. A man like me must dress well to look better, but a woman as pretty as you mustn't do anything to detract from her natural beauty. Your dress complements you perfectly. Let me see," he stopped and turned toward her, and with her arm still anchored in his, this forced her to face him. "Turn around." Somewhat abashed, she twirled for him. "Yes, indeed, just as I suspected. The color accents your hair, skin, and eyes quite well. That pinwheel blue and the orange-ish tint to everything about your—about you. You see," he continued, as they walked into the dining room, "people notice my suit, but the dress helps them notice you, not it." He gestured. "By the window?"

Blankenship pulled out her chair from a table next to one of the windows that looked out to the west and the Platte River as it meandered its way through the trees en route to the Missouri. The river was swollen and made the woods look like they were drowning in places. Like Atchison, Platte City seemed to be built on a slope that gradually led to the water. Always the water. Always toward the sea.

"I fear we may fall out the window into the river," Maria said, only half in joke. "Is it always this close to the main street?"

"Apparently not. The locals say it is flooded this year."

"The news in the East has not written enough about the weather. Has it been a wet season?"

"I have nothing to compare it with, my dear Maria! The Missouri is high, they say, but the Platte seems to be a bit of a problem. It floods easily. The soil is so rich here. I'm afraid that it seems to me the Missourians already have the best farmland on the continent."

"Yes, you can smell it."

Blankenship had set his napkin in his lap and his hands were returning to the table, but froze at this. His nostrils twitched, he froze again, and then began to laugh. And he laughed again.

Maria laughed. "What? What are you laughing at?"

Soon they were both laughing so much that the waiter, who had strode halfway across the dining room floor, returned to the kitchen.

"I fear you may be burned at the stake for saying such a thing."

Maria was not as amused at this as Blankenship thought she may be.

"I apologize if that offended you."

"No, it didn't." She smiled. "You aren't the first person to think that of someone in my family."

"Oh, my, has your family been in New England that long?"

"Oh, no, I am from Ireland myself. But, you see, in Ireland, certain . . . abilities . . . are lauded, not persecuted."

The waiter arrived at the table as Blankenship's eyes and mouth hung open. He managed to order for them. "Do tell! Do tell!" he said as a little girl might, nearly bouncing in his seat.

"Tell what?" She felt coy, and this was written all over her face.

"These abilities of which you speak. I must know!"

The waiter brought bread and butter, and Maria was still smiling coyly, her glances at Blankenship, teasing along his enthusiasm all the more. "My family—the women in my family—are able to do certain things that many people can't. Or, they don't know they can. I've never decided which. I've spent much of my life trying to pretend I don't."

Just as Blankenship's mouth opened to ask his question again, he saw a fork on the table move. Just an inch or so to one side. He looked at Maria, who was now smiling more coyly than ever. She was gorgeous. He looked down again at the fork. It moved to the other side, and her smile disappeared.

"Waiter! May I have some more water, please?" She glanced over at her fellow diner, and the glass of water by her hand quickly emptied itself of its water.

"You are the most beautiful woman in the world," said Adam Blankenship

Later that night, after a moonlit stroll along the swollen banks of the Platte, Blankenship stood with Maria outside the door to her room. She had been teasing him all the way about his being so overdressed; that if anyone encountered them along the gravel pathway that dipped in and out of the turbid puddles that reeked of catfish and sturgeon, they would have no choice but to consider them ghosts, apparitions from the North or even Europe; and, given this ghostly element to their appearance, they were safe, because no Missourian she had ever met would dismiss a ghost.

"You protect me by how unlikely your existence is," she said. "They would, like St. Thomas did Christ, need to touch you to believe you are real." She smiled.

"A Missourian's hand on this lapel? I think not!"

"Yes, well, it is a very nice lapel." She reached out and lightly slid her fingers along Blankenship's breast, down to his waist. The lines in his suit were striking. They fit his height so very well. And the fabric framed his bearded, dark face perfectly. For a man who had been to Mexico, California, and Missouri, he either had or was a top tailor himself.

"You are an anathema," she continued, her fingers still lingering where they'd come to rest. "In so many ways, you just don't belong."

"In more ways than you realize," he said, gently and politely moving her hand away.

Maria gave an audible sigh and slumped forward into his chest, breathing deeply once her nostrils touched him. She'd wanted to do this almost all night, almost ever since she met him. She'd resisted, repressed even, this urge, almost ashamed of it. When the Missourians boarded the steamer at Weston, she felt, as she usually did, defiant and confident. But once he intervened, she felt more compliant and insecure. Never in her life had she felt helpless. Never. Not during starvation in Ireland, oppression in Boston, and not even when the two came together in Kansas. But a man like Adam Blankenship made her feel the slightest bit helpless, because she knew she couldn't control how she felt for him.

She looked up. "Kiss me."

"No," he replied.

"Why not?"

"You are married, Maria, and we have a long journey tomorrow. A journey to reunite you with him."

All at once, a cascade of horror swept over Maria, draining her face of blood.

"Don't faint," he said. "Come, let's get you to your room."

"No! No!" She stepped back and wiped her face, straightened her hair and dress. "I am quite capable of that myself, thank you, Mr. Blankenship."

"Oh, Maria—"

"Mr.—Adam, I'm sorry. I apologize for my actions. I fear you must see me as horribly forward, perhaps even loose, but let me assure you…"

"There's no need, Maria, no need at all."

"I love my husband and have never—will never—betray him. I just don't know what came over me." She looked down, then back at him, and said conclusively, "You are a very charming man, Adam Blankenship."

"I am at ease with women, Maria." He smiled. "But never covetous." He had an implacable face as he said this, and she studied it a moment.

"I believe I understand."

"I'm quite sure you do. Now, Maria, we have a long day tomorrow. We must get some rest."

Maria couldn't sleep that night. She was worried about the journey, about Patrick and Roger, her sisters and mother, and herself. Perhaps her time away from Patrick had changed her. Perhaps their time in Atchison had changed them. It just wasn't like her to feel this way toward a man, even Patrick. For the first time in her life, she felt an undeniable urge to masturbate. And for the first time in her life, she did, and it was good, the silkiness, the moistness. She felt wickedly vulnerable throughout, fearing that at any moment her room may be raided by hairy-backed Missourians smelling of tobacco and they would carry her off to a filthy shack in the woods and rape her. The wind outside seemed to threaten entry, and all around her were enemies.

And for the first time in her life, Maria had an orgasm, thinking in the last few seconds not of Adam or the Missourians, but of Patrick standing tall in a doorway, a rifle in one hand and a dead chicken in another.

When she was done she laughed at this.

And then she cried.

She laughed because the mysteries of her psyche were really quite ridiculous, but cried because tomorrow, at sunrise, all the realities of her life were to fall upon her once again. There would be no more pretending with this man that she was a lady. There would only be the harsh truth that she was a pioneer.

***

They were almost five miles outside Platte City when Adam finally introduced Maria to the other pioneers. Though they were from Iowa, they had been too anxious to wait to rendezvous with Lane's Army and had attempted to cross alone. Turned back by armed farmers in the extreme northwest of Missouri, they eventually found Blankenship in Platte City and had waited patiently for four days for an individual to accompany them. They were a family of four with two small children, one boy and one girl, and Michael, the father, had spent his short career in newspapers before deciding to immigrate to Kansas.

"In order to help determine the future of the world," Michael said to Maria as they began their conversation in the sunny, chilly morning. "And restore democracy to the continent. And you? What brings an Irish lady all this way?"

Maria smiled. "Many things, I suppose. Food. Shelter. Security. Freedom."

"Aha! All the goods that are lacking in Kansas, I believe!"

"Yes." Maria chuckled. "That is a source of frustration for my husband and me both."

"And your brother-in-law?" interjected Mrs. Ross, Isabel. "Does he share your motives and opinions regarding the Kansas Question?"

It was the first time, in verbal conversation, that Maria had heard her home referred to in such a way. Seeing it in print in the Boston Library's periodicals room seemed divorced, almost de-realized from what was happening to her and Patrick and Roger, Del and Joseph James, Oliver John and Sarah Sally. The papers were one thing, people quite another, and somehow she'd forgotten that behind every written word there was a man. A man responsible for the letters being strung together, the words being hitched into sentences, the sentences into paragraphs, the paragraphs into columns, the columns with lithographs and sketches into "news." And here, on this strangely cold July morning on this stagecoach full of splinters and

loaded down with the Ross's guns and knives, she had met one of
those men. One of the men who helped turn Kansas into a question,
a crisis, an affair. One of the men who helped Kansas bleed.

"No, Roger is a young man. An idealistic young man from an
idealistic family, and he would sooner pick up a Sharps rifle than a
shovel or plow any day."

The Rosses smiled at each other, and Maria had a distinct
impression that they were relieved, that upon meeting their first
Kansan they were disappointed in her simple intents, her apolitical
and pragmatic reasons for living in the territory, and they were happy
to hear that the people Mr. Ross had been writing about in his small
Iowa publication were real.

"Excellent," said Michael Ross. "There are still newsworthy
people in Kansas!"

"Yes, there are," replied Maria without expression.

"Well, General Lane is bringing a veritable army of news with
him to the territory, Mrs. Dugan. I believe the summer of 1856 will
be remembered in the history books."

"You are probably correct."

"I know I am! I knew it! You see, Isabel, we came at the right
time. I told you so. Many newsmen," he said, turning back to Maria,
"prefer to report the news from afar. But not me. No, sir. I want to
be right in the thick of it. Ah! I can feel it now. The action! The
drama!"

Michael Ross stared off into the distance toward the western
horizon. In his brow and nose he reminded Maria of Dr.
Stringfellow, particularly the day he came and saw her bleeding,
pronounced her half dead, then left.

Beyond the rolling hills and established farms there was a river,
and on the other side of the river was their future. All of them. The
Dugans and Hawkinses, the Rosses and Stringfellows, even Adam
Blankenship and the untold millions who would come one day. And
so far it was only men like Mr. Ross, Dr. Stringfellow, and Roger
determining that collective future.

It was time for people like Patrick to have their say. If only they
would speak up.

***

As they left Weston, Blankenship noticed a young man following them on horseback. He quickly realized this man was actually two boys on one horse, and they seemed familiar.

"Remember our admirers on the street in Weston?" Blankenship asked Maria, who sat beside him. "I believe they are behind us."

Maria turned furtively and looked. Just as she did, the younger boy peered over the shoulder of the older, and she could see the same contrasting directions of their eyes. "Yes, that's them."

"They're watching to see if we make a turn for Kansas."

"We won't, will we?"

"Not for days. We're heading all the way up to Nebraska Territory before we even cross the river. I believe we will be a day or so behind Lane's Army, and they will show us the way into Kansas. I doubt very much these young men can follow us that far. I'm sure their mother expects them home for supper."

"They could alert someone else."

"Yes, that is what I fear. I think we need to confront them to allay suspicions. We'll tell them we've decided to settle in Nebraska."

"Won't they take exception to that as well?" Maria said after a bumpy patch of road. "Nebraska's future is also ruled by squatter sovereignty."

"The South has given up on Nebraska. They want Kansas. That was Douglass's calculation: the North would get Nebraska, the South Kansas." He pulled the reigns and the wagon slowed to a stop. "Let's stop here and let them overtake us. We're going to Nebraska, everyone." He looked each passenger in the eye and repeated, "Nebraska."

The two boys stopped a hundred and fifty yards short of the coach and discussed what to do. After a moment they rode alongside, the older one with his palm on the handle of a revolver at his side.

"Where're y'all headed?"

"Nebraska."

"What fer?"

"To settle."

"You sure chose an odd route to get there."

"I'll be honest with you, son—"

"Sir."

"Sirs." Blankenship's face shone with a wry smile, which the older boy noticed. "This young lady and this family were keen on settling in Kansas for her soil. But your comrades in Weston convinced them otherwise. I offered to take them up to Nebraska for a more peaceful settlement."

"Uh huh." He seemed remarkably unimpressed for someone so young. "And you wouldn't be fixin' on meetin' up with that rebel Lane, now would you?"

"Rebel?!" Mr. Ross wheeled around in his seat. "Senator Lane is not a rebel!"

"Sit down!" the boy bellowed in the lowest voice he could muster and drew his pistol, leveling it at Michael Ross, who quickly drew his own. "Put it down, old man or you'll be a-feedin' the worms a Missourah."

"Put yours down, son. You're just a boy. It would be a shame to have to shoot you."

"Michael!" Isabel Ross pleaded, tugging at her husband's coat.

"Listen to your old lady, Michael," the boy advised.

"Put it down, Mr. Ross," said Blankenship calmly. "We've no need for a violent exchange. We're just here to find some land."

"But Mr. Blankenship," Ross protested, "I'll not stand idly by while this little rodent—"

"Enough! Maria and I have no desire to die here so you can defend the name of someone we've never met. Either sit down and resume your trek to Nebraska, with these young men's permission, or get off my coach and shoot it out for yourself and leave us out of it."

Mr. Ross sat, slowly, reluctantly, and holstered his pistol. His wife and children whimpered in relief. "Well, now, gentlemen. It seems you've learned our names," Blankenship continued. "What are yours?"

"I'm Frank," said the older boy. "Frank James. This is my little brother Jesse. We come from a good family, Mr. Blankenship. We've got nothing against you. We just want our part of the world to be left well alone."

"Don't we all," muttered Maria.

XXVIII

Much of the rest of the trip through Missouri following their exchange with the James brothers was uneventful. "I should have shot him while I had the chance," Michael Ross was known to say years later, having realized this confrontation was with the future famous outlaws. "Train robbers they ain't," he would say, having slowly adopted the dialect of his new home. "Them boys is Confederate guerillas after all these years, trust me. They've been that way since they were young boys. Hell, I bet Jesse wasn't more than eight when I met him. And Frank, well, a nicer boy you never met. Even as he held that gun up 'gainst my head, I thought he was a sweet child." Over the years the story grew more friendly toward the brothers, as Ross told it. "They was just protecting their home, ya know. Can't blame 'em for that. Can't blame any of us, really. Them was different times, Kansas in the '50s."

North of St. Joseph they all began to relax. Though there were many hostile communities between them and Nebraska, the larger towns and cities were now behind them, and the rolling, well cared-for farms were what they had all hoped Nebraska and Kansas would one day become. They rode the rest of the day in silence, imagining what their farms might be like in some future season, themselves older, with children, even grandchildren. Maria imagined her cozy cabin with fresh milk in her tea, sitting beside her husband after a long, cold day's work. She imagined children running about, Roger bringing his new bride to the house, and the arrival of her family. She fell asleep in the bumping coach thinking of a little Ireland in Atchison County, with Dugans and Kennys everywhere.

And then she had a dream.

In her dream the Missouri flooded. The townspeople of Atchison built the levee as high as they could, reaching to the very pinnacle of the bluff where Lewis and Clark's man was bitten by a snake; where the shell fired from Major Long's serpent boat exploded, and where the Kanza buried their dead. But the waters overtopped it all. Even the residents who fled to that hilltop were washed away, slipping and clawing in the mud, snapped at by turtles and beavers and snakes, giant carp and catfish. The river wanted them and there was no escape. They floated away. All of them.

All the while, in Maria's dream, she and her family were sleeping, dreaming of rain. Ice melted beneath it, and green grew from it. All around them was water, wind, and sky, but beneath them was a dark, rich, musty soil. They dreamed they were rolling around in the mud, laughing, dancing, flirting, telling stories. They dreamed they were speaking in ancient tongues, and others came—poets, musicians, kings and monks, dark and light alike—and some stayed and some went. And when they woke they found they were alone in their little cabin in Kansas, their farm an island, the wild, weary world washed away.

And they rejoiced.

***

A few days later, they reached Nebraska City, ferried across the river, and turned the horses southward. Just outside the little settlement they saw a stack of rocks, a cairn of sorts, and Blankenship pointed at it. "There," he said, "that's our trail."

"How do you know?" asked Mrs. Ross.

"I was told to look for 'chimneys of stone' along the way. Lane's Chimneys."

"How far behind are we?"

"Hard to say. A day or two, I believe. But don't worry; if we don't catch them up, I shall take you to Topeka."

"That's very kind of you, Mr. Blankenship," said Mrs. Ross.

"Adam," Maria said quietly, "you don't have to do that."

"I'd very much like to," he replied. "I'm enjoying the company. Some of it, anyway." He winked at Maria.

The next day, however, they saw on the horizon a cluster of horses, men, and coaches. As they approached, they saw a small group hurriedly mount and ride toward them at a gallop, and realized this was it. They were now a part of Lane's Army of the North.

At their general's direction, Lane's Army was busy building an outpost along the trail, a cabin of sorts, but fortified with earthworks and cannon. It was just south of the border between the two territories, and Lane hoped it would do for the Free State cause what the towns of Weston and St. Jo did for the Pro Slavery community: create and protect a supply line. Supplies not only of ammunition, food, and comforts, but those of human beings themselves. This trail, with this army blazing it, would create an avenue for the North to flood Kansas.

As the riders approached Blankenship's coach, they drew their weapons and leveled them at the party. "Who goes there?" asked one of the men.

"Adam Blankenship of Illinois. I've escorted these Free State settlers around the Missourian blockade. We've come all the way from Weston to join you."

The men could tell instantaneously that Blankenship was telling the truth. Nothing about him, the way he dressed or spoke, nor any of the others, betrayed the slightest Southern sensibility.

"Very well then. Follow me."

The little party was escorted through a somewhat scattered mob of people, seeming at once both settler and soldier: there were more rifles than shovels, despite not being delivered the rifles they were promised by Lane all the way back in Iowa City.

Jim Lane was nowhere to be found, and Adam Blankenship scanned the crowd with increasing excitement, trying to find him. "He's got to be here somewhere. He's got to be."

"Why? Perhaps he's moved on?"

"This group is his past, present, and future, Maria. He wouldn't leave them alone. Not now."

"How do you know?"

"I'm an old friend."

Blankenship didn't have the time, nor the inclination just now, to explain that he and Lane had befriended each other in northern Mexico back in '48. Both colonels, they'd met—and drank—in officers' tents at various points in the long march to Mexico, and had found they had a lot in common.

"There. He's in the tent."

Blankenship found a flat, open space in the large camp, not too far to the periphery and thus vulnerable, and instructed the Rosses to set their tent. But he motioned to Maria to accompany him. "You'll want to meet Lane," he said. The two walked to the tent together. The sounds of work were all about them, and the sun sank low in the west. Mosquitoes buzzed about terribly, and many of the settlers seemed overly disgruntled by them.

At last they reached the tent and Maria saw immediately why Blankenship had known Lane would be there—it was an important tent in some way, though it wasn't labeled or otherwise demarcated as such. But its location in the camp, the amount of horses about it, and the two guards standing in front—whom she'd not noticed before—were the most militia aspect of an otherwise domestic gathering. It was a general's tent among a pilgrimage.

"Hello," Adam said to one of the guards. "I'm a friend of the general."

"Is he expecting you?"

Blankenship smiled. "I expect not."

"Name?"

"Tell him Blanks is here."

"Sir?"

"Blanks. He will know who I am."

The guard disappeared and in a moment Lane appeared at the flap, a smile beaming across his face. He seemed exactly as Maria had imagined, wooly and disheveled, nothing regal about him whatsoever. A buckskin coat was thrown haplessly about his shoulders, the lines and expression of worry had clearly been wrinkling his face though now they gave way to this uncanny smile.

"Blanks. At last you've found your mark."

"Indeed, old friend." They shook hands vigorously. "You're not an easy target to miss, I'm afraid."

"Yes, the crosshairs lie square across me in all directions. Both my back and my front. If I could only decide which way to turn," Lane smiled more than the joke was worth. "Please, do come in."

Inside there was a table, a map, a candle, and three other men seated about. It was clear they were in the midst of a heated conversation, and it became increasingly clear, as Adam and Maria took seats, that Lane had had tears in his eyes. It wasn't just smoke from a fire—he was upset. A contingency of federal troops had been sent from Ft. Leavenworth to intercept Lane's Army and prevent any armed encounter with Pro Slavery belligerents in Kansas, and both his financiers in Chicago and the Free State Party in Lawrence and Topeka, had no appetite to subvert the United States Government. They sent a friend of Lane's, a lame man by the name of Sam Walker, to inform him.

The three other men sat in total silence. Their bodies and their voices were perfectly still, and everything about them seemed austere.

"Walker," began General James Lane, "if you say the people of Kansas don't want me, it's all right, and I'll blow my brains out. I can never go back to the states and look the people in the face and tell them that as soon as I got these Kansas friends of mine fairly into danger I had to abandon them. I can't do it. No matter what I say in my own defense no one will believe it. I'll blow my brains out and end the thing right here."

A heavy silence fell over the tent, and nobody moved. Maria was probably the least impressed by this statement. She'd heard her father say such dramatic things before, and noticed the whiskey bottle on the table. She somehow knew Lane would do it, but he would say it a thousand times before he did. In her calculation, this was probably about the three-hundredth time, so she didn't think she'd be cleaning up any blood anytime soon. No, there was a negotiation going on here, and this was just a part of it. They all wanted him in Kansas, and they wanted to protect their rights and fight the Southerners if they had to; they just didn't want to commit political suicide by disobeying the military. This was a battle not only for freedom, but for political legitimacy. And disentangling the two had become the whole game.

"General," began the most austere of the men seated in the corner, grim-faced and dirty, sunburned and lean.

But the general interrupted. "Captain Brown, I am no general if I'm not allowed into the battlefield."

"General. You are a general, and the battlefield is all of God's green earth. You are on the battlefield. The battle for God's law knows no boundaries."

"But we still must find a way to escort him into Kansas," said Walker.

"Aren't we in Kansas?" interjected Blankenship.

But nobody was sure, and everyone knew it didn't matter.

"We'll hide him," said Maria before she thought about whether or not it was appropriate to speak. She also realized at this point that she'd helped herself to the whiskey just before saying it, and realized also that that was probably a little too familiar and out of place. But, oh, well. She helped herself to another.

"Hide him." She toasted herself.

Walker stood and directed his words at her. "And just who the hell are—?"

"Captain Walker, stand down," said Lane. "Little woman, what is your name?"

"Maria." She thought a moment, wondering if she should use her maiden or married name. "Maria Dugan."

"Dugan?" Lane thought aloud: "Do I know you? Your family?"

"The Irish are all about Kansas, General. Just like snakes." Everyone laughed, even Captain Brown, though he stopped himself before the others. "It could be another Dugan family." But Lane stared at her. She now realized whom he may know. "Roger. Perhaps you know a young man by the name of Roger Dugan."

Lane beamed. "Why, yes, yes, I do."

"He is my nephew, my husband's younger brother."

"Ah." Still he beamed.

She felt uncomfortable and wanted to change the subject. "Mutual relations aside, do you want to know how to sneak into Kansas or not?" She helped herself to another shot of whiskey.

"I could have guessed who you knew."

"Yes." Her mouth lay flat. "Well, if you want to help your fellow Kansans, Mr. Lane, I suggest we find a way to hide whom you know."

"How's that?"

"May I call you Sally?" The men looked at her quizzically. "Or Samantha, perhaps?"

Walker leaned forward. He looked like something emerging from a cave, seated in the shadowy corner. "You are not suggesting…"

"It's brilliant." At last, the other man had spoken. He sat so still, at the head on the far side of the little table, his forearms rested across the map, he was almost a statue. But now he spoke. "We must do what we must in the pursuit of the cause, Jim. I do not escape self-presumed 'authorities' by always standing ground. Sometimes I must hide and flee. God gives us what we require, and it is our task to make it fit."

"And for now," Maria stood, setting down her glass and pulling up one side of her skirt so they could all see it, "God has given us this. We must make it fit." She smiled and looked at Lane. "We must make it fit you, General."

***

Her plan was to take a different dress out of her trunk and use fabric from anything else, perhaps another bit of another piece of her clothing, to elongate it enough for it to fit the tall, long-limbed Lane. But it proved very difficult. Sewing by lantern-light in a tent in Kansas in early August was not only hot, but the mosquitoes were unbearable. It was almost embarrassing how much they annoyed her—she'd been in the east for far too long. Just as she feared she might, she had grown tender.

She couldn't finish it the first night, nor the next day, in fact. As the fortified cabin they were starting to call a "fort" emerged from the rolling hills of northern Kansas, the dress emerged from Maria's now swollen hands. She'd decided to let the mosquitoes gnaw on her knuckles as she sewed, thinking she would have to grow used to the venom again, one way or another, and now was as good a time as any. But her hands had become very tender, almost throbbing with the poisons of insects. It was painful to sew the dress.

During her hours of sewing, she nearly forgot about Adam Blankenship, and realized on the second night that she hadn't seen him all day. So after supper she ventured out into the night, looking for his tent. Hopefully, he hadn't left. She didn't get ten yards from her tent before he jumped out behind her from the shadows. "Boo!" he said. He'd been drinking.

"Oh, Adam! You startled me."

"I noticed."

"I'm going to miss you."

"As I will you."

"I can't ever thank you—"

"Stop. No need to thank me. It's my job. And I'm happy we made it."

"You doubted? I never noticed."

"It's becoming more difficult, Maria. I'm not sure what could be next."

"I know. Neither am I."

Without another word they embraced, and both turned and walked away. For a moment, Maria didn't want to leave. She wanted this part of the journey to last a little longer.

But on the morning of August 3rd, 1856, she helped the famous James H. Lane put on a dress and sneak into Kansas in order to evade federal authorities. She, Lane, and Captains Samuel Walker and John Brown rode cautiously across a swath of flattened grass in the prairies, a day or more behind their army. They followed the rock chimneys through the little settlements of Plymouth, Lexington, Powhattan, and Netawaka, careful not to be noticed on the little dusty roads and encouraged that there were few signs of any large group of horses other than their own company.

So encouraged was Lane, in fact, that he frequently exposed his face and spoke loudly with a broad grin during his endless chatter with Maria. She and Lane rode behind Walker and Brown, Lane mostly with his head bowed so his bonnet would cover his face (he'd refused to shave, and had barely washed), and every time he looked up at her, smiling and chattering innocently, she laughed. Walker would shush them. It was evident more than once that Brown was trembling with anger, certainly not fear, but he held his tongue and kept his body in rhythm with his horse.

"What brings a little Irish girl all this way, Maria?" Lane asked her.

"Her Irish husband, of course," she said, still chuckling from the last time he looked at her.

"And where is he?"

"Home. North of Atchison."

"Ah, yes, I remember Roger mentioning you both, now that I think about it. And tell me this: what brings you here, to me?"

Maria looked over at him. He kept his head bent and she rolled her eyes. "I've not come to you, General Lane. I am returning to my husband."

"Why did you leave him?"

"That's not your affair, Jim Lane," she said in a friendly way. "Don't you have a country to save from the evil clutches of your enemies? Shouldn't you be pondering on that at this moment?"

"Perhaps. But I thought I'd enjoy a little gossip." They both smiled. "They are your enemies, too, Maria Dugan of Kansas."

After a brief moment, she said, "Not necessarily."

"Of course they are. Tell me another thing: why doesn't your husband stand with us?"

"He does," she said, "at the polls."

"But the polls are stolen from us."

"Yes. Yes, they are."

"So why doesn't he stand for the polls?"

Maria hesitated. She knew how to say it but felt a pause to indicate reflection was perhaps expected. "It's a long way from Ireland, Mr. Lane. A very long way." They looked at each other and she smiled, not at his ridiculousness this time but his expression, as it showed he understood. She halted her horse, as did Lane, then the two men in front. "I'm afraid I must leave you all now," she said. "Atchison lies east of here."

"How do you know?" asked Walker.

"I can smell it," she said, turned her horse, and trotted off into the rising sun.

XXIX

Roger woke when he heard a knock at the front door. There were voices outside the room, and for the first time in almost two weeks, he felt warm, comfortable, and awake. He also realized for the first time that he'd been ill all the while; that now, as he opened his eyes and felt the growing heat of the August morning, he was home with his brother, safe and unhurried, unopposed and, for the time being, unneeded. No chore, no cause, not even a worry or concern awaited him on this summer day. His being ill had stopped time, paralyzed the world, and today would be the first day of a second life.

Roger had barely survived. A fever had gripped him, and he'd spent the last ten days in a delirium through which his brother had nursed him. His hallucinations were marked by paranoia about the jayhawk, and Patrick soon learned to stop asking questions about it. Nothing Roger said about anything made much sense during those ten days, but his older brother still felt there was something meaningful and significant about Roger's encounter with the big bird, whenever and however it had taken place. Soon, thought Patrick, if he survives, I'm sure he shall tell me all about it.

After the knock and the quick realization that he'd been ill and now was better, Roger began to recognize the voices outside the door. They entered his mind one after another as if they were filing into a room in a queue and he was receiving them to court as a king might. First, of course, there was that of Joseph James's, filling the room the way a full moon does relative to the stars; then Oliver John's laugh, which so often followed his older brother's voice, the rainbow about the moon on a misty eve; Delilah J.'s was next, uttering a sort of gasp of surprise and delight, which was accompanied by her baby, who began to cry. Then Roger heard his brother say with a little tremble, simply, "Love." And at last he heard Maria.

"Why, hello everyone! It's good to be home!" she said.

Roger smiled.

It was not until now—after the knock, the feeling of health, and the voices—that Roger finally thought of the bird that had been plaguing his dreams during the entire illness. And it was gone now, already a faded memory. He rose and opened the shades. Across the well-groomed fields lay the Great Plains and the sun, light and land stretching endlessly to the horizon. In every bit of turned soil, every blade of mowed grass, every grain of hewn lumber, he could see his brother's hand. He'd labored alone all spring and summer, intertwining himself with his land. Roger sat on the edge of the bed, and an image of Patrick came to him.

It was somehow also an image of their father, and of every man he'd ever met. It was a man made of corn and grass rising from the land like fowl in autumn.

***

Before long, the two families were seated at a feast. There was an air of excitement, intimacy, and plenty about the cabin that none had experienced but once before in their lives: last Christmas, together. Patrick and Maria had memories of holidays in Ireland, but the food had always been humble. Oliver John, Roger, and Joseph James had attended celebrations much larger than this, but the impetus for them had always been at the expense of someone else. They were the festivities of the victors over the vanquished, and they were always tainted by wounds and uncertain futures, not to mention the overt lack of a woman's touch. And Del, well, until last Christmas she'd never felt a part of anything, not even a meal.

"Pardon me, ya'll." Del rose and tapped her glass. "I knows it's a might unusual for a woman—a guest at that—to give the toast, but biscuits and gravy, I just can't help mahself!" Everyone chuckled. She was flushed and glassy-eyed, positively beaming as if she were pregnant. "I wanna say that until last Christmas, when we were all together last, I never knew a growed woman could feel the way I did. All tingly like a little girl a-seein' her first boyfriend in the schoolhouse, or out in the fields a-pickin' and a-plantin'. Jimmy knows how I was raised, so he knows I ain't never been a part of a family, not really, anyway. And I ain't never thought I'd be able to raise my children better than I was raised. I ain't never thought I'd a-own land, tend my own garden, cook on my own stove. Never." She paused and swallowed.

Joseph James kept himself from spitting.

"But that changed this winter," Del went on. "You Dugans is like family to me and Jimmy. And now with little Missy here," Melissa, the baby, cooed as if it knew it was being spoken of, "I expect there'll be more of us in no time. I know it's been a hard few months, hell, a hard year or two, but with Maria and Roger back, my little Oliver John back to a-walkin' and a-climbin' and such, Jimmy back to his senses and a-stayin' outa them stupid games them men is a-playin' all around the territory, and my mother-in-law outa bed, things is sure lookin' up!"

Everyone laughed, and Delilah J. held up her glass. "To us," she said, "let God and nature do what they will—ain't none of it strong enough to break apart a family like this."

Joseph James stood, also flushed and a little tipsy. "I could never a-put it like Del just did," he began, "but I'd still like to say that in my years on God's earth I have found that moments like these are precious and rare. In fact, this bein' Kansas and all, it seems mighty likely one of us ain't gonna make it to the next little feast of ours."

"Jimmy!" exclaimed Del, still standing, still smiling.

"No sense in a-hidin' from it, Del. It's true. The more we remember how close death always is, the more we remember how great it is to be alive. Ya never know when a tree might fall on yer leg, a brick on your head, you'll lose a baby or a wife or a brother—but it's moments like…" He paused and swallowed. "It's just moments like this…"

Patrick stood. "To us," he said, "the future of Kansas, the future of this country."

"To us!"

***

Later that night, after the women and children had all fallen asleep (even Maria, who had developed a habit of staying up late with her sister in Boston and had kept the habit out of nervousness during her trek back to Kansas), Patrick and Joseph James adjourned outside, lit a fire, and continued their conversation.

"Here, Paddy, have a glass."

"No, thank you, Jimmy." He was glad it had been offered, though knew it would be better if it hadn't.

"You haven't had a glass all night, my friend!"

"I know," he smiled, proudly, but retrained himself. "It's the only reason Maria is back."

Joseph James swayed as much in surprise as in drunkenness. "You have done well, Irishman. Quite well!" He produced a pipe and pouch of tobacco from his jacket.

"I will have a little of your pipe, if you don't mind. I don't think she's forbidden that." He paused and smiled. "Yet."

"It's yours."

Patrick packed and lit the pipe while Joseph James seated himself on a stump, threw a log on the fire, spat, and looked up. "Look at them stars, Paddy. Just look at them."

Patrick looked up. The smoke curled from his lips and disappeared into the dark night above. Before Maria, the sky in America had seemed lonely, frightening, and that sky had returned when she was in Boston. But now it was welcoming, brilliant and clear.

"I can never look at stars the same ever since the war, Paddy."

"You mean last December?" he asked, remembering his neighbor's lectures about the troubled nature of their new shared home.

Joseph James laughed. "Oh, Lord no! Lord, lord, lord, no, sir. That wasn't any war, Paddy! That was a bunch of drunken louses laying siege to a defenseless town. The Wakarusa War wasn't anything more than a big saloon quarrel if you ask me. No, I mean Mexico. Fightin' the Mexicans, oh, almost a decade ago now (my, my has it been that long?)"

"I'm afraid it has, so," he said, knowing that all men of a certain age can always bemoan the quick passing of a decade.

"That's what I mean, Paddy. I mean, look at them stars. They are the same—the exact same—as they were a decade ago. So much else has changed around me, just about everything, in fact, but them stars. I remember lying awake at night with Ninny in the desert, and after most of the rest of the men were asleep and the bivouac would die down, them stars would come out clear as day. On the way there, it was sorta comforting, ya know, thinkin' that no matter where I was out there in Indian country, the stars were just the same as they were back home in Missourah. My little Oliver John was a-lookin' at the same stars, my Del, my ma, hell, even my daddy, wherever the hell he was. Night made me feel good, like no matter how different my days were, my nights were the same out there than they were here."

"I felt that way when I first arrived in Kansas with Maria. I hadn't seen the stars since I left Ireland. Boston has none. It's just a lonely place, from your toes all the way to the Heavens. But in Kansas they seemed to encircle the earth again. I used to think perhaps my father was looking at them as well, so. If he is still alive."

"You Irish are quite the poets," Joseph James slurred. "What happened to your daddy, Paddy?" He smiled and took a swig from his flask.

Patrick puffed the pipe. "He was either hanged or sent to Australia by the English. We fled and came to America, my mother, Roger and I."

"What happened to your ma?"

"She died on the ship, with hundreds of others."

"Them damn English."

"Yes."

"Well, the stars changed after Christmas of '46 though. Changed for good."

"What happened on Christmas?"

"My first combat, Paddy. El Brazito. Wasn't much of a fight really, but a friend of mine I knew since we was little lost an eye. Just about the unluckiest sonofabitch you ever did see. A shell hit a few yards from him and a rock came up and hit him square in the eye, just smashed it right outa his skull. I'll never forget seein' his eye just a-danglin' there on his face as he tried to get back on his feet. After that, I ain't never felt comfortable at night again. Almost like there's a Mexican in every shadow."

"I know how you feel, Joseph. To have a gun to your—."

Joseph James's head fell to his chest and he snorted drunkenly, then he looked up at the stars again. "And you ain't never felt the same again, knowin' just how close you are to death."

"I knew that before, I'm afraid, like," Patrick said kindly. "As a boy, we were always afraid of starving. Every potato my father dug up from the ground that had the blight was another meal we'd go without. People were starving everywhere, marching down the road to the east, women as thin as skeletons and children crying, their tummies bloated." Patrick realized he reported this with little emotion. The smoke, curling out of his mouth and rising, dispersing into nothingness, seemed to take with it the pain of those days. "Then they came and took my father away one night, and it seemed they would shoot us all on the front stoop; then we marched to the sea, starving, and got on a ship with dead bodies all around us. And mother died. Roger was sick, and I almost lost him." He shook his head. "It was one trial after another. Boston was better, but not much. We were always afraid and unwelcome, sick and cold and tired. I don't think more than a month or two ever went by without a beating of some kind to someone I loved." Patrick stopped and smoked, then continued. Joseph James was listening more than he usually did.

"I've spent most of my life thinking I may not get another day, if that's God's will. So, Joseph," he said, turning to his friend, who looked cleaner in the moonlight than he ever did in the sun, "when you held that gun to my head, it didn't scar me. I am all scar. But it taught me a lesson. It taught me that I cannot escape the world. As you once said to me, we all came to Kansas to escape the rest of the world, but the rest of the goddamn world followed us to Kansas."

"Like a stray dog."

He laughed. "Like a stray dog. So it changed my world in another way. I've always known how close to death I am. Now I know how far from happiness I will always be."

"Paddy…"

"No, it's a good thing." He wasn't after pity. He hated it when people thought he was. "It teaches that moments like tonight are, as you said this evening, to be relished, because it's only a matter of time. I want a son. I want children to live on this farm and have a better life than I have. I want my family to find happiness someday."

"Yes. Me too, Paddy, me too. You'll have yer youngins one day soon, too. I'd a-bet on it." The two men stood and shook hands. "Paddy, I want you to know I have no mind to increase your suffering. I forgive your brother, and thank you for forgiving me."

"Thank you, Joseph. Thank you."

***

The next morning, over eggs, beans, veggies and greens, Joseph James asked Maria what he had wanted to ask all night. "So how did you git here anyways, Maria? The river's blocked off, I know, and that rebel Lane and his army is all over the north. *Sovereign* says that army is two thousand strong, and Lane is a real soldier. That is probably a man's army if there ever was one, and I'd hate to think…"

"Jimmy, it ain't polite to talk politics over eggs," interjected his wife.

"That a woman would get caught up in such an army?" Maria said. "Yes, I could see your concern, unless the general himself were a woman." The others looked quizzically at her. She chuckled to herself, and Patrick pretended his eggs were more interesting. "The truth, Joseph, and I tell you this only because I consider you a dear friend, is that said 'army' actually escorted me around the river and over the border. They gave me the horse outside."

Joseph James, without looking at Maria, swallowed his eggs, stood, opened the front door and spat.

"Don't mind him," said Del, "he just got a thing 'bout Yanks. Not you 'n yourn, just Yanks."

He returned to his seat. "May I have some more eggs, Maria?"

"Of course, Joseph."

After filling his plate for a third time, Patrick watching carefully to see what he would leave (which was minimal and which upset Patrick), he returned to his seat again. "It may just be from where I'm a-sittin', but I don't think you should be happy with this, Paddy."

Patrick didn't bother conceiving a response, but rose, taking the last of the eggs, and eyed Joseph James's plate enviously.

"What should Paddy's opinion on that matter be, Joseph?" Maria was drying her hands rather quickly.

"Jimmy …"

"Hush, Del."

"Don't you hush her," Maria said, "not in my house!"

"Maria, associatin' yerself with Lane ain't a smart—"

"I know what's smart for me and my family, Joseph. This 'army' you speak of is mostly just folks like us. Don't believe everything you read in the papers, Mr. Hawkins."

"I just think we all got to stick together…" At this point Joseph James looked over at Patrick, hoping he may intercede on his friend's behalf.

But Patrick merely motioned at Joseph's plate and was rewarded by his friend sliding it over.

"Exactly!" Maria sat back down, her back stiff, her hands clinging to each other in her lap. "We have to stop taking sides in this Kansas question, Joseph, at least with one another. You can support slavery all you like, but for Patrick and me it goes against our nature. We Irish have been enslaved for centuries. Patrick's father even signed Danny O'Connell's oath against the enslavement of the Negro. But one day these people will be gone, Joseph. Atchison and Stringfellow, Lane and Robinson, they'll all be gone. And Kansas will be left to us."

"And the niggers," said Joseph James, glancing over at Patrick, who had proceeded to pile his friend's eggs, potatoes, tomatoes, beans, and mushrooms onto a piece of bread.

"We are already here, Joseph. We already have our land."

Patrick had almost finished piling the plate on the bread, and said sloppily through his salivation, "They may not even be allowed into Kansas."

"Paddy, what's the point of opposing slavery then?" his wife asked.

"Just so they don't enslave the Irish next, love. But we don't need millions of blacks farming all of Kansas."

"I can't believe you just said that."

"I can," Joseph James interrupted again. "But that goes for all the world. Set them free and you've got a scourge on the land." He looked over again at Patrick, who had now placed another piece of bread on top of what was now a giant sandwich, and was pressing it down firmly. Joseph James looked perplexed. "What the hell is that? What the hell are you doing?"

"Irish stew," said Patrick, taking a giant bite.

XXX

Within a week, it began to feel as if the last year had never taken place. The convention in Big Springs, the shooting of Pat Laughlin, the tree falling on Oliver John, the Wakarusa War, the Pottawatomie murders, the Battle of Franklin, and the loss of Maria's child and her return to Boston, the birth of the next generation of Hawkinses, and even Maria's strange escort home were all surreal dreams now. For a short week in early August, all the Dugans and Hawkinses did was tend their farms, share their dairy and vegetables, make repairs to their cabins, and prepare more acres for future crops. And for the first half of the week, Roger had never been happier. He decided one morning, watching the sun rise while fishing, that he'd never leave the farm again.

By the time the sun rose twice more, however, he was restless. Farm work was hard and endless. He was poor, tired, and often hungry, not due to lack of food, necessarily, but due to how simple the fare was, and the lack of time to eat it. There was also something inside of him that began to return with his health, something he'd felt for years, and which he'd never been able to understand or express. It was an emotion, but Roger experienced it more like a mosquito bite or a sore throat. It was an irritation of sorts, a nagging sensation that distracted him from whatever activity or thought he was trying to focus on. Sometimes it made him clench all his muscles simultaneously, sometimes it made him squint then open his eyes as wide as possible, and sometimes it made him jerk his head suddenly.

To some extent, it was similar to the feeling he had when he saw a beautiful woman or when he shot the unnamed Missourian at Dutch Henry's Crossing. It wasn't so much like how he felt when he saw Oliver John's mangled leg, Sam Collins's practically headless body, or the night he realized what John Brown had done on the Pottawatomie, though it wasn't entirely unrelated either. One morning, while hoeing a row of beans, it occurred to him that the day he saw the giant bird, he felt the same sensation quite acutely. All the memories of his illness, and his dreams of the jayhawk, flooded back, and he raised his hoe above his head and brought it down on a vine of beans like an executioner beheading the guilty. And he cried out, clenching all his muscles, and felt better.

But not for long. He was soon marching toward the cabin, which lay perhaps an eighth of a mile across the field.

Patrick and Maria were nowhere to be found. He'd expected Patrick to come and help with the hoeing at some point, but he'd never arrived. And Maria was nowhere else, not in the kitchen garden, milking the cow, or slopping the pig sty. Roger had been left alone to do all the hard work. He stormed into the cabin and found them setting out afternoon tea.

"Roger," said Patrick, "you've saved me a trip. I was coming to fetch you for tea."

"I have some questions."

"Do you now, my boy? Well, ask them and I will try and answer them over some tea." He motioned to the table. "Maria and I were just asking and answering some of our own, in fact." Roger hesitated a moment, almost as if he were going to refuse, but then sat. "What sort of questions do you have? I dare say you seem a mite agitated, like."

"The bird."

Patrick stopped, his mouth hovering over his toast like a river around a bend. "Well, now. That's more than some questions, I must say."

Maria looked at the two men. She knew both well enough to know they understood the topic well enough, and also that it was an unpleasant one. She ventured a guess. "Have we lost some chickens?"

"No, I'm afraid that would be too simple," said her husband, setting down his toast and brushing the crumbs from his hands.

"It must be if you are to delay eating for it."

"Yes, I'm afraid it is. Roger, I don't know where to begin."

"You saw it. I saw it. I wasn't delirious with fever now, was I?"

Patrick shook his head and picked up his toast again. "Hard to say. I've often thought so, but I've come to think not." He paused, and before taking his bite, said, "Roger, I don't know what it is."

"What is what?" Maria's arm shot across the table as if to pull the food out her husband's mouth so he could reply. "Please, boys, what bird?"

Patrick looked at his wife and swallowed with some difficulty. "Maria, this is not easy to explain."

"Start from the beginning."

"Well—"

"There is a giant bird in the woods," Roger interrupted. "As big as a man."

"Should make a stew to feed us all winter," she replied facetiously.

"You should think. But it is not that sort of bird."

"I doubt very much that God has made a creature that you would not eat, Paddy."

Patrick looked away, slowly chewing his toast. "Well, I would not eat this one."

"This bird," began Roger, unsure of how to continue, "it, well, is, it is—it doesn't talk but—"

"'Tis a spirit, Maria," Patrick said. "This bird is the forest herself. The river, the sky, the grass. This bird is what the Kanza left behind, Maria."

Maria stood, seriously, her fingers upon the table like it was a lectern. "We are not in Ireland anymore, boys."

"Maria, this bird is somehow the cause of our troubles. Or, the troubles cause him. I don't know which."

"Nonsense." She began to nervously clear the table. "Have your tea and get back to work. There's no time for stories in America."

Roger turned to his brother. "Paddy, you said not to follow it," he asked trustingly.

"Yes, it will lead you to your demise. Many Kanza braves have been led away forever by this bird."

"How do you know that?" Maria said sharply while pausing her work, then continued to it just as sharply.

"Stories."

"Told by whom?"

Patrick hesitated, beginning to stand as if he were going to help Maria, then sitting again, as if he were going to continue eating. But he stopped and folded his hands. "A man I met last year. A man in the woods."

"What man?" Maria turned. "You never told me about a man in the woods."

"I was never sure he actually existed, lass. The bird as well. Until now. Until Roger saw it, and spoke of it."

"What man?" Roger sounded anxious.

"A Frenchman. An old trapper who settled here decades ago and married an Indian. He knows the stories of the Kanza. I met him by the sacred spring during the full moon."

"Stop it!" Maria shouted, pounding her fist on the table. "That is quite enough from both of you! There is work to do, and here I am stuck with the laziest poets from Ireland! Enough of your superstitious sacrilege. Get out there and finish your jobs, both of you!"

She grabbed her snake-killing shovel from behind the stove, and both men jumped up and headed for the door, shoving toast in their mouths and hats on their heads as they moved. "There are no stories in America! The past cannot haunt us here!"

***

During a visit to Atchison on the 17th of August, 1856, Patrick stopped at the post office and Bob Kelley handed him another letter.

"You shall see it is unopened," the postmaster said. "And that it is from Australia. Why an Irishman in Kansas should receive a letter from there, I do not know. I should most likely have found out, but did not."

"Why, thank you, Mr. Kelley," he replied, forcing sarcasm through lips that had begun to suddenly tremble.

"I trust, as you read my paper, you shall enjoy the harvest quietly on the Independence."

"I trust I shall." But Kelley's awkward attempt at kindness was lost on him. He had a letter from Australia, which could only really be one thing.

He carried it and several weeks' worth of the *Sovereign* home, stunned, and needed an hour or more to build up the nerve to open it. He also thought Roger might read it with him. It was only fair. They sat at the table over tea, Patrick reading aloud in an almost disembodied voice.

Boys,

I am alive.

I have been banished to Australia and have lived the last dozen years or more in relative peace. As such, I am sure you can imagine, I am terribly bored. Yet, I am well and think of you often. I am sure I would be proud of the men you have become.

I have learned much about you by exchanging letters with your uncles and aunts in Ireland in my attempts to find you. It is with a terribly heavy heart—I am crying as I write this—that I learned about Mother's passing. Being ripped from her and my boys was very much like death to me, but alas, death is not something that has any equivalent. I believe that the Lord told me of her passing. It was as if the sun became two shades darker. Our vision may adjust, but there is yet less light in the world.

I cannot imagine the difficulties you have overcome. Losing your father, your mother, and your country so early in one's life cannot be considered a blessing, even by the Vatican. And to have struck out into the American wilderness—well, if it is anything like the bush here in Australia, I imagine you are the toughest Irishmen that side of the Atlantic. A man always wants his sons to surpass him, and in this I am deeply gratified.

I know, too, that you are married, my dear Patrick, and congratulate you. Raising a family is the greatest blessing God has given us. I trust He will not allow it to be taken from you as it was from me. I understand, however, that the Troubles in Kansas are not wholly unlike those in Ireland. We read about them all the way across the world, and that my sons are there, in the middle of it, gives me both measures of pride and of worry. Please be safe, watch out for one another, and never allow the outside world to intrude upon your households. Make of your family a fortress, and let none pass.

I do hope you are doing all you can to oppose the brute slavery. I hope you remember Ireland well enough to know that when the powerful control the powerless by disallowing their right to own land, an entire race, an entire nation, can be enslaved, decimated, and starved to death. The English have done this to us, and their ancestors are doing it to the Negroes in America. You are next. They are your enemies, Patrick. They stole your father, killed your mother, and robbed you of your language and your heritage. Compromise is futile, as this is not a political question. It is a moral one.

Until the bright day when I put my arms around you both, and the sun restores its full luster, I am

Yours in God,

Pappa

The Dugan boys sat in silence at the table. The older brother, Patrick felt he should approach this as if it were to be expected, that, in the few years he had been on earth before Roger joined, he had learned something that could not have been learned anytime or anyplace else.

"Well, I suppose it's finally happened, so," he offered. Then, "I think I might have known." Roger appeared baffled, staring through the table into the floor, through the floor into the earth, and through the earth into the sky below.

"Maria, perhaps some tea would remind us we are awake, and not dreaming."

But before she could answer, they all heard a horse approaching quickly, nearly at a gallop, and its rider's heavy steps as he moved to the door. They knew who it was, and that the news he bore could not be good.

Joseph James, forgetting his manners, barged in the front door, began to speak, and backed out, muttering. He shut the door then he knocked.

"Who is it?" Maria called with a smile.

"You know sure as hell who it is, woman!"

"Joseph!"

Joseph James's face was quivering as he came back through the door, Oliver John following sheepishly behind, his limp all but gone and his feathered hat in his hand. "My apologies, Maria, but I ain't none too happy with you right about now. You done let a criminal into Kansas and endangered me 'n mine. That makes you a criminal yerself."

Roger stood and drew his breath, ready to speak, but Maria silenced him with a wave of her hand. "Tell us what you mean, Joseph."

"Jim Lane's a-rampagin' all through the territory. He and that army a his that you helped smuggle down attacked some Georgians in Franklin and stole Old Sacramento and used it on Col. Titus. Old Sacramento! My cannon, goddamnit! It's desecration!"

"I suppose that makes me a sinner and a criminal, then, doesn't it?" Patrick winced as his wife said this.

Joseph James raised a shaky finger and pointed first at her, then Patrick, then Roger. "Yer sure as hell right about that. Look here now, maybe when this is all over we can be friends again, but that you helped Lane, and you helped Old Brown, I cannot be a part of. Word is Lane is moving north, and I aim to join Stringfellow and Atchison and go and stop him. All of Missourah's on its way here and we'll beat that nigger-lover down into Hell. Then we'll find that old man and hunt him down like the treacherous dog that he is. If I see you," he pointed again at Roger, "we will not be friends. I have no more cheeks I can turn, boy. From here on out, we are foes."

He and Oliver John left, and the Dugans all looked at J.P.'s letter, which still sat innocuously on the table. And they looked at one another.

"I'm going," said Roger, turning around and grabbing a rifle that stood in the corner. He looked back at Patrick, who stared directly back into his brother's eyes. Pappa was coming home, and now this had happened. Patrick's choice was so easy, it was as if hadn't even made it. It came to him, obnoxious in color and sound, took him by the hand and pulled him into the woods ahead. Roger handed him the other rifle, smiling.

"I'll fix you something for the ride," said Maria, turning back to the stove.

"Wait." She pulled Patrick back in the door after she'd handed them their food. "I'm with child again, Paddy." She was beaming. "Go make Kansas a place we can rear him."

Out the window, the jayhawk stood in the pasture like a camouflaged statue, and yet she touched her belly fearlessly.

***

The Dugan brothers rode for Lawrence, the Hawkins brothers for Atchison.

Joseph James and Oliver John found a large gathering of Southern immigrants and Missourian Border Ruffians in the nearly-completed four-story hotel on the corner of 2nd and Main streets known as the Massasoit House.

Patrick and Roger found a similarly sized gathering of Free Staters and New England immigrants in the remains of the Free State Hotel.

"I say we ride through the county and find any damned abolitionist cabin we can and burn it to the ground," said a Kentuckian in the Massasoit House. "Then we'll ride south and meet Lane in Hell."

"We'll ride out to Osawatomie and join either Capt. Brown or Gen. Lane," said an Irishman in the Free State Hotel. "And on the way we'll do a little jayhawkin'."

"And let us stop at Dutch Henry's," said Roger. "There's a job there I didn't finish this spring."

"I know a Free State family just north of here I'd like to teach a lesson," said Joseph James. "They helped smuggle Lane into Kansas and one is friendly with Old Brown. I'd like to give 'em a little scare on the way if you fellas don't mind."

XXXI

At the crossing, Dutch Henry Sherman sat in his chair on the rickety wooden porch of his store with a rifle hid in a blanket inside the door, just as he had every day that summer of 1856. On this late August morning he was surprised to be bored. He'd had customers just about every day since before the first thaw, and most of them actually had business to transact, besides chewing on news and gossip and interrogating Henry for any information he may have on the enemy. And most of them paid for their goods. Very few had begged for credit, and even fewer had used armed robbery to obtain their supplies. Yes, it had been a good summer.

A little quiet now and then never hurt anyone, and Henry used this quiet to muse—marvel, even—on his own brilliance in setting up shop where he had. He'd come to Kansas almost a dozen years before, but rather than staking his claim where others would a decade after him, Henry and his brothers decided that travel in Kansas would be crucial, and that whatever towns came and went wouldn't matter. They would still need feed and seed and tools and beasts as they traded and bartered from hamlet to town to city and back again; and given the fact that, like water, human beings travel the paths of least resistance, the settlers of Kansas would follow those who came before them and blazed the trails to the west, to the gold of California and Oregon, the Eden of the Great Salt Lake, and the military roads that linked Fort Leavenworth to Forts Riley, Saunders and Scott. Yes, where roads meet a river is a fine place to sell a cow or a pound of salt, indeed.

A smile came across his face as he thought about how it had also been a stroke of brilliance to remove his brother William from the equation. Brown had offered Henry amnesty, saying "ensure your brother will be there and we will spare you." And he had made sure his brother, Dutch Bill as others called him, was there by not being there himself, telling Bill to stay with the "guests" while he went out in search of a wandering cow. Henry never saw what happened to his brother, but heard others talking about it in hushed tones at the crossing—his skull was flayed open and the river washed out its brains, there was a hole in his chest, and his left hand was missing. That bothered Henry a little, the thought of his brother trying to protect himself with raised hands.

Nevertheless, business was business, and Bill had forgotten that. At first, it made sense, breaking down cabin doors and threatening all those Easterners, because it seemed that they had everything shipped to them. They were terrible customers. But Bill let it get out of hand. He didn't see that the Free Staters had fairly won the race for that part of Kansas, and that those who came in recent months needed supplies every bit as much as any Missourian. More, even, if you thought about it hard. They would be great customers, eventually, if they could trust that the man they bought a horse from wouldn't show up in the middle of the next night with a gun demanding it back. Many were there to stay, but Bill didn't see that. He didn't see it. So he kept scaring away the customers no matter what Henry told him, and something had to be done.

Now, in the late August morning light, before the moisture and mosquitoes lifted from the prairie grasses, and the crickets were only starting to begin their chorus from the cottonwoods surrounding his store, Henry Sherman was looking forward to seeing either the four hundred Missourians that were rumored to be in the area, or any of Lane's Army that may still be roaming around. Either were welcome as long as they had money and reason to part with it. He figured the Missourians would head for Osawatomie if they couldn't find Lane, intent on finding anyone associated with Brown. Let them have it out up in town, he thought, and the survivors can come here for whiskey and flour. He had plenty of both. He even had iodine and gauze on hand, and plenty of that too, so if they needed to set up camp for casualties, well, that would be just fine. Just fine.

The only thing Henry didn't like about his location was that it was recessed some from the surrounding prairie, and didn't command much of a view. It was a low and therefore deep point in the creek, but slow, steady, and shady. It was a perfect point to camp, water the horses, and rest, as well as to cross, but not so good for reconnaissance. Wagon trains and armies didn't care about that as much, as they could always post folks on one of the ridges and see anyone else approaching for two or three miles. But once you dropped down into the bottoms, you were basically blind. And the taller the trees got, well, the harder it was to see. Henry wished someone would come, but it would be nice if he knew who they were before they got here. But instead he fell asleep.

He woke with a start, thinking he'd heard a horse. He swiveled first his head and then his torso about his chair, but saw nothing. Scanning farther off, then farther off, he still saw nothing. His own horse was out in the pasture, so it couldn't have been him. He remembered his mare that the Brown party stole the night they killed

William, and a little bitterness arose in him. The mare was never part of the deal, but they took her anyway. Oh, well. With all the lost business he would regain without his oaf of a brother around, the mare would be more than paid for.

Henry heard another noise from behind the cabin, eased himself just inside, grabbed his rifle, and turned around.

***

As the group approached the crossing, it became apparent that Roger was now in charge, at least of this little sortie, and Patrick couldn't help but feel proud. Seven men, many of them older than Roger by a factor of two, did exactly as he asked without question. But something inside told Patrick this was not only something to be proud of, but to fear. The Roger that attacked the chicken as a child; the Roger that tore apart the shack last summer; the Roger that seemed to find himself consorting with every violent man in Kansas—demagogue or criminal—scared Patrick. But the Roger that never, not even once, expressed a desire to leave Kansas; the Roger that did all this not for personal gain or even self-preservation, but only for what he believed to be right and just; and the Roger that believed with all his soul that good would always conquer evil—that Roger made him proud. Watching his little brother, Patrick could see their father in him, and himself. It was as if all the Dugans in Ireland coursed through his veins just now, and all the South should shudder.

"Here, take this," Roger said to a man, handing over his hunting rifle, as they regrouped behind a ridge with a view of the cabin. "Give yours to Paddy."

"That's a Beecher's Bible," said the man, referencing the Sharps rifles sent in boxes marked "Bibles" by the New England Emigrant Aid Society's Henry Ward Beecher. "I'm entrusted with it."

"Paddy can hit a rabbit from across the Missouri," replied Roger. "He'll cover me with the Sharps rifle, so."

"Always the missionary, I am happy to share the Word," smiled the man, pleased with his wit at a time like this.

They were all from New England, these seven men. Four had been present during the Wakarusa War, and one had been in a brief fight earlier in the summer, but that was the extent of experience. A bookseller, two lawyers, a small-time politician, and three men who preferred not to speak of their Yankee past made up their company. They could all ride horses and use a compass, and had been in

Kansas long enough to say they'd survived it, but Roger didn't trust them with his life. Only his brother enjoyed that trust.

"There, behind that tree," Roger motioned to Patrick. "And I'll slip down behind that thicket and sneak up on him."

"Henry's not a suspicious fellow if you have dollars in your pocket," said one man. "Why are we being so clandestine? We should just walk up and take him prisoner if we perceive him as an enemy."

"We—" Roger hesitated, shaking his head and correcting himself, "Captain Brown—killed his brother. We can't take the chance. He could be armed and ready for revenge."

"A ruffian is a ruffian," said another man. "We should just shoot him."

"He may know the whereabouts of the Missourians." Roger's leadership was more obvious than ever. "We will interrogate him on the way to Osawatomie."

"What about that tree?" Patrick motioned to Roger. "I think I can use that rock to steady my arm."

"That's farther, isn't it?"

"A little, but I'll be more stable."

With a nod from Roger, Patrick jogged up and around a depression in the ridge and positioned himself behind a large limestone outcropping and thicket of underbrush that surrounded two small trees. He could see Henry's hat move now and then around the corner of the cabin. It was indeed farther, farther than he'd realized. Patrick wasn't sure he could hit a man from such a distance, and became aware that Roger would be slipping down the hill between them and may get in the way of the shot. This wasn't good after all. Not good at all.

But before he could get his little brother's attention, Roger was already on the backside of the cabin. From here, he looked so small, so boyish. The trees, river, and prairie dwarfed him, like an infant being held by a giant. Patrick's whole body twitched to his left, as if it wanted to run down the hill and create a distraction for Henry to follow. But it was far too late. Roger was creeping up alongside the side of the cabin and was now just a few feet from Henry. The hat disappeared. He settled into the rock, which suddenly seemed soft, and took a deep breath while aiming his rifle.

Where Roger's skull met his spinal column looked very sweaty. Patrick could feel the direction of the hair and how it realigned itself with the bone's curvature when it was wet. There were two freckles, moles maybe, in that thicket of hair, and he could smell his brother's skin. The butt of the rifle began to feel like the back of his little brother's head. He could remember lying on the floor of the main room in their cottage in Ireland, scratching Roger just there, twirling his hair with his finger. Roger had a headache. There was sweat dripping into his eyes.

The boys could hear the floorboards of the wooden porch creak around the corner, and the hat disappeared. Their fingers found their triggers. It was time. In two steps they were around the corner.

Henry had his back to Roger as he leaned into the front door to retrieve his rifle.

As Henry turned, the Dugans saw the muzzle of a rifle in his hand.

"Lay down your weapon, Henry," Roger ordered.

"You have no right—"

"Lay it down or I shall shoot you in the face!"

***

At the farm, Maria sat on a chair on the rickety wooden porch with her snake shovel in her lap. She'd only seen the farm so quiet in the eerie glow of a storm as it stalled overhead. Chickens and pigs sat still, birds nested in trees and ceased their songs, and even the trees seemed to hold their breath. If they came, they would come from Atchison, and if they came now, she would hear them.

Maria marveled at their choice of land when they staked their claim all those months ago. Yes, she was vulnerable now, alone, but at least they had chosen their land well, almost as if they knew it should be defensible. Their cabin was perched atop a sloping ridge that ran west to east, and commanded perfect views of the approaches any Missourian may take. Any hostile rider from Atchison was likely going to cross the large pasture to the south, gain their bearings, slip back into the forest, and try to creep through the thin, scattered row of trees that ran along the ridge like the fins of a sturgeon. She'd told Patrick to clear them trees, dammit. At least she'd be able to blame him if she died because of them. And any hostile rider from the north would have to cross the Independence at one of only two or three shallow, slow points, and would be funneled through the trees and emerge in the large clearing at the bottom of the hill. There was nowhere to both hide and move to the north at all. It was pretty rugged country. You either stayed put in the forest or moved through their edges or out in the clearings, especially this time of year, when the undergrowth was thick and thorny.

It would also be difficult to find your way all the way around to the west of the cabin and try to sneak up from behind, and so, when she heard the noises in the forest to the west, she knew it must be something that was more than familiar with the land, but quite intimate with it. Easing her way around the back of the cabin, she peered out into the forest and saw Joseph James and Oliver John emerge from the trees with five or six similar-looking, hulking Missourians in tow. Quickly she decided that confronting them would be better than either hiding or trying to surprise them, but just as she stepped out into the open something grabbed her from behind. She felt feathers on her neck, and could feel a giant breast push up against her back, rising gradually as if she were an egg and a giant bird was going to hatch her.

"I got her, Jimmy!" she heard the bird cry out.

"Well done, Private." Joseph James rode up to the cabin, stone-faced. "I knew she'd a-hear us." Only then did she realize that the hands holding her tightly above each elbow were those of a man. "Drop that damn shovel, Maria. You know I ain't no snake."

"I must disagree with you about that." Her face was even stonier than his. "Neighbor."

"Goddamnit, woman, drop it!" He swung his rifle out and struck the shovel with a ferocity that shocked and excited her. Her voice quivered.

"Do what you will, you heathen."

"Yer menfolk done left ya, didn't they?" He dismounted. Ralph wandered a bit and he snapped back on the reins, cussing him, and handed the reins to another man.

"They went to protect me."

"Protect you? Good Lord, Maria, yer head's a-full of rocks. They left you a sittin' duck. Get her inside."

***

Inside the cabin Maria was told to sit in a chair while the men ransacked the house looking for maps, documents, anything that may be of use, particularly anything that pertained to James Lane or John Brown. They found all the food they could and shoved it in their satchels. One man went outside to butcher a pig and a chicken, and then collect all the eggs in the coop.

Joseph James stood in the doorway, supervising the looting. He was pleased, though he was often distracted. First, there were small pains of guilt, not so much for the Dugans, but for introducing Oliver John to this sort of behavior. He'd seen it a little in Mexico but Doniphan forbade it and the men usually enforced that policy amongst themselves. Then he was distracted by the idea that Patrick or Roger would come through the door any moment. But then, and for the majority of the time his men emptied his neighbor's cabin of its contents, he was distracted by Maria's legs.

She sat in a bit of a heap on the chair, just as she'd been rather indelicately placed a few minutes ago. Slumping more than she usually did, her pelvis more forward and back more arched, she looked tired and disheveled. Her skirt was pushed up her thigh by the rough handling and slumping, and her left leg was visible almost all the way up to her underwear. She wasn't wearing an undergarment, apparently. Del almost always wore one. She said the fabric of her dress wasn't comfortable enough against the skin to not wear one. The ransacking got louder, both inside and out, but Joseph James paid no mind, instead studying Maria's leg. So strong and muscular, shapely and pasty white.

When she bolted for the door, then, it took him a moment to realize it, dash for her and tackle her to the ground. By the time he got control of her, his body on top of hers, he realized the only way to protect himself from the power of her legs was to shove his pelvis between them as if he were making love to her. And again, he saw both thighs, wrapped around his, and had trouble thinking about anything else.

"You dirty sonofabitch," she said.

"How did you get loose?"

"I'm Irish," she said. "Irish gals are always loose."

"I don't want to hurt you, Maria."

"Really, Joseph? Because I sure don't mind hurting you right now."

Maria reached up and grabbed a frying pan that had fallen to the floor in the commotion. She hit him square in the head, and it rang out like bell as the men laughed and Joseph James fell unconscious.

***

The Dugan brothers and their squadron from Lawrence tied Dutch Henry to a chair inside the cabin and seated themselves around the cottonwood table. Why Henry could live here a dozen years without getting a new table made no sense to Patrick. It hardly served any purpose that a table would anymore—one couldn't place a glass, mug, or even a plate on it, the surface was so warped. The only purpose it served was to delineate the way people sat in relation to one another in the room. It was just a square that divided interlocutors.

"We want to know the whereabouts of any and everyone, Henry," said Roger, pacing across the table from his captive. "Have you seen Lane?"

"No."

"Word is there is an army of Missourians headed this way. Have you seen them yet? They would stop here for whiskey, I'm certain of it."

"Outa whiskey."

"That's a shame, because we could use some ourselves."

"Well, I do have—"

Roger slapped him across the face, produced a small muzzle-loading pocket pistol from his belt, cocked it, and pushed it into his neck. "Where are they?"

"Close is all I know." Only the first word sounded nervous. "I don't know where and I don't know where they're headed."

"Osawatomie."

"Your guess is as good as mine."

"Guess or I will shoot you, God help me."

"Osawatomie."

"Leave him tied here," Roger said to his men, holstering the old pistol. "We'll ride for Osawatomie. And if we don't find them there, we'll come back and kill him."

XXXII

When Joseph James came to, Maria was tied to the chair and he could hear horses being mounted outside. He sat up with a start and held his head.

"Don't worry. They aren't leaving you. And you aren't hurt badly." She glared at him. "Unfortunately."

As he stood and gently re-tied her hands before striding out the door, Maria thought about having his body on top of hers, of being so completely incapacitated it was impossible to move. There was a corporeal force, a brute strength and power in Joseph James that Patrick Dugan did not possess. And it was attractive. She had to admit it. Had she been truly scared perhaps she would not have admitted this to herself, but given that she somehow knew that no matter what he did she would outsmart him, and that he would never really hurt her because deep inside he was as sentimental as her husband, and he loved her as much as she loved him. What an idiot he was. She laughed to herself. What a loveable idiot.

"We're leaving you here," he said as he came back in through the door.

"Fine."

"And taking all your food."

"I see that."

"You may just starve in that chair, Maria."

"So be it."

"I talked them out of raping you."

"I suppose I should thank you then." An impertinent smile held itself steady on her face.

Joseph James stood a moment and swallowed his spit.

She could tell from the brim of his hat that he was quivering with anger, just a little. He snatched it off his head and stomped out the door.

"Say hello to Del for me!" she called.

She listened to the horses ride off to the south, and laughed. Maria laughed and laughed, until she heard the jayhawk alight on the roof—scratch, scratch—and hop down onto the ground in front of the door.

***

A half mile outside Osawatomie, the Dugan company came upon John Brown and a small band of followers. Roger thought they had found them without being noticed; their rifles stood up against the trees, wood had been gathered but the fire was not yet lit, and blankets were not yet unrolled. He knew from the way the rock ring around the fire was built it was Brown, because one rock stood apart for the grinding of corn, with yet another, hand-sized rock set aside for breaking the kernels. Roger felt a sense of triumph in finding Brown's camp without being seen.

But just as he turned over his left shoulder to tell Patrick and the others this, and that while they should be cautious nonetheless, he felt a tap on his right shoulder.

As he wheeled to see what it was he felt his rifle being seized. It was Brown.

"Why, I know you, and we are friends." The old man didn't smile, but handed the rifle back to Roger.

"We are." Roger did smile. He turned and saw that his entire company was surrounded by Brown's, a half-dozen to a dozen. "And I see you're not surprised."

"No. And it isn't wise to lead all your men into an unknown camp, young man. You should hold four back to cover, while one or two investigate."

"We just happened up on you."

"Upon our trap, that is. Come, let's eat."

Patrick found himself standing more and more upright as he saw the old man speak to his little brother. He had read about Brown the villain in the *Sovereign*, and had always shuddered to think of Roger's sojourn with him last winter. Only now, perspiring so badly he couldn't feel whether something on his face was a bug or a bead of sweat, standing among the dappling shadows and shafts of light that each leaf on each tree marked on the prairie grass below, did he realize that he also blamed this mysterious man for nearly killing his brother. Roger had given so much to this gray, stiff, almost non-human person, and it became obvious that he gave Roger little humanness in return. John Brown fancied himself some sort of god, and Patrick didn't like it. He didn't like John Brown. Not for what he did, necessarily, but for what he thought he did and for what he thought he was.

As they sat down around the fire and the sky turned orange with evening, Patrick thought of the convention at Big Springs. Seeing how this movement came to be, and how this Free State Party operated, ruined everything righteous in its cause. He remembered how Jim Lane seemed—and then later proved to be at even a national level—a zealot and provocateur when compared to Charles Robinson, and it made him sick to compare Brown to these men, because it made Lane seem the moderate. And now it all made sense to Patrick, this odd Free State movement. By jailing Robinson the Law and Order Party and the official territorial government, and by extension the U.S. Marshal's Office, the War and State Departments, and the White House itself, had removed almost all reason from the righteous. Robinson was a man who could control Lane and Brown, and though others such as Pomeroy tried to fill this role, they could not. Just or no, Patrick was in the company of murderers. He could fight to protect his home and his right to live freely, but he could not fight to protect this man.

"No, thank you," he said with almost an unthinking automation when Brown offered him a corn pellet.

"This is a soldier's fare, Mr. Dugan."

"I'm not hungry."

"Food for the warriors of God."

"I'm no crusader, Mr. Brown. I'm a farmer." He could feel his brother's stare behind his right ear. He had to stand; it was so humid and hot around the fire, he could barely breathe.

"We are at war, Mr.—may I call you by your given name?"

"Patrick."

"The namesake of Saint Patrick is no crusader? I find that disappointing, to say the least. But we all fight for a cause, however large or petty we make it. Nevertheless, we are at war, so I must ask you to call me Captain Brown."

"I've not enlisted in any army, sir," replied Patrick. "I am only here defending my home and my family. I consider that to be a great cause indeed."

"I see. Then you are on your way through, then? Well, thank you for joining us for supper. We hope you will continue to fight alongside us."

Brown stood and shook hands with Patrick.

Roger stood as well, and spoke. "We are an independent company supporting the cause, Captain," he said. "We're looking to join forces with whosoever may be in position to oppose the Ruffians, wherever they may be."

"Lane's command is in Lawrence," replied Old Brown. "You may find them amenable to your suggestion." Brown looked down, then back up. "And just how shall we refer to your independent company?"

Roger didn't hesitate. "The Jayhawkers."

"Very well, then." Somewhat to the Dugan brothers' surprise, the other men they had arrived with stood as well, brushing off their pants. Their number included another, as well, a very large man with an even larger gun. The men paused as he stood, both knowing it meant he was defecting from Brown's command to Roger's, and because his weapon was just so big. "We shall find somewhere to sleep in Osawatomie and ride for Lawrence in the morning," said Patrick after a pause.

Brown cleared his throat, said, "There is a mill in town owned by the Emigrant Aid Company. Samuel Pomeroy is the Society's representative. If he asks tell them I sent you there."

"I know him," replied Patrick. "I served with him at Franklin." The words fell out of Patrick's mouth like inedible food, so strange they felt.

"Excellent."

On the ride toward town, they all introduced themselves and learned their new compatriot was a man by the name of Freeman Austin. He towered above the others, his legs so long he didn't need a horse. He kept up just fine.

"Call me 'Pap'," he said. "And a mighty thank you for a-lettin' me join. That there is one crazy old man, lemme tell you. Runs a fine command but I ain't livin' on no corn pellets until this thing is over. Hell, no. I'm starving!"

One of the other men handed Pap some food—ham and carrots and a baked thing that passed for bread—and he ate it greedily as he strode alongside the other men and their horses, still talking.

"This here is a man I call 'Kill Devil'," he said, indicating his rifle. "If he wasn't on my side I'm afraid old 'Kill Devil' may-a thought that old Brown was the devil and fired accidentally while we slept. I had to keep him away from his balls there for a while jes to make sure."

"What sized balls are they?" Patrick asked.

"A whole ounce," he said through a mouthful of food, pulling some out of a satchel. "Lookee here."

"Sweet Mother in Heaven!" Patrick leaned down and took two and felt their weight. "You could hunt a bear or bison with that!" Patrick dreamed of killing a bison someday and eating it all winter. He tired of the chore of finding pheasant, deer, beaver, muskrat.

Muskrat tended to be easy picking along the banks of the Independence but they didn't taste all that great, even with Maria at the helm of the stove.

"Yessiree. Only trouble is, they don't fly too far. Gotta get up close to the devil if you wanna kill 'im."

***

Little did the Dugans know, however, that when the Hawkins brothers and their small company rendezvoused with the rest of the Atchison Guards at Leavenworth a few days before the Dugans arrived at Osawatomie, they found a huge army under the command of General John W. Reid riding west on the Santa Fe Trail. They were heading for Osawatomie. Reid had squatted along the Pottawatomie only to be driven out by Brown earlier that year. He and hundreds of his friends were returning for revenge.

Just as the Dugans finally found the mill and bedded down for the night, a scouting party of Missourians crossed the Marias des Cygnes River, four miles northwest of the town.

Patrick woke and found that ticks were crawling all over him, the last of the Missourians found the south bank, and Captain Reid and his lieutenants drew up a plan for attack. Just as Roger woke to pee, and saw the stars in the east were weakening with the approach of second-to-last sunrise, the Ruffians sent out another scouting party toward town, their leader deciding to join them personally. And just as Pap Austin woke with a start from a bad dream, slapping a mosquito and twisting a tick from his neck, Captain Reid and his small party encountered John Brown's son Frederick on the road one mile east of Osawatomie.

"Morning boys!" he said cheerfully. "Are you heading for Lawrence?"

"I know you," said Captain Reid, "and we are foes."

With that he shot the young man in the chest. Frederick was dead before his head found the Kansas soil, and the Battle of Osawatomie had begun.

***

Word reached the Jayhawkers at the mill, Brown's men just east of town, and the rest of the men and women of Osawatomie that four hundred Missourians would be in town by sunrise. Brown and others ran among the cabins gathering recruits, and by the time the first ray of light touched the first blade of grass there were forty-one men along the main street of the town.

Along with the mill, the Emigrant Aid Company had built a small blockhouse that could be used to help protect the settlement, but when the Free Staters learned the Missourians had a cannon with them, and realized they were outnumbered ten-fold, they withdrew to the north of the town and formed a line on the south bank of the river. Their backs to the water, they hunkered down in the grass and began to sweat in the already-hot August day. As the light expanded across the sky and the insects in the trees began to quiet, Patrick spotted the first of the enemy.

The Missourians came into view, one by one, spreading across the horizon like it were a painting melting in the sun. Patrick looked over at his little brother. Roger's jaw was clenched and he was strangling his rifle. Only now did Patrick fully realize that one of them could die today. He hoped it was him, looking at the band of hair behind his brother's ear. But then he thought of Maria. Roger would not be able to stay on the farm and tend to it the way he should. He just couldn't do it. Maria would be alone. The thought of it was intolerable. But so was the thought of Roger dying. This fight wasn't worth it.

Word came along the line that Brown asked everyone to hold their fire until the Missourians were within two hundred yards. Many of the men had Sharps and Sheridan model rifles that had longer ranges, but at this distance the older muskets would also be effective. Brown and others knew their only chance was to inflict heavy casualties upon the first charge, hoping to repel the Missourians through fear and perhaps ignorance as to how many men lay in wait in the woods along the river.

Patrick thought about it. Two hundred yards wasn't very far. At two hundred yards, the Missourians would be firing into the timber and full speed. No, this just wasn't worth it, and he shimmied on his belly over to his brother to tell him so. But just as he spoke, the Missourians fired their cannon into the center of the Free State line.

"What?" Roger yelled, a little too loud now.

"This isn't worth it, lad!" But again his words were muffled by small arms fire.

"What?" Roger was clearly getting irritated. He was trying to focus on his first real battle experience, and now his older brother wanted to talk about it.

"I said—!" He was interrupted this time by a bullet whirring between them.

They both buried their faces in the brush.

"Shut your mouth, Patrick, you langer! Can't you see we have something to do?"

"This isn't worth it, Roger!"

"Not now, Paddy! Not now!"

They both looked into the distance. There seemed to be a charge coming to their right, but nothing in front. "I don't want to lose you, Roger! Not like this!"

"Shutup!"

"I don't want to lose Maria!"

"Then leave!"

The cannon was fired again, this time closer to them, and he heard it tear through the branches, leaves, and bark of the oak, birch, and buckeye trees along the water. Birch bark rained down on them like cinder and ash from a far off fire. The heat of the day was apparent again.

"No! If you stay, I stay! I'll fight for you, Roger!" Patrick was crying.

Roger looked over at him, ready to shoot him and put him out of his misery himself. His older brother's tear- and sweat-stained face, with its sepia tones and vertical lines, looked almost camouflaged in the grass. Roger smiled, and then laughed. He looked again and laughed again. Patrick laughed too.

And the cannon fired again, even closer this time. It was just to Patrick's right, and one of the men who had marched with them all the way from Lawrence tried to dig himself further down into the soil with his knees and elbows. A ball bounced in front of Patrick. He picked it up.

"Grape shot!" He smiled and held it up for Roger to see. They laughed. "What are we, squirrels?"

"Move!" A man approached from their right, motioning for them to move left along the timber. "Move!"

Roger looked up and saw, distant though it was, Joseph James riding Ralph. He was holding his distance and scanning the woods with his eyes. Patrick grabbed Roger by the shirt and tried to pull him to his feet or knees so he could shift left along with the rest of the line, but Roger slapped his hands away and hunkered down. He was going to kill that damned Joseph James once and for all. Now was his chance. Patrick hopped over him and assumed a similar position, now on Roger's left. Men stumbled over both. Both Dugan brothers realized the Free Staters were now returning fire. Patrick fired aimlessly.

But Roger took aim. As he held his neighbor in his sights and began to squeeze the trigger all manner of memory came and passed through his mind. Joseph James making them kneel in the grass one year ago; the mangled body of Sam Collins; the writhing of the man he shot in the shoulder at Henry's crossing; the sickness he'd felt after learning what Brown had done that night a few months ago; his father's voice and warmth; and finally, the jayhawk. As Roger's rifle discharged, he felt something feathery about it, about himself, about the ground on which he lay. Kansas was a nest of monsters, a haunted, eerie place whose woods were alive with millennia of hunts, births, deaths, marriages, floods and droughts and tornadoes and the sun's full fury. Here one could feel the continent shifting on the seas of lava, the earth spinning through the void.

He missed. Ralph heard the ball whizz past his ear and tried to dump his rider, but Joseph James held to the saddle.

And Roger felt stunned, wondering just how, and why, he had missed.

XXXIII

For another hour the Battle of Osawatomie was a stalemate. The Pro Slavery army attacked from their left flank and the Free Staters shifted toward theirs, returning fire as best they could. The cannon helped spur the battle toward the east as well, but did little damage.

The Hawkins brothers stayed generally to the right flank of their forces, never moving in much closer than two hundred yards. Joseph James was proud that they were no longer a drunken mob, but thought the attack could be more organized and aggressive. He could tell Reid was trying to feint left and outflank to the right, and failing. He could also tell there were fewer men in the woods than Reid seemed to think. He thought they should just come at them with everything they had. With a river to their backs, the Yanks had little option for retreat; and if there were several hundred men, evidence of them would have been in town and around the area. But there were no tents in the prairies or torn up creeks from a cavalry of any considerable size. No, they had surprised these men just this morning, and they had scrambled into squadrons and for cover as best they could. But Joseph James had been told to hold his ground to the right of the cannon, and that was what he would do. He was delighted to follow clear orders that, while overly cautious, were clear enough.

Just as the sun rose high enough into the sky to make the day's heat even more apparent, the Free Staters began to run out of ammunition. Finally, hearing the decreasing frequency of return fire from the woods, Reid seized his chance and ordered all his forces into the woods to "finish off those Yankee bastards."

Free Staters jumped into the river and scrambled their way up the steep, muddy banks on the other side. Some were caught and held. Some were shot in the river. Some were hunted down, put on their knees, and executed in cold blood.

Patrick and Roger didn't cross the river, but heard the cries of their comrades and ran as fast as they could down the bank to the east. It was surreal, and they both felt automated in thier movements, impelled onward with little actual volition of their own, until they stopped running, and fear shook them like the earth were opening. Somehow they found themselves back at the mill with Pap Austin and, after a few moments of collecting themselves, they realized the fight was over and the Missourians were razing the town. Many were heading back toward their home state with wagonloads of loot and wounded. A large body of them were coming straight for the mill, perhaps to check it for munitions caches or just for sacks of flour. But Pap had other ideas. He stepped outside and fired Kill Devil right at them. One man fell—was knocked back, more like—and Pap yelled at them. "Plenty of men in here!"

Patrick and Roger looked at each other, eyes wide. This crazy man with his huge gun had done them in. But the Missourians halted, tracked back, and gave the mill a wide girth. They had no intention of opening a second, confused and misdirected battle. Realizing this, and feeling dizzy and slight of breath in the stone structure with little air movement whatever, Roger stepped outside and slunk around the corner to rest and catch his breath. But just as he sat back against the wall he heard a ball scream by his head and tear the native stone into shards, some of which scattered against the side of his face and dazed him. He heard another shot, but was too disoriented to open his eyes, much less return fire.

But someone did. It was Patrick. When Roger was able to regain his bearings he saw three or four Missourians about three hundred yards away hammering the side of the mill with small arms fire, his brother lying next to him, firing madly, his face so full of courage and resolution it looked like those he'd imagined on ancient mythical soldiers he read about them as a boy. Had he not been so terrified, he might have laughed at his brother's transformation.

But he could also see the hulking back of one of his attackers, as he lay in the grass, and from the horse that wriggled against his hitch behind, that one was Joseph James. He could then see Oliver John's feathered hat in the grass, peeking up just as it had that fateful day that now seemed so far in the past. Something exploded inside him, an anger he remembered feeling as a toddler. Screaming, doing all he could to keep himself from racing across the grass to attack his neighbor, he loaded his rifle and shot at Joseph, regretting he'd missed just an hour before. Patrick, his face distorted with the fury of battle, rose and shrieked, ready to charge and fight his neighbors hand-to-hand.

But Pap Austin stepped out from around the corner and fired one of Kill Devil's ounce balls into the dirt just in front of the Hawkinses and their two or three compatriots. Pap screamed the same scream, and the Hawkinses were mounted and riding east before anything else could happen. Briefly, as Joseph James looked back, helping Oliver John mount Ralph behind him, he locked eyes with Roger, and both began to breathe again.

The Battle of Osawatomie may be over, but for the Hawkinses and Dugans, the war had just begun.

***

Somewhere in that timber were men who wanted to kill me, thought Oliver John Hawkins as he followed his brother north and east. They and the few Carolinians who had joined the Missourians at Leavenworth were now just reaching the Atchison area and rejoining the Guards. Oliver John liked the men. They drank and laughed and their horses meandered all over the road. They patted one another on the back often and playfully made fun of one another's beards and legs as they swung in the saddle. They were funny.

Where they were going exactly, Oliver John didn't know. Toward Atchison at first, and now the other direction. They had learned during their time in the south that hostilities were increasing north of the Kaw, and that was where they lived with Del and Sarah Sally. Not to mention little Missy. She was almost crawling now, sitting up all by her lonesome. Oliver John missed his niece, though she was more like a little sister than a niece. That was because Jimmy was more like a dad than a brother. He smiled at the thought.

"What're you a-smilin' at boy?"

"Nothin', Jimmy. Where're we a-headin?"

"Grasshopper Falls, son. There's a bunch a Free Staters there that're a-havin' troubles minding their own business. We're there to teach 'em what fer."

Several dozen men from Atchison arrived in Grasshopper Falls that early September day, and the Hawkins brothers occupied themselves mostly in just watching them. They pinched the backsides of the women and made the children cry, and when they found a man they would beat him up or just threaten to do as much. Sometimes it was funny to Joseph James. Other times he bit his lip and spat, sighing and rubbing his beard. It didn't seem to be the way to teach men a lesson, but it would have to do for now. The day started out cool but got hot pretty quickly, and by the time they were done and camped outside the town, along Slough Creek, Oliver John was tired. He went to bed just about nightfall.

Around two in the morning, Oliver John had to urinate. He'd taken to drinking coffee around the campfire on this trip, and it always woke him up at night. It had cooled off again, and he remembered how much he liked this time of year. The ups and downs of the temperature, the anticipation of the change of seasons, and the relative abundance and variety of food were wonderful. Sure, there was a lot of work for a farmhand in September, but it kept you busy, your body tight and lean, and you slept well at night. Even the insects started to disappear this time of year, or at least, you could bet that they soon would.

He decided to walk a little farther from the camp, enjoying the night. The moon was only a few degrees above the eastern horizon, just a sliver of a thing cupped down toward the ground like the rind of a watermelon resting on a table in a dark cabin. He had eaten melons that day, in fact, and could still feel the stickiness on his fingers. The stars were brilliant and stretched wide across the sky. Oliver John breathed deeply. His hip still hurt now and then from the accident, but not now. For this he was most grateful. To be free of pain meant so much. He loved being alive.

He lay down on the grass and looked up at the stars. To feel the earth enclose him and the sky open into endlessness—this was love.

Oliver John Hawkins thought about what he loved just in time to lose it. A bright flash, a smell of burning, and a deafening sound later, he had exactly what he wanted. The earth closed and the sky opened. No bugs, even, to make him regret it. Yes, it was well worth it. All of it.

***

For us, and those we love, death sends the earth reeling into places unknown; vast, dark, cold, starless voids in space; spinning so out of control all that what once was is grotesque, almost unrecognizable as non-existence. But not even the slighted hitch in the gears of time, nor the faintest of breezes; not even a whisper of a cry from the world comes when we die, so strong is the feeling the world was created for us. And so on went the world, and Kansas, and the tussles of men and boys as they fought over things that would one day become rotten and horrible, as they would soon be to those who loved Oliver John Hawkins.

The Dugan brothers rode three terribly hot days straight and reached Lawrence on September 3rd. There they learned that the Free State leadership, knowing the Missourians would wage a final assault on Lawrence and finish what they'd twice failed to complete, had decided to preemptively strike the Pro Slavery capital of Lecompton. Governor Robinson and others were still held prisoner there, and they intended to rescue their prisoners, restore their government, and once and for all stand their ground. Osawatomie had been a terrible defeat, and it would not happen again.

Patrick and Roger chose to join a larger band this time and rode with a Colonel James A. Harvey and his "Chicago Company." The Chicago Company was to rendezvous with Lane's Army near the official territorial capitol the following day. Lane had taken an alias of Cook but everyone knew him to be the same Jim Lane that led the Army of the North from Iowa. Harvey did not find Lane there, however, and instead turned his attention north, toward Grasshopper Falls, deciding to stop whatever Pro Slavery outrages he could find.

"That's getting closer to home," said Roger to his brother.

"I know. I should be there."

"No, you're defending her better here."

"The Hawkinses will be there."

"Atchison?"

"Yes."

Roger considered this, but was decided. "No, they'll be wherever Stringfellow is. My guess is we shall meet him with Harvey, Paddy. Meet them both, once and for all. We will save our farm and our cause by facing them at last!"

***

Like a woman whose man has left her bed, Joseph James woke with a start at 3 a.m. and reached for Oliver John. His blanket roll was empty and was cold—it had been empty for some time. Something was wrong. He sat up and looked around the camp. All the fires were out and not a single sentinel could be seen. Palmer hadn't set a watch, damn him. He'd let his men loot a town, get drunk, and pass out. It was dereliction of duty.

Knowing his brother's penchant for having a weak bladder under pressure of coffee, he set out the way he thought Oliver John would walk to urinate.

He was nowhere to be seen.

The moon stood above the trees, now giving the sky an appearance of a wry smile. Something was wrong. Terribly, terribly wrong. He spat.

"Oliver John! Oliver John, where are you, boy?!" he whisper-yelled.

Nothing. Nothing but bugs and stars and a breeze.

And then, horses.

Not twenty yards behind him, Joseph James heard and smelled a band of horses close in on the camp he'd just left. There were twenty or so men sleeping there, and soon Joseph realized they were surrounded, but he was not. He jogged carefully, but quickly, away from the camp, toward the moon. He could only hope Oliver John had wandered into the forest and was also away from the surrounded encampment of drunken Carolinians. Damn them. Damn them all.

And then Joseph found he was right. He stumbled in the grass over something that felt familiar, even to his booted foot. He remembered his brother wandering about their various cabins around Westport at night, finding cool spots on the floor—or even out in the yard—to sleep. And he remembered stumbling upon his sleeping body from time to time, almost like a black dog lying underfoot around the campfire at night. He felt sick and green. Oliver John hadn't done this in years.

Reaching down into the black grass at night, he felt that his brother was wet, limp, and unnaturally still, even for a sleeping person. He held his hand up in the moonlight. It was covered in red.

"No."

He reached down again and felt the all too familiar contour of his brother's body. His arms and waist, slightly disfigured hip, and then his neck. It was soft, wet, lukewarm, and mutilated, like a butchered pig. He held his hand up in the moonlight again. It was blood. Definitely blood.

"No. Oh, God, no."

Joseph James gently picked up his little brother under the arms and propped him up in the moonlight. His head nearly fell off. He'd been shot through the neck at close range, and the spinal column was shattered. He let Oliver John slump into his chest and ran his hand through his brother's hair. His hands knew that skull so well, from when it was not even fully formed, through when the hair was soft with boyhood, and was only now becoming hard and proud and wiry with age. His wrists had touched those ears a thousand times, and his chest knew that nose poking into it.

"No, please, God no, don't do this to me. Please God, no, don't do this to me."

Commotion rose from the trees around the camp, and Joseph knew exactly what was happening. The entire company was being taken prisoner without a fight. They were all asleep and had no chance of defending themselves. The Free Staters—the Dugans might be with them, damn Irish sonsabitches—had at least shown mercy in not slaughtering them as they slept. Had he been them, he would have slaughtered them. He would now.

He dragged his brother's body into a thicket of hickory trees and watched the silhouettes of men rise, at gunpoint, congregate, sit, stand, congregate again. He began to weep, holdings his brother's body in his lap like Mary did the Son of God after His death, rocking himself, too sick even to spit. He heard laughter and saw, by the firelight and the curious coincidence of the weak moonlight finding its way through the trees just so, a man hold the company's flag up. It was the bright red flag that Oliver John had carried into Lawrence in May, the flag that had been his sin and his pride alike. It was captured. Oliver John's flag was in the hands of the enemy, as was his mortal life.

Joseph James looked to the stars, picked up his brother's feathered hat, kissing it, and prayed for the first time in many years. He prayed that Oliver John's soul was in the lap of something altogether different.

***

At first, Colonel James A. Harvey thought James H. Lane was the exact man needed to settle the Kansas Question. He had met him in Chicago and raised funds for the National Kansas Committee with him. But now that he'd failed to hit back after Osawatomie, when he had the chance, failed to show at Lecompton, and was balking on the idea of attacking Leavenworth, he wasn't sure anymore.

Harvey was going to return to Lawrence, no matter what Lane or "Cook" or whomsoever else told him. All of the South was coming to Lawrence yet again and his general was nowhere to be found.

Two Irishmen in his company were hesitant, however. They were brothers from a farm up near Atchison and wanted to stay north of the Kaw to help ensure the Pro Slavery guerilla bands were controlled. They acquiesced, nonetheless, after discussing it aside, under a great elm tree. It seemed the younger one held sway over the elder. It was odd.

When they reached Lawrence, however, they were immediately contacted by Lane and asked to reinforce him up near Hickory Point, where he had cornered one hundred Pro Slavery farmers in three log cabins. Small arms fire wouldn't do it. Lane wanted the old four-pounder they called "Sacramento." He wanted to give these men the same lesson he'd given their friends at Ft. Titus—a taste of their own medicine.

And so Colonel Harvey's Chicago Company marched overnight toward Hickory Point, flying the flag of their enemy, his dearest war prize in tow. Though they had captured—and then released upon condition of their leaving the territory—two dozen of these men just two days ago, apparently a few had gotten away and exacted revenge on Grasshopper Falls with another squadron or two that were camped in other parts of the woods. One man (it was said he was the older brother of the sole fallen enemy in the little skirmishes north of the Kaw in recent days) in particular had wreaked great havoc. They had done to Grasshopper Falls what they had done to Osawatomie just ten days previous. It was gone. Grasshopper Falls, Kansas, was no more.

But once again, when Harvey arrived, Lane was not there. It seemed Lane was all bark and no bite. He preached like a soldier and fought like a preacher. No matter. The enemy was still holed up in those three cabins, and Harvey let them have it.

One cannon blast tore through the blacksmith's shop and killed a man, injuring two.

But as they reloaded and fired again, they found it did little damage to the two structures that lay farther away. They had to move in, and fast.

He ordered five mounted men around the right flank to try and hold the road so his captives couldn't flee. He then deployed five others to the left to scout the woods south of the town, to do the same and also to watch for sniper fire. And he ordered the cannon forward.

But just then the elder Irishman came on horseback. "There," he said, pointing to the corner of a building in town. "I know that man and he's a deadly fighter. Looks like he has a Sharps rifle. Move slowly, so." And he rode off again to the left flank to recapture his detail.

And the Irishman was right. Every time the men tried to wheel the cannon forward into town, the strange, hulky man beside the cabin rang a shot off the muzzle of Sacramento. He also seemed to be aiming for the Southern Rights flag they flew over it. He was a veteran, no doubt, of Mexico, but perhaps also of Wakarusa. He had a vendetta against these things. Against his past.

From the Dugans' vantage point on the left flank, they could see both their neighbor and their brothers in arms.

They could see Joseph James holding the cannon back with sniper fire, and see that Harvey kept the men inching Sacramento—and the flag of the Atchison Guards—forward.

One or two men were hit non-lethally. Finally, the cannon was fired. But it did little damage. It was still too far away.

"Patrick," Roger said, reloading his musket as he had somehow lost his Sharps rifle. "It's him. He's keeping them back. We have to move in."

"I know it."

Roger moved to rise from his position crouching in the brush but Patrick grabbed his elbow and held him back. There was firmness in his gentleness that Roger had not felt before in all their years together. He looked at the hand, then at his brother's face. "I shall do it, boy."

"Paddy?"

"I know, lad, I know. But God has put me here. I must, so." They scanned each other's eyes, and souls, the way brothers can. "I must and you know it."

It was as if all the times they had ever looked each other in the eye was relived, and Roger realized that excepting his mother's, Patrick's were the first he ever saw. A dim memory of Patrick as a boy came to him, with bulging, pock-marked legs and a concave chest. He wished they were still boys, still in Ireland, still with their parents. Suddenly he knew what Patrick had been feeling all these months in Kansas, and wished he could leave then and there, return to the farm and forget all about slavery and sovereignty and the ownership of land.

"We can leave right now, Paddy. Go home."

Patrick looked back at Joseph James, still firing at the cannon from his superior position from behind the cabin, still keeping it back.

And Joseph James looked in their direction. Even from this distance, they could see fire in his eyes. He was making his final stand.

"No, we can't. And you know it, boy."

Roger nodded.

Patrick moved forward.

Roger grasped his hand. "What shall I tell Maria?"

Patrick thought a moment, then said, "Tell her I couldn't keep my mouth shut."

XXXIV

At times, the glowing inferno of rage subsided in the breast of Joseph James Hawkins. But these were short-lived reprieves, and served the sole purpose of allowing him to breathe. Breath gave the inferno oxygen, and on it raged, consuming his soul like bone-dry cottonwood limbs. Every time he saw the flag of the Atchison Guards, he was reminded of his little brother's mangled throat. Every time he saw the cannon, he was reminded of Little Danny Baumgartner's mangled eye littered with dust in the Mexican desert. And every time he fired his weapon, he was spurred on by an overriding desire for vengeance, for every bullet to tear the enemy from limb to limb, explode him into tiny bits for the coyotes to swallow by the mouthful.

Even that was not enough. Joseph James wanted them not just dead, their bodies scattered across the land; he wanted them to decompose and decay immediately. He wanted them dust and judged and to burn in the fires of Hell.

His only concern was that not every man would be killed by bullet or sword. He prayed earnestly that at least a few of them would be left unarmed and that he could fight them with his hands, tear their skin from their faces and shove it down their throats, crack their bones in his teeth. Joseph James wished he were a wild animal digesting every organ and cell in his enemy so they could burn not only in God's Hell, but burn first and foremost in his own. He wanted their souls to convulse and shake in unimaginable torture and terror.

Oliver John's body was wrapped in hemp cloth and lying in a wagon behind him, his feathered hat in his older brother's coat pocket. Joseph James began to envision himself as protecting not just his comrades, their town, their cabins, or even the wagon or Oliver John's body itself—he was still fighting for his little brother. Del and Missy and even Sarah Sally were in his thoughts, and somehow he felt that if he killed every last one of his enemy, perhaps he would not have to bring the body home. Perhaps he would not have to die as well. In his peripheral vision he saw something move on the gentle slope to his right. It was a man. He recognized his boots, his way of moving, angular like some sort of African giraffe. It was Patrick. It had to be.

And it had to be him or Patrick. Only one could return to Atchison. God had seen to it.

He turned and fired into the brush.

***

As Patrick scrambled along the slope on the enemy's right flank, looking for a place where he could take cover and determine his next move, he saw that Joseph James had spotted him, and somehow also knew that he would know exactly who he was and know exactly his intent.

The end of the world was personal now. Patrick could see the earth around him, and the sky sloping toward it like water rolling toward the sea. All of his life was here now, with him—not just Roger, who he could feel behind him—but his mother and father, Maria and his children (the one he lost and the one he now fought for). He felt as strong and unmoved and unmovable as a tree, as dangerous as a sword. Light and strong, supple and poised, he knew from somewhere deep inside him that he would pass this test that God had given him this September day.

By sheer luck, the slope had a hollow in it right as this happened and all Patrick had to do was get on his stomach. The shot rang out above him, tearing through the leaves of the oak brush. His head appeared above the cusp of the hollow and another ball tore through the brush. At once he became aware of his mouth (how dry it was), and his tongue (how swollen it was); his hunger and his thirst. His arms trembled as he held his upper body up on his elbows. His legs ached from walking and his thighs from chafing in the saddle. Tired and weak, he removed his hat, thinking it helped Joseph James identify him and see him hidden in the bush, and slowly raised his head again.

Joseph James was crouched now against the back of the cabin, reloading his rifle.

Now was his chance. Generations of Dugans, the bravest heroes of an indomitable race, coursed through his blood and impelled him forward.

Scrambling out of the hole, he glanced to his right and saw Roger moving in on his belly. He must get down into position before Roger found himself in Joseph's range and he decided to fire there first.

With a swift movement, he stood and bounded down the hill. He felt he was not himself, but a deer of some kind, swift and sure of foot, his feet finding every perfect spot to land, avoiding all rocks and tangles and hollows in the earth. It was as close to flying he ever felt. All his hunger and thirst and fatigue were gone. His muscles rippled with anticipation and strength. Somewhat to his own surprise, he heard himself screaming wildly, his face contorted again with fury.

Joseph James looked up just as Patrick was upon him.

Only when Patrick raised the rifle above his head and struck the first blow did he realize he had somehow decided not to pull up and fire, but to attack as if the rifle was a club, and he remembered then his father telling him stories of ancient Irish warriors charging down verdant yet rocky hillsides with clubs. All of his ancestry flowed through him. This was right. It was good. It was deadly.

But Joseph James held his rifle up and blocked Patrick's, no fear in his face whatsoever; there was a smirk about him, a sort of entertainment at his normally sober neighbor's animation. But as the blow struck and broke the pieces of his weapon, a concern came to his eyes and he rolled over, kicking and clawing to get away. He too screamed, a different, lower-toned scream, and was soon on his feet, stout, low to the ground like a badger. He swung back at Patrick's middle section and hit him hard in the ribs, blowing the air out of him.

The butt of the Irishman's rifle came across Joseph James's face and cut him in response. But he ducked the next blow and tackled Patrick around the waist.

Both men's guns dropped and they wrestled in the dusty earth behind the cabin where other men shouted and shots rang out into the September afternoon.

Joseph James, some thirty pounds heavier and four inches shorter, got the upper hand, but could not still his opponent enough to hit him cleanly.

Patrick broke free and was able to stand. He looked around for a weapon and realized he was standing on his rifle. He picked it up and leveled it just in time to stop Joseph in his tracks.

The two stood for a moment, knowing that now a decision was to be made.

"Oliver John's body lies in that wagon!" Patrick could see the boy's feet and the cloth around his legs. He recognized the boots. The very same boots he'd helped the boy into when he was able to walk again last Christmas. He now saw the feather of his hat in Joseph's coat. "And now you will kill me!"

A moment passed.

"Do it! Do it, you damned white nigger coward!" Joseph James Hawkins spat. Blood poured from his face and his mouth.

Patrick was about to shout something back, what, he didn't know. But he was interrupted by the cabin suddenly coming to light in a blaze. Men poured out of it. Under Harvey's orders the Free Staters, including Roger, had pushed a lighted coach up to it. Sacramento unloaded her heavy load into the cabin. Splinters and glass and gravel flew about them.

Patrick hoped Joseph would run, but he didn't.

"Do it! I killed your wife, Patrick! Maria is tied to your chair in your kitchen, bleeding to death and I put her there! Shoot me, you damned coward! Shoot me, for the love of God, right here!" He beat his breast.

Patrick heard distinctly the jayhawk shriek overhead. He made sure his rifle was ready.

Hearing Roger shout to his right, he looked over. The boy was crawling in his own blood. The Pro Slavery men had shot him in the leg beneath the wheels of the alighted wagon. He was desperately trying to crawl to safety.

And now enough time had passed that Joseph James changed his mind. He grabbed the rifle and almost tore it away.

"If you don't, I'm going to kill Roger! That little sonofabitch deserves it!"

Patrick felt the weapon torn away, as if his hands were numb with frostbite. He watched, frozen, while Joseph aimed at Roger as if he were killing a dog. But Roger stood. And Joseph looked back at him.

"Save your brother, you coward! Save him!" He held his fire.

But Patrick was immobile. Not with fear, and not so much with indecision but with disbelief. This was not right. This was not good. It may be deadly, but death came to every man. This was the end of the world anyway. There was little sense in fighting it.

But just as he decided to acquiesce, he found himself leaping and grasping hold of the gun with a strength he never thought could be his own.

Joseph was stunned, as if a gorilla had taken the gun away from him.

Patrick leveled it and fired. Joseph James Hawkins fell with a red thump upon the soil of Kansas, smiling.

***

Del had waited so long for her husband's return she didn't know the day anymore. Something was wrong. Everything in her body and her house told her so. She'd always had the gift, as her grandmother described it—the gift of knowing. From Sarah Sally's incessant whining and aches to little Missy's fever; from the odd way the bugs in the trees and frogs in the grass would fall suddenly silent at night, only to rise to crescendo once again, to the changing breezes and the eerie smells rising from the river; and from the way George Sherman Hawkins had arrived, sitting down at the kitchen table and smoking his pipe as if he had built the cabin, intended to stay, and said calmly and with incredible politeness through his ashen beard, that he would wait for his sons to arrive, she knew life would never be the same.

She didn't think her husband dead. The tealeaves told her it was not so. The muddy trail from the cabin to the shallow well that was turning hard and brittle said he lived. But someone was. Someone was. She knew who but could not bring herself to think it, knitting at night as her mother-in-law talked in her sleep—complaining even then of the coarseness of the sheets and the whirr of mosquitoes in the cabin—and her daughter flopped about the bed like a red carp on a bank heating in the sun, gasping for air, and the big disgusting man that deigned to consider himself her father-in-law, George Sherman Hawkins, snored in the dark. She couldn't even think of his name.

And so when she heard the horse near daybreak, and the steps outside, and when she opened the door, she was not surprised to see the scene that would define her, before and since. The scene that would be to her as the crucifix was to Catholics. It was Joseph James, bathed in blood from his shoulder, carrying Oliver John's body wrapped in cloth, a hollow and empty look in his eyes. They had changed color, from a lively blue to a dull gray, dulled by a suffering that could never be forgotten, and they would never be the same again.

Nothing would.

"Oliver John," she said softly, taking him from his brother's arms at last. "Oh, my sweet little Ollie. Of course it was you."

***

Roger was taken to Lawrence for medical attention. The ball had torn into the flesh on his lower leg and broken his shin, but it was clear he would survive and walk again in a matter of a few months, if not weeks. Patrick was exhausted. Twice he mounted Zion to ride for home, but soon found he was too tired for such a dangerous ride. Somewhere out there were yet more Missourians. He would rest and ride like the horsemen of centuries past for Atchison in the morning.

The Battle of Hickory Point ended mostly a stalemate. The Pro Slavery forces surrendered once the cabin was set afire, and many of the men on both sides spent the evening drinking whiskey. Another Missourian about Oliver John's age was killed, and several Free Staters suffered wounds such as Roger's. But most were able to gather their things and either leave or set up camp for the night, eating flapjacks and ham.

Patrick sat apart silently. He felt sick watching the two mortal enemies bond over violence and liquor. His brother lay injured, his neighbor dead, because of these childish men.

And he knew Joseph had been lying about Maria—he knew she was alive—but he also knew she was not safe.

He'd followed the jayhawk with the rest of the idiots in Kansas and was paying for it dearly. He needed to get back to the farm and never leave it again.

Around midnight he was able to stagger off into the brush by a creek and vomit. Men laughed, thinking it was the whiskey. The cool water felt refreshing, and he drank. It became quiet, the laughing men having left, and all that could be heard was the trickling of the water over the rocks and breeze through the leaves and grasses of the wide prairie.

Patrick was not surprised to see Paschal in the flickering of the campfire light, the jayhawk in the field behind him. It was as if he'd been sitting on that rock beside the creek for a thousand years. The bird seemed to be his consort, or a pet, perhaps.

"Irishman! You survive!"

"You told me not to follow it." He wiped the vomit from his chin with his sleeve.

"Yes." Paschal laughed. He laughed again and looked over Patrick's prostrate body. "You have company. It seems your journey continues, Irishman." And he picked up his satchel and left.

Patrick turned.

Behind him were seven soldiers on horseback.

"Stay on your stomach."

Patrick did as he was told.

"Now stand."

He did as he was told.

More dragoons were rounding up the rest of Harvey's command and forming them into ranks. "Join the ranks. You're under arrest for treason and attempted murder. We're taking you to Lecompton for imprisonment."

Patrick Dugan was marched southward with nearly one hundred of his fellow men over the sloping hills in the pitch dark night of the new moon. As they crested one, he could see the men spread out over the field like ghosts moving in to a place of death. Ahead of them was the jayhawk, but none of them seemed to see it. Standing there, lifeless and indifferent, it jerked about in its automated way. The men-ghosts seemed to be following it to the south.

Suddenly it was gone, but the ghosts marched on.

Glossary of Principal Historical Characters

Pardee Butler. Reverend Butler immigrated to Kansas from Ohio in 1854 and settled a dozen or so miles west of Atchison. His outspoken views supporting the abolition of slavery were entirely unwelcome in Atchison in 1855 and 1856, and on two occasions he barely escaped death by mobs. In 1855, he was sent down the river on a makeshift raft as a warning to like-minded individuals, and in 1856 he was tarred-and-feathered and set out upon the plains to make his way home. He refused to remain silent, preferring to preach to his congregation about the evils of slavery and write several op-eds in eastern newspapers. The town of Pardee, Kansas, is named after him, and his extensive autobiography contains incredible details of territorial Kansas.

Robert S. Kelley. A lawyer by training, Kelley was a founding member of the Atchison Town Company, its first postmaster, and junior editor of the *Squatter Sovereign*, its infamous newspaper. He was active in Pro Slavery militias but inexplicably declined commandership of the Atchison Guards in June of 1856. He was a part of the mob that sent Rev. Pardee Butler down the Missouri River in August of 1855, claiming decades later that he rigged a vote to save Butler's life.

Grafton Thomassen. Thomassen owned and operated Atchison's first saw mill. His slave drowned in the river in the summer of 1855 and he accused a lawyer and known Free Stater from Ohio, J.W.B. Kelley, of inciting her suicide. After beating Kelley nearly to death, Thomassen's actions were applauded by Atchisonians and they circulated a statement of support, forcing townspeople to sign it or face mob rule.

Paschal Pensoneau. Considered the first permanent white settler in Atchison County, Pensoneau was a French fur-trapper, trader, and interpreter who had long lived with the Kickapoo Indians. He fought in the Mexican-American and Blackhawk Wars, for which he was awarded land in Kansas Territory near the present site of Potter. His house served as the county's first polling place, though he later moved west with the Kickapoo when their reservation was diminished.

David Rice Atchison. Known as "Old Bourbon," Atchison was the first United States Senator from western Missouri. He served as President Pro Tempore of the Senate and was a proponent of the Kansas-Nebraska Act of 1854. A lawyer by schooling, he once represented Mormon prophet Joseph Smith and later served as a general in the state militia that suppressed the violence of the Mormon War of 1838. As ardent as any Pro Slavery man in the West, Atchison rallied for Missourian emigration to Kansas and supported violent defense of the Southern cause through secret societies known as "Blue Lodges," among other monikers. Though he was not an official founder of Atchison, he was instrumental in its creation and close friends with J.H. Stringfellow and others of the Town Company, who named the town after him. After losing his Senate seat in 1855, he turned his full attention to "Bleeding Kansas" and led troops in both the Wakarusa War and siege of Lawrence in the spring of 1856, where he personally ordered the cannon "Old Sacramento" fired on the Free State Hotel. His actions during these engagements were denounced by Territorial Governor Wilson Shannon and the bicameral Committee on Kansas Affairs.

Charles Robinson. An agent of the New England Emigrant Aid Society, Robinson helped found the Free State Party, write its constitution, and was elected territorial governor by that party. He organized the defense of Lawrence during the Wakarusa War of 1855 and negotiated the truce that ended it. The next May he fled, following the shooting of Sherriff Jones, was arrested in Missouri, and held for several months by the Pro Slavery legislature under charges of treason.

James Henry Lane. Former Lieutenant Governor of Indiana, Lane also served as a member of the United States Congress and as a Colonel in the Mexican-American War before moving to Kansas in 1856. A renowned orator who was very active in territorial politics, he helped form the Free State Party, write its version of the state constitution, and was elected to the House of Representatives under it, only to be denied the seat once arriving in Washington. He subsequently went on a speaking and fund-raising tour and returned to Kansas with armed men from Iowa and Illinois, "Lane's Army of the North." Their route into the territory was known as "Lane's Trail" and approximates the current path of Highway 59 from Topeka to the Nebraska border.

Patrick Laughlin. Laughlin was an Irish immigrant involved in the organization of the Kansas Legion in the northeast part of the territory, a secret military arm unofficially supporting the Free State Party. During one of its meetings he was accused of treachery to the Legion by a man named Sam Collins, whom he shot later that night, an incident that actually took place nearer Doniphan than Atchison. Laughlin later moved into Atchison where he became a tinsmith and was widely known to have killed Collins, but was never prosecuted.

John H. Stringfellow. A Virginian by birth, Stringfellow was a doctor from Missouri who helped found Atchison in 1854. He was active in Pro Slavery militias and the territorial government, serving as its Speaker of the House. His Atchison-based newspaper, the *Squatter Sovereign*, was as vehement a Pro Slavery publication as any in the Territory, often associated with the motto "Death to all Yankees and Traitors in Kansas!"

George Million. Million owned one of the first two tracts of land in the future site of the town of Atchison and sold his land to the Town Company, joining it in the process. He operated a ferry across the river for many years as well as several businesses in town, including the Pioneer Saloon.

Samuel Jones. Appointed in the summer of 1855 by Acting Governor Woodson, Sam Jones was the first Sheriff of Douglas County. A Virginian with staunch Pro Slavery views, Jones assisted in destroying ballot boxes during the elections of 1855 and used his office to promote the views of Southerners and repress those of Free Staters. He was personally involved in both the Wakarusa War and the May, 1856 sack of Lawrence, which largely started as a result of Jones's being shot by a Free State sniper while sitting in his tent one night. It was widely reported that he had been killed and his death became a rallying cry for Missourians intent on destroying Lawrence.

Wilson Shannon. Former Governor of Ohio, Shannon also served one term in the United States House of Representatives and as Minister to Mexico before becoming the second governor of Kansas Territory, successor to Andrew Reeder. Though he helped negotiate a truce that ended the Wakarusa War, his administration was marred by the violence of 1856. He resigned before President Franklin Pierce could fire him in June, fleeing as the territory descended into chaos.

John Brown. One of the most prominent figures in American history, Old John Brown was a zealous abolitionist from New York and saw himself as a key figure in God's plan to purge the Union of slavery. He followed his sons to Kansas in 1856 and orchestrated the shocking murder of five unarmed Pro Slavery men in the "Pottawatomie Massacre" as a reprisal for the siege of Lawrence. He is credited with winning the first battle of "Bleeding Kansas" at Black Jack Springs, an engagement some believe to be the first battle of the Civil War. He then helped organize small defense companies and became a Captain in the Free State Militia. His son was the first casualty of the Battle of Osawatomie and he became known nationally as "Osawatomie Brown."

Alexander W. Doniphan. A lawyer and western-Missouri politician, Doniphan was colonel of the 1st Missouri Dragoons in the Mexican-American War. From 1846-1848 he led his men west from Ft. Leavenworth, Kansas to New Mexico, south to the Sacramento River, and east to the Gulf of Mexico in one of the longest marches undertaken by any army since Alexander the Great. His command won the Battles of El Brazito, Monterrey, and Sacramento despite being a volunteer force that was largely distrusted by the rest of the army. In the Battle of the Sacramento River, a Mexican cannon was captured by his men, labeled "Old Sacramento," and hauled back to Missouri where it stood silent in the armory at Columbia for nearly ten years, until it was stolen and pressed into service by Atchison's Kickapoo Rangers in the May, 1856 siege of Lawrence. It was then captured by Free Staters at the First Battle of Franklin and used against the Missourians in the Battle of Hickory Point. Doniphan is also well known in Mormon history for his refusal to execute Mormon prisoners in 1838, including the prophet Joseph Smith, despite being ordered by Missouri Governor Lilburn Boggs to do so.

Samuel C. Pomeroy. An agent of the New England Emigrant Aid Society, Pomeroy was involved in the founding of Osawatomie and served as a Captain in the Free State militia and Secretary of the Lawrence Security Committee during the absence of Lane and Robinson in May of 1856.

"Dutch" Henry Sherman. Actually a German by birth, "Dutch" Henry settled with his brother in a cabin where the California and Oregon Trails crossed Potawatomie Creek, before the

Kansas-Nebraska Act of 1854 officially opened the territory for white settlement. "Dutch" Henry's Crossing, as it became known, was a rendezvous place for Pro Slavery "Border Ruffians" in the area, a way-stop and dry good store for travelers, and one of the cabins targeted by John Brown and his men in the Potawatomie Massacre. Henry escaped only because he was out on the prairie retrieving a wandering cow, but his brother William and all other inhabitants became victims of Brown's men. There is no historical evidence he was complicit.

John W. Geary. The third Governor of Kansas Territory, Geary was the last to be appointed by President Pierce. When he arrived in Kansas in September of 1856, he inherited a region on the brink of civil war. He acted quickly to disarm the militia his predecessor, Acting Governor Woodson, had mustered and stopped yet another attack on Lawrence. Nearly a hundred prisoners were taken shortly after the Battle of Hickory Point and held for trial near Lecompton under his authority.

Frank and Jesse James. Notorious western outlaws, the James brothers were children in a vehemently Pro Slavery household in Platte County Missouri during the 1850s. Neither are known to have raised a gun in anger until the Civil War, and in some ways, never to have surrendered them afterwards.

Andrew H. Reeder. The first governor of Kansas Territory. Appointed by President Franklin Pierce, Reeder was a lawyer from Pennsylvania, a Democrat, and proponent of the Kansas-Nebraska Act and the concept of squatter sovereignty. His tenure as governor was marred by the frauds of the territorial elections of 1855.

Daniel Woodson. In his capacity as Secretary of Kansas Territory, Woodson served as acting governor in the absence and between the terms of Reeder, Shannon, and Geary. An orphan and newspaperman from Virginia, Woodson was a strong Southern sympathizer and quickly acted to appoint sympathizers to territorial offices and sign the Pro Slavery legislature's laws whenever he was in office. During the tumult of the summer of 1856, he relied on Pro Slavery militias to control the expanding violence, who engaged and arrested solely Free State men.

Acknowledgments

This book would not have been possible if it weren't for my family, who encourage and inspire me, not just to write this book but to write about family. It also wouldn't have been possible if it weren't for the writers and historians of the past, and most importantly, for the brave people who staked their lives in the West, including my great-great grandparents who served as inspiration for the main characters. I would not have been able to publish it if it weren't for those who read early drafts, including Lucas Miller, Jeff Chacon, Floyd Jones, Aaron and Sean Maslow, Jonna Gjevre, and Kim Baack. Thanks is also due to Nik Morton, Jane Finch, and the best editor and writer I know: Joan The Ruthless, who is anything but.

And almost nothing in my adult life would have been possible if it weren't for Traci Gibson.

Bonus Material:
www.songofthejayhawk.com